9-04-09

AUG 2007

$200
F107

This item is no longer property
of Pima County Public Library
Sale of this item benefited the Library

Jon Cleary is often referred to as one of the statesmen of Australian storytelling. He was born in Erskineville, Sydney, in 1917, and has been a self-supporting professional writer since the 1940s, working in films and television in the United States and Britain.

He is also one of Australia's most versatile writers. His most famous novel, *The Sundowners*, the epic tale of an Australian outback family, has sold more than three million copies, and his work has been translated and published in 14 countries. With his Scobie Malone crime series he was labelled 'the best practitioner of Australian crime fiction' by the *Sydney Morning Herald*. A number of the recent Scobie Malone stories have been optioned for a television series.

Jon Cleary has collected a number of literary prizes, including the coveted Edgar Award, the Australian Literary Society's Church Medal for Best Australian Novel, and the Award for Lifelong Contribution to Crime, Mystery and Detective Genres at the inaugural Ned Kelly Awards.

In 2004, Jon Cleary's most recent Scobie Malone book, *Degrees of Connection*, won the Ned Kelly Award for Best Crime Novel.

ALSO BY JON CLEARY

The Sundowners
You Can't See Round Corners
The Beauford Sisters
High Road to China
The Golden Sabre
Season of Doubt
The City of Fading Light
The Pulse of Danger
Peter's Pence
Miss Ambar Regrets

Featuring Scobie Malone:

The High Commissioner
Helga's Web
Ransom
Dragons at the Party
Now and Then, Amen
Babylon South
Murder Song
Pride's Harvest
Bleak Spring
Dark Summer
Autumn Maze
Winter Chill
Endpeace
A Different Turf
Five Ring Circus
Dilemma
Bear Pit
Yesterday's Shadow
Easy Sin
Degrees of Connection

MORNING'S GONE

Jon Cleary

This first world edition published in Great Britain 2007 by
SEVERN HOUSE PUBLISHERS LTD of
9–15 High Street, Sutton, Surrey SM1 1DF.
This first world edition published in the USA 2007 by
SEVERN HOUSE PUBLISHERS INC of
595 Madison Avenue, New York, N.Y. 10022.

Copyright © 2006 by Sundowner Productions Pty Limited.

All rights reserved.
The moral right of the author has been asserted.

British Library Cataloguing in Publication Data

Cleary, Jon, 1917-
Morning's gone
1. Politicians - Family relationships - Australia - Fiction
I. Title
823.9'14 [F]

ISBN-13: 978-0-7278-6506-9

Except where actual historical events and characters are being described for the storyline of this novel, all situations in this publication are fictitious and any resemblance to living persons is purely coincidental.

All Severn House titles are printed on acid-free paper.

Printed and bound in Great Britain by
MPG Books Ltd., Bodmin, Cornwall.

For Gerald Wells
1918–2004

Chapter One

1

GOD IS OKAY — MATT DURBAN BLESSED HIM.

The big calico sign was strung between two trees a kilometre out of town, a heavenly blessing, or vice versa, made visible.

'Pull up!'

Des Lake brought the big Ford to a slow halt, careful that the car behind it, with the media in it, would not tail-end them. Lake had been driving Matt Durban for some years now, but it was only in the last few months that the media had begun to tail-end them.

Matt Durban got out of the car, moving with the slow grace that some men are born with and manage to retain as the arthritis and the kilos increase. He was a handsome man with thick dark hair only just tinged with grey. The eyes were shrewd, used to looking for answers and reasons behind questions, a politician's eyes; but they were also kindly and people recognised that. He had *presence*, which had grown with him over the years.

'Look at that!' The voice, too, had grown over the years. He turned back to the three reporters and the two cameramen who had got out of their car. 'Who do you reckon did that? A supporter or an enemy?'

'Could be both,' said Jack Shakespeare, from the ABC. He was as tall as Matt and good-looking and twenty years younger; his cynicism as yet was not a tailored fit. 'The first bit of lettering is different from the last bit.'

Matt gave him the famous Durban smile. 'Jack, does it matter? I'm sure God is on my side.'

'Bullshit,' said the man from Channel 9. He was small and middle-aged and not handsome, but he knew politics inside out and the camera forgave him his lack of photogenic appeal.

Matt turned the smile on him. 'Of course it is, Mick. But bullshit makes the world go round. You blokes should know that.' He looked back at the sign, now fluttering like a Mexican wave as a breeze blew up. Then he got back into the Ford, shouting over his shoulder to the media men, 'Let's see if Collamundra has got pearly gates!'

There were two men in the back seat of the Ford, neither of whom had got out when Matt had. They were of similar build, lean and medium-height, but one was grey-haired, almost white, and the other had a shaven skull and was much younger. The elder man, Tony Casio, said, 'Matt, why can't you turn a blind eye?'

Matt Durban turned halfway round in the front seat. 'Tony, I've been turning a blind eye for the last twenty-five years. If I'm going to win this race, or whatever you want to call it, I'm not going to do it by closing my eyes and ears. I'm for truth.' He looked at the younger man, Hamilton Jessup: 'Ham, you can spread that around as a slogan: I'm for truth.'

'Sure, Matt. Sounds great. Simple.'

'Too simple,' said Casio. 'You think they'll believe it, the voters?'

'Tony,' said Matt, still in good humour. 'Slogans are never meant to be believed. Even Moses knew that.'

Des Lake was looking at his worn, creased face in his driving mirror.

'What are you doing?' asked Matt. 'Checking on those bastards behind us?'

'No, I'm looking for the innocent boy I once was.'

Matt laughed and slapped him on the shoulder and the two men in the back seat looked at each other and rolled their eyes. Matt Durban had been laughing and slapping men, even enemies, on the shoulder ever since they had come to work for him. Only twice had an enemy swung a fist at him in retaliation, both times the same man. Had swung and missed.

The two-car caravan drove on into Collamundra. The sky was as bland as blue wallpaper, a cruising eaglehawk its only decoration. In the far distance, brown grassless hills lay like sleeping cattle.

'They need rain,' said Matt.

'Talk to God about it,' said Tony Casio. 'You're in touch.'

'Only occasionally,' said Matt. 'He's too busy listening to the Americans.'

They drove in past the cotton spread, white snowfields under the hot sun; past the glass-cabined cotton-pickers, moving slowly like heavy snowmobiles; past the used-car lots and the farm equipment yards and then, at the entrance to the main street, the iron statue of the World War I digger.

'There he is,' said Matt. 'Bayonet at the ready. Notice he's facing east, towards the coast? He knows you can't trust those buggers down there.'

'That's where your voters are,' said Tony Casio, who could count votes in a blacked-out room. 'Not out here.'

'That's why I'm here, why I've come back. If I'm going to lead the party, I want everyone to understand me. The voters out here have been telling us they've been neglected for a decade. If I can show 'em I've got a listening ear, maybe one or two will change their vote, come the election. I want to work for everyone,' he said and tried not to sound pious.

Casio looked at Jessup. 'We're gunna have our work cut out.'

Jessup grinned. 'You never worked in a union office, Tony. I'm case-hardened.'

They were in the wide main street now, cruising slowly, looking for the town hall, where the mayor and the local party secretary were to be waiting for them. The street was lined on both sides with cars and trucks, angle-parked; there were only four cross-streets, only one with a set of traffic lights, that seemed to blink in surprise at their own use. Virtually all the stores on both sides of the street had corrugated-iron awnings, like barricades laid flat against modernity. The first store had gone up in 1851 and it was still there, a weatherboard that was now, white-painted with a fancy glass door, a gourmet café. Collamundra had always been a wealthy town, though there had been years when the wealth had been hard to hold on to. Now, with the recent drought and the prices of cotton and wool dropping, it was drawing in the purse strings.

'There it is!'

The town hall, cream-painted stone, had been built in 1902. It had a solidity to it; it would never crumble, come what may. There was a clock tower, the hands tied together at midnight or noon. One looked for a line cut into the stonework: *Time Flies, But Not This*. The party secretary stood on the front steps, like a limpet on a rock-face.

'Matt!' He came plunging down the steps, his plump face bursting with bonhomie. He was the ideal front man, but he was genuine, though isolated out here in the backblocks. 'Great to see you! I tried to get the town band —'

Matt, out of the car and on the footpath, put his arm round the shoulders of the other man. 'Gary, cut out the bullshit. We don't have a town band, do we?' Then he turned back to the other men who had got out of the cars.

'Gary McGrath, meet my minders, Tony Casio and Ham Jessup. And Des Lake, my chariot driver. And these —' A big smile for the media: 'These are our historians, from the ABC, Channel 9 and the *Herald*. Truth-tellers, all of them.'

'Within reason,' said the man from Channel 9.

'Gary —' Matt still had his arm round McGrath. 'Who put up that sign out along the road? About me and God. Or God and me, whichever way you want to put it.'

'Me and a coupla the fellas. Things need stirring around here, Matt. We thought some of the God-botherers might kick up a stink, then you could sprinkle holy water on them — you're still a Catholic?'

'Still. Devout as St Paul.'

'And with just as many messages,' said Tony Casio.

'Where's the mayor?' asked Matt.

'Inside, in his office. He —'

'He doesn't want to be seen with me out in the open?' Matt looked up and down the street. 'I'm the prodigal son, Gary. Doesn't he know that? Be careful what you say in front of the historians.'

'No, he's really looking forward to seeing you again. He's tied up at the moment with some women from the CWA —'

'What've you got planned for our man?' asked Casio.

'A dinner tonight. This afternoon a visit to our primary school, let the kids respond to him as an ex-teacher —'

'Blessed are the children, bring 'em unto the politicians — what the fuck have kids got to do with this?' Then Casio looked at the historians, already grinning, tapes at the ready. 'Forget you heard me say that. He's gunna read to 'em —'

'What?' said the man from the *Herald*. He had been only six months in the press gallery and found it much more difficult than covering football clubs. 'Something from *The Magic Pudding*? Or *The Decameron*?'

Matt gave him the big smile. 'Terry, I've never read either of those two classics. No, I'll talk sport —'

'The national religion,' said Casio. 'The Bible according to Shane.'

'Don't let's get off on the wrong foot, Terry,' said Matt. 'We're one big happy family.'

'My boss won't be pleased to hear that,' said the Channel 9 man; then looked at the cameraman: 'Don't quote me.'

'I'm a silent movie man,' said the cameraman.

'Let's go in and interrupt the mayor,' said Matt, leading the way. 'I can ask the Country Women's ladies if they'll bake me some scones. I used to love scones.'

'And he's been sconed a lot of times,' said Shakespeare.

And they all went up into the town hall, one big happy family, as political junkets always are. Unlike other arenas, the knives only come out when they separate.

2

Matt Durban, smile at the ready, every-inch-and-then-some-left-over a father figure, went out to the local primary school, stood amongst the youngsters in their yellow sun-hats like a well-dressed scarecrow in a field of daffodils, and asked them questions they understood and told them stories of monsters and hobbits and elves, all of which the historians recognised as portraits of some in Canberra, not Middle Earth. The visit was a huge success and all Matt had to do was wait eight or ten years before his audience could vote.

Driving back to town Casio said, 'Why can't all voters be under eleven years old?'

'A lot of them are,' said Jessup. 'Mentally.'

Matt turned to them: 'Tonight, you two button your lips and be acolytes at my altar. No cynicism, no bullshit.'

Des Lake grinned in his driving mirror. 'You two are gunna have hernias.'

At six o'clock that evening Matt, having showered and shaved, lay on his back in his room at the Mail Coach hotel. In this room, or one like it, he had first gone to bed with Ruby Rawson. It had been Collamundra Cup week and the room had been lent to him for an hour by a young man posted to the local high school for six weeks as a relief teacher. It was the first time Matt had *gone to bed* with Ruby; the other times had been down by the river or in the back of her father's car in the garage at the back of the Rawson house. That had been twenty-five years ago and Ruby was dead, with her ivory-handled nail-file buried in her heart . . .

His phone rang. 'Yes?'

'What do you mean, yes? I haven't asked you yet —'

'Talk about Anytime Annie —' He smiled, loving her at 400 kilometres. The image of her was as clear in his mind as if he were carrying a photo. Strangely, he had never carried photos of her and the children, as if the images in his mind were enough. 'How're things? Missing me?'

'I always do. Why did I have to marry a politician?' He loved the sound of her voice, soft and throaty. Out in the hallway he heard a woman laugh, a parrot's screech. 'There was a poet wanted to marry me —'

'I'll dream up some verses. How're the kids?' He had come straight here from Canberra, instead of going home.

'I took Nat to lunch today, she's fine. And Richard called. He'd just come back from a fake sortie, whatever that is.'

Richard was a pilot officer in the RAAF. 'I never know what those Air Force buggers are talking about. For a week there I was the acting Shadow Minister for Defence —

remember? — and they all seemed to be speaking Esperanto. What time do you get in here tomorrow?'

'Eleven o'clock. Will you be at the airport?'

'Where else?'

'If you see Teresa tonight, give her my love. Not all of it — keep some for yourself.' Then she hung up, always on the right note.

He put down the phone, sat for a while as he always did after talking to her. Tomorrow she would be coming home to, in a way, re-start a journey that had begun years ago. Carmel's parents and her sister Teresa and Teresa's husband were still here in the district, out on adjoining properties along the Noongulli River. Carmel's two brothers had long ago moved on, one to the Gold Coast, the other to grow grapes across in West Australia. Matt himself had no family here, even though he had been born in the district. His mother had died when he was fifteen and he had had no siblings. His father, a teacher like himself but the principal of the high school over at Cawndilla, the shire centre, had died ten years ago. He and Carmel had come home almost every year, but never as publicly as his visit now.

When his father died, there had been a hundred people at the graveside, all friends, and he, the only relative. He remembered how, that day, he had walked over to the grave of Ruby Rawson; but her grave had been neglected, weeds instead of flowers remembering her. Her family, like himself, had left town after her murder.

There was a knock on his door and Tony Casio poked his head in. 'Time to go. What speech are you gunna give 'em tonight?'

He smiled, getting up and dressing. He had once been a casual dresser, careless of fashion, but Carmel and politics had smartened him up. He had a figure that could wear a suit off the rack; tonight's gear was from Henry Buck's, no change from sixteen hundred bucks. 'Number 22. Don't you ever get a sour taste in your mouth, from your cynicism?'

'Never. I think of it as medication.'

They went downstairs, passed through the narrow lobby that backed on to the main bar of the hotel. The bar was full, noisy with chatter and poker machines. Some of the drinkers saw Matt and Casio and raised their glasses in salute. Someone shouted, 'Welcome back, Matt!' and he saluted in return.

Out on the pavement he said, 'Nobody's turned their back on me yet.'

'You reckon?' said Casio.

'Why, what's the matter? Where's the dinner tonight? At the town hall?'

'In a private room at the arse-end of the RSL. Matt, all Gary McGrath could rustle up were fifty-two starters. Out here it ain't Labor territory, Matt, you know that. The price was fifty bucks, plus drinks, and all he could get, from far and wide, was fifty-two faithful. And not all of them are faithful, just relatives of your wife.'

'Are the historians going to be there?'

'The ABC, Channel 9 and the *Herald* guy. The TV cameraman and the *Herald* photographer have gone off with a couple of the local talent. I hear the locals are accommodating.'

'Some of them were,' said Matt, remembering Ruby Rawson. 'Not all of them . . . Is there anyone coming tonight from the local rag or radio station? Otherwise, why'd we come?'

'The guy from the *Cawndilla Courier*, it comes out twice a week. He's a Labor man, he says he'll see you're on Page One, he'll make you sound like a cross between St Paul and Henry Five at Agincourt. For Labor, Aussie and St Gough!'

'Tony, you're a treasure!'

'That's what my mum used to say. God's Little Treasure, she called me. I never found out what God called me.'

Matt laughed and as always it sounded happy. He put his arm round the shoulder of his minder and they went down the main street to the private room at the arse-end of the Returned Services' club.

The room was not large, with paper streamers, a decoration from some previous booking, still hanging from the ceiling. A portrait of the Queen, taken fifty years ago and the colours now faded, was at one end of the room; at the other was a World War I hero, the sepia faded till he looked ghostly. It was not a room to raise the spirits.

The faithful and the unfaithful were still having drinks when the politician and his minder arrived. Ham Jessup was circulating, seeing that everyone had a drink, loosening their faith or their scepticism, whichever affected them. When Matt walked in the door Jessup turned and spread his arms, as if to say, Lo, Our Hero! Everyone also turned and for a moment Matt felt that warm glow that hits every politician when everyone is smiling at him. Tony Casio, a student of world politics (or anyway, world politicians), had once remarked that the local smiles were slower than one saw on American voters' faces, but then, he had added, American smiles were always brighter, they had better teeth.

Paddy O'Reilly, Matt's father-in-law, approached with a small, weatherbeaten man who came up only to O'Reilly's armpit. 'Matt! You haven't met Bruce Curtis, have you? He's National Party, but he said he'd come tonight if I paid for his dinner. Worth millions, but he's a miserable bastard.'

Matt smiled at the little man. 'You should meet some of the miserable bastards I meet down in Canberra.' He shook hands, appreciating the firm grip of the man. 'I'll try not to sound too bolshie tonight.'

'That young bloke of yours told me you're all for truth.' He had a high, thin voice, as if he had spent all his life shouting at skies that didn't rain, at grass that turned to dust. But then, as O'Reilly had said, he was worth millions, so it must have rained some time. 'I'll settle for that. I might even give Paddy his fifty dollars.'

He moved away and O'Reilly said, 'It's good to see you again, Matt. Your visits are getting longer and longer between.'

'Paddy, I'm up to my neck in things now —'

'We're not complaining, we see Carmel and the kids and she explains. How's it feel, this new situation? We used to dream we'd maybe see you running the country some day, remember?'

'There's a long way to go —'

O'Reilly nodded. He was an inch or two taller than Matt, who was six feet; both of them still thought in inches, not centimetres. He had a broad Irish face, with a long upper lip and a complexion always susceptible to skin cancers; there was one now on the end of his long nose. The O'Reillys had been here in the district for almost 150 years and Paddy, though not worth millions, didn't have to count his dollars before he spent them. Matt liked him and the feeling was reciprocated.

'Is Eileen here?'

'Nup, she's got the 'flu. She sent her love. But Teresa and Col are here. Gary McGrath says he's put Terry beside you at dinner.' Then he raised his glass of whisky. 'Good luck, Matt. I hope I live long enough to see you in the Lodge.'

Matt drifted on through the gathering, working it with ease. He never overdid the charm, because it was natural; and people saw that it was. Then it was time to sit down to dinner. McGrath was on his right; Teresa, his sister-in-law, was on his left. She kissed him on the cheek and smiled at him (there was an O'Reilly smile; Carmel had it). She was ten years younger than Carmel and was as beautiful. Almost.

'Why are you O'Reilly women so beautiful?'

'Matt darling, there's no need to spread bulldust around me. I'll vote for you.'

He smiled. 'How are Mark and Luke?' The O'Reillys were good Catholics and the four children all had saints' names: Carmel, Teresa, Mark and Luke. When he had first met them he had wondered if he should genuflect.

'Mark is a developer now, up on the Gold Coast — he says he's bought white shoes and he won't be voting Labor any more. Luke is still growing grapes and is thinking of bottling under his own label. Drop the wine tax and he'll vote for you.'

Matt looked down the table at her husband, a quiet, good-looking man who, a philosopher, knew that the present was only a split second between the past and the future and so always took his time in everything he did. 'Col looks fine, as usual.'

She nodded, smiling: Carmel's smile. 'I see that he does. Just as Carmel does the same with you ... Why are you running against Becky Irvine?'

'Becky? How would that sound — Prime Minister Becky?'

'Okay. Rebecca. She's been at the well longer than you have.' He looked blank and she went on: 'Biblical.'

He had a dim memory of the Bible: 'Didn't she prefer one twin over the other? The one who lost out was blind.'

She ignored that. 'Why are you running against her to lead the Party?'

'I was asked to.'

'By the blokes. There are men who would die of shock if ever we had a woman Prime Minister. Other countries have them — Britain, New Zealand, India, some European countries. What have you got against Becky — Rebecca?'

'Nothing.' Nor did he; but he would have preferred to run against a man. 'Nothing at all — we get on well together. But she's made no impression on the voters —'

'She has on women voters —'

'Feminists like yourself —'

'Don't give me that crap — no, not you —' She smiled at the waitress putting the first course down in front of her.

'You had me worried there for a moment, Mrs Hailey.' She was plump and middle-aged and Matt had a faint memory of her as a slim girl he had once danced with at the local hops.

'Would you vote for Mr Durban?'

'If he put his shoes under my bed.' She winked at both of them and went away, a waitress as independent as Boadicea and other women leaders.

'There, you see? You were always a ladies' man,' said Teresa.

'No,' he said. 'I was always one lady's man.'

'I know — I'm sorry, I didn't mean it like that. But you were always — always *nice* to women.'

'Even to feminists,' he said and gave her the big smile.

When everyone had got to the coffee stage he stood up and, without notes, gave them his speech. He had a good voice that carried without his having to raise it; it had been a useful voice when he had been on the backbenches. Now he used it to effect. Tony Casio had written the speech for him, he had read it twice, and he gave it as if it were extemporaneous, with pauses in the right places as if he were trying to remember what to say next, jokes inserted as if he had just thought of them. He had been doing it for years and now the act was as smooth as a well-oiled machine. His audience loved it, even the National Party millionaire, who looked across at him and gave him a thumbs-up.

As they stood up to leave Teresa said, 'You're a lovely bullshit artist, Matt.'

'Which Becky Irvine isn't,' he said, but smiled. His face was starting to ache from the smile, but soon he would be escaping to bed and the truth of himself. 'The voters don't like their leaders to be too intense. It worries them.'

'I love you, Matt,' she said and kissed him. 'Just don't get carried away.'

Then Col Hailey, steady as a rock, came up. 'These O'Reilly women are always giving advice.'

'What would we do without them?' said Matt.

3

Next morning he rose early and before breakfast went out to the local cemetery. It was on the slope of a hill facing west, as if the dead had spent all their lives looking at sunsets and the pattern wasn't going to be broken. It was a well-kept cemetery, the graves as neat and ordered as a regimental parade. A row of bottle-brushes ran down one side of the graveyard, a line of jacarandas down the other; neither now in bloom. At Christmas, Matt thought, the whole scene must look cheerful, though he couldn't remember how it had looked when he had lived in Collamundra. He had once made love to a girl amongst the graves, but he couldn't remember the season.

His mother's and father's graves, side-by-side, like a marriage bed with headstones instead of a headboard, were well-kept. He guessed that would have been done by Eileen O'Reilly, who had always respected the dead. The inscriptions on the headstones, still clearly visible, book-ended two lives just in dates. On his mother's, 1934–1970, and his father's, 1930–1994. Nothing about pain and love and happiness, just used-by dates.

He blessed himself, said a prayer for the two who had loved him and he them, then turned to go. And saw the lone figure standing by a grave at the far end of a row further down the slope.

He had driven himself out in the Ford and the path to the gates where he had left it ran just below the line of graves where the man stood. He paused a moment, wondering if he should disturb the man, who seemed to be staring intently at a headstone, as if there were some sort of message on it for him. Then the man looked up towards him, but didn't move. Matt began to walk cautiously, wondering if this was some zealot come to waylay him on a political point. Down in Sydney there was always the hand that came out of the crowd to grab him and snarl a question or accuse him.

He was half a dozen paces short of the man when the latter said, 'Hullo, Matt.'

Matt stopped, stared at a memory: 'Bert? Bert Carter?'

Carter nodded, remained standing beside the grave he had been tending. It was Ruby Rawson's grave and the last time Matt had seen it (when, he couldn't remember) it had been neglected as a tiny rubbish dump. Now it was as neat as Matt's parents', with fresh flowers in the stone vase at the base of the headstone. On the headstone itself the lettering was highlighted in new gold paint: RUBY RAWSON, 1959–1979, REST IN PEACE. Nothing about her reputation, her murder, the family that had left town for the coast after Bert Carter's acquittal and were somewhere out there in the suburbs of oblivion.

'I come out here once a week,' said Carter, looking down at the grave. 'Nobody looked after it till I come back. I loved her, Matt. Just like you did.'

No, I made love to her but I never loved her. 'It was a long time ago.'

'Yeah,' he said and coughed, putting his hand over his mouth as if he were about to sob. He was two or three inches shorter than Matt and twenty-five years ago he had been a rugged eighty-five kilogram inside-centre for the local rugby team. Now he was almost skeletal, a goal-post of a man. 'I've come home to die, Matt.'

Matt, used to shock, still felt the thump. It was part of his job to attend funerals, comfort the grieving, sometimes give a eulogy. But here on this deserted hillside, among the already dead, you did not expect a man to tell you he would soon be in his own grave. Graveyards were not for dying in.

'Christ, Bert, I'm sorry —'

'Lung cancer. My grandmother used to say, when I was fourteen, fifteen, those things will kill you.' His grin, now that Matt took notice of it, was ghastly. 'You think I could sue the tobacco companies?'

Lost for something to say, not usual with him, Matt fumbled, then said, 'Your mum and dad still alive?'

'Sure, in their late seventies now and twice as healthy as me. They still have the property out along the Cawndilla road, still running it themselves. I help — well, try to help. It nearly killed 'em years ago, you know. When I was charged with —' He gestured at the grave, unable to say *murder*. 'That was why I went away when I was acquitted. As far away as I could get.'

The murder had shocked the town and it had been doubly shocked when Bert Carter had been charged. It had not been the first murder in Collamundra, but the last had occurred twenty years before and the facts of it had faded. Collamundra, the people had told themselves, was a peaceful town, one where everyone respected everyone else. Or almost . . .

'Where'd you go?' Again for something to say.

'The States. I got a green card and worked in Kansas City, in the saleyards there. Remember I was an assistant auctioneer here, remember?'

Suddenly it struck Matt that Carter was talking to him as if they had been old friends; which they had never been. Christ knew how lonely the man had been over the past twenty-five years. Matt felt a sudden sadness for him, almost *was* a friend.

'I married a girl from down south in Missouri.' He pronounced it Missour*a*, which someone at the US embassy in Canberra had once told Matt was the American way. 'It didn't work out. No kids, fortunately. I was still in love with Ruby.' He looked down again at the grave, as if she were listening and he was trying to make the point to her. 'You know how it is. Was.'

No, I don't know how it was, not with her.

Then Carter looked back at him, seemed to struggle for a smile on the thin, flesh-sagging face. 'You've done well, Matt. Who'd of believed it?'

'Not me.' But he didn't believe that.

'If ever you run for prime minister, I'll vote for you. If I'm still alive —'

'Don't talk like that,' he said banally.

'How else do you expect me to talk?' For a moment he looked angry, as if Matt had insulted him.

'I'm sorry, Bert —' He wondered how he would talk if faced with his own death. He was still healthy, very much so, and the future still ran over the horizon.

Carter looked at him, then suddenly put his hand to his face and began to weep. 'Oh Christ, I'm so unhappy! Have been all my fucking life!'

Matt hesitated. He had always been good at sympathy; or practised at it. But all he could do now was stand awkwardly, say apologetically, 'I've got to go, Bert.'

Carter, still with his hand over his face, waved in dismissal. Matt stood a moment, not wanting to leave the other man alone, but knowing he could do nothing if he stayed. A crow flew over them, cawing harshly, and down on the road below the cemetery a car went by, horn blowing as if whoever was in the car was saluting the dead. Or mocking them.

'Give my best to your mum and dad,' said Matt and went on out to his car.

In it, before he started the engine, he looked back. Bert Carter still stood above Ruby Rawson's grave, hand to his mouth, shoulders hunched. As if he had only just buried her.

Chapter Two

1

'You love my tits, don't you?' said Ruby, filing her nails.

'I love every fucking inch of you. And I use the adjective advisedly.'

'You trying to give me an English lesson?'

'I'd like to give you French lessons.'

Matt had always liked his own repartee, but it was a soufflé with a lead centre. Nobody else ever commented on it. Except Ruby, who thought it very unfunny and told him he should *pull his head in.*

Which she did now: 'Pull your head in. We can't do anything — Sharon is out there in her bedroom. I'll bet she's got her ears pinned back, waiting to hear you start panting.'

'We could tell her we were doing our homework.'

Ruby gave a mock groan and went on filing her nails. The nail-file was an heirloom that her grandmother had given her: it was twenty-five centimetres overall, with a carved pearl handle. It was the sort of fashion implement that a French courtesan might have used, Madame Du Barry or Diane de Poitiers, pointing it at suitors to emphasise a remark. Ruby always carried it in her handbag, which was large, almost a satchel, and whenever Matt upset her she would take out the file and work on her nails. She might have made a courtesan, but she missed by three centuries.

She was a pretty girl with a complexion that tanned well and thick blonde hair that she used as a sailor might use a semaphore flag, always tossing it, especially when men were looking at her. And men did look at her; or at her body. It was the sort of body that caused tumescence in the young men of the town and frustrating memories in the old. Middle-aged men went home to their under-developed or over-developed wives and wondered why all women's bodies were not like Ruby Rawson's. Matt could not keep his hands off her.

They were in the lounge room of the Rawson home; still called the lounge room by Ruby's mother, not the living room. It was a large rambling house, an Edwardian relic whose interior Mrs Rawson had modernised without ruining the character of the house. The Rawsons had come to Collamundra from Melbourne four years ago, imbued with that superior sense of good living that wafted up from the south. They had bought a coffee lounge and grill in the main street, brought a better sense of what was good food and good cooking that, they said, was natural to Melbourne. It had prospered and they were working there tonight. But Sharon, Ruby's fourteen-year-old sister, was out there in her bedroom, keeper of the morals she herself was busting to break.

Ruby stopped filing her nails and took his hand out from under her shirt. 'That's enough, I'm getting excited. Wait till tomorrow night. There's a movie I wanna see. *Grease*.'

'Great title. What's it about — a lubritorium?'

'A *what*? I dunno what it's about. It's got a new feller in it, I saw the trailer. John Something-or-other —' She rolled her eyes, as she often did when movie stars, *male* movie stars, were mentioned.

'I can't, not tomorrow night. There's a Labor Party meeting on, it's the third Tuesday in the month.'

'Oh, bugger! Can't you pass it up?'

'I can't, I'm the Secretary.'

'How many of you are there? Eight, ten? You're a joke.'

He eased himself out from behind her, pushing her away. 'Don't get insulting. Your old man votes Labor, he told me. Okay, this is National Party territory, but one day things will change.'

She put the nail-file away, did up the buttons on her shirt. 'I dunno why you bother —'

'I'm ambitious.' He had never talked like this before with her. There had never been any encouragement; she lived for the moment. She was not unintelligent, just limited in her interests. She rarely read a newspaper and never read a book. With her he had always turned off his own mind, content just with the physical. 'I'm not going to be a schoolteacher all my life. One day I'm going down to Sydney, maybe to Canberra —'

'Doing what? What about *us*?'

Us? He had never seen her as a fixture in his life. He was not her first lover and he would not be her last. He hedged, not wanting an argument, not here in her parents' house and with Sharon, ears wide open, in a back bedroom. 'I'd come back for you — after I'd got started —'

'Started at what? Being a politician? You don't think I'd wanna be married to a politician, do you?'

'I haven't asked you yet —' And knew in that moment that he never would. Their romance or affair or whatever you called it was suddenly at an end. He was surprised that he felt a certain relief, his sense at last up out of his crotch. He would not be coming here to this house again, her tits and the rest of her were history. People, if they knew, would call him a cad, a real bastard, and maybe he was. But he knew she would not be broken-hearted, men lined the road ahead of her . . .

'Bert Carter once asked me to marry him.' She was sitting with her knees together, prim as a nun, one of the older ones. But she knew nothing of nuns or convents, the Rawsons appeared to have no religion. In the heat of passion she would exclaim Oh Christ! Or Oh Jesus! but she might just as easily gasped the name of some film or pop star. 'He's honest with me —'

'He's a nice bloke —' Any reserve was welcome. He pushed in Bert Carter from the bench: 'Get him to take you to see *Grease.*'

'I might do that,' she said and took out the nail-file again.

He was not used to making awkward exits. 'Well —' Then he bent and kissed the top of her head. 'See you —'

'Just like a bloody politician — I'm not a fucking child —'

But that was exactly what she was, a girl who thought happiness lay between her legs. Thinking that, he again felt a real bastard; but he knew it was the truth. He left her then, sorry (in a way) that it was ending like this. But she was not the first girl he had turned his back on and she might not be the last. The politicians' beacon, the light on the hill, threw shadows in which, he knew even then, women wept.

2

The Labor Party meeting was held in a back room of the town hall — 'underground', as one wit had once described it. As soon as he entered the room Matt saw the black-haired girl seated at the bottom of the long table. She glanced up at him, but seemed uninterested. He sat down across from her and gave her the Durban smile and she acknowledged it, as if she had seen it, or copies of it, a hundred times.

'We have a guest tonight —' Gary McGrath was the same age as Matt and chairman, for tonight, of the meeting. He had a pink cheerful face that would grow pinker and plumper as he grew older; he was the sort of man who would never change, just the mould of him growing larger as the years piled up. Always the happy man, always on the sunny side of the street.

'Dr Hennessy couldn't be here tonight, he's over at the hospital delivering twins. Carmel O'Reilly is sitting in for him just to take notes. Gents, Miss O'Reilly.'

The eight other men, including Matt, smiled their greetings and she smiled back. Her smile lingered on Matt, almost mocking, and after a moment he nodded and said, 'You're very welcome, Miss O'Reilly. Doc Hennessy should be delivering more babies.'

'I'll tell him.' She had a low, throaty voice that one could never imagine being raised in a shout.

'Take no notice of him, Carmel,' said McGrath. 'He talks like that to all the girls. He's our Lothario —'

'I once had a bet on Lothario,' said one of the members. 'Ran third in the Collamundra Cup, back in '67 —'

'Can we get down to business?' said McGrath. 'Read the minutes of the last meeting, Matt.'

The meeting lasted an hour and, like all their meetings, went round in circles. They were subversives in National Party territory, a *maquis* that never got out of the bushes. Only one of them had the passion to want to escape.

Matt walked out of the town hall with Carmel O'Reilly. He put his hand under her elbow as they went down the steps and she smiled at him as if he meant it as a joke. But she said, 'You're a ladies' man, I'm told.'

'Who told you that? I'm as pious as the Pope.'

'They told me that, too. About your corny jokes.'

He looked at her, then smiled. 'Okay, it's all true ... I've been trying to remember you. The last time I saw you, you would have been — what? — ten or twelve? I was still in high school.'

'I went off to boarding school in Sydney.'

They had paused at the bottom of the steps, examining each other. She saw a well-built, tallish man, dark-haired, worn a little long, as if he were easing his way out of the Seventies and its hairiness. He had a broad, good-looking face that, practised or not, seemed to have an always-ready smile.

He was trying to place this girl who was nothing like the young girl he had occasionally seen around town back in their schooldays. True, he had not been interested in twelve-year-olds; Year 11 and 12 girls had been his mark then. *This* girl was beautiful, no two ways about it.

'You live in town or out with your folks?'

'With them. I've got our ute, I drove myself in.'

'You like some coffee? Or a drink?'

They had begun to walk down the street. The night air was still warm and stars crowded the sky. 'I'd like some coffee. That was pretty dreadful stuff you served back there at the meeting.'

'We're Labor, billy-tea is our cuppa —'

'Oh, there's the Kurrajong — how about there?'

'Well — no, not there —'

She smiled: perfect teeth, he noted. 'It's owned by your girlfriend's parents, that right? I know about you, Mr Durban.'

'Don't keep calling me Mr Durban. Matt ... No, she's not my girlfriend, not any longer. We broke it off last night.' They were opposite the Roxy theatre, where Ruby, maybe with Bert Carter, was enjoying John Something-or-other. 'Just in time.'

She laughed this time, a full-bellied laugh. 'You really should start a new line — Matt. Just try being yourself — whatever that is.'

He stopped. She went on a pace or two, then she, too, halted and turned back to him. 'What?'

'You're really beautiful. No corny line, just the truth.'

She had dark blue eyes with lids that might, in other circumstances, be heavy; a perfectly straight nose with just the right length; high cheekbones and a defined jawline; and a full-lipped mouth that, if she let it, was an invitation. Her hair was blue-black and thick and worn in a bob with a fringe. Her figure was full, but not as blatant as Ruby's, and her legs were slim and good.

'I like your hair. It reminds me of Cyd Charisse. She was in an old movie with Fred Astaire and she had her hair cut like that.'

'I'm glad you noticed. I saw the movie on TV and I copied it. I just don't have her legs and I dance like a flat-footed kangaroo.'

They had arrived opposite her transport, a white Holden utility that looked brand-new. On the door, in distinct letters, was: Cavanreagh — P.J. O'Reilly Pty Ltd.

'Cavanreagh. A nice spread, I always look at it every time I pass it. Where did your dad get the name?'

She looked across the street. 'There's a café, let's go and have some coffee.'

Without waiting to see if he agreed she stepped off the kerb and began to cross the road. A car screeched to a stop as she held up her hand, then pointed to the pedestrian crossing on which she walked. Matt, grinning, feeling a little sheepish, followed her. The four hoons in the car hooted and the driver blew the horn and Matt bowed and kept on walking.

When they reached the opposite pavement he said, 'Down in Sydney, did traffic stop for you?'

'All the time. It's only old ladies and men they run over.'

The café had been owned by the same Greek family for the past sixty years. The grandparents, who had come here to Collamundra from Larissa, were dead, but their heirs,

Greek–Australians, had carried on, never changing the long room except for a new coat of paint every two years. There were still old-fashioned booths instead of smart tables out in the open, as if the original designer had believed in privacy, though small towns had a hard time concealing their secrets. The long counter still had its original marble top. There were two espresso machines, but they were the only evidence of keeping up with the times. On the walls were coloured prints of the Parthenon, the amphitheatre at Delphi and Mount Athos. There were no ghosts of Greek gods in the booths. Matt, who came here often, always thought of it as a museum, one that should be preserved.

They sat down and Carmel, as if the question had only this moment been asked, said, 'Cavanreagh was the village in Galway where the family came from. My great-great-grandparents were tenant farmers for some absent English lord. Then the potato famine hit them and they were forced off the land. The family myth is that my great-great-grandfather knocked the bailiff out cold, stole his money and then he and my great-great-grandma robbed a bank on their way across to Cork.'

'Bonnie and Clyde O'Reilly?'

She acknowledged the joke. 'If you like. Instead of going to America, as most of them did, they came out here. He had enough money from the bank hold-up, or wherever he got it, to buy that land out along the Noongulli. It may be all myth, but that's the Irish for you.'

'You look Irish, the blue eyes and the black hair.'

'Black Irish. That's another myth. When the Spanish Armada was scattered by Francis Drake — you know any English history?'

'I teach English and history.'

'Well, some of the Spanish ships went up the Irish Sea, round the top and came down the west coast and some of them were shipwrecked. The story is the shipwrecked sailors never went home to Spain, but got into bed with the colleens and hence —' She flicked her hair. '*Quien sabe?*'

A granddaughter of the Greeks, black-haired and brown-eyed, brought them coffee, winked at Matt and went back behind the counter.

'Is there any girl in town you don't know?'

'I don't know you. Why have you stayed away so long?' He sipped his coffee, which was always good in this place. 'How long have you been back?'

'A month. I've only been working for Dr Hennessy for two weeks, while I make up my mind what I want to do ... I stayed away because I wanted a career, but I couldn't make up my mind what I wanted to be. I thought I'd like to be a model, but I found that too boring. So I went abroad ... Have you ever been overseas?'

'Once. A month on the west coast of America. Where did you go?'

'Italy, first. I spent two weeks as an au pair, but the signora wanted a skivvy, a servant who'd do everything from washing the floor to washing the car. So I left her and got a job at a language institute teaching English.'

'I'm told Italian fellers are very attentive to women.'

'You're really probing, aren't you? Yes, they are ... My mum, who's a good Catholic, was very happy I was living in the same city as the Pope. I wasn't ... You know an English writer, G.K. Chesterton?'

'I've heard of him, but never read him.'

'He was a Catholic convert — they always take it more seriously than those of us born into it. What are you?'

'Catholic. Not a very serious one.'

'Well, he made the pilgrimage to Rome and then wrote —' She paused, sipped her own coffee. 'I have to remember it ... Any man who spends a twelvemonth in the shadow of the walls of the Vatican and still retains his faith need have no fear that the gates of Heaven will be closed against him ... It goes double for a woman. All those celibate old men telling women what they should do with their bodies.'

'How did your mother feel when you told her that?'

'A bit disappointed. I'm a born-again, dead-again, born-again, dead-again Catholic, I think. I believe in God and I hope He believes in me ... I'd like another cup of coffee. All this autobiography is making me thirsty. I haven't talked to a man like this in I dunno how long.'

He signalled for more coffee, then went back to studying her. He couldn't remember any girl intriguing him as much as Carmel O'Reilly. 'What happened after Rome?'

'I went to Paris for six months, then to London for six months.'

'Why did you come home?'

She looked at him, as if debating how much more she should confide in him. Then: 'I had a man let me down. A very nice Englishman who went back to a fiancée I knew nothing about.'

'Ah.'

'Yes, ah.' She waited till the girl who had brought their coffee had gone away, then she looked past him and down towards the front door. 'And ah again.'

He looked over his shoulder. Ruby Rawson had come in with a solidly-built, boyish-looking young man: Bert Carter. Ruby paused inside the doorway, as she always did, as if looking to see if anyone interesting, meaning anyone interested in her, was present. Then she saw Matt, frowned, said something to Carter, and came down to the booth where Matt and Carmel sat.

'A Labor Party meeting?' But she was looking at Carmel.

'Yes,' said Matt. 'We're discussing pensions for unmarried fathers. You an unmarried father, Bert?'

Carter grinned, lit a cigarette, said, 'Not yet.'

'What happened to *Grease*?' asked Matt. 'They run out of lubrication?'

'The projector broke down, they've given us passes for tomorrow night,' said Ruby, still looking at Carmel. 'You a member of the Labor Party?'

'As of tonight,' said Carmel. 'You should join. You too, Mr Carter. I've seen you out at the stockyards.'

Carter grinned, waved his cigarette. 'Christ, no! I'd lose my job. They'd set the bulls on me.'

'I'll see you tomorrow,' said Ruby, looking back at Matt. 'Enjoy your coffee. It's not as good as the place down the street, remember?'

'Why aren't you there?' said Matt, but Ruby and Carter, the latter grinning and shaking his head, had moved on to a booth at the back of the café.

He looked back at Carmel and she smiled and said, 'You've got a problem there.'

'It's finished.'

'She doesn't think so. You may have a lot to learn about women, Mr Durban. Trust a woman to know a woman.'

He studied her. 'Do you know men as well as that?'

'No, but I'm progressing. You're the simpler sex.'

'Thanks, on behalf of the simpler sex.'

'My pleasure.'

They were coming to ease with each other. They talked for another ten minutes, finished their now-cold coffee and stood up to leave the café. Matt looked down to the last booth where Ruby and Carter were seated. She was facing Matt and he frowned at the look she was giving him. He was accustomed to antagonism in the schoolroom, but not hatred. And that was the look on her frozen face.

Bert Carter turned and looked over his shoulder. Poor bugger, thought Matt.

Then he turned and followed Carmel out of the café and across the road to her utility. She opened the door, turned back to him. 'Do you want to see me again?'

Experienced though he was, he was not used to such a direct approach. But he was also quick to recover: 'Tomorrow night?'

She was studying him. 'Am I making a mistake?'

'I dunno. What mistake?'

'I've only been back a month, but I've heard all about you. You and your girls. Have you got a faithful bone in your body?'

There was some repartee answer to that, but he couldn't think of it. 'Somewhere, yes.'

She continued to look at him; no girl had ever given him such a long stare. Then she leaned forward and kissed him softly on the lips, got into the ute and slammed the door.

'You're quite a girl,' he said, still feeling the touch of her lips on his.

'I'm not a girl. Ruby Rawson is a girl, I'm a woman. You'd better learn the difference, Mr Durban. Call me tomorrow at the surgery,' she said and drove off, pulling out in front of a car that, horn blowing, had to squeal to a stop.

Matt looked after the disappearing utility, then turned to the driver of the car who, window down, was yelling, 'Who the hell was that bloody idiot?'

'A woman,' said Matt, smiling. 'They rule the world.'

3

Ruby Rawson, in the family's silver Mercedes, was parked outside Collamundra High. It was a co-educational high school that went only as far as Year 10; Year 11 and 12 students took the bus to Cawndilla High, twenty kilometres away. Collamundra had produced an Olympic relay sprinter, a Wallaby rugby reserve, three petty criminals and a girl who, within three years of graduation, had produced two sets of twins. It had not produced anyone of real note, or indeed any note, in politics, business or the arts. But both Ruby and Matt were ex-pupils.

She was waiting for him now, as other girls had waited for him when he had been a student. The school bell clanged and five minutes later the classes spewed forth. In their brown tunics and yellow shirts (the girls) and brown trousers and yellow shirts (the boys), they came out of the two buildings like the overflow from a muddy dam. Ruby looked at them with no nostalgia for her days in that uniform.

Four boys, Year 10 fifteen-year-olds, testosterone on and off like a light globe, paused at the gates and laughed at Ruby.

'Waiting for Mr Durban?' yelled one. 'He's gay! We're what you want, Ruby!'

She gave him the thumb (the middle finger salute not yet having crossed the Pacific) and they all laughed and ran off down the street, holding their crotches. She sometimes wondered what it would be like to have a fifteen-year-old make love to her; she had read that men's tumescence, whatever that was, went downhill from their teens. But she wasn't going to waste her time finding out.

It was another five minutes before Matt came out. He was in shirtsleeves, his tie loosened, a canvas satchel filled with books and papers slung over one shoulder. He was out of the gates before he recognised that it was Ruby behind the wheel of the Mercedes. He halted, frowning.

'I want to talk to you,' said Ruby. 'Get in.'

'Ruby —' He moved closer to the car. 'There's nothing to talk about —'

'Get in or I'll scream!'

He looked right and left. Fifty metres down the street the four boys stood watching him, brown-and-yellow hyenas waiting to laugh. He sighed, then went round the car and got in. Before he could buckle his seat belt, Ruby had started the car and taken it away from the kerb with a screech of tyres. Just as Carmel had done the night before. He would have to look for a girlfriend with a horse and sulky. But he was not in the mood for repartee: there were no jokes ahead.

'Where are we going?'

'Where we can talk,' she snapped, not looking at him.

The school was on the edge of town and within two minutes they were out in the countryside. She swung off the main road, down a dirt track and in another few minutes she had pulled the car in beneath the shade of a red gum and they were on the banks of the Noongulli. She switched off the engine and turned to him.

'Why did you stand me up last night for that O'Reilly bitch?'

He sighed again, used to her temper. On the other side of the river the cotton fields stretched away like displaced snowfields. This was only the district's second crop; there were promises that the white harvest would eventually stretch for miles. The countryside was changing and many of the older settlers, like the O'Reillys for instance, were not ready for it. He looked back at Ruby, who was not ready for a changing relationship.

'Ruby, she was at the party meeting, standing in for Doc Hennessy. I didn't know she was going to be there. For Crissake, I hadn't seen her since she was twelve years old. Last night was the first time I'd ever spoken to her.'

'I saw her kiss you goodnight when she got into her ute.'

'You were spying on me? Jesus, Ruby —'

'No, I wasn't! I was just coming out of the café —'

'With Bert Carter.'

'Yeah, with Bert Carter!'

'Did you kiss him goodnight, give him a feel?' Jesus, he thought, we're like a couple of twelve-year-olds. 'Ruby, pull your head in. You and I are finished, but it has nothing to do with Carmel O'Reilly.'

She took a deep breath and calmed down. 'Why are we finished?'

He searched for the word; his vocabulary in such circumstances was limited. 'We're — we're incompatible.'

'Oh, don't play the fucking English teacher with me!' Her temper burst out again. 'The last four months, screwing me three and four times a week — right here where we're parked — we weren't fucking *incompatible*. And I use the adjective advisedly,' she said, trying to imitate his tone of the night before last.

He had to smile. 'Top marks, love. Now drive me back to town.'

She leaned closer to him. 'Touch me —'

'I can't —'

'Why not?'

'Wrong time of the month.'

She hit him across the face, so hard that his nose began to bleed. He took out his handkerchief, held it to his nose. His eyes were watering and she was a blur in his gaze. But he kept his voice steady:

'That's it,' he said, opened the door and got out. He reached into the back of the car, took his loaded satchel and slammed the rear door. 'Go home, Ruby. Find someone else; you'll have no trouble doing that.'

She stared at him, then abruptly she started up the car, swung it away from him and went back up the track in a swirl of dust. He stared after the car, then looked at his handkerchief; his nose had stopped bleeding, but felt sore. He checked that it wasn't broken, then stood for several minutes staring across the river. And seeing nothing, his mind too clouded to take in any vision. Then he turned and began to walk up the dirt track to the main road. He waited there for ten minutes for a lift, but all cars and trucks seemed to have retired for an early night. Then he saw the white ute coming from town. It pulled off the tarmac opposite him and came to a halt.

'She dumped you?' said Carmel as he crossed the road to her.

'Who?' You had to be careful when discussing one woman with another. He had learned that much about them.

She smiled at his naive answer. 'Ruby Rawson. I passed her coming back into town, going like a bat out of hell. What happened to your nose?' There was no sympathy in her smile. 'Oh, Mr Durban, you should be more selective about your women.'

'Any suggestions?' He was fencing with her, not sure of her sympathy.

'What's in your pack? The books and papers.'

'I have to mark them.'

'When?'

'Any time. I hand them back next week.'

She studied him; he could have been a prize bull out at the stockyards, being sized up before a bid was made for him. As if to underline the metaphor, a semi-trailer went by carrying cattle to the abattoirs at Cawndilla. He could not remember ever being graded like this.

Then she jerked her head. 'Get in. Come and have dinner with us.'

'Us?'

'The O'Reilly clan. You know my mum and dad, they won't mind me bringing you home.'

He went round to the passenger side of the ute, got in, slammed the door and looked at her. 'Bringing me home — isn't that what girls used to do in your mother's day?'

'They still do. But don't get ahead of yourself.'

Then she let in the clutch, shot the ute back on to the road and they sped towards Cavanreagh. He sat beside her, saying nothing, wondering if he was speeding off a cliff and ambivalent about the fall.

4

Cavanreagh, the O'Reilly spread, covered 8000 acres (the locals still did not talk in hectares) and so far the clan had not fallen to the cotton fever that was taking over the district. The homestead, stone and brick, was at the end of a long line of coolibahs, now green with leaf.

'I thought you'd have shamrocks lining the drive,' said Matt.

'Pull your head in,' said Carmel, echoing Matt's words to Ruby. 'No Irish jokes, okay?'

Paddy and Eileen O'Reilly welcomed Matt and did not seem surprised that Carmel had brought him home without warning. Paddy and Matt sat out on the wide verandah of the house, each with a beer, while Carmel and her mother prepared dinner. Teresa, their twelve-year-old, was away at school in Sydney and the two sons, Luke and Mark, who worked on the property, were both married and lived in town.

'But both of 'em are getting restless,' said Paddy, sipping his beer. 'Why is it you young 'uns think things will be better elsewhere? You thinking of leaving us?'

'Not yet.' He didn't know Paddy well, but he always felt at ease with him.

'Gary McGrath tells me you're gunna run for mayor.' Paddy was an occasional member of the Labor Party, sometimes letting months pass between meetings.

Matt looked out over the paddocks, green as Ireland (well, almost) after the recent heavy rains. He loved the bush, but he was no sheep-and-cattleman, nor a cotton farmer, and he never would be. Dealing in people, harvesting votes, that was what interested him. Running for mayor was, though he had told nobody except his father, just a training run for other ambitions.

'You'll be up against St Paul,' said Paddy.

Paul Zetland had been mayor three times running. He saw every road out of Collamundra as leading to Damascus; he was forever having visions and writing letters to voters. Matt knew there was little hope of beating him, but he needed the exercise.

'It's a gesture, Paddy. Now and again they need to be made.'

Paddy O'Reilly looked at Matt shrewdly. Had Paddy's grandparents gone to America instead of Australia, he would have been in Tammany Hall instead of the cattle plains of New South Wales. He could not have resisted the temptation. 'You're starting to sound like a politician. That what you wanna be?'

He had never confided this to anyone but his father: 'Yes.'

Paddy looked out over the paddocks, dim now in the yellow-grey twilight; then he looked back at Matt: 'It'll be a long road. From here.'

'Ben Chifley started on a railway track. Abe Lincoln was a country lawyer.'

'Sure, and Adolf Hitler was an army corporal. My point is, you need someone behind you. Way out here, Matt, in the Labor Party, you're at the arse-end of the world.'

Matt grinned. 'One thing I'll say for you, Paddy, you're all encouragement.'

'I'm pragmatic. It's not an Irish characteristic, but it's crept in somewhere. Still, good luck.'

Then Eileen O'Reilly called them in for dinner and for the next hour-and-a-half Matt felt himself being drawn into the warm pool of a family and a black-haired girl whose smile was as enigmatic as a dryad's.

When dinner was over and the table was cleared Carmel said, 'I'll drive you back to town.'

It was a fifteen-kilometre drive but he wasn't going to say no; he wanted to be alone with her. He said goodnight to her parents, went out to the white ute and got in beside the black-haired siren. Before she turned on the ignition, she said, 'You kept looking at me all during dinner. What were you thinking?'

If she could be so direct, so could he: 'I was thinking of you as a siren. On a rock, luring shipwrecked sailors.'

'Are you shipwrecked?' She switched on the engine, looked at him again, then took the ute down the long avenue between the coolibahs, now black in the season of night.

'No.' *But I could be*; but that would be juvenile repartee. 'Do you always drive as fast as this?'

Out on the main road the countryside went by in a dark blue sliced by the broadsword of the headlights. 'It's a reaction to traffic in cities — Sydney, Rome, London. I used to own a third-hand Civic and I rarely got out of second. You scared?'

No, I like fast women. But that, too, would be juvenile stuff.

He directed her to where he and his father lived in town and she pulled the ute in before the neat weatherboard house in the tree-lined street. She switched off the engine and looked at him for the next move.

'Can I see you again?' he said.

'If you want to. But I'm not going to be a library book, something you take out when you've nothing better to do.'

'I think you've got the wrong impression of me,' he said, though he knew she was right.

'No, I haven't. But I think you could be changed —'

He gazed at her: a longer stare than he could remember ever having given another girl. Then he leaned across the bag that sat between them, across the books and essays on *Coriolanus* (another politician) and Australian poets, and took her by the shoulders and kissed her. Her mouth opened at once under his and he felt a shudder go through her as if he had touched a nerve. His hand went down to her breast and she left it there for a moment. Then she pushed his hand away and sat back.

'Wrong side,' he said. 'I'm a right-handed lover.'

'Don't let's get technical. It's early night yet.' Then she looked past him and down the street. 'Your girlfriend is spying on us.'

He turned, looked over his shoulder. On the other side of the wide street, in the darkness under a tree, he saw the silver Mercedes.

5

When he went into the house his father was in the kitchen preparing his usual before-bedtime pot of tea. It was a ritual with him, almost like a prayer ceremony, though he was not given to many prayers. It was not he but Matt's mother who had been a Catholic and sent Matt to church and on the search for salvation.

'Where've you been?' he said, nodding at the satchel as Matt put it on a chair.

'Out at Cavanreagh, the O'Reillys. Their daughter Carmel drove me home.'

'The one's just come back from wherever she's been? I saw her the other day when I was down at Doc Hennessy's with my thumb.' He had sprained his thumb gardening, a hazardous occupation. 'Good-looking girl. You've got lipstick on your chin.'

Matt took a tissue from the box on top of the fridge. For two men who lived without benefit of a woman, it was a remarkably neat kitchen, a place for everything and everything in its place. There were even two aprons hanging on a nail behind the door, striped butcher's aprons, not frilly pinafores. The rest of the house was as neat as the kitchen.

'I went for a walk a while ago, stretch the legs,' said Keith Durban. 'Your girlfriend Ruby was parked down the street. I nodded to her, but she ignored me.'

'That's finished.' Since Matt was eighteen his father had never interfered in his choice of girlfriends, as if they were shoals he had to learn to negotiate on his own. But he knew that his father had not had much time for Ruby.

'I'm glad to hear it,' said Durban senior and managed not to sound like a schoolteacher.

He was an inch or two shorter than his son and slimmer, a dark-haired, good-looking man whom women found attractive without ever managing to throw a rope over him. He was still in love with his dead wife, though she had been gone ten years. He took women to dinner and sometimes to bed, but never in Collamundra nor Cawndilla, and his son had never met any of them. He was self-contained but not selfish.

He poured tea for each of them and they sat down at the kitchen table.

'This came for you today,' he said and pushed a letter across to Matt.

Matt opened it, read it and said, 'Bugger!'

'What is it?'

'The Education Department. I told you, I'd applied for a transfer to Sydney. I didn't expect it till next year at the earliest. They want me to report to —' He checked the letter again: 'Plain Hills High as soon as possible. Next week.'

'Plain Hills — where's that?'

'I dunno, they don't say — it could be one of the new ones. Bloody bureaucrats.' He sipped his tea, black with no sugar and made with leaves not teabags. He reached for the biscuit tin, at an Iced Vo-Vo. Wilma Durban had been a woman with old-fashioned tastes and bequeathed them to her husband and son. She was still here in the house, for Keith if not for Matt. 'That puts the kybosh on running for mayor.'

'The voters will miss you,' said his father with mild sarcasm. Then, looking at his spoon going round in his cup: 'I'll miss you, too. But good luck.'

Matt looked across the table at him. 'It's only a means to an end, I've told you that. Canberra is the target.'

'It'll be a long road. But as I say, good luck. And you can always come back.'

Matt grinned. 'I dunno. I'm teaching the kids the American author Thomas Wolfe — the Thirties one, not the one who's writing today. He wrote *You Can't Go Home Again*.'

'A pity,' said Keith Durban, secure in home.

6

The affair, the romance (Matt wasn't sure yet what to call it) progressed quickly. He took her to dinner, to the movies (she liked the aging Paul Newman), to a country dance; but never in Collamundra, always in Cawndilla or neighbouring towns. There was fumbling in the front, sometimes in the back seat of his Corolla, but that was as far as he got — 'I'm not going to make love in a car,' she said. 'That's out. O–U–T.'

Then his father went away on a two-day education camp and that night he picked her up at the surgery and took her home. He had prepared dinner because his mother had taught him how to cook; Carmel looked with surprised approval at the *coq au vin*. They ate, drank a bottle of shiraz between them and went to bed.

'Don't rush it,' she said as he undressed her.

He said nothing, peeled her and marvelled at the lush beauty of her. She looked at the enlarged intruder between them and said, 'No wonder you've been successful.'

'You're talking too much.'

'Yes,' she said, 'yes, I am.'

He was experienced and he was surprised, though he said nothing, at how experienced she was. When it was over he realised he had made love to a woman, not a girl.

'Well,' she said as she lay back, getting her breath, 'that's a beginning.'

He raised his head from her breast. 'Beginning of what?'

'Whatever you want to make of it.'

'I love an enigmatic woman.'

'How many do you know?'

'One.'

She kissed him tenderly. 'You have a lot to learn, Matt. I'll teach you.'

They made love again, recovered, got up and showered, dressed and he took her out to drive her back to Cavanreagh in his car. They got in, he switched on the ignition, then looked in his rear-vision mirror.

Down the street, on the opposite side in the darkness under a tree, was the silver Mercedes. He said nothing, put the Corolla into gear and drove off.

Over the next two weeks he saw Carmel four, sometimes five, nights a week. He took her to dinner in Cawndilla, had dinner out at Cavanreagh, made love on a bed of woolsacks on the banks of the Noongulli, but never at the same spot where he had made love (?) to Ruby Rawson.

Several times he saw the silver Mercedes and once Ruby accosted him in the street. He kept the encounter to as low a level as he could and she, seething with anger, surprised him by not blowing her top in public.

But when she left she snapped, 'It's not over, you creep! You'll see!'

Chapter Three

1

Two nights later it rained. The cloud dams that had built up from the west after sunset suddenly burst. The rain poured down in the way that made farmers believe in heavens if not in God. By dawn the downpour had eased off to a steady drizzle, making the morning as grey as grief.

Matt and his father were at breakfast, getting ready to leave for their respective schools, when the knocker on the front door clanged loudly, demandingly. They looked at each other, frowning, then Matt got up, went down the short hallway and opened the door. Two police officers stood there, rain dripping from their hats, their slickers glistening like glass shawls.

'Bit early, Matt, sorry about that,' said Ken Shuster, the senior man. 'We come in?'

'Sure,' said Matt and stood back. 'What is it? Some kid from school in trouble?'

'Worse than that,' said Shuster and waited till they were shown into the living room off the hall: 'Ruby Rawson's been found out by the river. She'd been stabbed by what we think was her own nail-file. Big job, with a pearl handle. You know it?'

Matt nodded, sat down, almost collapsing into an armchair. 'Jesus!'

'Sit down, fellers,' said Keith Durban and took a chair beside his son and opposite the two police officers. 'What's this got to do with Matt?'

The two officers looked uncomfortable. They took off their hats and slickers, looked around for somewhere to drop them.

'Just put 'em on the carpet,' said Keith.

The two men hesitated, then did that. Shuster and the constable, Dick Lucas, had known Matt Durban since childhood. Lucas and Matt had played together in the district rugby team and Shuster was the team secretary. These three were *mates*.

'This is bloody awkward, Keith,' said Shuster. 'But we've got to start somewhere ... Matt, when did you last see the — the deceased?'

Matt looked up, shook his head. 'Come on, Ken, cut out the official crap. Not *the deceased*. Ruby ... I dunno. A coupla nights ago.'

'You'd taken her out?'

'The other night? No. Come on, Ken — you'd seen us together. For about three or four months, something like that. But we broke it off three weeks ago.'

'Why?'

Matt took his time: this was the Big Lie, the beginning of the lies he would tell in the years ahead in politics; but at the moment he was seeing no more than the immediate present. And last night, when Ruby died. He didn't look at his father as he said, 'I'm leaving here next week. I've been transferred to Sydney, to Plain Hills High down there. She didn't want me to go.'

His father was looking at him, his face a mask. Dick Lucas said, 'Why? Were you engaged or anything like that? Unofficially?'

'No. Between us it was — I dunno, what d'you call it? An affair.'

'Did you ask her to go with you?'

'No. That was never on, she didn't want to leave Collamundra.'

'Did she have another boyfriend? Someone from another day?' said Shuster.

Matt frowned. 'Come *on*, Ken. Are you asking me to dob someone in? She knew lots of fellers, she was popular —'

'With the guys? Yeah, I guess she was, we saw that. But not with the women?'

'I dunno about that. I never discussed her with any woman.' Carmel was blocked from his mind, behind a locked door. 'Had she been — been raped?'

'The doc says no. She'd fought with whoever did her in, but there was no sign of rape or anything like that.'

'Were there any — clues?' Keith Durban hesitated before he said the word, as if embarrassed by it. 'Evidence?'

'None that we've found. Strictly between us, okay? They found her in her dad's Merc. The rain wiped out any footprints, anything like that. No, we're starting from taws, but that's between us, okay?'

'Of course. There was no evidence in the car?'

For Crissakes, Dad, leave it alone!

Shuster was still in good humour. 'What's your point, Keith?'

'I'm trying to prove there isn't a skerrick of anything to connect Matt with this. Last night he was with me, over at Cawndilla. There was an area teachers' meeting. We drove over together about seven and we came home just on eleven. Just as the rain started to really come down.'

'That's good enough for us,' said Shuster and he and Lucas stood up. 'Thanks for your co-operation, both of you. But we had to start somewhere.'

Matt showed them to the front door, stood on the verandah as both men paused to put on their slickers against the still-falling drizzle. Lucas said, 'You looking forward to going to Sydney?'

'Yes and no. I'll let you know when I come home for the next holidays. As for Ruby —' He made a meaningless gesture. 'It shouldn't have happened to her. I hope you catch whoever did it.'

'We will,' said Shuster. 'It's a small town. Come and have a drink with us before you leave.'

'I'll do that,' said Matt.

He watched them drive away, disappearing into the drizzle, then turned to find his father standing in the doorway. 'Why'd you tell them Ruby didn't want to go to Sydney with you?'

'It wasn't that she didn't want to go to Sydney — she'd have been in that. It was the other thing, that I wanted to be a politician. She couldn't understand that. And — I guess I was selfish — I looked at her and knew she would never fit in to what I wanted.'

'Why didn't you tell them that?'

'Dad —' He looked straight at his father.

Who looked straight back at him; then nodded his head. 'I see your point. I noticed you didn't mention Carmel.'

'No, I didn't. The town's going to be full of gossip from now on — why bring her into it?'

'Is it serious between you two?' Keith Durban had met her only a couple of times.

'I don't know for sure. It could be. But now I'm going off to Sydney . . . '

His father nodded. 'Okay. Now come on, let's wash up. We're running late.'

Life might be unravelling, but a neat house had to be kept.

Ruby Rawson's murder was the talk of the school, the subject for the day. Matt was aware of everyone scrutinising him, even the other teachers, and he did his best to look like a man upset but with his feelings under control. He was shocked at what had happened to Ruby, but most of all he was sorry for her. She had been the town bike, or pretty close to it, but she had not deserved to be murdered.

Desdemona Smith, the school principal, called him into her office at the lunch-break. She was a formidable woman, bulky, medium-height, with a bosom that was a balcony, her square-jawed face glowering above it like old newsreels of Mussolini looking for a contradiction.

But her looks were misleading; she was a kindly woman. 'Matt, that's terrible news about Ruby Rawson. I hear the police went to see you this morning —'

'Des, don't jump to conclusions —'

'Matt, I'm not. To be frank, I thought you'd picked the wrong girl in town, but —'

'Des, yes, you're right. She was the wrong girl, but I'd woken up to that three weeks ago. We'd called it off. She wasn't happy about it, but I stayed away from her. Whatever Ruby was, and I know a lot of people didn't think much of her, she didn't deserve to be — to be murdered.'

'No. No, she didn't deserve that. She was here when I first came to this school and she was a handful even back then . . .' Then she picked up a letter from her desk: 'There was this from Sydney this morning. You're being transferred —'

'I told you I'd applied. I didn't think it would come through this quick —'

'Quickly. Don't forget you're an English teacher, watch your adverbs.' But she was smiling, trying to put them both at ease. 'It's just as well, Matt. I mean the timing. The kids will talk — and their mothers. It could be difficult for you if you stayed on.'

'Des —' He looked at her, a mother figure despite the Mussolini image; he had always got on well with her and liked her. 'Des, do you think I'm to blame? Not the murder, but —' He waved a helpless hand.

'For encouraging Ruby — if she needed encouraging? No, Matt. Men do half their thinking — or non-thinking — below their navels. I'm just glad you woke up in time.'

He smiled, the first genuine smile of the day. 'I love you, Des.'

'Don't get any ideas,' she said and smiled back.

That afternoon, after he had got home from school, he phoned Carmel at Dr Hennessy's surgery, but there was no answer. He hung up, pondered whether to ring Cavanreagh and decided against it. Carmel may have gone shopping or just gone home early because there were no appointments. He was seeing her tonight and that would be the time to discuss Ruby's murder, not over the phone.

His father came home just as he walked out the front door to get into his car. 'How'd it go today? The kids give you any curry?'

'No. But they gave me plenty of looks ... I'll be glad to leave, Dad.'

'I couldn't agree more. Where you heading now?'

'Out to see Carmel.'

'A word of advice. You'll have to bring up Ruby's murder, but keep it short. She won't want to hear the details.'

Matt grinned. 'Mum really educated you, didn't she?'

'Right down the line.'

The rain had stopped and Matt drove out to Cavanreagh through a silvery dusk. Carmel was waiting for him on the steps of the homestead verandah. 'Let's go for a walk,' she said as he stepped out of his car.

They walked down the long drive, night creeping in on them, isolating them. Out on the main road, headlights went by like swift fireflies, the sound of the car's engines like a faint buzzsaw in the dark silence.

Carmel's own silence lasted for almost a hundred yards, then she said, 'How do you feel? About Ruby?'

'Shocked, like everyone else. Why?'

'Darling —' It was the first time she had called him that out of bed. 'Have the police been to see you?'

'Yes. But, like they said, it was routine, they had to start somewhere. I was over at Cawndilla last night with my dad. There's nothing to worry about.'

They walked another fifty yards before she said, 'I wasn't thinking there was. It's the town — it's a small country town, people talk —'

'I know that. I tried to get you this afternoon at the surgery —'

'I left early, the doc had no appointments. But this morning in the waiting room —' She shook her head. 'People were more concerned about what had happened than they were about their own complaints. They didn't mention you, but they will —'

'I'm going to dodge all that —' They had reached the front gates. A huge truck-and-trailer went by with a thundering *whoosh*, lights all over it like a runaway Christmas tree. He leaned on the stone gatepost, held her hand as the silence rushed back in: 'Love, I'm leaving for Sydney the end of the week. My transfer has come through, a year ahead of schedule.'

Her hand tightened on his; he was surprised and winced at the strength in her grip. 'Oh —' It was a gasp, as if he had punched her. 'You never mentioned it —'

'It was a year down the track. I'd have told you about it sooner or later. It just happened sooner, much sooner than I expected.'

Again she was silent in the dark silence. Then: 'You're going to take it?'

'Carmel —' It was almost like talking to a pupil. 'I told you about my ambition — I want to get into politics, serious politics, not just council stuff. I can't do that from here, unless I changed to the Nationals and I'd rather cut my throat than do that. I need a job in Sydney while I try to make my way in a Labor Party branch down there — the transfer gives me that. It's going to be a long haul, I know that, but I'm patient —'

They began to walk back up the driveway. Somewhere out in the paddocks a nightjar gave its gobbled cry and, as if in answer, a bull roared. This was country peace, he thought, and wondered if, down the long track ahead, he would miss it.

'What about us?' said Carmel after another fifty yards' silence.

'I'll miss you —'

'Thanks,' she said dryly.

He laughed; in later years she would always be able to make him laugh. In the tangled web of politics it would be she who would remind him that he is not laughed at, that laughs at himself first. But all that was a long way down the track.

'No, I'll more than miss you — I'll — I dunno —' Suddenly he heard himself say, 'Will you marry me?'

She stopped, turned to face him. In the darkness they could barely see each other; the coolibahs crowded in, listening. 'Matt, you're talking off the top of your head —'

'No, I'm not.' Just as suddenly he knew he was not; he knew, as certain as anything he knew, that he wanted to spend the rest of his life with her. 'Okay, it's sudden — but I mean it. Marry me.'

Silence; the trees crept closer. Then: 'No. Not yet. I'll think about it. But not yet.'

He took her in his arms and kissed her, like pressing a seal on a pact. 'I do love you. That's the truth.'

'And I love you. But right now, everything's too — too

shaky. When we marry, darling, I want it to be forever. On solid ground.'

'When will that be?'

'I don't know. All I know is, not *now*.'

2

He said goodbye to Carmel on the Friday night. They had dinner with her parents at Cavanreagh, then he drove her out to the banks of the Noongulli and they made love on a bed of woolsacks. They were a mile downriver from where Ruby Rawson had been murdered and he shut out of his mind any memory of her. Carmel's love-making was fierce, but he was accustomed now to the moods of her love-making. She alternated between tenderness and rage and he liked the unpredictability of her.

'Don't try this with any other girl,' she said, lying on top of him. 'Ever.'

'Never,' he said, half-amused, half-serious.

Somewhere a kookaburra laughed and Carmel raised her head. 'They don't laugh at night —'

'It's not laughing at us. His wife has just asked him, how's about anothery?'

She bit his ear. 'You and your corny jokes! Get rid of them before we marry.'

He grinned, pulled her closer. 'How's about anothery?'

Later he took her back to Cavanreagh, said goodbye to her at the steps up to the verandah, promised to call her every night and twice on Sundays. Then drove away down the long avenue of coolibahs, the beginning of the longest road of all.

Saturday morning his father carried his bags out to the Corolla and stacked them in the rear seat.

'How was it yesterday when you said goodbye to your classes?'

'Two of the girls cried and none of the boys made any jokes. I was touched, to tell you the truth.'

'You were a good teacher, Des Smith has told me that. Don't lose the knack.'

They shook hands, they were not the sort of males who embraced, and Keith Durban said, 'Did you hear the news on the radio this morning?' He always tuned in for the breakfast session on the local station. 'They've arrested Bert Carter for Ruby Rawson's murder.'

'Oh shit! Bert? Christ, he wouldn't kill a snake!

'Well, they've taken him in.' Keith Durban closed the car door on his son. 'I think you're getting out of here just in time —'

Matt thought about that, then nodded. 'You're right. If I was still here, they might call me —'

'They may do that. Call you back as — what do they call it? — a character witness —'

'I was never a mate of Bert's —'

'I mean Ruby —'

'A character witness for Ruby?' He frowned at the thought of it. 'Jesus, everyone in town knew what she was like —'

'But no one is going to say that about her, not now she's dead. You should read more court reports, mate. The worst bugger in the world is murdered and suddenly his family and his friends discover he was St Francis of Assisi. Ruby will be a born-again virgin by the time Bert's trial comes up.' He patted the car door, as if making sure it was tightly shut. Against the future. 'Stay down in Sydney, don't come back, not even for a weekend. I'll come down to visit you. Good luck.'

So Matt Durban, twenty-five years old, optimistic, in love with a girl and with the future, drove out of Collamundra on the long, long road to Canberra. He laughed at the thought (and others would have laughed louder) but he didn't deny it. *I charge thee, fling away ambition. By that sin fell the angels.* Shakespeare may have had it right; but there were no angels in politics, and that was where he was heading. Collamundra, the town, the wide paddocks, the cotton fields, the Noongulli, fell away behind him. Crossing the Blue Mountains he began to sing, not a pop song but an old Rodgers and Hammerstein number written before he was born.

That night he booked into a motel in Blacktown, on the edge of the city, the edge of tomorrow. Sunday morning he drove out to Plain Hills High. It was on the Windsor Road, a comparatively new school with buildings not yet worn by weather, bureaucratic neglect nor student vandalism. The principal, Derry Jakes, was there waiting for him.

He was a big, round, cheerful man, a Mr Pickwick in blue jeans and a bright red shirt. 'Better to see you this morning rather than coming in cold tomorrow. It's a good school, now we've got it sorted out. We've got a mix here and it wasn't easy to begin with. We've got kids from the Hills district —' He waved a hand to the north-east. 'And from Out There —' He capitalised it, waving a hand to the west. 'Parents with what-you-want and those who haven't got it, but want it. I shall deny I ever said that, if you quote me.' His smile was almost a caricature, teeth in a watermelon. 'They're all good kids, all wanting to get on. There are the exceptions, but that's par for the course. As I'm sure you know.'

'I'll cope.' Walking through the empty schoolyard, through the empty classrooms, it was easy to see that. The test would come on Monday when he faced dozens of sceptical minds.

'I'm sure you will. You'll be teaching Years 10 and 11, English and history. I teach both in Year 12. In English give 'em plenty of Shakespeare, even though some may ask you why. He's always good for a quote, though off the top of my head I can't remember anything he ever said about teenagers. Give 'em some of the moderns, too — Arthur Miller, Tennessee Williams, our bloke Williamson. I never give 'em Beckett or Pinter. Too many silences. Adolescents don't understand silences, they think they are black holes from the universe. History — I give 'em English, European, American, even a bit of Asian when I can find books on it. I never tell the class this, but I never take history for the full truth. History is just a novel with real people as characters. But again, I'll say I never said that. You got any interests? Sport, movies, what?'

'Politics.'

An eyebrow went up. 'You're not a Commie? Or a Greenie?'

'No, Labor.'

Jakes nodded appreciatively. 'So am I.' He put out a hand. 'Welcome, comrade. As St Gough would say. One other thing — you married, got a partner?'

'There's a girl, but she's back in Collamundra.'

'Keep your mind on her. There's one or two of the mums here who have too much time on their hands — so they might try putting their hands on you.'

It was Matt's turn to raise an eyebrow. 'I had none of that at Collamundra.'

'Well, I suppose they are all virgins out there, even the mums.' But he was smiling: 'You'll survive, Matt. Good luck and welcome.'

That night Matt rang Carmel: 'I think everything's going to be okay. The head seems a nice bloke . . . I'm in a motel at the moment, but I'm going to look for a one-bedroom flat —'

'It's none of my business — but can you afford it?'

He had never discussed money with her. 'Love, I'm not on the breadline. I've been saving ever since I started as a trainee teacher. And ten years ago my mother left me some money. I've trebled it since then.'

'A socialist who speculates?'

'I love you. Will you marry me?'

'I'll think about it. I wish you were here. I'm feeling *moist* —'

'Not *now*! I'm on my knees, saying my prayers —'

They hung up, both laughing, which is one of the sounds of love.

Next day he began school. The girls in Years 10 and 11 looked at him as naked flesh: they could have been cattle judges. He gave them the big smile and they gave him their vote and anything else he wanted. The boys, the same age but younger, were more cautious: he was authority and that was always to be suspected. But he got through the day without incident and went back to the motel tired but happy. He ate at McDonald's, nodded to a couple of Year 11 girls with their boyfriends, studied them covertly and wondered what lay ahead down *their* roads, went home (home?) and fell asleep within minutes.

Wednesday he moved into a one-bedroom furnished flat in a block of four in Parramatta, twenty minutes by car from the school. The flat looked as if it had been furnished at an end-of-year sale at Ikea or Norman Ross; few items matched, but they were still in good condition. The bed was a double, the mattress solid and comfortable; the linen and the towels were unstained and not threadbare. He rented a television set, stocked the cupboards and by Thursday evening was *home*.

He had spoken to Carmel every night, enjoyed the teaching and the school atmosphere, identified the one or two mums with clutching hands (sirens on the Windsor Road?), nodded g'day to his neighbours, all young like himself, and Friday night there was a knock at his door.

He opened it, expecting it to be one of the neighbours, and there stood Carmel, a suitcase on either side of her.

'Is there room for me?'

And so another step on the road was taken.

3

At the end of another week his father rang. 'I'm coming down on Saturday. Can you give me a bed?'

'Dad . . . Carmel is here with me.'

'H'm.' A pause; then: 'Permanently?'

'Yes. I'm asking her to marry me, but so far she's holding out.' She was sitting opposite him and made a face.

Another pause in Collamundra; then: 'I'll come down anyway. Book me into a motel.' Another pause: 'You happy?'

'Very.'

'That's all that counts in the end.'

Keith Durban came down to Parramatta and went out to dinner with Matt and Carmel. He and Carmel got on like old friends and at one point Matt asked if they would like him to get lost.

'Son,' said Keith, sounding grandfatherly, 'you had better get used to other men showing interest in your girl.'

'He doesn't have to worry in the least,' said Carmel, reaching for Matt's hand.

'I didn't mean that he would,' said Keith. 'Other women will take an interest in you, too. People are more inquisitive these days than they used to be, publicly inquisitive. Watch out when you get into politics.'

Then, putting a toe in the water, Matt asked, 'What's happening with the Rawson murder?'

'Do we have to talk about that?' said Carmel.

'No, not *talk* about it. I don't want a discussion on it. But how are things stacking up against Bert Carter?'

His father turned up his hands. 'The police are letting out nothing. He's out on bail, reporting every day to the cops, but he's given up his job out at the stockyards. His mum and dad told me he's *shattered*. Nobody believes he murdered Ruby, they think it was someone from out of town. The trial's been moved to Bathurst. Working at the stockyards, they can't find anyone for the jury who doesn't know him.'

'I hope he gets off,' said Matt.

'So do I,' said Carmel. 'Who wants dessert?'

'You can see why I want to marry her?' said Matt to his father. 'Always practical.'

'She'll need to be if she follows you to Canberra. Will you?'

'Follow him to Canberra? No. Side-by-side, but not *following* him.'

Keith gave her the Durban smile. 'Mr and Mrs Prime Minister. There goes the misogynist vote.'

That night in bed Carmel said, 'Do you still think of Ruby?'

'What? God, no! Tonight I was thinking of Bert Carter, not her. Are you jealous of her?'

'Not just her. Every girl you went with.'

He held her to him, feeling the quivering in her that might burst into tears or temper. 'All the girls I knew are a blank sheet. I think you know that.'

'I do,' she said and kissed him as gently as she might have a child.

Next morning Matt went round to the motel to say goodbye to his father. 'You got on well with Carmel.'

'You've got a good one there. Hang on to her, wedding ring or not.' He put his bag into the boot of his car, a Peugeot. For some reason he had never explained to his son, he always bought a European car. Neither of them talked cars, so his choice never came up. 'Have you contacted the local Labor Party lot yet?'

'Tomorrow night.'

'Good luck.' Then, as he was about to get into the car, he paused. 'I wish Mum had lived to see you now. And Carmel.'

'So do I. Tell me —' Matt felt uncomfortable. 'Were you two as happy as I remember?'

'You'll never know how happy.' He got into the car, slammed the door. 'Look after yourself and Carmel. Good luck tomorrow night.'

Monday night Matt went to the local Labor Party meeting. He asked Carmel if she wanted to accompany him and she said, 'No, you test the water first. They're not interested in me. They'll be sizing you up and I don't want to stand back and watch that.'

'You may be doing a lot of it in the future,' he said, half-joking.

'That will be time enough,' she said and kissed him. 'Good luck.'

So he went alone, walking through the rain-swept streets, a damp start that might be a long journey. The meeting was held in a single-storey building owned by the local social club. It had a large hall where dances, bingo and, on election night, celebrations or wakes were held. Politically, it had all the emotional warmth of an empty warehouse. But the meeting brought in over a hundred members, which made the Collamundra Labor Party look like a sewing circle.

The secretary, Danny Voce, introduced Matt to the gathering and everyone smiled and applauded. He stood up, gave them the smile that would become famous, and said, 'I'll work with you to elect our State and Federal members —'

'Do you have any political ambition yourself?' That from a committee member sitting beside Danny Voce, a leather-faced man who, one knew, carried sharp questions with him like a scabbard of swords.

Matt was not naive: he knew that the State party didn't need enemies from outside: it had its own roll-call. Faction-fighting was a party sport; blood sometimes ran like water. This man asking the question had faction-fighter written all over him.

Matt hesitated; then took a chance: 'Yes. Some time in the future, maybe not too far down the track, I'll aim for Canberra —'

The temperature dropped. There was silence and the members looked at each other as if another 'flu epidemic had been announced. The leather-faced man slapped his hands round his body as if looking for swords. Then a woman's voice at the back of the hall yelled, 'Attaboy!' and somewhere in the body of the meeting a single member clapped two or three times, then the clapping suddenly died as if the traitor, whoever he was, had been seized from both sides.

Matt sat down in his chair at the end of a row, wondering if he should dash out into the night. But a woman behind him leaned forward and patted his shoulder and he decided to stay.

When the meeting was over Danny Voce took Matt into his office and closed the door. It was a small room papered with past triumphs, election posters for the last forty years. The ideal room for Danny Voce to say:

'Matt —' He was a portly man with a fringe of blond curls running round three sides of his head. He had no ambitions of his own and so was able to run the branch and the meeting with an iron hand. He was the mechanic that every political party needs.

'Matt, you must tread carefully. At least twenty of our members have ambition or aspiration, whatever you want to call it, some for Macquarie Street and our esteemed State bear-pit, some for Canberra and running the whole country. If you're set on Canberra, don't broadcast it. Work silently till someone higher up the ladder, down at headquarters, notices you and taps you on the shoulder and lets you know you've been chosen. I'll keep an eye on you and if I think you're worth it, I'll help you.' He was a widower with no children; his family were the voters. 'But remember, the Labor Party has as many enemies inside it as outside it. It's the nature of our game.'

Matt recognised someone who might turn out to be a best friend. 'You're my mentor, okay?'

'Okay. Now have you heard this one —?' Danny Voce collected jokes as other people collected paintings or books or tattoos. 'Back in the Fifties, when Florida was in the middle of its building boom, new hotels going up every week, all with fancy names, these two Jewish ladies from New York met for the first time beside a Miami pool. They talked for a while then the first lady said, "Have you been through the Fontainebleau?" And the second lady says, "I don't think so. I'm still going through the menopause."'

And he fell back in his chair laughing, his belly rising and falling with each gust.

Matt laughed at the joke, as much to please Voce as at the joke itself, and went home to begin his first study in diplomacy, a subject he had not thought necessary in Labor circles. Carmel asked him how he had fared and he told her of his baptism:

'I've been daydreaming — I thought everyone would

welcome me, an eager beaver, charming, good-looking bloke like myself —'

'I welcome you. Come to bed and shut up.'

Over the next week Carmel got a job as a receptionist with a local doctor. Matt traded in his Corolla and bought a second-hand Holden which, the dealer swore with hand on heart, had been driven only by a clergyman to Sunday services. Which made Matt wonder why more used car salesmen didn't go into politics.

Matt and Carmel slowly got used to Parramatta. It was a city with its own history; but only twenty-five kilometres up-river from Sydney, it had difficulty establishing its identity. It was surrounded by suburbs of the bigger city. Its Lord Mayor exchanged Christmas cards with the rulers of Andorra and San Marino, two other territories surrounded by foreigners. Matt began the task of becoming an immigrant who fitted in.

The weeks went by and slowly everything progressed: their love and satisfaction with each other. Living together is different from *going* together: tolerance has to be learned as well as trust. And, as they found out, sharing a bathroom is the ultimate test.

Outside their flat, Matt was accepted into Plain Hills High and the Labor Party endorsed him as someone who might, in the future, make a substantial contribution. Carmel never went to the meetings with him, but she showed interest in matters and started to sound like a Labor voter. Which was the first thing any Labor aspirant needed.

Then came a long holiday weekend and they drove down to Canberra. Neither of them had ever been to the national capital and they were impressed by it, the largest country town in the nation. The many trees were thin with winter and a cold wind blew down from the ranges to the south. Parliament was not sitting and they walked through the empty halls of Parliament House, empty but for other tourists, who, like themselves, didn't count. This was the House where, in 1927, a royal duke with a stammer had proclaimed that Australia at last had a national capital. Melbourne, which up till then had thought *it* was the national capital, suffered a severe earth tremor. It was here that a governor-general, who liked a tipple or two, had dismissed a Labor government. Matt remembered the newcasts of that fateful day and the dismissed Prime Minister standing here on these steps surveying the cheering, weeping mob like a Roman emperor waiting for his chariot. Keith Durban, an occasional heretic, had remarked, 'Look at him, enjoying every moment of the drama,' and Matt had had to agree with him.

But a new temple was already planned for the hill behind this House and Matt and Carmel walked up to see the first excavations, like the planting furrows of his own ambition. Carmel held his hand, her back turned to the wind, and said, 'If you never make it, how will you feel?'

'I don't know,' he said, his own back turned to the wind, as if the wind were caution. He looked down at the city, as neat as any mapmaker could make it, and wondered where its heart, if any, was located. 'But I wouldn't be the first who's failed. A feller named Bryan, William Jennings Bryan, ran three times for US president.'

'What happened to him?' She had always been more interested in the women in history, not the men. She didn't think of herself as a feminist, but she knew neglect when she read it.

'He finished up pleading the wrong case in what was known as the Scopes trial. About evolution. He won the case against monkeys as our ancestors. Don't let me become a lawyer, a bush one or a Philadelphia one. I might argue a case I don't believe in.'

'I thought politicians did that all the time,' she said, but smiled and moved closer to him as if protecting him against the wind that, she now noticed, came from over the hill where the new temple would be built.

'They do, but with their fingers crossed behind their backs.'

'Don't ever become cynical,' she said, as if his idealism was her charge. 'Pragmatic, but never cynical.'

They drove back to Parramatta in a quiet euphoria, at least on his part, as if Canberra, an unlikely source, had presented a vision. He talked almost all the way of what lay ahead, what he wanted to do and she listened and nodded and smiled. And sometimes her eyes glazed over, but he didn't notice, keeping his own eyes on the road ahead, both actual and dreaming. Women have perfected non-listening, as well as listening, as an art. Carmel had learned that from history.

Matt began to work on a subject that he felt had long been ignored by those who ran the country, the nation's long northern border. He knew it was a subject that, then, did not excite the voters, but he had developed the long view, which his father, heretical as ever, had told him was un-Australian.

While he was still a trainee teacher he had gone with a small group to Darwin and then down the north-west coast. He had stood in wonder at the vast loneliness, along the coast and behind it. He had stood on a headland, the rest of the group camped three miles back in the scrub, and felt like the only man on the planet. Then out of the loneliness of nowhere a plane had appeared, heading north-east. He waved to it as it went over and the plane's wings wagged in reply. On their return to Darwin he had learned it was a Flying Doctor Service plane taking a dying pearl diver back to a hospital that hadn't been able to save him. It was on that trip that the germ of an idea was planted and he had been watering it ever since.

He went to Danny Voce with his plan. 'Danny, I think we should have a national coast guard, the way the Yanks do. Walter Peal is coming in next Monday. You think you could get him to give me half an hour?'

Walter Peal was the local member, had been in Canberra twenty years, been a minor Minister and was now a Shadow Minister, though the shadow was said to be thin and at times blurred. It was complained, by his critics, that he had settled for the comforts of his job.

Voce looked at Matt's notes and map. 'It's a good idea, Matt. But it has two things against it. One, it would cost a heap of money. Two, if it's a good idea he's not gunna suggest it to the government, he'll hold on to it till we're back in power.'

'Danny, I know that.' There were in Voce's office, with the door closed. 'I'm not trying to impress the voters, nobody out there is going to listen to me. I'm trying to impress Peal, so that he'll go back to Canberra and mention me to his mates in the Shadow Cabinet.'

Voce looked at him admiringly. 'You have the right spirit, son. But I have to warn you about Peal. He's a stuffed shirt, he wears a fancy handkerchief in the pocket of his dressing-gown. And he's so bloody socially correct! He wouldn't fart if he was alone on the Nullarbor Plain. He *will* listen, but you'll have to be careful —'

Matt smiled. 'Danny, except for my first night here, have I put a foot wrong?'

Voce smiled in return. 'No, you haven't. I'm never sure whether you're fair dinkum or a door-to-door salesman, but you know how to win friends and influence people. A bloke named Dale Carnegie preached that years and years ago. The Yanks have made an art of it. But like another

Yank, the first Roosevelt, Teddy, they carry a big stick, just in case.'

'I teach American history, Danny, bits of it. I'll never carry a big stick.'

'What will you carry?'

'I dunno. Maybe just a big smile.' And he flashed a sample and the posters around the office walls seemed for a moment a little brighter, as if applauding him.

Walter Peal came to the Monday night meeting, moved amongst the members like a Vatican cardinal. He was not a tall man but gave the appearance of being one, he held himself so straight and stiff. He was handsome and knew it, with a head of famous red hair that he carried like a beacon.

Matt at last, with Danny Voce's help, managed to get Peal into the small office. He closed the door. 'Mr Peal —'

'Walter.' But it was like God saying, *Just call me God.*

'Walter —' Matt produced his notes and map. 'Twenty-five coast guard patrol boats —'

Peal listened without showing any expression. Then: 'Have you costed this?'

'Roughly.' Matt gave a figure.

'Do you believe in the Little People?'

Matt was puzzled. 'Dwarves? Elves?'

Peal smiled tolerantly, as on a dumb child. 'No, the people at the bottom of the social heap. We build a battleship and some social worker asks how many pensions and unemployment cheques that will cost. It's a good idea and I'll take it back to Canberra with me. But . . . Can I have those notes and map?'

Matt produced a large envelope. 'Copies are in here.'

Again the smile, this time appreciatively. 'You're well prepared. I shall mention you when I get back amongst my colleagues. You're a schoolteacher, aren't you?'

'Yes. English and history.'

'Do you know much about Asian history?'

'Yes.' But he didn't. Asia was hundreds of blank pages in history's book. In China he had heard of Confucius, but never read him; had heard of Genghis Khan and read a bit about Mao Tse Dong. As for the other Asian countries, with the exception of India, he would have had trouble placing them on a map, let alone quoting any of their history. He made a mental note to look at Asia tomorrow.

'Bone up on it. Do you think you could work well in Canberra?'

'I'm a political animal, Walter.'

'We're a breed apart, aren't we?' said Peal and their smiles lit up the room, bathing just themselves in the glow.

Matt went home to Carmel, hugged her and said, 'I think the call may be coming.'

'A call has come,' she said, freeing herself from his arms. 'A letter from Bert Carter's lawyers. They want you as a witness for him.'

4

'Will you come with me?'

'No, I can't,' said Carmel, making hot chocolate for them before they went to bed. She was not as neat as Matt and his father about the house, but she managed to keep everything in its place. 'Dr Puget is on hospital duty this week and I have to stay and run the office. Also —'

'What?'

'I don't want to see you in the witness box. I — I was in a courtroom once, a girlfriend had been raped — it was in London —'

'You never told me —'

'It's something I wish I could put out of my mind. I hated the whole scene — the man in the dock who did it, the witnesses, the jury, the judge sitting up there as if not interested — well, that one was like that. And the lawyers — I dunno, almost impersonal. And my friend sitting there, the primary object . . . I don't want to come, darling. You go, get it over with, then come home . . .'

He took the mug of cocoa, stirred it. 'It won't be over and done with if Bert is convicted. Nobody will ever convince me he killed Ruby —'

'Let's pray he gets off. I'll say some prayers for him. You, too.'

'You think God ever listens to us?'

'I don't know. I've never had a prayer answered yet. Except when I prayed you'd be mine.'

He grinned. 'You make a good cocoa.'

So Matt got two days off from school and drove back over the mountains to Bathurst. The town, a small city, had all the solidity that some country towns achieve as their older buildings, the town hall and the courthouse and the banks, take on the shape of monuments. Wealth, inauspicious, surrounded it and its citizens had the comfortable look of people who trusted the future as much as they knew the past. But, of course, as Matt knew, there were always undercurrents, bores of uncertainty leaking through the soil.

He booked into a hotel, had lunch and went to see Bert Carter's lawyers. Shell & Lucci had offices in a two-storeyed stone building across from the courthouse. The building suggested its occupants might be solid, dry men; but both Shell and Lucci were young, bright and, Matt suspected, ambitious. Something like himself.

'We're arguing the case, between us —' Hugo Shell was tall, thin and energetic. 'Mr Carter couldn't afford a barrister, not one from down in Sydney. They charge ransom fees.' He rolled his eyes, as if about to dream of ransom fees.

'We want you as a character witness for our client. Bert says you will vouch for him —'

'I'll do that, if he wants me to. But I was never close to Bert, he was just a bloke I knew about town, about Collamundra —'

'Good enough,' said Albert Lucci, younger than Shell, plump and black-haired. 'The thing is, you *knew* the deceased. Ruby Rawson.'

'What d'you mean, *knew* her?' Matt hadn't missed the inflection.

'Well —' Shell, despite looking like the archetypal laconic Australian, was all twitches and nervous gestures. Lucci, on the other hand, though Naples-born, was not all Latin hand-flapping but had the sardonic manner of a Mafia *don*. 'Well, you knew — you knew her history —'

'For Crissakes, she was only twenty, what sort of history would she have had?'

'Come on, Matt,' said Lucci quietly, 'you know what we mean.'

'Yes, I do.' He was keeping his temper. He was surprised at how, suddenly, he wanted to protect — what? Not Ruby's virtue, certainly not that. Her reputation? That was indefensible, certainly back in Collamundra. But she was dead, in the worst of circumstances, and all at once he did not want to see the ghost of her revived and talked about. 'Can't we leave her out of it? I don't want to talk about how it was between us —'

Shell and Lucci looked at each other, then both nodded. 'Okay, we understand. We know what it's like in small towns. But we're trying to have Bert walk free — we *know* he didn't kill her. Did she ever mention another man to you? You weren't her first and we don't think our client was her last.'

'Had she had sex before she was killed?'

'The police report says no, unless a condom was used. There was evidence of a struggle, but no sign of rape or anything like that.'

Matt closed his eyes, shook his head. Ruby, for all her faults, did not deserve to be discussed like this. He remained silent for a few moments, then he opened his eyes and said, 'Look, Ruby was the town bike, Anytime Annie. When I started going with her, there were a lot of people who didn't like it. I was a teacher at the local high school, I should be setting a better example. But Ruby began to look like a one-man woman — *me*. I can't say she didn't look at other fellers, but I was the regular and after a while I think people began to think of me as her —' He was stuck for the word, or embarrassed by it.

'Saviour?' prompted Lucci.

'Well, I dunno they thought that far. But yes, I think they were less critical —'

'Did you talk marriage?'

Matt managed to hold back his exclamation. Lucci looked different now, sounded like a priest in the confessional. Bloody Italians: they were chameleons. 'No. We — I never thought of it. We broke up because I was going down to Sydney.'

'Amicably?' Lucci again, the lawyer this time.

'No-o.'

Shell flapped his hands. 'Did she turn to some other man? Someone, maybe, from out of Collamundra?'

'I wouldn't know. When I saw her, she was usually with Bert Carter.' There was no need to mention the stalking in the silver Mercedes. 'But Bert —' He shook his head again. 'I think he loved her. *Really* loved her.'

'We think so, too,' said Lucci. 'And that's why we think we can get him off. Desperate lovers kill, but Bert is not the desperate type. Do you think so?'

'No,' said Matt.

Then Lucci said, almost as a throwaway, 'You're now living with a girl from Collamundra?'

Matt was suddenly very still, holding his temper. 'Yes, I am. But she never knew Ruby, other than to see her in the street.'

'You took up with her before or after you broke it off with Ruby?'

'After. She'd been away from Collamundra for years. School in Sydney, then she went overseas. What's she got to do with this?'

'Matt —' Shell was doing his best to be affable. He offered more wine; well, more coffee. But coffee had never been a drink for confidences. 'We are only asking the questions the prosecutor may ask —'

Matt was suddenly glad Carmel had not come with him. 'She's my — my partner —' A new word just coming into vogue, but still sounding like a commercial union. 'We are going to be married. And it all began after — I repeat, *after* — I'd split with Ruby.'

'We understand, Matt,' said Lucci, now a romance counsellor. 'We'll protect you as best we can. After all, all we want is for Bert Carter to walk out of the court scot-free.'

'How strong is the case against him?'

'It has holes. Bert saw her on the night of the crime, but only for half an hour. They had words and he says he went off in a huff — he went home. Unfortunately, his mother and father weren't there, they'd gone to Bathurst for the night, so he's got no one to corroborate his story.'

'We think Ruby got in tow with an out-of-towner, someone passing through. Did she pick up fellers?'

'No.' Matt tried to make it sound emphatic, but Ruby had always been easy game. Once, during an argument, he had called her a probationary nymphomaniac and she had tried to stab him with the outsized nail-file. But that was history and should be buried with her. 'No, I don't think so.'

'The odd thing is,' said Shell, 'there were no fingerprints on the nail-file that killed her. It could've looked like suicide, except there was evidence of a struggle — her shirt was ripped and one shoe had been kicked off. Ruby's prints were on the nail-file, so it looked as if the killer had had his hand over hers. All the evidence against Bert is circumstantial. We're pretty hopeful for him.'

'So am I,' said Matt, wishing now he had not come.

The trial began next morning. Bert Carter, dull-eyed, seeming to have shrunk, was brought into the crowded courtroom. Local murder was rare and the retirees and the unemployed and housewives taking a day off from the hoovering and the laundry occupied all the public gallery. Matt, as a witness, was kept out of the courtroom. He sat outside in his car, waiting to be called. Town life went on about him: people shopping, people making money, an old man crossing the main street, stopping, then shaking his head as he went back to the kerb he had just left. By lunchtime argument and counter-argument in the court were still being heard. Lucci came out and took Matt to lunch at an Italian restaurant down the main street.

'Things are going well, we may not need to call you. I'm afraid Ruby's past reputation is going against her. You like pasta?'

'My girlfriend makes it. Irish pasta, it has everything in it.'

'You said she never knew Ruby?' Lucci was winding pasta on his fork.

Like trying to wind me, thought Matt. 'No, she didn't. I don't think she ever said two words to Ruby.'

'Have either of you been back to Collamundra since you left?'

'No. Why?'

'Matt, we're trying to divorce you as much as possible, you and your girlfriend, from Collamundra. We don't know the Crown Prosecutor, he's from Sydney, and I'm trying to anticipate anything he may ask ... You want a glass of red with the pasta?'

'Yes ... How long will the trial last?'

'A couple of days at least. We want the jury to get used to the sight of Bert, that he's an unlikely-looking murderer.'

'Aren't there a lot of unlikely-looking murderers?' The glass of red tasted bitter.

'Of course. But it's still a good ploy.'

Matt spent the afternoon waiting, but was not called. He rang Carmel at six o'clock: 'I'm here for at least another day.'

'Does it look bad for Bert Carter?'

'The lawyers are hopeful. They say some of the jury are starting to look sympathetic ... I wish you were here.'

'Hurry back,' she said; then: 'I'll say some more prayers for Bert. I love you,' she said and hung up.

Matt spent the next morning still waiting to be called. Lucci took him to lunch again, but the lawyer was the only one with an appetite, making short work of a steak.

'It's going well. We've had one of the stockyard workers who says he phoned Bert at home at the time Bert says he was there. Around the time the police have said Ruby was probably murdered. It's looking good —'

'When will you be calling me?'

'We may not need to ... Another glass of red?'

At three o'clock the jury retired and at four o'clock they were back in the courtroom. Fifteen minutes later Lucci came out of the courthouse and approached Matt, who was walking up and down, impatient at the delay in being called.

'It's all over,' said Lucci. 'He was acquitted.'

'Thank Christ.' Matt was surprised at his own relief. 'I'd like to see Bert.'

'I don't think he wants to see anyone — he's, well, basically, he's collapsed. His mum and dad have already taken him home ... Thanks for coming, Matt. What do we owe you?'

'Nothing. You've paid me, getting Bert off. What do the police think? Who killed Ruby?'

'Person or persons unknown. It was probably someone from out of town, someone passing through. The police checked everyone who was in Collamundra that night, the hotels and the motels, but they couldn't trace all of them. Person or persons unknown, Matt. Go back to Sydney and do your best to forget it all.'

'I'll do that. Give my regards to Shell.'

He got into his car, then got out again as Lucci walked away, and went down to the post office and called Carmel. 'Bert was acquitted. I didn't have to appear.'

There was a gasp, then she said, 'Great! I'm glad for his sake. And I'm glad you didn't have to appear ... Are you coming home now?'

'Two, three hours at the most. We'll go out for dinner.'

So he drove back over the mountains, east again, feeling a dead weight of the past drop off him. He came down the long winding road from the top of the ranges, the city laid out in the distance like an illuminated map. Once down on the flat highway he speeded up, thinking of Carmel.

When he walked in the door of their flat she was waiting for him, wearing only a thin wrap. She flung her arms round him and kissed him fiercely, her body trying to graft itself to his. He pulled his head back, laughing. 'God, you must be *extra* moist —'

'I'm *creamy*!'

He picked her up and carried her into the bedroom, where, for the next hour, he thought he was in a sexual Cyclone Tracy.

At last he lay back and stared at the ceiling. The day had been full of suspense and emotion, culminating in the last hour where everything, emotion, orgasm and love had hammered him into exhaustion. Then he turned his head.

She was lying on her side, her eyes dark with mystery. Then she smiled and said, 'The honeymoon's gone on long enough. Let's get married.'

Chapter Four

1

They were married a month later, in the school holidays, at Cavanreagh. Both Matt and Carmel were twice-a-year Catholics; going to Mass only at Christmas and Easter, as if they knew that God (forget the Vatican) knew they were the only dates that counted. Father Mulligan, the Collamundra parish priest, was a liberal-minded man for whom any Catholic was worth hanging on to. He even agreed to their being married out at Cavanreagh, which was what Carmel wanted, instead of at the church in town.

A hundred guests turned up and it rained all day, but nobody complained. A mini-drought had been predicted and the rain drowned the prediction. The grass would grow, the livestock would fatten and out in the cotton fields the Noongulli would not have to be drained to fill the irrigation channels.

Keith Durban and Paddy O'Reilly gave speeches, both laced with bad and obvious jokes about marriage that the male guests laughed at and the women looked at each other and raised their eyebrows. Matt replied with a speech that, Carmel told him later, was 'as smooth as cream, fattening but not nourishing'. Which, as he told her, was the recipe for most wedding speeches.

'Politics,' he told her with a smile. 'Just practising.'

They went up to the Gold Coast for their honeymoon, were blinded by white shoes and vacation shirts, but looked at each other and plain sight was restored. They enjoyed each other as if new lovers and for a week politics, schoolteaching and the doctor's surgery were forgotten. Then they came back to Parramatta and earth.

A week after they got back from the Gold Coast, sitting sipping their after-dinner coffee, Carmel said calmly, 'I'm pregnant.'

He paused, his cup halfway to his mouth. 'You sure?'

'I'm a practical girl — most of the time. I work in a doctor's surgery, I know how to do certain tests. It must have happened the night you came back from Bathurst —'

'But you've been on the Pill —'

'I must've forgot that day . . . Aren't you glad?' She looked at him as if suddenly apprehensive.

It had been a bad day at school. A hulking sixteen-year-old, ticked off for his behaviour in class, had threatened to punch him and then stalked out, telling him to shove his English and his history up his arse. In the next session a first-generation Aussie boy, son of English migrants, had called a Lebanon-born girl a wog bitch. Derry Jakes sent for him.

'Things are going to get worse, Matt. These kids are the sons and daughters of the rock-and-roll generation — Christ knows what *their* kids will be like. By then I'll be retired, out on the golf course with a club in one hand and a beer in the other, talking about the Good Old Days. What are you going to do with the kid Bateman?'

'When he comes back tomorrow I'll offer to take him out the back of the toilets and belt the shit out of him —'

'An appropriate place. But practical?'

Matt grinned. 'No, I'll handle him. He's a bully, but he's a coward, he'll back down. As for Sitwell, I'll take him aside and teach him a little history . . . '

Now he looked across the table at Carmel. 'Yes, of course I'm glad. What'll it be, a boy or a girl?'

She laughed, as much from relief as from merriment. 'God, I don't know! At the moment it's just a tadpole. I'll wait till the last month before I find out whether I'll be knitting blue things or pink things.'

He got up, went round to her and kissed the top of her head. 'Mother —'

She elbowed him in the stomach. 'You'd better start practising to be a father.' Then she lifted her face to his: 'I couldn't be happier.'

'Likewise,' he said and held her to him.

Later he lay in bed, eyes wide open to the darkness, Carmel already asleep beside him. Another step had been taken on the road, one that, he had to admit, he had not even thought about. Ambition had made him selfish: that was one of its ingredients. He was suddenly afraid, not of responsibility, but of failing his child.

A month later he received an unexpected invitation to dinner from Walter Peal. 'Bring your wife. I'd like to meet her, so would my wife.'

He consulted with Danny Voce. 'What's it mean? Does he make a habit of inviting workers to dinner?'

'No,' said Voce, secure in his own little domain. The most trusted ally for an ambitious man is a friend with no ambition. 'I think you are about to be anointed. I know he's been making discreet enquiries about you, he's been on to me as well as some down in Sussex Street.' The Labor Party Kremlin. 'I think you can start packing your bags.'

So Mr and Mrs Durban went to dinner with Mr and Mrs Peal at Darcy's in Paddington, where the prices were not exactly McDonald's-like. The owners and the waiters welcomed the Peals as if they were shareholders and the Durbans got equally pleasant treatment.

Georgia Peal was not what Matt had expected. She was the rebel daughter of an ultra-conservative Liberal family, a bohemian who, in search of Bohemia, had landed on the milder shores of Canberra. She was a good-looking woman in a horsey sort of way and wore a suit that, Carmel guessed, had been hand-crafted and cost what Carmel earned in a month. Mrs Peal wore very little jewellery and it was discreet at that, but the Bulgari watch on the thin wrist told how expensive time could be.

Peal wasted no time: 'How would you like to come and work in Canberra full time?'

Matt looked at Carmel, who said, 'I go where he goes.'

'Of course,' said Peal, and his wife nodded approvingly. 'I should have asked, would the two of you like to come to Canberra? Matt?'

'What would I be doing?'

'To start with, you'd be a general dogsbody, till you learned the ropes. Then research and — can you write speeches?'

'He can recite Shakespeare backwards,' said Carmel, like a good agent.

'Shakespeare, backwards or forwards, would only frighten the voters. Australians are suspicious of eloquence —'

'Lower your voice,' said Georgia Peal. 'We're surrounded by voters.'

Peal smiled, patted her hand, then looked back at Matt. 'There was that American chap, I've forgotten his name, he shouted *Give me liberty or give me death*! If I stood up in Parliament and shouted that, they'd send for the pound-keeper.'

Matt smiled. 'I'd like a little free rein, nothing that would embarrass you.' He was taking his time, though he knew from the tone of her voice that Carmel had already committed them. He was eager and pleased at the invitation, but he was learning the uses of pauses. 'I'm doing sums in my mind.'

'Of course. What's your salary as a teacher?' Matt told him and Peal went on, 'You'd get two thousand a year more than that. And rents are cheaper in Canberra. So you'll come?'

Matt looked at Carmel, who nodded, then he looked back at Peal. 'When do I start?'

There were smiles all around and Georgia Peal said, 'I think this calls for champagne, don't you, Carmel?'

'My favourite way of celebrating,' said Carmel, not looking at Matt.

Mrs Peal signalled to a waiter. 'Alberto, champagne all round.'

'Domestic, of course,' said Peal, just in case there were some Labor voters amongst the other diners.

The rest of the evening was like the establishing of a small family; it was obvious that both Peal and his wife liked the younger couple. Later, driving back to Parramatta, Matt said, 'Have I done the right thing?'

'It's what you've always wanted.'

'Yeah. But now I'm to take the first step — step off the cliff ...' He had slowed down, driving carefully as if on a road suddenly vague. 'Do you want to be — I dunno, live that sort of life? It's like no other sort of business. Danny Voce has told me — it's back-stabbing, stroking egos, turning a blind eye to principles ...'

'You know how you sound?'

'How?'

'As if you'll enjoy every minute of it.'

He laughed, leaned across and kissed her and went through a red light.

Keith Durban and the O'Reillys were told next morning that they were to be grandparents and that Mr and Mrs Matt Durban's new address would soon be Canberra. Both bits of news were greeted with warmth.

'But,' said Keith Durban, safe in Collamundra, 'keep your head down for the first six months.'

'Dad, I'll just be a dogsbody in the office of a shadow minister. You don't start raising your head till he's the actual minister in government.'

'Sure, but you're at the bottom of a learning curve. Take it easy. Look after yourself. And Carmel in particular.'

'You think I'd ever neglect her?' He was hurt.

'No. But women can feel neglected and the husband never guesses it.'

'When did you become an expert on women?'

'Your mum taught me,' said Keith and hung up.

Matt said goodbye to the school, even to the school bully, Jason Bateman, who surprised him by shaking hands with him and wishing him all the best. The girls wept and two of them offered to go with him and he blew them kisses and escaped before they raped him. The last farewell was to Derry Jakes.

'I'm sorry to see you go, Matt. You're a good teacher and you'd have been a better one. The swollen heads in the Education Department are changing the syllabus, throwing years of good teaching out the window, making it *easier* for the pupils — Christ, why should we make it *easy* for them? Life after school isn't going to be easy . . . '

'Derry, stop banging your drum. I might've made a good teacher, but my heart wouldn't have been in it. I was born to be a politician.'

'Christ, what a birthmark!' But Jakes shook his hand with warmth and wished him all the best. 'Drop me a line occasionally. Or a phone call. Keep in touch with reality.'

Matt went home and Carmel had everything packed; not much, but everything. They said goodbye to their neighbours, whom they had not got to know well, and on a morning in late winter, the trees in their street like naked scarecrows, they set out on the road that might be potted, washed out or forked.

Chapter Five

1

They rented a house in Belconnen and for the first time had to buy furniture. Carmel's pregnancy had begun to show and Matt, belatedly, had begun to appreciate that he now had responsibilities. Along with the other furniture they bought a cot and he looked at it as if it were — a treasure chest?

'What's the matter?' said Carmel.

'Just wondering ... If I last, what he or she will think of me?'

She took his hand. 'Darling, first-time parents always have that thought. The Virgin Mary probably had the same thought when she looked at the manger. Don't be afraid ... '

'I'm not,' he said, but couldn't put aside the thought: how would ambition and fatherhood live side-by-side? Which would shine brighter, the light on the porch or the light on the hill?

The house they had rented was modest and had no hall; one stepped straight into the living room, as into their flat back in Parramatta. Carmel wasted no money on buying furniture that would last; it was as if she had decided, without consulting him, that this was no more than a whistlestop. Virtually all their neighbours were public servants and they knew the flotsam and jetsam that came through the small city.

Matt settled into Peal's office without causing waves. There were two other staffers: Chris Indelli, a man in his forties who hadn't had an illusion since he got out of short pants; and Bernadette Brown, a pretty, bosomy girl who had all the enthusiasm and energy of a cheer-leader, an American breed just beginning to appear at local sporting events. Peal himself was not a demanding boss, since ambition had run out and he knew he would rise no higher in the Party.

Politics were relatively quiet, the Vietnam War was over, and both Government and Opposition were waiting for the next election. Matt raised a few questions for the shadow minister to ask in the House and gradually the word spread that there was a new kid on the block who should be watched.

The parliamentary session came to an end and Peal threw a small drinks party before he went back to Parramatta to show the locals how much he had their interests at heart. Carmel, leaning back against the weight of her pregnancy, still looking beautiful in a female Buddha sort of way, came to the party and instantly found a chair.

Georgia Peal, looking like a duchess out of her element but unfazed by it, came and sat beside her. She looked around her with invisible lorgnettes: 'I'm used to all this. Will you get used to it?'

Carmel looked around her, equally composed. 'I'll cope, Georgia. I've been reading the stories of the women who surrounded the French kings. These are all little kings — no offence to Walter —'

Georgia Peal smiled. 'He'd be pleased to hear himself described like that.'

Carmel went on: 'One or two of the silly ones lost their heads, but the shrewd ones never lost *themselves*. I'll be okay, Georgia. Not French and regal, but okay.'

Georgia looked at Carmel's swollen belly. 'I remember when I had my first. Walter had just been elected to State parliament — which was a bear-pit compared to this.' She waved a hand at Canberra in general. 'I'm not a religious woman, but I prayed the baby would not grow up to be a politician. He didn't. He's a junior banker in London, married to a lovely girl who's a snob, votes Tory and phones his father every week to ask how things are in the Colonies ... There's Bernadette at work and play again.'

Carmel looked across at the bosomy girl offering Matt a drink. 'Is she a flirt?'

'I haven't heard that word since I was at school. Yes, I think she is. And more. She's like those French women you mentioned, but without their brains. She wants to be the prime minister's wife. Doesn't matter who the PM is.'

'I don't think she'll get anywhere with my Matt,' said Carmel, but keeping an eye on the other side of the room. 'He's been fending off girls since he was in primary school.'

'He is good-looking, isn't he? And he's developing as a charmer. You're a very lucky girl, Carmel.'

'I know,' said Carmel and flashed a smile across the room at Matt to remind him where his chains were.

Later they went home and went to bed and she put her hand between his legs.

'The family jewels,' she said and squeezed his testicles till he gasped. 'Don't ever think of trading them outside of this bed.'

'What? What're you talking about?'

'That girl at the party. She was all over you like a rash.'

'She's just friendly. She's a virgin, her name's Bernadette, after the saint.'

'I wouldn't trust her within a mile of Lourdes, she'd pollute the water. Her real name is Salome. I'll bet she wears her G-string back to front.'

He looked at her, seriously. 'Do you really think I'd look at another woman?'

'It happens. There are some men who can't make love to a woman who's seriously pregnant. And we know what you're like, five nights a week and twice on Saturday and Sunday.'

'You're making out I'm a pervert —'

'I'm not complaining. Sex is one of my most serious interests. But pregnancy can get in the way, something that doesn't affect men. I'm not the lissom siren you fell in love with —'

'Was that what you were?'

'You still have a lot to learn about women —'

'They'll vote for me, you watch.'

'I hope they do. But they'll be voting for me, too. I'll keep reminding them.'

He laughed, loving her. 'I think you're just as ambitious as I am. You want to be the prime minister's wife.'

'That's what Georgia Peal said tonight about Salome. But you're wrong. All I want to be is *your* wife, now and forever, amen.' And she kissed him fiercely, shoving her belly against his.

'Amen,' he said and held her to him.

They settled into the city and its atmosphere. They made friends, went to small parties and to dinners. Matt went to see the Canberra Raiders play, though rugby union, not league, was his game; fitting into the capital scene, not yet a somebody but gradually shedding the cloak of a nobody.

Then one summer morning at three o'clock, Carmel woke Matt: 'It's coming! Get the car out!'

They got to the hospital an hour before their son was born. Matt looked at the small bundle with delight and apprehension; he was twenty minutes into fatherhood and he wondered how he would respond. He had not gone into the labour ward for the birth; he was a coward when it came to blood and pain. They showed him Richard Keith Patrick Durban, though the infant was not yet burdened with those names, and he shook his head in wonder and a little fear. Then they wheeled Carmel out past him and he stopped the gurney and kissed her on the lips, soft and not passionate, just relief and love.

'You did wonderfully,' he said.

'Of course she did,' said the nurse pushing the gurney. She was young but looked as if she might have been at the birth of Cain and Abel; she wore experience as her uniform. 'What did you expect?' Then she patted Carmel's arm. 'Men! They should go through it some time!'

'He's learning,' said Carmel and gave him a smile that was like a hook round his neck.

Time passed and Richard progressed from being a pissing, shitting, always hungry bundle of joy to the semblance of a voter. Matt loved him and the infant responded like a voter, gurgling at every remark his father threw at him. Carmel, calm as ever, watched the progress with amusement and relief. The three grandparents came down to Canberra, greeted the child as if he were the New Messiah, left gifts and a trust fund for him, and went back to the Real World, as Keith and Paddy called it. The world spun on its axis, the United States got a new president, a Hollywood actor who beat a peanut farmer, and the rest of the world made jokes that fell flat as it realised that America had got the man it wanted and needed, someone to tell it optimism and not pessimism. In Britain the new Prime Minister was a woman, a grocer's daughter, for God's sake. The walls of clubs of St James and Pall Mall shook and out in the English shires retired army colonels wondered if it was too late to emigrate to the Colonies. And the Australian Labor Party got a new leader.

He was a vain, charismatic man who would have stood and pressed the flesh of every voter in the land, living or near-dead; he would have glad-handed Venus de Milo, if she hadn't been handicapped. He had a wife whom everyone, man and woman, respected and liked. Suddenly the party was rejuvenated and even Chris Indelli climbed out of his cynical trench and began to talk about the new sunshine. Matt continued to make quiet progress, which Peal always broadcast to the mandarins, because nothing stiffens an aging politician's idea of himself more than a promising protégé. The mandarins, readying themselves for power, standing straight again, walking more purposefully, took time out to mark the name *Durban* in their notebooks.

Then, with an election looming, Walter Peal was diagnosed with cancer. He called Matt into his office. 'Close the door, Matt. Then sit down while I tell you what I have in mind.'

What he had in mind was that he would be vacating the Parramatta seat and he was recommending that Matt should stand for preselection.

'It won't be easy, you know that. You'll be classed as an upstart, too young, still wet behind the ears. I sometimes wonder at what our power brokers would have done with Pitt the Younger, PM of England at twenty-four.'

Matt smiled at the thought. 'Had heart attacks.'

'I've seen the list of other starters and you beat 'em, hands down. Our venerated Leader knows of you, he sees something of himself in you . . . Flattered?'

'Always,' said Matt. 'It's bullshit that flattery gets you nowhere.'

'You're reversing the meaning of the phrase,' said Peal, but smiled as if he knew the truth. 'Anyhow, you have my backing and you'll have the Leader's. All you have to do is watch your back, make a good speech at the preselection meeting and, chances are, you'll be the next MP from Parramatta.'

'I didn't want to get the opportunity this way. What's the prognosis —?' He nodded at Peal as if the cancer were visible.

'Not good. Maybe six months. I'll be going younger than I expected, but I've had a good run.' He sat back in his chair and his eyes glazed for a moment, as if he were experiencing pain. He had aged suddenly, as if the cancer were piling on the years; even the famous head of hair was thinner and now almost white. Matt, who hadn't looked death in the face since his mother had died, was suddenly uneasy; as if Walter Peal might die right there in his chair. But Peal recovered, said, 'Georgia will take it hard. Keep in touch with her, she's a fan of yours.'

The Durbans closed up their Canberra house and while Matt went to a motel in Parramatta, Carmel and young Richard went home to Collamundra and Cavanreagh. Matt set up his office in Danny Voce's office and on his second day there got a visit from one of the Sussex Street heavies.

'You're jumping the queue, you know.' Arthur Urling had a weatherbeaten face (it was difficult to tell whether it was drink or blood pressure that gave it its hue), a large belly and an intimidating manner. 'We've been grooming our man for five years. There's such a thing as the rules of succession.'

'You sound monarchical,' said Matt, unfazed by the other man's manner. 'I thought we were supposed to be republican?'

'Don't smartarse me, son —'

'You asked for it, Arthur,' said Danny Voce, who was sitting in on the meeting. 'We want Matt to get the preselection and you blokes had better learn to lump it.'

'We won't work for him,' said Urling, getting redder in the face. He was not a political boss, just a manager and he was used to managing those who did what they were told. 'And don't ask us for funds.'

'We have our own,' said Danny Voce. 'I've been cooking the books.' He winked at Matt. 'It's an old political trick, as you know.'

'You're a bloody disgrace to the Party,' said Urling and departed, taking the sunset of his face with him.

Danny Voce grinned at Matt. 'You're home and dried, Matt. But when you get to Canberra, don't disappoint me.'

'You've been here in this office how many years? Ten, fifteen?'

'Coming up twelve.'

'Have you ever been disappointed?'

'Half a dozen times. Someone once said, "Disappointment is the parent of despair".'

'Keats,' said Matt, remembering his English.

'Whoever. He was wrong — my disappointment has been a sterile parent. I've never despaired, Matt. Neither should you.'

The campaigning began, though the world at large and even most of Parramatta was unaware of it. Matt spent the days shaking hands, beaming the smile that would become famous in later years, and when the voting began he had the preselection sewn up. Danny Voce had run the campaign with all the skill of one of the better generals. Matt was chosen with a twenty-five per cent majority over the other three candidates, with the Sussex Street nominee coming bottom of the heap.

Carmel, leaving the baby at Cavanreagh with its doting grandparents, came down for the vote and, when the result was announced, stood beside Matt and, with her smile and looks, added to his promise. *What a lovely couple*, said the women members, and their husbands looked at Carmel and wondered why sex appeal was so low down on the list of political priorities. Down at Sussex Street, among the male diehards there, the thought was worse than a stroke.

Carmel stayed the night at the motel with Matt. Whether it was the joy of his success or the release from not having to get up in the middle of the night to tend to young Richard, her Mount of Venus was volcanic and Matt was smothered with love and sex. Exhausted, he fell asleep under her, convinced he was the most fortunate man in the world.

Next morning they drove back to Cavanreagh. It was a beautiful day, white clouds lending shape to the sky. The cotton farmers were sowing for next season; the fields had spread and the irrigation channels shone like cutlery under the bright sun. For a long moment, as they drove down the main road into Collamundra, Matt wished he were representing *this* electorate; but that was hankering for the impossible. This was, and always would be, National territory. The locals might be proud of him, but only in an offhand way, like a wayward cousin who had made good as, say, a smuggler or a bank bandit.

As they drove into Collamundra, past the iron digger still on alert towards the east, Matt looked out at the town as if it were already fading from his memory. They passed the Rawson coffee lounge and the ghost of Ruby stood dimly in the doorway.

Carmel, who was driving, saw Matt turn his head and look back and she said, 'That's all past, darling.'

He turned back to look at her and nodded. 'I know. I just hope that someone, some time in the future, won't mention it.'

She took her eyes off the main street. 'You think they will? What will they have to talk about?'

He shrugged. 'Nothing. But people have long memories, especially in the bush ... I wonder how Bert Carter feels?'

'Maybe we'll never know.' She went back to concentrating on her driving. 'Mum told me that he disappeared the week after his acquittal. His mum and dad are still here, still working their property.' She nodded back at the town as they drove out of it on the road to Cavanreagh. 'The Rawsons, too, have gone. It's history, darling, close the book.'

He leaned across and kissed her. 'Why are you such a comfort to me?'

'Because you're mine,' she said and for a moment let the car coast while she looked at him. 'That's enough.'

Keith Durban came out to Cavanreagh for dinner and while they waited for it to be served, being good old-fashioned Aussie men, he, Paddy O'Reilly and Matt sat out on the wide verandah, each with a beer in his hand, like living symbols of the rightness of things. Light was dying on the now-thin clouds at the edge of the long plains and Matt felt again the silence, almost physical, that came out of the heart of the continent.

'I'll miss this,' he said.

'What?' said Paddy O'Reilly.

'*This*. The silence.'

'You'll never get that down in Canberra,' said his father.

'I'm told there's a bloke on the Coalition backbenches who hasn't opened his mouth in eight years.'

'I'll vote for him,' said Keith.

Then, for no reason at all, the talk turned to money. Over the past decade or so it had become a major topic, as if the population had just discovered it, another cure-all. It was Paddy who brought it up: 'I only ask this because of Carmel and the baby. But how are you fixed for money?'

'Okay,' said Matt, surprised at the question. 'My MP's salary will be double or more of what I earned as a teacher.'

'Bloody disgraceful,' said his teacher father.

'And I've got shares that are on their way up. Your wedding present, we put that into shares. Despite what the banks warn, I think the economy is going to go up and up for a while longer.'

'H.L. Mencken —' said Keith.

'Who?' Both Matt and Paddy looked at him.

'An American editor back in the Twenties and Thirties, a sardonic sonofabitch. He said bankers have the haunting fear that someone, somewhere, might be happy.'

'The buggers come out here every six or seven years, when there's a drought, and mention the overdraft.' Paddy O'Reilly finished his beer, slaking the drought, and stood up. 'Righto, let's go in to eat. Dinner's ready.'

'How do you know?' asked Matt.

'It had better be,' said Paddy, Irish to the core.

Before he went in to dinner, Matt went into what had been Carmel's bedroom before she left home. The baby was lying in its cot, still awake, eyes fixed on the old-fashioned night-lamp on the nearby dressing-table. Matt tickled him under the chin and young Richard smiled and gurgled.

'Pray that I'll never let you down,' said Matt softly.

'I'll shoot you if you do,' said Eileen O'Reilly just as softly from the doorway.

He turned. 'Did you ever have any doubts, Eileen?'

'Often.' She was a good-looking woman who had bequeathed, with dividends, her beauty to Carmel and her younger daughter Teresa. She had no vanity, but she was sure of herself, just as Carmel was. She had a low-pitched voice and a tendency at times to look absent; not just absent-minded, but absent, as if a long way away. 'Paddy and I fought like Kilkenny cats when we first married and I often wondered if we would last. I was a trainee nurse from the city, we met over his broken leg in Royal North Shore. Our family lived in Wahroonga with lots of trees and security, my father was a doctor, a specialist — I had *city* stamped all over me. Then I married Paddy and came out here to drought and falling wool prices and — and *loneliness*.' For a moment she drifted away, then came back: 'I hated it all, but I loved *him*. Then the Korean War broke out and wool prices jumped and I was pregnant and . . .' Her voice trailed off; she was absent again. Then she straightened up, or seemed to, though she had not physically slumped: 'People without doubts are idiots. But you're no idiot.'

'Thanks,' he said and moved to her and kissed her on the cheek. 'You bloody O'Reilly women know how to make a man feel good.'

'Remember that,' said Eileen to the baby.

Chapter Six

1

Then an election was called and Labor was the new government. The defeated PM, a stone-faced man ('the Member for Easter Island', as a bitter-tongued opponent once described him), shed a tear and at once the voters realised he was more human than they thought. His gracious lady led him away into the twilight of defeated Leaders, where sins of commission and omission merged into airbrushed memoirs.

The new PM, hyperventilating, swept around the party room on a surf of clapping hands, and his lady, equally gracious as the departing queen, finally led him away towards the dawn that couldn't come soon enough for the faithful. Australian elections don't bring out bunting and bands, as in America, nor do they have shooting as in some Latin elections. The voters vote and go home, tune in to the Saturday night movie and nod placidly but appreciatively as the election results are flashed up on the TV screen. Sometimes the results are flashed in a strip, like subtitles, below Harrison Ford saving the world yet again. Perspective must, always, be kept.

Matt and Carmel, at the Labor social club in Parramatta, celebrated with all the local faithful. Matt, despite being a new boy, kept up the majority that Walter Peal had accumulated over his years. Danny Voce read out the new commandments and everyone cheered and had another drink and another. Chris Indelli and Bernadette Brown came up from Canberra for the night and reacted in their opposite ways.

'All the best, mate,' said Indelli, shaking Matt's hand. *Mate* was the obligatory mode of address on such an occasion; mateship was the only religion, at least for tonight. 'I'm moving across to the new Minister. I was hoping it would be you —'

'Too soon, mate,' said Matt. 'I was never in consideration. Debts and homage have to be paid. But don't quote me . . . '

'Your day'll come,' said Indelli and moved on to congratulate Carmel.

Bernadette, bosom at the ready, cleavage as brazen as an old-time brothel's red light, kissed Matt as if he were a client, an embrace that shocked some of the older faithful. Over her shoulder Matt saw Carmel raise the barrel of her finger and shoot him.

Bernadette, forward-passing her breasts, was gasping, 'I'm going to be in the secretarial pool — I can still work for you —'

'I'll look forward to it —' Matt was trying to stay ahead of the overtaking breasts.

'I'll be available any time —'

Then the Vice Squad moved in. 'Bernadette, can I have my husband for a moment?'

'Oh yes, yes! You're so lucky!'

'Ain't I just?' said the Lucky One and led Matt away. 'Got your breath, darling? What's that bulge in your pants? You were enjoying that.'

'I was just being polite.' He was all innocence. 'I wasn't trying to throw her to the floor.'

'You didn't need to. She was halfway there. Those tits of hers must be a weight.'

He put his arm round her waist, kissed her cheek. 'I'm all yours. Trust me.'

She bit his ear and the faithful cheered and had another drink. Domestic, of course.

So life changed for the Durbans. They had already discussed how things would be different if Matt was elected to Parliament. He would spend more time at his electoral office than his shared office in Canberra. An MP was many things to many people: counsellor, creditor, appellant, boundary rider; there were always fences to be mended. He was on call twenty-four hours a day and it was always a relief to sail back to the horse latitudes of Canberra.

They gave up the rented house in Belconnen and, taking out a heavy mortgage that sank the structure a foot further into the ground, they bought a three-bedroomed house with a view of the Parramatta River. It was a 1920s house of blue-brick and had once been described as a California bungalow, though the natives back in the 1920s knew no more about California than the antics of Charlie Chaplin, Mary Pickford and Fatty Arbuckle. It was double-fronted with a wide verandah looking out on the river; its large plot had lawns back and front and a neglected garden. There was no swimming pool, which prompted the neighbours to remark that the Durbans were either non-swimmers or reverse snobs. The street was a mixture of solid bungalows and fibro cottages; Tuscan villas were still far over the northern horizon.

Carmel, with an eye to the long term, bought furniture that had quality and would last. She went to local art shows and bought paintings that instantly turned the artists into Labor voters. The neighbours, most of them non-Labor voters, greeted the Durbans with suspicion, but Carmel soon won them over, especially the husbands. Matt spread his smile and did his best not to offend. Richard, of course, was an asset, all smiles and fluttering fingers. When he was old enough to go to day-care he would be a glad-hander equal to the PM.

Matt had to decide where he would stay while Parliament was in session. He did not want to share a flat with another Member, which was a usual thing in the capital. Though a very public man and at ease in public, he valued his privacy. There was the small item of wanting to phone Carmel every night and he did not want someone else sitting across the room from him while he told his wife he loved her. So, declining a couple of half-hearted offers to share a flat with him, he came to an arrangement with a motel where he could rent a room on a weekly basis, which was covered by his expenses. He settled into a life that he had already begun to realise had its drawbacks. He missed Carmel and the baby and rang every night for comfort and long-distance love. All of it, of course, marked down to an MP's expenses.

He was within walking distance of the House and his office, but on occasions he rented a car, again putting it down to expenses. He was learning the convenience of the taxpayers, God bless 'em.

The new Minister for National Security sent for him the first week Parliament was in session. At the swearing-in of the new government Matt had been introduced to the other members, many of whom were strangers from other States, known to him only by their television images. Joe Rothschild had been in Parliament twelve years, was from Victoria, a twenty-five-year union official, a sane voice amongst some of the insane clamour of that State's unions. He was a small, thin man with a wicked grin, which he called his moneylender's smile, and a smoker's cough. He was a Jew, but only by circumcision and circumstance.

'I'm like a lapsed Catholic,' he told Matt. 'My old man came out from Poland in the 1930s, but he never wore the yarmulke and went to synagogues only for weddings. You're a Catholic?'

'Off and on. Twice a year, Christmas and Easter. I went every Sunday for six weeks before the election.'

Rothschild grinned appreciatively. 'A pragmatist — the best way to approach religion ... Walter Peal told me you had something interesting about a coast guard patrol?'

'It just so happens I've brought the material with me,' said Matt, smiling, and Rothschild grinned in reply. It was apparent even then that they were men who were going to work well together. 'Twenty-five coast guard patrol boats, based on the US Coastguard Service boats, but slightly larger because their patrols will be longer. They'll patrol our north and north-west coast from Cape York as far west as Port Hedland —'

'How much?'

'Each boat? Five to seven million —'

'A hundred and fifty, seventy-five million? Social Services would be at my front door with their own patrol boat. Not to mention Health and Education in their little canoes ... Matt, it'll have to go on the back burner. It's just been okayed that the Navy are to get new submarines —'

'Submarines? Christ, that sort of war is over —'

'Matt, generals and admirals and air marshals fight the last war. It's boffins who fight the next war.'

'Did the boffins suggest the submarines?'

'I don't know. But we're a new government and for the present they're keeping their heads down. Those heads you see popping up above the trenches are the Defence brass.'

'But you're the Minister for National Security —'

Rothschild grinned again, tolerantly this time. 'Matt, I'd been promised a frontbench seat. When the PM counted up the candidates, he had one left over. Me. So we created the Ministry of National Security and now we're trying to find something for me to do. I'm sure we'll find something, but we're taking our time. I once worked at the Melbourne Zoo and we had a warning there. Never stand behind an elephant, you never know when it's going to shit or sit down. The Ministry for National Security may turn out to be an elephant, a white one. We dunno yet.'

Matt sat back, looked at the older man with wry amusement. 'Joe, did you ever have any ideals?'

'Sure.' Again the moneylender's grin. 'When I was eighteen or nineteen I tried to join the Altruists' Party. But I couldn't find it ... Matt, in trade unions ideals are like my wife's single string of pearls — worn only on safe occasions. Bear that in mind.'

'I have a lot to learn —'

'You have. One thing — never try to be Don Quixote. Leave the windmills to the press gallery.'

So Matt took away his file, marked it 'Pending' and forgot about it.

Then Carmel was pregnant again.

'I wish you wouldn't keep sneaking these kids in on me —' He had come up from Canberra for the usual weekend.

'We talked about it —'

'When?'

'One night when we were in bed here. You said yes, yes —'

'I was talking about coming, not fatherhood —'

But they were both laughing and he was happy, for her and for himself. Another child would put pressure on the budget, but he was still buying shares and they were still rising, still paying dividends. He was never going to be rich nor wanted to be, but it seemed he had a talent for the right investment. An estate agent had told Carmel that their house was on its way to increasing its value by fifty per cent. The road ahead had roses growing beside it, voters tending them.

'What do you want?' he asked. 'Boy or girl?'

'A girl. I think, come next century, next millennium, if you like —' It was a word just beginning to touch the tongue; after all, it had been a thousand years since it had last been used. Something people, even linguists, tended to forget. 'Women are going to rule the world. It'll take some time, but they will. Wait till the Americans have a Madam President. Even out here, as PM —'

'Fat chance,' he said, secure in male domination. 'If Heliotrope or whatever we're going to call her goes into politics, I'm leaving.'

'Fat chance of that,' she said and wrapped her legs around him.

He fitted into the government benches as if they had been made for him. He was given the opportunity to ask a question or two besides the usual Dorothy Dixers; but backbenchers are not encouraged to get above their station. Still, he was patient, a virtue he had learned as a teacher; he was sure that his day would come when he would be on the frontbench. In the meantime he fitted in. He cultivated the press gallery, but not too obviously, and they marked him down in their notebooks for future reference.

One night he was in his room at the motel, had just put down the phone after talking to Carmel, when there was a knock at his door. He got up, opened it and there was Bernadette, large envelope in hand and three buttons of her shirt undone.

'Those notes you wanted typed up —'

'Tomorrow morning would have done —'

'I'm booked tomorrow morning —' As if she were a female Minister; or a hooker. She hadn't yet handed him the large envelope; she fanned herself with it. 'God, it's hot!'

Dangerous though it was, he wanted to laugh. 'All I can offer you is a Coke —'

All the invitation she wanted was a splash of water. She came into his room and, after pausing a moment, he closed the door behind her. He got her a Coke, poured one for himself and sat down on a chair opposite her. He was not going to sit on the bed and he was glad she hadn't.

She sat at ease, one good leg crossed over the other good leg. They talked of the day's events in Parliament, which had been testy and tacky. The Opposition, still smarting at being kicked out of government, which they thought of as their natural, God-given right, since they were much more God-fearing than Labor, had indulged in random shooting and some Government members had lost their cool.

'It's been a hectic day for us girls,' said Bernadette. 'It's just as well we like the men we work for.'

'You work too hard,' he said, meaning she worked too hard at being noticed by men. She was Ruby Rawson with political overtones.

'I hear your wife's pregnant again?' She was looking at him over the rim of her glass. She was as obvious as a red light.

'Yes. Six months.'

'It must be frustrating —'

Salome couldn't have been as obvious as this; John the Baptist's head would have laughed and told her to get lost. 'Not really.'

'What do you do to — to *relax*. While you're waiting?'

He was amused, but wary. 'Waiting for what?'

'You *know* —'

'Fatherhood?' He finished his Coke, stood up. 'I'm tired, Bernadette.'

She was not dumb, she caught the double meaning. She put down her drink, half-drunk, and stood up, pulling her shirt tight. 'I'll see you tomorrow —'

'You're booked tomorrow.'

'Of course.' She was experienced in knock-backs; unlike Salome, she would not ask for heads to be chopped. 'Thanks for the drink. I usually drink something stronger.'

'Tough titty,' he said, which was a lapse considering how she was built.

'How would you know?' she said, smiled and left.

He just hoped no one had seen her depart. He showered, got into bed and lay looking at the ceiling. The temptation had been there in the groin, he couldn't deny it, but he felt pride that he had resisted it. Self-congratulation is more prevalent in the male animal than in the female. A lion's roar is just remarked by a lioness with a roll of the eyes. 300 kilometres to the north Carmel was sound asleep in her own dream.

Next day Matt was lolling on the almost empty backbench when Rebecca Irvine came up from a couple of benches below him and sat beside him. Down on the floor there was desultory fencing between Ministers and their Shadows, but the topic under discussion wasn't going to appear in tomorrow's newspapers. It was another of the doldrums days that oozed in Parliament every so often.

'Matt —' Rebecca Irvine was ten or so years older than Matt. She was a plain woman who had made the most of what she had; her hair and make-up complimented her and she was always well-dressed. She was a trade union lawyer from Victoria and bore fading bruises of a male environment. Which meant she knew men: 'Mind if I give you some advice?'

'Not at all. My wife tells me I should always listen to feminine advice.'

'I'm not being a feminist.' She gave him a smile, but it *was* a feminist smile. 'When you are letting a girl out of your motel room, sonny boy, always turn the light out before you open the door.'

He gave her sharp attention: 'What are you getting at?'

'I was staying at your motel last night — my shared flat had a broken pipe in the kitchen. I came back there just as you let Miss Nameless out of your room.'

'Would you believe I was showing her the door?'

'I might —' But she looked at him dubiously.

'You know the girl. I hadn't invited her — she turned up with some papers she could quite easily have given me this morning. I gave her a Coke and told her I was tired — she got the hint and I showed her the door.'

'Fair enough ... But be careful of her, Matt. She's known among our golfer MPs as the Australian Open.'

He laughed and got a warning look from the Speaker. He bowed his head in apology and looked back at Rebecca Irvine: 'I'll be careful, Becky.'

'Do that, Matt. I've seen you with your wife — you're the best-looking couple in the Government. Don't spoil the image.'

He smiled and thanked her and she went back down to her bench.

2

Life went on, small footnotes to history were written. The Seventies, one of the worst-dressed periods in history, faded, unregretted, from memory. The Sixties, when hair and clothes first got out of hand, conversely now began to be remembered as the Big Bang of Creation, when Woodstock was the Garden of Eden and all music and even sex were invented. Keith Durban, back home in Collamundra, dug out his old LPs of Benny Goodman and Artie Shaw and Gerry Mulligan and, like some dread conspirator, pulled the blinds down and shut the windows against the New.

On the other side of the world the United States had a president who dozed off during Cabinet meetings while Down Under the nation had a prime minister who looked as if he never slept. Carmel gave birth to Natalie Eileen and Matt was showered with congratulations by fellow MPs, all male, as if he had been the one who had gone through labour. Carmel, a girl with a sense of calendar, had given birth while Parliament was in recess and so Matt was at home when the baby arrived.

'That's the lot,' she said, still in the maternity ward. She was still beautiful, the strain of the labour — it had been a natural birth — already gone. She had chosen a public hospital rather than a private one and she was in a ward with three other women. It was a proletarian touch she had suggested. She was becoming a politician's wife and, though she never mentioned it, she sometimes felt a fake. She would have had the same devotion if he had been a banker, which, thank God, he was not. She had her father's suspicion of banks and bankers. 'With you away so much, two are all I can handle.'

'I feel a bastard each time I leave for Canberra —'

She smiled, tolerantly. 'Darling, no bullshit, please —'

'Watch it. The baby might be listening.'

'She'll hear much worse than that as she gets older . . . I'm not a voter who can't make up her mind about what you are and what you do. How are things down there? How's Salome?'

'I dunno. She doesn't work for me any more, she's out of the pool. She's gone to one of the Ministers.'

'Lucky him. Does his wife know?'

'He's divorced.'

'Lucky Salome.'

'Why are we talking about her instead of Natalie Eileen?'

She smiled, stroked his cheek. 'I'm just testing you, darling. There was no reaction. You're over her.'

'I was never under her —'

The other three mothers turned their heads in astonishment as Mr and Mrs Durban roared with laughter. What a lovely couple, they said, and even the Liberal mother in the end bed said she would vote for him at the next election.

A month later Walter Peal died. Matt and Carmel went to the funeral in the Uniting church and Matt, at Georgia's invitation, gave the eulogy. He had come to have affection for the older man, taking the starch out of the stuffed shirt. On his visits to Peal, confined in his last months to his home, the older man had gradually revealed that he, too, had had ambition — 'But it died, Matt, and I don't know why. Satisfaction with what I had, perhaps. Georgia and the voters' votes. Don't let *your* ambition die —'

Georgia Peal was touched by the eulogy and took Matt and Carmel aside. 'You were his protégé, though he probably never told you . . . I'll miss him. We were more than a couple, we were lovers. You two be the same.'

Carmel kissed her. 'Thanks, Georgia. We'll keep in touch.'

Which they did, taking her to dinner once a month. Once she asked if she could bring her father. 'He's eighty-eight and a stuffed shirt and still thinks Menzies was God in a Henry Buck's suit. But he's interested in you, Matt. He thinks you have promise.'

'Of being a stuffed shirt?'

But Henry McKinley proved to be a sprightly old man with a sense of humour and an eye for beauty. 'You make your husband look better, Carmel —'

'I think so,' said Carmel, turning up the gold light on Matt. 'He needs it occasionally.'

The old man looked at Matt: 'Can't you fellows shake up our side of the House? We don't seem to know whom we want as leader. I'd vote for Sinclair, but he's from the country and the city slickers wouldn't stand for that.'

'We have enough trouble on our side,' said Matt. 'That's why we're glad they're brawling on the other side of the floor.'

'I never understood why anyone would go in for politics,' said Henry McKinley. 'I was a lawyer, where the abuse is civil.'

Then, over on the distant east coast of the United States, an Australian yacht won the America's Cup. England, back in 1805, couldn't have celebrated the Battle of Trafalgar with more enthusiasm. The PM flew over to Perth, where the yacht had been built, and was only prevented from granting the nation a month's holiday by sober-sided aides. The entrepreneur who had financed the Cup challenge was added to the other candidates for canonisation. Six years later the wind would go out of his sails and he would go to jail for business tacking on a wrong course. But that was in the future and it was against the national psyche to worry about that.

Matt, who had difficulty in telling port from starboard, who got seasick on the river ferry, managed to look excited and waved his little flag along with everyone else. Yacht sales shot up and harbours became cluttered with skippers who, like Matt, wondered which was port and which was starboard. Euphoria, that on-again, off-again intoxication, came back and yachts collided with each other, but everyone was happy, happy, happy.

Then, almost overnight, the front pages changed their tune. In Beirut, a city vaguely remembered by some Australians from World War II, almost 400 US marines were killed or wounded in a suicide bomb attack on their barracks. For the first time a minor US State Department officer spoke of the 'war against terror', an age-old custom given a new name. Matt wondered how submarines would counter this new form of warfare.

But he still had a long way to go before his voice would be heard and heeded. The local voters loved him, but throughout the rest of the nation he was a nameless face on the backbenches. And it began to hurt.

'Mate —' said Danny Voce, the voice of experience. 'Your day will come. Jesus Christ was thirty before anyone took any notice of him.'

'I'm not aiming to be crucified —'

'You will be, mate, if you try to jump the queue. Just be content with what you've got and wait for the beckoning finger.'

'Whose will that be?'

'I don't know, mate. But accidents happen. We'll pray for one.'

'I thought you were an atheist?'

'Only between prayers.'

Chapter Seven

1

Richard was now six-and-a-bit, going on twenty-six, and Natalie was coming on five and Matt was still on the backbenches. There had been another election and he had been returned with an increased majority; so someone, Carmel said, liked him. But the frontbench seemed as distant as ever, a far shore where he might never land. There was friction on that frontbench and nobody turned an eye towards the men and women at the back.

'Sometimes I wonder if it's all worthwhile,' he said one night when he was home for the weekend. Carmel had progressed as a cook, was now almost a chef, and the home-cooked meals were a change from restaurant meals and fast food in his motel room. 'Basically —'

Carmel looked at him: 'Basically? At the end of the day?'

He grinned. 'You see? I've been down there too long —'

'I think I'd like to be prime minister,' said Richard. 'Basically —'

'Don't you start,' said Carmel.

Later she and Matt sat in front of the television and watched the *7.30 Report*, where the PM had just been interviewed.

'He looks older,' said Carmel. 'His face has got more lines in it.'

'He'll last. He loves the job —'

Then the two children came in to say goodnight. They were both good-looking kids, promising to be better-looking than their parents. Richard, according to his teacher, was bossy and a born leader and Natalie, according to *her* teacher, lived in a world all her own.

'Nothing will ever worry her,' the kindergarten teacher had told Carmel; and looked dreamy for a moment, not usually a state of mind amongst kindergarten teachers. 'Such bliss!'

The two children now stood in the living room doorway in their pyjamas. Richard said, 'Daddy, do you and Mum ever fight?'

This was as bad as a complaint from a constituent. Matt looked at Carmel, then back at his son. 'Never. Why?'

Richard turned to his sister, as if continuing a discussion between them: 'Jason says his mother and father fight all the time.'

'Who cares?' said Natalie dreamily.

'Who *cares*?' cried Carmel. 'Where did you hear that?'

'Miss Judy says it all the time.' Miss Judy was one of the kindergarten teachers, evidently as dreamy as her star pupil.

'I'll have a word with Miss Judy on Monday. Now come on, into bed. What are you going to do tomorrow, it's Saturday?'

'Basically —' said Richard.

'There you go again! It's the end of the day, so off to bed!'

Left alone, Matt looked around him. He was surrounded by solid comfort. His investments had prospered and he had increased them; with his parliamentary salary, they were solidly middle class, upwardly mobile as the now hackneyed phrase had it. Carmel had furnished the house for the future; she had an eye for quality. There were some good paintings on the walls by artists who, she said, were keepers. The bookshelves held middlebrow reading, including her joke:

The Perfumed Garden between Germaine Greer and Susan Sontag. Matt had a well-paying job that he liked, a wife he still loved dearly, two kids he also loved — but why was he still not satisfied?

Carmel came back and sat down beside him, drawing her legs under her. Her hair was cut shorter now, Cyd Charisse faded into a dim silent movie, but the style still suited her face. Her eyes still held their secrets, but not from him. He liked — the mystery? — of her, though he was not sure that it was no more than surface mystery.

'What's on your mind?' she said.

'Why are you always reading my mind?'

'Because it's so available.' She reached across and took his hand. 'Are you unhappy?'

'Not at all.' It was a half-lie. 'It's just that, basically —' She slapped him. 'It's just that I'm, well, I dunno, *standing still.*'

'You knew when you ran for Canberra that it was not going to be quick.'

'I know. But ... I wonder if I'm standing on the sidelines of the way the world's going. Not politically, I don't mean that ... I've been talking to some of these fellers, young blokes just out of uni, coming down to see us in Canberra. It's this new thing, the IT business. Information Technology. They reckon over the next five or ten years it's going to take off like a rocket. Old technology is going to go out the window.'

'What do you know about it?'

'Nothing. I'm a technological idiot. But computers are already making a huge difference — firms like Apple and Microsoft. And things will grow out of them. Any information you want, *anything*, will be available. George Washington's middle name, how many runs Don Bradman scored —'

'Important stuff? Gee, I can't wait —'

He sat back from her. 'You're not impressed, are you?'

'No.' She took her time before she went on. At times she could be impetuous, but there were other occasions when she hesitated, gave consideration to what she was about to say: 'Because every time someone moved up from the backbenches, you'd be thinking that should be me. You're a political animal, darling. That would always be on any computer screen you looked at.'

'And you don't care?'

'Yes, sometimes I do. But I know it's in your blood ...' She paused again, was looking at him but, he sensed, not seeing him. Looking down the long, long road: 'I have no ambition to be the prime minister's wife, not like some we know. But if it happened, I'd be happy for your sake.' Her eyes were again focussed on him. 'Women spend more time being happy for their husbands than vice versa.'

'You've been reading Germaine Greer again.' But he reached across and pulled her to him. 'How could I have been so lucky?'

Two days before he was to go back to Canberra, Luke Jamieson came to see him in Danny Voce's office. He was a tall bony young man with untidy red hair and a face that looked curiously lopsided, as if he were speeding round a sharp bend. He edited a small weekly newspaper run on a shoestring budget. He was a crusader with a tiny paper banner.

'Matt —' He was on first-name terms with everyone, whether they liked it or not. 'We've got a problem —'

'We?'

'The electorate. People who care about our city, our environment —'

'Luke, I'm all for saving trees —'

'Trees, nothing. This is *people*.' He was sitting forward in his chair and you knew that was how he always sat; on the edge, ready to jump off into causes. He had big hands on the ends of thin arms and they clawed at each other like battling crabs. He was all energy. 'There's a row of workmen's cottages out along the river, been there since the 1880s. River workers, punt men and the like, they lived in them. Now pensioners live in them. And that bastard —'

'What bastard is that?' The world was full of them, as he had learned.

'Nick Badon —'

Matt raised his eyebrows, not in surprise but at the thought of what was looming. Nick Badon was a man of indeterminate origin: he might have been a Greek, a Turk, a Lebanese, even a Phoenician, if any of them were still around. He was from the watery *pot-pourri* of the Mediterranean and he waved no national flag. He was one of the biggest developers in Sydney and he was a generous supporter of the Labor Party. He had even given a sizeable sum to Matt's own campaign. Matt had never met him, but Danny Voce had told him how much money Badon threw around. Of course, being an even-handed man, he threw money at the Liberals and Nationals too. As Danny Voce remarked, there was no one more middle-of-the-road than a developer. Provided, of course, both sides of the road were ripe for development.

'What's he got in mind?'

'He wants to buy up the cottages, knock 'em down and build a block of luxury flats. The pensioners will be thrown out on the street —'

'Luke, don't start the violins just yet. I'll have Danny Voce look into it, then we'll see what we can do.'

Luke Jamieson looked suspicious, his face even more lopsided. Matt had now had experience of the dedicated: the conservationists, the animal rights leaguers, the gay and lesbian rights advocates. None of them at first recognised the obstacles that had to be overcome; all they recognised was the caution of those in authority: 'You don't sound too keen —'

'Luke, I'm a slow starter. A feller like Badon, big time, you don't rush into a fight with him. I'll have Danny find out what's what, what backing he's got, then we'll start planning.'

Jamieson was a true zealot; he was only half-convinced. 'I dunno. I know what politics are like — you scratch my back, I'll scratch yours —'

Matt was patient, kept his temper: 'Luke, tighten your violin strings, but keep it in its case. I'll be in touch in a fortnight, when I come up here again. Check with Danny.'

On his last night before his return to Canberra, Matt and Carmel went to bed early and made love twice before ten o'clock. Carmel had just rolled off him for the second time when Natalie, dreamily, said from their bedroom doorway, 'Are you fighting?'

'No, darling,' said Carmel, the quicker to recover. 'Just playing.'

'Great,' said Natalie and went back to her own room.

'I'm glad it wasn't Richard,' said Matt. 'He'd have wanted to know, basically, what it was all about.'

'I'll see you at three o'clock,' said Carmel and went to sleep.

He went back to Canberra, where the Treasurer, a man with enough confidence to have flown a punctured balloon, assured Parliament and the country that the economy was steady and healthy and the new millionaires were welcome for tax purposes. Matt made discreet enquiries about Nick Badon and was told, just as discreetly, that he was a man with clout. Meaning money that could be used for influence.

'This is a local matter, Matt,' Danny Voce told him from Parramatta. 'State and council level. I think you should sit on the sidelines, don't put on a guernsey.'

'I'll talk to you when I get back.'

As he had since first coming to Canberra, Matt got up each morning and did a five-kilometre walk. Sometimes he saw Bernadette and she would wave to him and occasionally blow him a kiss. Sometimes she would be with the Minister, trailing behind her, breathless, like a St Bernard in a tracksuit. As he got to the end of his walk out along the lake, Matt would pause and look back at the new seat of parliament growing steadily, sunk into its hill like a bunker.

He came back to Parramatta late on a Friday afternoon and at eight o'clock, when he had just finished dinner with Carmel and the children, Danny Voce was at the front door.

'Can I see you, Matt?' His full-cheeked face looked as if air had been let out of it; he seemed even to have lost some of his pink colouring. 'I didn't want to talk to you down at the club —'

'Come in,' said Matt and led him through to the living room. Carmel came in from the kitchen and he said, 'Love, keep the kids out. Danny has something he wants to tell me.'

Carmel looked at Danny. 'Don't spoil our weekend, Danny.'

'I wish I wasn't going to —'

She remained in the doorway, part of the Durban team. 'What is it?'

Voce looked at both of them in turn. He was a man accustomed to bad news as well as good, but what he was about to tell them had shocked him: 'Luke Jamieson has disappeared. They found his car, with the keys in it, out behind his office. But he's disappeared.'

There was silence for a long moment, then Matt said, 'He leave any note or anything?'

'Nothing. The police are treating it — their word — as suspicious.'

'Wait a minute. The kids are in the bath.' Carmel disappeared.

Voce nodded at the empty doorway. 'You think we should trouble her with this?'

'Danny, we're a team. We don't make a big deal of it, I mean in public, but we discuss everything. She's a strong woman, Danny.'

'I've noticed,' said Voce approvingly.

Then Carmel came back, bringing coffee and some Scotch Fingers, Matt's favourite biscuit. 'Okay, Danny, you can start now.'

'Thanks,' he grinned, sipped his coffee and told them what had happened in the past week: 'Luke ran a story, under his name, on what Nick Badon was trying to do to those workmen's cottages. Two days later some stand-over guys turned up at his office, told him they'd shut him down if he didn't shut up. He told them to get stuffed — he rang me right after it and told me what had happened. He tried to get the building unions interested, but they're too busy, so much work going on — one of their officials told him to get back to them when the boom was over. It'll be too late then —'

'When did Luke — disappear?' asked Matt.

'Last night. He lives next door to his sister, over in West Ryde. She said he didn't come home — like I told you, his car's still at the back of his office. She knew about the stand-over tactics and threats and she called the police. They're sympathetic — one of the cops' mothers lives in the cottages.'

Matt took his time: 'What do you want me to do?'

'Luke shouldn't of come to you in the first place, but he said he got nowhere with our State member nor with the council. Talk to Macquarie Street, to Sussex Street. Find out if Nick Badon is getting support down there.'

'Danny —' Matt was all patience. 'Federal and State politics are two different countries. The Libs down there would tell me to get lost. So would our own blokes in Sussex Street. I'm not exactly their pin-up boy, since I ruined their rules of succession.'

Voce nodded. 'I see your point. But —'

'We can't just turn our backs on Luke,' said Carmel. 'Wherever he is.'

'I'll talk to the police,' said Matt.

Voce stood up. 'I know how we're placed, Matt, but we can't sit on our arses —'

'I'll see he doesn't,' said Carmel and ignored Matt's annoyed look.

Next morning, at Carmel's insistence, he went to see the police. They were not hopeful that Luke Jamieson was still alive, but they had no idea where he might be. 'We're going to drag the river,' they said, 'but that would be an obvious place to dump him. If we ever find him, it'll be someplace else. They made one mistake — they left his keys in the car. If he'd gone off on his own, for some reason, he'd have taken his keys.'

'Good luck,' said Matt.

'We always need that,' said the police.

Carmel was worried. 'I only met Luke once or twice — at Party socials. He was — he was *intense*, but not a bore. He was never afraid to protest — I read his paper every week —'

'Why are you looking at me like that? You think I don't protest enough?'

'If your mates down in Sydney —'

'I have no mates down in Sydney. As I told Danny, Federal and State are two different countries — he knows that as well as I do. Leave it to the police, but I'll do what I can.'

But that didn't satisfy her: 'I'll go to the local council, get them to put a ban on those cottages —'

'Stay out of it.' He was becoming short-tempered.

'No! You're always spouting off —'

'Spouting off?'

'Yes!' She was worked up, he couldn't remember when he had last seen her like this. Except in love quarrels, which were few and far between. 'Spouting off about *big* issues! Little issues count, too — they're the ones that affect little people ... For God's sake, listen to me! Little people! I'm talking like a bloody mealy-mouthed politician —'

'That's what I am? A mealy-mouthed politician?' His brain and his mouth weren't connected. He could hear himself arguing like — like a mealy-mouthed politician.

'For Crissakes, stop repeating me! No, you're not — but you're in danger of becoming one —' She simmered down, drew a deep breath. 'Don't let's quarrel. I feel this is important — Luke might have been murdered because someone wants to make money ... Don't you feel *something*?'

He was silent, almost for too long. It had just occurred to him that he might not be feeling *something*, that he was outside the situation, that he had fallen into the trap for politicians: stay on the outside, looking in. But if Carmel was *in*, then so must he be: 'Yes, I do. I feel bloody helpless — the tiers of government have put me on the outer —'

'Then let me do it!' She was all exclamation; he knew, only too well, the passion in her. 'I'll be a concerned citizen or whatever they call them. I'll go and help Luke's paper —'

'There's only two of them on it, he told me. Himself and a girl, a Vietnamese.'

'Okay, it'll be two girls! She'll know how to run things —'

He took both of her hands in his; he could feel the energy in them. 'Love, be careful —'

'I shall be! Darling, please — I *want* to do it —'

'Okay,' he said reluctantly, afraid for her. 'But be careful.'

'I will be,' she said, quietening down. 'But it has to be done —'

Then young Richard was standing in the doorway in his pyjamas. 'Are you two fighting?'

'Basically,' said Matt, 'no.'

Early Monday morning he flew back to Canberra. Coming in from the airport he shared a Commonwealth car with Joe Rothschild, whose perk it was. 'You look worried, Matt.'

Matt told him about Carmel's crusade. 'It could get dirty, very dirty.'

'Dirty work should be left to men. Unless, of course, she's Mrs Thatcher. Boy, would we give her the works if she was in our Parliament.' He was an all-Aussie male. 'Still, you should tell your wife to leave that sort of fighting to the blokes.'

'Does your wife take your advice?'

Rothschild grinned. 'She turns a deaf ear to it. Right now she's doing her best to lose me the Catholic vote. She's all for abortion on demand.'

'Is she Jewish?'

'No, she's Catholic, a nice convent-bred girl.'

'So's mine. Why are there so many rebel Catholics?'

'The Jesuits should have let the women in. That would have shaken the Vatican, arguing with a woman Jesuit ...' He dwelt on the thought, like a mental orgasm, and Matt, beside him, nodded in approval. 'Let your wife campaign, Matt. This country needs more women in public life. But don't quote me.' Again the moneylender's grin. 'Not till I've retired.'

Matt went through the motions as a backbencher, sitting on a committee, once asking a Dorothy Dix question of Joe

Rothschild who gave the answer — 'I appreciate the Honourable Member for Parramatta raising that question' — as if he never met Matt. There were letters from constituents, Caucus meetings: all the appearances of working hard, but he knew he was just coasting.

Each night he called Carmel: 'How are things going?'

'Terrific!' She was still in exclamation mode, as the press gallery, with its one-page thesaurus, would have described it. 'Fleur —'

'Who?' Names were becoming more exotic.

'Fleur Tan, she's Vietnamese. Luke's girl — well, she's not his girlfriend, she's his dogsbody, she's a journalism student. She's taken over as editor and I'm *her* dogsbody. I drop the kids off at school and work at the *Gazette* till it's time to pick them up again.' Her enthusiasm was like heat down the line: 'I'm loving it!'

'You had any visits from anyone?' He couldn't keep the concern out of his voice.

'Just supporters, mostly women.'

'Keep your tin hat on and watch your back. I love you. Now can I talk to Richard and Natalie ... Hi, son. How were things today?'

'I was in a fight today,' said Richard. 'Apple Perkins.'

'Who? *Apple?*'

'That's his name, his mum's a what-do-they-call-'em, a hippo.'

'A hippy. What happened? You get hurt?' He kept the concern out of his voice, the teacher still there in him. 'What were you fighting about?'

'I dunno.' Careless as a Roman gladiator. 'Just something. I broke his nose, I think.'

'Oh shit!'

'What? Were you swearing?'

'Nothing. Put Mum back on.' A moment, then Carmel was on the line again: 'Did he break another kid's nose?'

'No.' She was laughing. 'One of the teachers broke it up, she said it was just a scuffle. But he's aggressive, she said, he's leadership material —'

'At six-and-a-bit? Jesus! Put Natalie on ... Hello, love. Did you know Richard was in a fight today?'

'Who cares?' said Natalie dreamily and he got off the phone laughing, glad there was someone in the family with her feet off the ground.

2

Friday night he went back to Sydney as usual. Carmel had engaged a babysitter, who turned out to be the *Gazette*'s stand-in editor.

Fleur Tan was a small, slim girl, plain and not deterred by it; there were other things in life besides romance. She was a serious girl with a sense of humour and she and Carmel were already the best of friends.

'She was only Natalie's age when she and her family got out of Vietnam. Her dad's still violently anti-communist, but Fleur is a rebel, like Luke was —' She hesitated before she said *was*, as if reluctant to admit that Luke Jamieson was gone forever. 'She's a treasure, darling. Really.'

Matt shook hands with Fleur, liked her at once. 'Our two aren't angels, Fleur —'

'I'm the youngest of six, Mr Durban. I babysit for my brothers and sisters — I can show you the bruises. Your two are angels compared to some of my nieces and nephews —'

'Carmel tells me you two are going for the Nobel Peace Prize.' But then he said, 'I shouldn't joke. There's still no word on Luke?'

She shook her head, her plain face suddenly plainer.

'Be careful, Fleur,' he said, suddenly concerned for her. Only God knew what dangers she, unwitting, had fled from in Vietnam.

'I'm trying to be.' She had a pleasant voice, but she would never be a television journalist, at least not on the commercial channels; she was not photogenic, image counted as much as news content. Even the male television journalists were getting better-looking. 'But I owe it to Luke . . .'

'We all do,' said Carmel, and after a moment and a glance from her, Matt nodded.

He took Carmel to dinner at a restaurant in Hunter's Hill, where, out of his own bailiwick, they were anonymous. They enjoyed the dinner and the intimacy of each other and went home to bed and closer intimacy.

Saturday morning he went to his electoral office, heard complaints; made promises; worked, without solutions, on the crosswords of other people's lives. Then he went home for lunch. In the afternoon Carmel took the two children to see a revival of *Mary Poppins* and Matt went out to mow the back lawn. They employed a once-a-month gardener, but there had been heavy rain since his last visit and the grass needed cutting. The gardens along each side fence were a blaze of colour, camellia bushes in full glory. Matt was glad of the exercise, the surroundings and the chance to turn off his mind.

He had been mowing only fifteen minutes when Arthur Urling came down the side path and round the corner of the house. Matt stopped mowing and the sudden silence was a wall between the two men. Then Matt chopped a hole in it: 'A social call, Arthur? No, you'd never make them.'

'No, not a social call.' Urling was in jeans and a checked shirt that seemed to match his complexion. He was all self-assurance, as if intrusion into other people's backyards was a habit. He looked around the yard, seeming to pause to admire the surroundings, then back at Matt: 'Nice place you have.'

'The fruits of honest toil,' said Matt.

'Still with the smartarse talk, eh?' He paused, then said, 'I'm here to do some negotiating.'

'You like a beer?' Matt was doing nothing to be sociable, but he knew the advantages a drink could have in a — in a negotiation. He went into the house and came out with two beers that he hadn't bothered to pour into glasses. 'Take a seat.'

They sat on the back patio, under a grape arbour that showed no promise of producing grapes. Though the Durban house had a wide front verandah and a view of the river, no one ever sat out there. That had been a custom now gone; the back patio, if one had one, was the meeting place. It was a calm, early winter day and the air carried weekend noises: another lawn mower somewhere, a children's party further up the street, some kid three doors down practising his drum raps in the family garage. Ideal climate for cut-throat negotiations, which Matt suspected it was going to be.

'Are you here from Sussex Street?'

Urling shook his head, put his finger to his lips; he was almost a caricature of a conspirator. He's been too long in the game, Matt thought.

'No, I'm here as a private adviser. A — what do they call 'em? — a consultant.' His grin was a cartoon.

'From Nick Badon?'

'No names, no pack drill. Matthew, your friend's little rag —' He made the *Gazette* sound like a scrap of notepaper. 'It's getting in the way of progress. Inevitable progress. The future.'

'You sound like a TV commercial,' said Matt, keeping his

voice and his temper steady. 'We happen to think it's protecting the past.'

'The past? What the fuck's the past got to do with it? It's gone —' He swept away a couple of centuries with a big ham of a hand. 'You said *we*? Your wife and you?'

'Leave my wife out of it.' He still kept his voice steady.

'Her and that Viet tart are keeping the rag going, still banging the drum about those old cottages.'

Down the street the kid in the garage was still banging his drums as Matt said bluntly, 'Did you know Luke Jamieson was going to disappear?'

Urling took a mouthful from his bottle of beer, swirled it around in his mouth as if it were mouthwash, then swallowed it. He's practised in delay, Matt thought, he's been this route before. He waited while the older man took his time and up the street the birthday party erupted in screams of delight. Matt found a certain comfort in the everyday noises.

At last Urling said, 'I dunno anything about that. Personally, I think he just decided he'd gone too far and — and *disappeared*. It happens.'

'The police don't think so.'

'You've been to them?'

'No, they came to me,' he lied. 'They have their suspicions as the saying goes. One of the cops' mothers lives in one of those cottages.'

That surprised Urling; he took another swallow of beer, went through the same mouthwashing tactic. 'You're sure of that?'

'Dead sure. That sort of — what's the word? — *personalises* the problem, as far as the cops are concerned. You'd better go back and tell No Name, No Pack Drill that things could get nasty. Tell him it'll be inevitable, like the future.'

Urling put the beer bottle on the patio table, stood up. 'You're shitting in your own nest, Mr Durban.'

The drummer in the garage was working himself into a frenzy. Matt loved the kid, whoever he was. 'Maybe.'

Urling looked at the bottle. 'Heineken. You don't like Aussie beer? The voters wouldn't like to hear that.'

'A voter gave me a case of it,' Matt lied and up the street the partygoers gave a cheer. 'Tell Nick Badon the cops are not going to rest till they find out where Luke Jamieson is buried. See yourself out.'

When Urling had gone Matt sat there under the grapeless arbour, feeling the sudden trembling in his hands. He was not a man who frightened easily and he was not afraid for himself. But all at once Carmel (and Fleur Tan) had to be protected. And for five days of the week he would not be around to see that that was done. He was suddenly aware of silence: the lawn mower, the party, the drummer had disappeared.

He got up, went into the house and called the local police. 'Is Sergeant Belucci on duty today? This is Matt Durban.'

'He's on duty, sir, but he's up at the stadium, keeping an eye on things. The Eels are playing the Sea Eagles. You know what those Eagles supporters are like.' The duty constable, a woman, was obviously an Eels fan.

'Sure. It's the sea air gets to them.' He shot an arrow into the Parramatta air: 'Would you know which of your mates has a mother living down in River Row cottages?'

'It's me, Mr Durban. Sharon Huxley.'

The women's army was gathering; they should send for Mrs Thatcher. Or — no, not Germaine Greer. He shook his head and got back to basics: 'Sharon, what time do you knock off?'

'Five o'clock.'

'Could you come and see me?' He gave her the address. 'I won't keep you more than half an hour.'

'Mr Durban, I'll give you the whole of my holidays if it keeps them from demolishing my mum's house.' Another Boadicea. 'I was born in it. I'll be there.'

Matt was in the kitchen, making himself a cup of tea when Carmel and the children came back from their matinee. He looked at the three of them and Carmel caught his look: 'Something up?'

He shook his head, a warning, and said to the children, 'Did you enjoy the movie?'

'I think I'll learn to fly,' said Natalie and spread her arms, but didn't take off. 'Without an aeroplane. You don't have to pay.'

The first down-to-earth statement Matt had ever heard her utter. 'And you'll be able to do it, I'll bet. You like the picture, Richard?'

'Girl's stuff,' said Richard. 'All that singin' 'n' dancin'.'

'Well, you better get used to it, buster. There's always going to be singin' 'n' dancin' ... You enjoy it?' he asked Carmel.

'Mary Poppins had the right idea. There are advantages to being able to fly away. You finish the lawn?'

'Yes. And I had a visitor —' The children had gone inside to their rooms. He told her about Arthur Urling. 'I've asked the young woman cop, the one whose mother lives in the cottages, to come and see us. She'll be here in half an hour.'

Carmel, usually strict when it came to television-watching, plumped the children in front of the TV set, and had coffee and cake waiting in the kitchen when Constable Huxley arrived.

She was a tall girl who carried her uniform well; and looked confident. 'My dad was a cop, too.'

'How did the Eels go?' asked Matt as they sat down.

'They won. Sergeant Belucci sent his regards. He's given me the okay to help you any way I can.'

Matt took his time, trying to establish calm: 'Sharon, I had a visitor today, a Mr Urling —' He went on to recount the conversation with Urling. 'My wife and Fleur Tan are shoving their necks out —'

'Very carefully,' said Carmel.

'Except for yesterday's edition,' said Constable Huxley, slicing coffee cake with the fork Carmel had provided. Carmel still had some old-fashioned habits. 'You named names.'

'Jesus!' Matt hadn't seen the latest edition of the *Gazette*. He turned on Carmel, scared (for her) as well as angry: 'Why?'

'Fleur got carried away — I didn't know till the printers delivered the paper. She named Mr Badon.'

Matt took his time again, putting a lid on his fear and anger. Then he looked at Sharon Huxley: 'I think this is where you people have got to step in. I don't mean a detail on Fleur and my wife, but just let it be known you are now the Praetorian guard —'

Constable Huxley looked blank and Carmel said, 'He used to be a schoolteacher. It breaks out occasionally, like hives.'

Matt ignored her. 'A visit now and again to the office in daylight, the night patrol might drive by . . . Mr Badon is not going to take on the police.'

'We can do that.' When she stood up to leave Constable Huxley said, 'We've almost given up hope of finding Luke Jamieson. Our guess is that he's under a concrete pour somewhere.'

Carmel shuddered. 'I didn't think murder could be so cold-blooded —'

'It often is, Mrs Durban. I've learned a lot, maybe too much, since I joined the Force. My mother says she prays for me every night, as she did for Dad ... Praetorian guards, eh? I like that. Sounds interesting.'

'They were all men,' said Carmel. 'Wore short skirts.'

'Gays?'

'Possibly,' said Carmel. 'You never know with those ancients. The Greeks were at it like rabbits —'

'Homosexual rabbits?' said Matt. 'That would've been more effective than myxomatosis ... For the record, the Romans didn't encourage homosexuality. They encouraged everything else — throwing Christians to the lions, orgies, conquering lesser tribes ... But fellers holding hands?' He shook his head.

'The schoolteacher again,' Carmel told Sharon Huxley. 'Come by the office some time, Sharon. Fleur makes good coffee.'

Matt took the policewoman down the hall, let her out the front door, closed it and stood with his back to it and looked at his wife: 'For Crissakes — naming names!'

'Pull your head in,' said his wife. 'I knew nothing about it — Fleur got carried away. She phoned the printers after we'd sent them the copy, had them put in Badon's name.'

He put his anger away, put his arm round her as they walked back down the hall to the living room. 'Be careful, love.'

'I will be.' Then to the children, sitting on the floor in front of the television set. When she had left them they had been looking at a cartoon on the ABC: 'What are you looking at, for God's sake?'

'The football,' said Richard.

'Three men just had a fight,' said Natalie. 'Lots of blood all over them.'

'I think I'll be a footballer,' said Richard, who changed ambitions daily.

Matt felt the family close around him, like three sets of arms, and all at once he felt safe. And hoped it would last ...

3

It did. Nick Badon, perhaps frightened off by the Praetorian guard, turned his attention to other developments. Australian developers, short of finance, still learning to think big, were at last flexing their growing muscle. Wide open land still lay ahead of them and some of the more adventurous were reaching for the sky with office buildings.

Luke Jamieson's body was never found. Fleur Tan, finding the finance somewhere, took over the *Gazette* and made it even more successful than it had been under Luke's editorship, though it was still hand-to-mouth publishing and Rupert Murdoch had nothing to worry about. Carmel still did work, unpaid, at the paper. Richard moved up another class at school and, said his teacher, was almost too bright for his age. Natalie, dreamily, moved from kindergarten to year one and all the six-year-old boys fell in love with her, something she accepted without a moment of doubt.

Matt went about his chores as a Member, rising steadily in the ranks even if still on the backbenches. Then, in August 1987, after a talk with the *Financial Times* man in the press gallery, he rang his accountants in Sydney.

'George, sell all my shares. The lot, today —'

'Matt, are you out of your head?' George Mailer was a young man on a rising wave; accountants, like developers, were breeding faster than rabbits. 'The market's still going up, the tip is it will run till December at least —'

'George, *sell*. I've just heard that our richest man has unloaded all his shares. He either knows something or he's got his finger to the wind or he's guessing. But his judgement is good enough for me. Sell.'

'You're making a mistake, Matt —' What were accountants for if not to advise? George Mailer couldn't understand why accountants had not been called in on the Ten Commandments. 'Okay, it's your money —'

Indeed it was and it moved from the stock exchange to his bank. Two months later the bottom fell out of markets all over the world; an atomic explosion was only a squib cracker *bang*! to the crash of falling shares. Nobody jumped from skyscraper windows as they had done in Manhattan in the 1929 havoc, but the moans of despair sounded like tornadoes. Porsches and Ferraris suddenly appeared on used-car lots; pawnbrokers hadn't seen so much jewellery since the French Revolution. Computers were smashed in fits of rage, as if the screens had lied; stockbrokers and accountants began wearing protective armour. On one dreary rainy day, October 20, the Australian stock market lost 55 billion dollars, a huge sum in national accounting at the time. Armageddon was just around the corner, said churches that had lost *their* investments. The following Sunday the churches were full of supplicants, praying for the Lord to revive the market. The country was on its knees everywhere, even the atheists.

Matt was surprised at how much money he had saved. He had not been the sort of investor who watched his portfolio like a miser; he had let George Mailer offer advice and patrol the exchange. He was not yet a millionaire, though he was well on his way; something he would have to keep from the voters. Carmel was impressed by his financial acumen and at once began adjusting her budget.

Parliament was subdued. The Opposition yearned to criticise the Government, but Labor could not be blamed for what had happened in Europe, Asia and the United States. Wall Street had lost 700 billion on the day. President Reagan was woken from another of his naps and declared, with his usual optimism, that everything was gonna be all right, that morning again in America would turn into a sunny afternoon at the end of the day. In Central Africa, where poverty was endemic, the locals wondered what all the fuss was about.

Then came the Christmas break and all the MPs went home, glad to escape. Matt and Carmel closed up the house and went up to Palm Beach to join Paddy and Eileen O'Reilly in the big house they had rented.

'Dad —' Carmel, who had proved to be a careful girl with a dollar, looked around her. 'Whatever are you paying for this?'

'Don't ask,' interrupted Eileen. 'I talked him into it. He's become such a tightarse —'

'Nan,' said Richard, 'that's swearing!'

'And I'll swear some more if you interrupt me again.'

Richard grinned; he had inherited the Durban smile. 'Swearing is a safety valve —'

'Now who's being a smartarse? Where'd you hear that?'

'Mum —'

It was a good week, just what Matt needed. His father came down from Collamundra, and Matt felt the comfortable bond that can never be found in the political family. They spent every morning on the beach, which this year was not crowded. Money, what was left of it amongst the wealthy, stayed home and fewer houses were rented. The nation's richest man was not sighted, but his vacation house on the southern hill looked as if it had had a new coat of paint, with gold touches.

'The estate agent who rented me this place,' said Paddy O'Reilly, 'has lived in Palm Beach for forty years. He was telling me that back in 1942, during the Jap submarine scare, you could've bought the whole of the Palm Beach peninsular north of Avalon for 15,000 quid, maybe 200,000 dollars in today's terms. The bloke who owns this house wants to sell it, he'll take a hundred thousand for it.'

'I was twelve years old then,' said Keith Durban. 'My dad was away with the Ninth Division in the Middle East, Tobruk. It was another age, another world.'

Matt had never known his paternal grandfather; he had been killed at Tobruk. 'It's fading. The only time we remember it is on Anzac Day.'

'That's the way it goes,' said Paddy, who had served in New Guinea as a nineteen-year-old commando. Then abruptly he said, 'You've become fat, Matt. Fat and complacent.'

He, Keith and Matt were still sitting on the beach under a large umbrella. Paddy was wearing a lot of sun-cream and wore his wide-brimmed Akubra hat. He was still lean and fit, no wrinkled skin, no flabby muscles. He was not the sort of grazier who sat on his verandah and let his men do the work.

'Fat?' Matt was still in condition, with a strong chest and muscular shoulders. He looked down at the two children playing on the edge of the surf, then back at his father-in-law. He tried to keep the resentment out of his voice: 'And complacent?'

'Yes.' Paddy's gaze was direct; he was not one to dodge an issue or an opinion. 'I've been following what goes on down in Canberra, watching the TV broadcasts, listening to the radio, reading the columnists. You never get a mention. You're doing bugger-all but sit there on the backbenches as if that's the end of the road.'

'Paddy, you have no idea —'

'Don't gimme any bullshit about having to wait your turn. Our esteemed PM didn't wait his turn — he came in and showed 'em who should be boss. Waiting your turn is what they do in the Coalition, the — what do they call it?'

'The rules of succession,' said Matt, but he wasn't smiling. 'Paddy, what do I do? Shoot a Minister or two?' He was not used to criticism; or had begun to resent it. 'I have to wait till I get the call —'

'I've seen it happen,' said Paddy; he was speaking quietly, with no excitement. 'Blokes who sit on their arses, get comfortable with the salary and the perks, settle for being an MP — it's happened to you, Matt. Get off your arse and be *noticed*. You've got more talent, more nous, than half the backbenchers and you just *sit* there, sunk amongst them —'

Matt had never been spoken to before like this, not even by the PM or the Treasurer, a man with a vitriolic tongue. He looked at his father, who had remained silent. 'What do you think?'

Keith took his time. 'I think Paddy has a point.'

Matt was surprised as well as hurt. Surprised not at the bluntness of Paddy (and his own father), but that he had not noticed the folding of blankets of acceptance about himself. Had he really slipped so far down into the comfort of doing nothing? Well, virtually nothing.

As if reading Matt's mind, Keith said, 'The perks have coddled you. But come the next election, will the voters vote for you?'

'I've looked after it, the electorate. They've got no complaints.'

'Okay,' said Paddy, smearing more sun-cream on himself; but no soothing cream on Matt: 'They vote you back in and you go back and sit there doing nothing again. We're concerned for you, Matt —'

'Who? Who's concerned for me?'

Down by the water's edge Richard and Natalie shouted and yelled with delight. Further out surfers rode the waves, mindlessly happy in what they were doing. All along the beach families, couples, singles, lay in the sun, not a care in the world visible.

'Me, Keith here, Eileen. And Carmel, too, I'll bet, if we asked her. You're there for *us*, for the kids down there —' Paddy gestured towards Richard and Natalie, who looked up and waved, as if they thought he had been waving at them. 'You're our man, we had hopes for you, and you're stuffing it all up!'

'Jesus!' He suddenly lost his temper. 'I didn't start out to be a fucking knight in shining armour!'

'I think you did,' said Keith quietly. 'Somewhere along the way you took it off. You've settled for the Hugo Boss suit —'

'Fletcher Jones. I don't throw money away on clothes.' It was a stupid, juvenile answer, but his brain wasn't working too well.

'Well, when you go back in the New Year,' said Paddy, 'try the shining armour again — Fletcher Jones might have some in stock. The helmet mightn't fit —' Then suddenly he grinned. 'Christ Almighty, we're really giving it to you, aren't we?'

'But with the best of intentions,' said Keith, who knew how to pour oil on troubled waters.

Then the children came up from the water and it was time to go back to the house for lunch. Matt gathered up the towels, gathered himself. He would have to talk to Carmel tonight, his best sounding board.

After dinner that night they left Eileen to shower the kids and put them to bed and they walked down the winding road to the street that fronted the beach. The pine trees that lined the road stood like jagged battlements against the moon and at the surf club a party had already begun. At dusk the surf had flattened and now there was just the slap-silence-slap as the sea gummed the shore. Cars were parked fronting the beach and down on the sands parties were beginning to stir as someone turned up a radio and Tina Turner silenced the sea.

'Am I fat and smug?' he asked.

'What?' They were walking hand-in-hand and her grip tightened.

'Your dad — and mine — they told me today that I was. That I was just filling a space on the backbenches. They said you and Eileen thought the same.'

Carmel said nothing for about twenty paces; she could be volatile, but she could also take her time. Down on the beach Tina Turner gave way to someone just as raucous. Then: 'I don't discuss you with other people, not even Mum. But she did bring it up and I listened, because what other people think of you, politically and personally, is my concern. But yes — I think Mum and Dad and Keith have a point. Maybe,' she added as a consolation.

'Jesus!' Then it was his turn to walk in silence for a while. Then he stopped, still holding her hand: 'How did it happen?'

'I don't know. I don't think I noticed it till Mum mentioned it. You just seem to have settled into a rut, you go through the motions. I don't think there's any complaint from the electorate, but we — well, we all expected more of you.'

'You want me to still aim at being PM?' He had to confess: it had become almost a joke in his own mind.

'I don't care — no. Yes, I do care. You had ambition and we all thought you had what was needed at the top —'

'What?'

'I dunno. Enthusiasm, broadness of vision, a recognition that the world is changing . . . Somehow, darling, I think it's been lost.'

Intelligent men often become lost in the maze of self-perception; the signposts are often obscured by mists of vanity. The political benches over the years, on both sides of the House, had claimed men who had lost their way and their ambition. A safe seat was not only a comfort but a trap. Voters were not interested in a man's ambition; they were only interested in themselves and he was their champion. A politician's personal target was not theirs; their arrows were aimed closer to home. He had gone to sleep, dosed by voters whose only ambition was their own well-being. He had the grace not to blame them.

'Okay, when I go back in the New Year I'll start making waves, get noticed.'

'I'm not driving you, shoving a broom in your back. Whatever you want is what I want. But it's afternoon, morning's gone. I don't want you asking when the sun's setting, at the end of the day, as you men say, why did you become fat and lazy. That wouldn't be the man I married.'

He leaned close and kissed her. Down on the beach some radio jock had been bitten by nostalgia. He was playing Peggy Lee, voice seductive, singing *Why Don't You Do Right?*

Chapter Eight

1

On the other side of the world, politics, oblivious of Canberra, went about its business. The Americans gave aid and hardware to the Taliban, a group Australians had never heard of, in Afghanistan, a country most of them couldn't find on a map; it was aid to help kick the bloody Russians back behind their own boundaries and so it was a good thing. In Iraq a US Under-Secretary of Defence named Rumsfeld shook hands with the tyrant Saddam Hussein and offered chemical aid against the goddamn Iranians and Canberra could see no harm in that. God, in one of His cynical moods, gave the world another spin on its axis.

Down Under, the new year came in with trumpets and banners and rhetoric and a fever of patriotism. It was the double centenary of the nation's founding. Aborigines, who arrived 40,000 years earlier, sat on the sidelines and smiled indulgently at the new kids on the block and their flag-waving and the brass bands and the Prime Minister, hair bouffant, walking on water. Mrs Thatcher sent a message of congratulations and said how fortunate it was that the first settlement had been the work of the British. President Reagan, who seemed to spend his time stepping into or out of a helicopter on the White House lawn, paused to send best wishes for the future and remarked, in passing, how

Errol Flynn, a great Australian, had helped win World War II in Burma and other places.

In the rest of the world small wars and terrorism and poverty and disease went on as usual, the Four Horsemen of the Apocalypse still galloping, but for January 26, 1988, Australia was the greatest country on earth; or, as the new word had it, on the planet. Government and Opposition members shook hands and some even embraced, much to the horror of their minders who did their best to keep the horrible sight from media cameras. If this sort of thing got out of hand, only God knew what the future would be. Euphoria reigned and rained.

Then Parliament reconvened and slowly the country came back to earth, Matt went back to Canberra, *sans* fat, *sans* smugness. He raised again the vulnerability of our northern coastline, costed and elaborated his plan for a fleet of coast guard vessels. Joe Rothschild listened and so did the Defence Minister; the Treasurer listened and then said it would all cost too much. But Matt had been noticed again and by the middle of the year he was marked for promotion. At the next Cabinet reshuffle he would be closer to the frontbench.

But there were times when there were elbows that had to be used.

'Matt,' said Joe Rothschild, a man with more bruises than a litter of fallen fruit, 'you'll have to get used to the fact that fighting amongst ourselves is natural to our Party. It might have something to do with the other fact that there were so many Irishmen in at the beginning.'

'I try to be neutral —'

'Sitting on the fence in the end just gives you a sore crotch. The trick is to take sides, but always be at the back. Soldiers at the back of a battalion are always the last ones wounded.'

'How did you get to the front in the unions?'

'I just stepped over the dead and wounded,' said Joe Rothschild and smiled.

Matt went out to dinner occasionally with other Members, but he formed no lasting friendships. He was affable and popular, but he was, at heart, a loner. Or merely content with what he had to go home to each weekend.

He went to embassy receptions, occasionally again going to a meal with men from the embassies, second or third secretaries, men, like himself, on the way up. He broadened his knowledge of the rest of the world, became more tolerant of other countries' attitudes. He did not become an internationalist, he was too native for that, but his intelligence widened.

Then, each weekend, he went home, felt again the safety and comfort of Carmel and the children. It might be afternoon, no longer morning, as Carmel had said, but the sun was still high in the sky.

2

'I'd love a Lamborghini,' said the Japanese ambassador, 'but the Foreign Office insists I have a Lexus.'

'They take it for granted I'm an ex-All Black,' said the New Zealand High Commissioner. 'But I only played badminton for Otago High.'

'Australian women are the biggest devourers of the Pill,' said the Brazilian ambassador. 'I tried to persuade my wife to stay home in Rio, but she insisted on accompanying me.'

Matt had come to this cocktail reception at the residence of the British High Commissioner just because the evening otherwise looked empty. He was tired of watching television, the local cinemas were showing only disaster movies and he had read himself almost blind. He was lonely for Carmel and the kids. And so he had accepted the invitation to this reception and now stood in a corner, sipping a chardonnay and listening to the balloons of wit floating about the large room.

'You look bored, Mr Durban —' The High Commissioner, a man in his early sixties, as urbane as a Harrods floorwalker, had appeared out of the crowd.

'No, no, Sir Donald —' Then Matt grinned and was relieved his host returned the smile. 'Doesn't it wear you down sometimes?'

'Matt — it is Matt, isn't it? I went straight from Oxford into the FO I started as the messenger boy at our embassy in Beirut and progressed, third secretary, second secretary, first secretary, up the ladder till one day I was an ambassador, a minor one in a Middle East country. All along the way the receptions were the same, some with more intrigue than others, some frightfully bloody dull. Then I was offered this post and I realised I'd reached Nirvana. You're familiar with Nirvana?'

'Not over at Parliament House —'

Sir Donald smiled. 'I've been on the sidelines of politics all my adult life. It's fascinating to watch. I'm glad I'm a spectator and not a participant.'

'There are no politics in diplomacy?'

'Of course not. We're just the messenger boys.'

'Still? After how many years?'

Sir Donald smiled and turned as a well-dressed, good-looking woman approached. 'Ah, Mrs Herx, you know Mr Durban?'

'We've waved to each other across the House once or twice.' She had a low but distinct voice, as if she might have been coached in elocution at school. 'Hello, Matt.'

'June —'

'I must move on,' said Sir Donald. 'Enjoy yourselves.'

He departed and June Herx smiled and said, 'What did he mean by that?'

They were casual acquaintances with little in common in terms of their voters' needs. She was a Coalition backbencher from a far north Queensland sugar farm electorate. She was in her early forties and a decoration on any parliamentary bench.

'I've been meaning to talk to you, Matt. You and I have something in common.'

He was pleasantly surprised at her company. Good-looking women often put a stamp on a man, sometimes undeserved. But he was wary of her, feeling Carmel's ghostly hand on his shoulder: 'How come?'

'Our unprotected northern borders.' She moved a little closer to him; he could smell her perfume, which, he guessed, was not made from sugar juice. 'I'd like to talk to you about what you know and what you have in mind.'

'What's your interest, June? Are the sugar farmers worried about New Guinea invading us? They'd cop it first.'

She gave him a benevolent smile, showing her experience of men. 'Don't joke, Matt. You know as well as I do that the Indonesian military think we're a pain in the arse. They look at all that empty land up in the north and think how they could populate it and develop it better than we're doing.'

'We're palsy-walsy with Suharto.'

'But not with the military.' She looked around her, as if looking for Indonesian military hiding in the bushes of the crowd, then back at him. 'Let's go and have dinner. My shout.' He hesitated and she smiled. 'Matt, I'm a happily married woman and I know you're a happily married man. It will be strictly political business.'

He hesitated, then nodded. They moved out of the crowd and as they went out the door he saw Sir Donald smiling at him in approval. Matt had come by taxi, but she had her car, a late model Volvo.

'My husband bought it for me. He thinks it gives me the proper staid look for a woman alone in Canberra.'

They went to dinner at a small restaurant where other MPs and the press gallery did not hang out. The waiter recognised them both, but that was usual in Canberra; after all, as someone had said, it was just a big country town loaded with outsiders. He took their orders and went away.

Matt had noticed what she had ordered as her pre-dinner drink. 'My wife always has champagne to start her off.'

Her smile this time was not benevolent but charming. 'Matt, don't keep reminding me you're happily married. Are you always this cautious?'

He relaxed, gave her his own smile. 'Yes, I guess so. You hear gossip about affairs — some of the names would surprise the voters. We manage to keep the scandals quieter than the Brits and the Americans ... Why are you, as a woman, so interested in our north?'

'A woman? I didn't think you'd be so one-eyed — or are you misogynistic? No, I don't think you are. But women have made their marks in fields you men think are yours — and yours only. Mrs Thatcher hasn't done too badly. And Golda Meir did well. And Catherine the Great. And Boadicea ... Do you want me to go on?'

'Okay,' he grinned. 'What's your interest, as an MP, in our north?'

'What are your chances of getting your plans for a coast guard watch, getting them through Cabinet?'

'Bugger-all, looks like. Defence would love to have all those extra boats, they love having money spent on them. They swoon when they think about the money Reagan spent on Star Wars ... But the Treasurer and the PM get on well with Suharto and they think it would be a waste of money. I have it on good advice that the Indonesians surveyed our north-west coast, years ago, back in Sukarno's day. But it's not just them. Drugs are coming in every week from New Guinea —'

'I know.' She looked at him across the rim of her champagne glass. It was not vampish, but he had the idea that she had been looking at men like this since she was adolescent. She was a natural in the battle of the sexes. 'Some of my constituents up in the Gulf tell me of boats coming in and the police just can't get near them. Even planes flying in to airstrips out in the mulga.'

'Some day, maybe not tomorrow, maybe in ten years' time, there'll be immigrants trying to sneak in, not bothering about visas. The world is on the move and nobody seems to be taking much notice of it, least of all us.'

The waiter brought them their main course: roast duck for her, venison for him. She ordered the wine and he noticed it was a top-of-the-range shiraz. She was evidently not short of money and he wondered what her husband did.

'Is your husband in sugar?'

She smiled again: she was ahead of him. 'Yes. He's also into a dozen other things. He's a Czech, he was a professor of economics, the youngest at Prague University. He got out when the Russians moved in in 1968. I — we — can afford this.' She touched the bottle of wine. 'Do you usually judge women by what they spend?'

'I have my benchmarks. My criteria, if you like.' He was wondering again about her; she didn't seem particularly passionate about the northern borders. Curious, yes, but not passionate. He wondered if it was her husband or the sugar farmers of her electorate who had prompted her? He asked bluntly: 'Do you have ambition?'

She considered for a few moments, sipping her wine. 'Not really. I'm not even sure I'll run again. But you're ambitious, aren't you?'

He nodded, sipped his own wine; it was good: the taste of ambition? 'I can't see any point, otherwise, in coming down here.'

She raised her glass. 'Well, in ten years' time or whatever it takes, I'll vote for whatever you want to be.'

'PM,' he said, but watered the conceit with a smile.

When it was time to leave she paid the bill, left a generous tip in cash rather than on her credit card, and walked ahead of him out of the restaurant. He was aware of other diners looking at them and he guessed they had been recognised. He saw no one from the press gallery and he felt a relief.

Then just as he got to the door he saw Bernadette at a side table with her Minister. She raised an eyebrow, gave a thin smile and then an almost imperceptible shake of her head, a silent *tut-tut*.

Then he was out the door and June Herx was saying, 'Do you want a lift? You could wait ages for a cab.'

He hesitated, then said, 'Sure.' He didn't want to be standing here waiting for a cab when Bernadette and her Minister came out. 'I stay at —'

He got into the Volvo, had difficulty in finding the lock for the seat belt. 'Let me,' June said and leaned towards him to buckle him in. He was close to her and could smell her perfume. He felt a stirring in the crotch, but it was only slight and it was not going to lead him into difficulty.

'We must do this again,' she said as she started up the car. 'I'll let you pay next time.'

'Yes,' he said, but had already made up his mind there was not going to be a next time. She might be happily married and so was he, but temptation hovered around her like perfume.

She dropped him at his motel, leaned across and kissed him on the cheek. 'Stay ambitious, Matt.'

'I'll do that,' he said and went inside and called Carmel, like an act of contrition. He didn't mention June Herx.

3

Next morning he was in the office he shared with Alex Filkins, another backbencher. There was a pile of mail on his desk; the voters back home had too much time on their hands. There were also invitations (commands?) to open a fete, a new classroom, a new wing to a nursing home. He and Alex also shared a secretary and Doris, a down-to-earth woman who had been in Parliament House for twenty years, had seen Members come and go and knew that all life here in the House and Senate was transitory, was going to be busy.

Alex Filkins looked at the pile on his own desk. 'I think I'll be glad to see the last of this. They tell me that just over the horizon there's gunna be something called e-mail that's gunna make this look like a few birthday cards. Jesus!'

He was a short, nuggety man, an ex-rugby league halfback with a square-eyed face that suggested he was something of an innocent; which he was not. He was the member for a marginal seat and the latest polls showed that at the next election he would probably be on his way out; another example of the transitory life here. What had once been a solid working-class electorate had been infiltrated by upwardly mobile (he still used that expression) bastards from only God knew where. Yet he was not downhearted; he had never been ambitious for higher status and he would be satisfied with his pension. He was a seat-warmer, but everyone liked him. Everyone but the upwardly mobile bastards.

'Just imagine what it's gunna be like when Them Out

There all own computers . . . Hullo, Doris, what's worrying you this time?'

Doris stood in the doorway, half-filling it. 'I've been here too long to be worried by anything . . . The boss wants to see you, Matt.'

'The PM?' Matt was surprised.

'No. When I mean Him, with a capital aitch, I genuflect.' She had gone to a Catholic school and pronounced it *haitch*. 'No, Mr Rothschild. He said he wants to see you — *now*.'

Matt looked at Filkins and shrugged. 'I haven't a clue. Am I supposed to have leaked something, Doris?'

'The last time a Minister confided in me I was young and innocent and a size 10.'

'What did he confide in you?'

'None of your business. Better get a move on, he's waiting.'

Matt went round to Joe Rothschild's office, hurrying but not looking as if he was the Minister's lapdog, coming at a whistle. He was flipping through his memory, wondering what had suddenly come up that had brought on this urgent call.

Rothschild was seated behind his desk, comfortable-looking as always; come Armageddon he would be comfortable, ready for anything. With him was a big man who might have been a second-row rugby forward or a Mafia hitman. Except that he looked affable, at ease.

'Matt —' said Rothschild. 'You know Guy Fortague from ASIO?'

'We haven't met,' said Matt, wondering why the man from Security and Intelligence was here. He had seen Fortague in the House occasionally and had been told who he was. The big man, black-haired and dark-eyed, stood up and Matt shook hands with him: 'Why am I here?'

'Tell him, Guy,' said Rothschild. The older man looked unusually grave, the wicked grin totally absent. 'Sit down, Matt. It'll save your knees buckling.'

Matt sat down, almost warily, suddenly having the feeling that he was in a schoolroom again; only this time he was not the teacher. Fortague sat down again, took his time; one almost expected him to take out a tobacco pouch, fill a pipe, light it. He was a big man, but not ponderous.

'You were observed having dinner with June Herx last night —'

'Observed?' Matt was on guard, fencing.

Fortague had a pleasant smile, one designed to put you at ease; even his dark eyes smiled. 'We tend to have our own vocabulary. You were *seen*. Have you had dinner with her before? Taken her out?'

'No. Last night was the first time.' He thought a moment, then added, 'And the last.'

Rothschild was impassive, but Fortague raised an eyebrow. 'You had a row, a disagreement?'

'No, nothing like that. I just decided I was a married man, a happily married one —' He looked at Rothschild, who nodded. 'I don't think she had any ideas about an affair or whatever you want to call it, but I decided I wasn't going to be put in a situation where people might think there was one. You know how people talk —'

'Indeed,' said Fortague. 'We sometimes wonder if we should slip a word to people we know are having affairs —'

'No names, no pack drill,' said Rothschild, an echo of Arthur Urling, but he smiled this time.

'Where's this leading?' asked Matt. 'Are ASIO into morals now?'

Rothschild shook his head in warning, but said nothing.

'No, Mr Durban,' said Fortague, unruffled. 'There are no morals in our business. Don't you read spy stories?'

'No.'

Fortague nodded approvingly, as if he, too, had no time for spy stories. Then abruptly he got down to business and leaned forward. 'What did you talk about last night?'

'Ah —' Matt began to see some light. 'About northern borders and the problems —'

'What problems?' Fortague cut in, still leaning forward.

'Possible future problems. She asked me about my suggestions for a fleet of coast guard vessels up there —' He looked at Rothschild, who nodded again, this time encouragingly; then back at Fortague: 'A plan that was vetoed because of costs. She agreed with everything I said. What are you getting at?'

'We'd like you to go on seeing Mrs Herx.'

'No way!' Matt shook his head; but then had to ask: 'Why?'

'We've had her under surveillance for some time. We suspect she is working for — well, let's say someone else.'

'She's a *spy*?' Matt couldn't keep the disbelief out of his voice. He was not naive. There had been the Petrov affair back in the Fifties, front page stuff; it would have been even more sensational on television, had the country had TV back then in the Dark Ages. There had been some quiet stirrings since then, junior diplomats deported, but those affairs had been handled with a minimum of fuss. But June Herx — a spy?

Fortague nodded, sat back. 'We think so. They come in all shapes and sizes.'

'But *how*? She's not on any committee, she's not with Foreign Affairs. She approached me because —' He stopped. 'Wait a minute. Am I looked upon as an expert on our northern borders?'

'Joe here tells me you have a pretty good knowledge of them.'

Matt looked at Rothschild, who remained impassive; then he looked back at Fortague. 'Only in a general way. I've been up there only once, when I was a trainee teacher. I went to Darwin and then down as far as Wyndham and came back through the Kimberley. I dunno the Gulf country at all. I've been planning to go back, but never got around to it. All I know is from maps and reading reports . . . '

'You wouldn't be the first expert on a place he's rarely been to . . . We'll give you declassified material that you can discuss with Mrs Herx. We want you to draw her out —'

'Wait a minute.' Matt held up a hand; he was in the kindergarten of extravagant gestures, but he was learning. 'Why is she a — a spy?'

'For the same reason that at least half of them are. Money.'

'Money? I got the impression she's loaded. Her husband, she told me, he's into quite a few things besides sugar —'

'He is, he's a very wealthy man.' Fortague was sitting back, comfortable again. Rothschild was still silent, but there was no mistaking his interest. 'He's kicked her out. She had an affair with one of her constituents and Mr Herx is evidently very strict about marriage vows. They've kept the split quiet, but he's tied up his money so she can't get a penny of it —'

Matt shook his head in wonder. 'How do you blokes know all this?'

Fortague looked pained: 'We know our job . . . All she has is her MP's salary and she's a lady with very expensive tastes.'

Matt was still suspicious: 'What do you know about me?'

Fortague smiled. 'Only the very best of references.' He looked at Rothschild, who also smiled. 'We'd never blackmail you, Mr Durban . . . Will you help us?'

'What happens if I say No?'

'Nothing. But if you say Yes . . . You're an ambitious man, Mr Durban —'

'Who told you that?' With a suspicious look at Rothschild.

The latter shook his head, smiled. 'Not me, Matt. But you've never tried to hide it, have you? You carry a placard, Matt, sooner or later someone's gunna notice it.' He paused, then said, 'Take the job, Matt.'

Matt, instead, took his time. He ran several things through his mind, then said, 'On one condition — if I go courting Mrs Herx, I tell my wife why.'

Fortague took his own time about that, chewing his lip. 'Wives talk. They have their women friends, their mothers —'

'If my wife heard you make those remarks, she'd throttle you. She's circumspect, Mr Fortague, she can keep a secret — she'd make a good spy. I tell her or there's no deal.'

Fortague looked at Rothschild, then back at Matt: 'It's a deal . . . Take Mrs Herx to dinner again —'

Matt's pocket clenched; all the money in his bank hadn't loosened its grip. 'Hold it. Who picks up the expenses? She has expensive tastes, as you said. She likes champagne for starters and last night we had a fifty-dollar bottle of wine.'

Fortague made a mock wince. 'Try and wean her off that. Do they still make Porphry Pearl at two dollars a bottle? Just send us the account. And thanks, Mr Durban, you'll be appreciated. Now here is the declassified material I mentioned —'

'You must've been sure of me.'

'We make mistakes, but not many.'

4

Matt went home for the weekend. He had spent the last day of the week in the House, hardly listening to the exchanges but covertly looking across the chamber at June Herx. Once their glances crossed and she smiled and he smiled back. He was still uncertain if he was about to do the right thing.

When he went home he hesitated telling Carmel about June Herx and decided to wait a night or two. Saturday morning he did what was called his surgery at his electoral office, promising voters to look into complaints, to try and fast-forward immigration complaints, to talk with the Treasurer about how taxes were hitting small business. Cynically, but never voicing his cynicism, not even to Danny Voce, he had from experience divided the electorate into those who couldn't-care-less and the born-to-be whingers. But everyone had to be listened to.

'It's the wages you pay,' Danny Voce told him. 'Now, this afternoon there's this fete —'

So he took the children to the fete, giving Carmel a rest from them. He bought ten tickets in each of four raffles — 'If you win,' Danny again advised him, 'you give the prize to the nearest kid you see. But not your own.'

'My kids will grow up and be Coalition voters. Can I charge these tickets off against expenses?'

'Matt, you must be the tightest-arsed bastard since Uriah Heep. I'll see what's in the petty-cash box.'

That night, bringing in a Dial-an-Angel girl as babysitter, he and Carmel went out to dinner. He relaxed, shutting his mind to everything but the pleasure of being with her. Then they went home to bed, and made love quietly so as not to invite an audience from the kids. Then he lay back, got his breath and said, 'I have to tell you something. I'm seeing another woman.'

'Big Tits Bernadette?' She, too, was exhausted.

'No, an older woman. Older than you. Middle-aged, almost.'

She was silent for a long moment, but he felt the sudden stiffness in her and then she said, quietly but fiercely, 'You'd better be joking or I'll kill you!'

He turned his head and looked at her: 'Now *you're* joking —'

'No, I'm not. You're mine and I'll never let anyone else have you!' She was on her elbow, leaning over him. 'Understand? Now, are you joking or not?'

He stared at her, at the fierceness in her face; then he reached up and stroked her hair: 'Love, I'm joking. You're the only one —' Then he told her of June Herx and the ASIO approach. 'It's strictly business, all I have to do is see how much she will tell me —'

'She's a *spy*?' She sounded as incredulous as he had sounded a few days ago.

'She's not Mata Hari —'

'Who?'

He sighed. Carmel was intelligent and well-read: she knew Elizabeth Bennett and Anna Karenina and Madame Bovary, but she did not know Mata Hari. He had begun to realise, when teaching, that World War I was as remote as the War of the Roses. 'She was a famous spy — June Herx is nothing like her.'

'What's she like to look at?'

Were James Bond and George Smiley ever questioned like this? 'She's blonde and good-looking and well-dressed and she wears expensive perfume.'

'You sound as if you've been studying her pretty closely. I don't know that I like this. Do you have to do it? Take her out?'

'No, I don't *have* to. But ASIO tell me I'm doing my patriotic duty —'

'Balls. Why don't they get one of their own men to work on her?'

'I'm not *working* on her. They picked me because *she* picked me.'

She was still leaning on her elbow, gazing at him. 'If you so much as undo one button of her shirt —' She ran her free hand across his throat. 'Understand?'

'You ever thought of going in for espionage? As a hitwoman?'

She gave him a wicked smile and rolled over on top of him again.

Monday morning he went back to Canberra and called June Herx. He hesitated before he picked up the phone: dangers, small, maybe even large, lay ahead. Then: 'June? I'd like to discuss further what we were talking about the other night.'

'I didn't think you had any further interest?' She sounded cool.

He took his time: how long did it take to become practised in counterespionage? 'I've got some of the Defence boys backing me and we're hoping we can get the Treasurer to change his mind when he brings down the Budget. The more backing I can get, the better the chances.' He was surprised how convincing he sounded.

She took her time, then said, 'All right. Same place, same time.'

No: Bernadette might be there again with her Minister. 'Let's try another place.' He named a good restaurant on the edge of town. 'Eight o'clock. My shout this time.'

He could *hear* her smile: 'I never thought otherwise.'

He rented a car for the evening; he did not want her driving him back to the motel again. He felt a perverse shame that he was warding off temptation; but Carmel was sitting on his shoulder. He would charge the car to ASIO and felt no shame about that.

He was waiting for her in the restaurant, eyes searching for someone from ASIO keeping tabs on him; he had told

Fortague of the meeting and the latter had wished him luck. Looking around now, it seemed that no one was interested in him and he wondered if Fortague was now trusting him to work alone. When she was brought to his table by the waiter, the latter looked at him with what could have been a smirk and Matt wondered if *he* was the ASIO surveillance man, *observing* him.

She had champagne to start with; perversely Matt thought of ordering French champagne, but reason prevailed. They had *boeuf a la Provençale* with a forty-dollar, not fifty-dollar, bottle of wine. Gradually he felt comfortable with her; she was totally at ease with him. He passed on the information that ASIO had given him. She sipped her wine, nodded appreciatively, then said, 'Where did you get this extra information?'

He realised he was going to have to tread carefully; he was not used to dealing with spies. 'I've had someone up in Broome who's been writing to me for some time.'

'And he suddenly wrote to you over the weekend?'

He was used to fencing with sceptical voters; he gave her the Durban smile. 'June, do you lay all your cards on the table at once?'

She returned his smile. 'No-o. But I don't want to tie my name to something that's half-baked. You're sure of all that you've told me?'

'Absolutely.'

She put down her glass, picked up her fork. 'Tell me more.'

So he did and the rest of the dinner passed pleasantly. He paid the bill, glad that ASIO would be picking it up, and they went out into the cold night air.

'You want a lift back to your motel?'

'No, I have a car tonight.'

She smiled, then said, 'Come back to my flat for a nightcap.'

'I don't think so, June.'

'Why not?'

'You know why not. What's that perfume?'

'Arpége. Why?'

'I told my wife about it. I thought I'd buy her some.'

'Touché.' She kissed his cheek, opened the door of her car and got in. 'If your friend from Broome writes again, let me know.'

He watched her drive away, then walked across to his own car, got in and drove back to his motel. The car was a Honda Civic, not something James Bond would have driven. Still, in his first effort at counterespionage, he felt he had done all right.

Back at his motel he called Carmel: 'Would you wear Arpége if I bought you some?'

'That's what *she* wears? No, thanks. You'll never be a diplomat.'

'When did you hear of a Prime Minister who was a diplomat?'

'Metternich.' She had done European history at school, had a habit of remembering odd bits and pieces.

'He doesn't count. He was Austrian, not Australian ... I love you.'

'I know you do. Just be careful with that Arpége. If I smell it on you, you're dead ...' Then she gurgled and he could see her smiling. 'Darling ...'

5

Next morning Matt was in his office, already at the bottom of the pile of mail on his desk. Alex Filkins was somewhere showing a constituent around the House, a voter come to see what he thought he owned. Outside autumn sunshine lit the trees as they blazed their last colours before winter drained them. Sometimes, Matt mused, there was peace in Canberra.

Then Doris was in the doorway. 'The Minister's office — *now*!'

'Doris, why are you starting to sound like a prison guard?' Then he looked at her: 'No, you're not. What's it about?'

'I dunno. Grace, his secretary, called and said he wanted you over there at once and not to stop to talk to anyone on the way. Don't shoot me, I'm just the messenger.' Then she softened: 'Maybe you're going to be promoted.'

'Wouldn't that be nice,' he said and went out of his office expectantly.

He went round to Joe Rothschild's office. Somehow, he was not surprised when he walked in and found Guy Fortague there. But he was surprised at how concerned they both looked.

'Sit down, Matt,' said Rothschild. 'In case your legs buckle.'

'You said that last time I was here.' Matt sat down and looked at Fortague. 'You've arrested June Herx?'

'No,' said Fortague. 'Last night she was murdered.'

'Jesus!' Matt blinked, as if the ASIO man had flung cold water in his face. 'How? Who by?'

'We don't know yet, who by, but we have our suspicions. Well, more than that —' Fortague, surprisingly, seemed ill at ease. 'They found her body only an hour ago, in her flat. She'd been strangled, pretty brutally. The media will be on to it any minute now and you may be questioned. Did you go back to her flat last night?'

'No, I did not!' Matt was fluttering between being angry and being afraid. 'Christ Almighty, I told you I was going to keep it as — as professional as I could. She invited me back and I turned her down ... Who's handling it — the murder?'

'The Federal police. We've talked to their boss and they're keeping our name out of it.' A moment, still looking uncomfortable, then: 'We may not be able to keep yours out of it.'

Anger bubbled up inside him. 'Well, thanks. Thanks a fucking lot! I didn't want to be in this, from the beginning —'

'Get off the boil, Matt,' said Rothschild quietly. He looked disturbed, but he was not going to erupt. 'None of this was on the cards. They wouldn't have put you in this situation if they had known she was in danger.'

'You never guessed she might be?' Matt looked at Fortague.

'No, we didn't think they'd do anything — not *here*. Matt —' Fortague was obviously concerned. 'We'll do our best to protect you —'

'How? I had nothing to do with her murder —' Then a thought struck him, cold as a dagger: 'What if they come after me?'

'We don't think they'll do that — they've killed one of their own, what are they going to gain by killing one of ours?'

'I was never one of *yours* —'

'Yes, you were, Matt. Maybe unwitting, but you were. Whoever murdered her suspected her of being involved with you. We don't know, we're only guessing, but we think they knew I had been to see you —'

Matt was finding it hard to believe the situation. Canberra was not a place for spies, for espionage and counterespionage. That happened in other capitals a long way away. There was intrigue here, maybe even spying of a sort, but it was domestic, party against party: politics.

'We'll see you get protection,' said Fortague.

Matt struggled to control himself: 'How do I get protection? Your goons following me —'

'Matt —' said Rothschild warningly.

'Well, for Crissakes, how do you expect me to react?' Matt turned on him. 'You dobbed me in for this —'

'What's done is done and we've got to wear it.' Joe Rothschild had not raised his voice, but there was no mistaking the authority in it. He was the old union boss, you did what he told you.

'Keep a low profile,' said Fortague, like an infantry captain warning a private to lie low in the trenches. 'We'll have the Federal police interview you at their headquarters, instead of coming here —'

'Thanks —' Matt's voice was as dry as a saltpan. But, conversely, he felt he was on an ice-floe with the others pouring kettles of hot water at its edges. He was going to sink ... 'What about the media? Where do they interview me — on top of Black Mountain? You've really put me in the shit!'

'Matt —' said Rothschild patiently. Matt was tired of his patient tone, but there was nothing he could do about it. 'You've had a smooth trip so far, really smooth. Other people have got kicked in the arse, fallen down a hole, been caught in the wrong beds. None of us are born-again Christians, clapping our hands, never committing any sins. You're in the shit, yes, and it's our — well, no —' He wasn't going to take the blame. He nodded at Fortague, who didn't duck. '*Their* fault. But we're all supposed to work together and that's what's gunna happen this time.'

'What do I tell my wife?' said Matt quietly.

'Tell her the truth,' said Fortague, as if the truth were a variable commodity, like the dollar. 'Up to a point.'

'Sure, I'll do that.' Matt stood up, slowly, unsure of his legs. But they didn't buckle. 'When do I see the Federal cops?'

'Why not now?' said Fortague, who sounded as if he had arrived with an already prepared schedule.

Matt sighed. 'Why not?'

And he and Fortague drove over to police headquarters, where Mr Durban was evidently expected. The enquiries were as perfunctory as if he was to be charged with a parking offence.

'And that's all?' said Matt when the questioning had finished.

The inspector, a man with the tired look of a cop who had witnessed every sort of crime, nodded and closed the one-page file: 'You're in the clear, Mr Durban.'

Matt looked at him and Fortague: 'Do you know who killed Mrs Herx?'

Fortague and the inspector looked at each other, experts in a field that was a vast uncharted map to Matt. Then Fortague said, 'We think so. But at the inquest it will be murder by person or persons unknown.'

'And you'll leave it at that?' Matt knew he sounded naive, but he was floundering in this case.

'Matt,' said Fortague as if talking to an old friend, one who had lost the plot since their last meeting, 'at the level this thing is at, pragmatism is the order of the day. We know who did it, they know we know, and we leave it at that. It's called diplomacy.'

'Whatever happened to idealism, morality, things like that?' Even in his own ears Matt knew he sounded like a novice priest, one who had never read church history.

'Idealism is something dreamed upon by people who rarely have to practise it,' said Fortague and looked at the inspector, who nodded. 'I'll drive you back to your office.'

On the way back, through a day where the sun shone through air as unpolluted as possible, except for politics and diplomacy, Fortague said, 'Matt, I go home at night and take out my conscience and give it a good wash. I have three kids and I try as much as possible to protect them from seeing it. Are you an idealist?'

Matt thought a moment: 'A practical one, yes.'

'Good luck,' said Fortague, but sounded as if he thought Matt was setting out on an uncharted sea.

'Am I or my family in any danger?'

Fortague shook his head. 'What would they profit by going after you? Matt, in our business there are checks and balances. It's like accountancy, but a little more dangerous.'

As Matt got out of the car he said, 'What about the media? What if they come asking questions?'

'Our people will already have been in touch with them, telling them to tone it down. International relations and all that. Just stay away from the TV cameras. Faces give away more than words.'

Whatever influence ASIO and the Federal police used, the media did not call upon Matt. It seemed that June Herx had had a regiment of dinner companions; certain other shirts were impregnated with Arpége. Her body was shipped north to Queensland and she was buried, with her reputation, amongst the sugar cane. There were no interviews with Mr Herx and Matt never did find out if ASIO told the husband why his wife had been murdered.

Matt went home to Parramatta for the weekend break and Carmel studied him carefully, as wives do: 'You look as if you've been dumped in a big surf.'

'I have been.' They were in bed, the place for secrets. 'I'm not used to having women I know murdered —' Then he stopped.

'Don't mention Ruby Rawson. I told you — that's history. But I see what you mean about this Mrs Herx . . . '

'It's just — well, her murder was terrible. But the way it's been covered up. I've lost my illusions, or what few I had.'

'Darling, they've been disappearing for a long time. You'll manage without them. We all do.'

'Who's we?'

'Wives and girlfriends.' She kissed him. 'Now let's get down to business.'

Laughter was part of their love-making; they sometimes played parodies of love scenes from old movies:

'Did the earth move for you, my bunny?'

'Did it ever! Play it again, Sam.'

Happiness is an aphrodisiac.

Chapter Nine

1

Time slipped by and then Parliament moved into the new Houses under the hill that was topped, some remarked, by a Hills Hoist, a national emblem. Led by Moses, hair bouffant, up to the Promised Land, the members wandered through all the extra space, ears shut against the rumours of its cost over-run. It was only what they deserved and in time the voters, who had paid for it, would come to recognise that truth.

Matt was one of the few who missed the old, cramped house down on the flat. But he and Alex Filkins and Doris fitted into their new surroundings, though for a week or two they sometimes got lost amongst the corridors. But, like new settlers, they were determined to struggle on. Extravagance, at voters' expense, is no hardship.

'I feel as if I've won the lottery,' said Alex Filkins.

'Enjoy it,' said Matt and settled down to do the same, snuffing out his nostalgia for the old House.

The months passed, the economy sluggish but no concern of Matt's; he stayed away from finance and budgets, where so many politicians fell into the quicksand. Joe Rothschild let it be known, quietly, that he would be retiring at the next election taking his pension poultice and going home to live out a quiet old age. Small wars still happened, like sores breaking out, on the other side of the world, but the echoes were too faint for ears in the southern hemisphere. Then the Berlin Wall fell, not with a crash but with a crumble. It was as if an almost silent earthquake had closed a chasm that had lasted too long. Germany, it seemed, was coming together again; but the two Germanys stood on either side of the Wall and, almost afraid, looked at each other as strangers. Further east, beyond the Danube, Communism began to sink, especially in Russia where the locals were suddenly free to enjoy some of the customs of the Free World: corruption, extortion, organised crime and other divertissements.

'Out here we'll sit on our hands,' said Joe Rothschild. 'Never a comfortable position, but always a safe one. There are advantages to being in the Antipodes.'

'Did you ever wish you were over there?' asked Matt. 'Working on the Big Stuff?'

'Never. I'm an old union man, Matt. Small worlds are safer and easier to control.'

'I wonder if some day I'll have your cynicism.'

'You will, Matt. It comes to all who serve and wait.' And he grinned, Machiavelli in a blue serge suit and an old union tie.

So another veneer was painted on Matt's ideals.

Came the Christmas break and Matt and Carmel closed up their house and went to spend two weeks out at Cavanreagh.

Teresa, Carmel's younger sister, was home from university. Matt had seen her on and off over the years, but she had been away at boarding school and then gone to university at Armidale in the north. He got on well with her, but he didn't *know* her.

'What are you going to do after university?' he asked.

They were out by the yards, watching Richard, sure in the saddle, trotting a horse round the ring. Teresa had Carmel's looks: *almost*. She was beautiful but missed being distinctive: like ninety-five per cent of models, Matt thought. She was intelligent and, like Carmel, Matt guessed, would graduate in the psychology of men.

'I'll go overseas for a year on a working holiday, then come back here and be a station agent. I'm doing business administration at uni.' She looked at him as she leaned on the rails of the yard. 'When are you going overseas? Aren't you entitled to what you call study trips?'

'I've been putting it off. I could've gone last year, but I want to take Carmel with me. Your mum says she will look after the kids . . . Don't get too flash, buster.'

Richard, standing in the stirrups, had set the horse prancing. 'I think I'll be a professional rider.' Another year, another ambition. 'At shows and things.'

'You'd better start saving then. Horses cost money.' Then Matt looked back at Teresa. 'Do you have a boyfriend?'

She looked sideways at him with amusement: a Carmel look. 'Several. Are you trying to protect me or something? I have two big brothers who've tried it.'

'How'd they go?'

'I told 'em to mind their own business. But —' She looked sideways at him again, her own look this time: 'I envy you and Carmel, what you've got.'

He stared across the yard, at Richard on the horse, then beyond the yards; down by the woolshed, Carmel and Natalie, the latter holding a lamb. 'Yes,' he said. 'I hope you have the same luck.'

Later he was in the big kitchen with Eileen, who was preparing lunch. It struck him then, as they stood there, that he and Eileen rarely had moments together, yet he knew they were compatible. She was slicing a ham, none of your packaged slices for her; this was an old-fashioned kitchen with old-fashioned values.

'We couldn't afford Palm Beach this year,' she said. 'The rents are getting ridiculous and, besides, we just don't have the money to spare. How are things with you and Carmel?'

'Moneywise?'

She nodded. Eileen at times could be vague, but then she would contradict herself with a heavy approach.

'We're okay. We've paid the house off.'

'Already?' She seemed surprised; then suspicious: 'You're not turning into a money-maker, are you?'

He laughed. 'Eileen, how much spare time do I get to go out making money on the side?'

'How much spare time do you have for Carmel and the kids?' She would have been a champion frontbencher, she could shift her aim like an Olympic trapshooter.

The shot went home. He admitted sheepishly, 'Not enough. But Carmel understands.'

'Do Richard and Natalie? They're not littlies any more.'

'I don't know. They haven't complained so far, but maybe that's because Carmel has told them not to. I sometimes wonder how pollies' families stay together.'

'You chose to be a politician.' She didn't say it accusingly, just matter-of-factly.

He nodded. 'I didn't exactly *choose* it, not the way some blokes choose between being an accountant and a — lawyer. I was — I guess the word is *infected*. Does that sound a bit fanciful?'

'No.' She was now at work on a salad, which she would douse with home-made dressing. 'Where I think your infection is dangerous is your ambition.'

'Last Christmas you all said I'd let it die.' Half-humorously, he wondered if he was up against Irish logic.

'That was last year. Pass me the oil and vinegar.' She took the two bottles, held them up and looked at them. 'These two mix. Family and ambition sometimes don't.'

He was hurt, but he said patiently, 'Eileen, if it ever came to a choice between Carmel and the kids and ambition, I'd come back to Collamundra and start at something all over again.'

'I'm glad to hear it.' She was pouring oil. 'But you'll never come back to Collamundra, not to live. It's too small for you now.'

After lunch Matt and Carmel drove into town. The children had gone with their grandfather out to the far reaches of the spread to bring in a sheep killed by a dingo.

'We oughta shoot the dingo,' said Richard belligerently.

'You couldn't shoot an elephant,' said Natalie in her dreamy voice. She was now eight years old, but had already decided the world wasn't worth worrying about.

Richard, on the other hand, was willing to take on the world. Matt sometimes worried at his aggression, but relied upon Carmel to keep it in check. He loved both children, his heart leaping every time he came home to them, but he knew, in the leaping heart, that they depended on Carmel and not on him. He sometimes worried that, as they grew older, and saw their world with different eyes, that they would look on him as the outsider.

Carmel was driving and he sat beside her, looking at her profile against the passing paddocks. She was in her thirties now, a full-blown woman but not blown out of shape. The chin was still firm, the cheekbones still clean, the figure almost the same as when he had first gone to bed with her. She felt him looking at her and she turned her head and smiled.

'I like being looked at by you.'

'How do you read my thoughts?'

She went back to watching the road; she still drove at speed, but safely. 'I've learned to do it. When you're away from me — and you are most of the time —'

'Do you resent that?' He was cautious.

'Not really. Sometimes. Physically, not emotionally. Well, maybe that, too. But it's what we've both chosen —' She looked at him again, slowing the car slightly. 'Don't worry about it ... But when you're away, I start thinking about what *you* might be thinking. Not trying to be telepathic, but just — I dunno. Just trying to be inside your head. And I think it works —' She concentrated on the road ahead. 'Don't you? We rarely, if ever, argue. And it's not because I'm trying to be a knee-bending, compliant wife. I'm not, you know that.'

'And how,' he said and kissed her ear.

They came into the town between paddocks where sheep and cattle still grazed. The cotton fields were on the other side of town, closer to the river. Foreign owners had moved in there, including Japanese investors. But the town and the district was still Collamundra, as it had been for almost a century and a half. The town hadn't grown since Matt and Carmel had left it, but neither, unlike other country towns, had it shrunk. It just suggested it was *there* and always would be. Matt had deserted it, but it was and always would be *home*.

They parked the car, angle-parking, got out and instantly a girl was standing on the footpath behind them. 'Mr Durban!' And then, as an afterthought: 'Mrs Durban!'

Matt frowned at a distant memory. She was red-headed, distinctly pretty and with a body that was also a faint memory.

'Verity Dodds! Remember, you used to teach me in Year 10!' Then, again as an afterthought to Carmel: 'All the girls were in love with him!'

'Just as well I got him out of town,' said Carmel.

'You're in Parliament!' She was building a picket fence of exclamation marks.

'Someone has to do it,' he said, but wondered if Verity Dodds was interested in irony. 'What are you doing now?'

'Vet science up at Armidale!'

Well, there you go. And he had thought her an airhead. Carmel said, taking charge, 'That's great, Verity. Shove the men aside.'

'I'm trying!' she said and went off along the street, swinging her hips like — like, omigod, Ruby Rawson.

'Get your eyes off her bum and think about her brain,' said Carmel, inside his head again, if a little blurred. 'At the next elections girls like her, making money, being independent, will be asking questions and wanting answers.'

'You want to be my campaign manager?'

'You could do worse,' she said and he knew she was right. But he wouldn't want her to be; knew that he wanted, as much as possible, to keep his political and family life apart. He wanted the retreat of family life. The light on the porch was still as strong, if not stronger, than the light on the hill.

'Go around and see your dad,' said Carmel. 'Remind him he's coming to dinner tonight out at Cavanreagh.'

'What are you going to do?'

'I have to do some shopping for Mum. And I'll go down and say hello to Dr Hennessy. Meet me back here in an hour.'

Matt went off along the main street, waving to people who recognised him and remembered him. Then as he turned the corner into his father's street, what had been *his* street, a uniformed cop and a man in plainclothes stood in front of him.

'G'day, Matt,' said Ken Shuster. 'You know Wally?'

Whether by accident or design, Matt had stayed away from the police during his visits home. He had severed all ties that had linked him to Ruby Rawson and the police had been a reminder of her.

'Sure. How are you, Wally? You a detective now?'

Wally Mungle was a half-blood Aborigine who had been at school with Matt; they had played together in the school rugby team. He was slightly built and shorter than Matt and Ken Shuster; he had dark sad eyes but a beautiful smile, which he showed now. 'Trying to be.'

'Things quiet?' Matt asked Shuster.

'Quiet enough.' Then, almost too casually: 'You ever hear from Bert Carter?'

Matt was surprised by the question. 'Bert? God, no. I did hear he'd gone overseas, but Christ knows where. Why?'

'Oh, just an idle question. We even check on you down in Canberra.' He grinned. 'You're doing all right.'

'Thanks. Well, I'm on my way to see my dad. Look after yourselves.'

He walked on down the street, all at once curiously ill at ease. Did Ken Shuster, after all this time, think he had something to do with Ruby's murder? He looked back over his shoulder. The two cops were still back there at the corner. Then Shuster raised a hand in a wave, they turned and were gone. Matt paused under a tree, leaned with one hand against its trunk. Then a voice said, 'Nice to be home again, Matt?' and there was a woman leaning on her front gate, smiling at him, welcoming him. Out of long ago he remembered her: Verity Dodds' mother.

'Always glad to be back,' he said. 'The town never changes.'

'And ain't we glad of that!' Mrs Dodds had taught her daughter the uses of exclamation marks. 'There's your dad over there! Always watering his garden! Say hullo for me!'

Matt said he'd do that, crossed the road. Keith Durban was in his front garden hosing the roses that bloomed against one fence. 'Your mum's favourite flower,' he said and Matt had heard it scores of times. It struck him now that it seemed his father's only tribute to sentiment. 'You're looking well.'

'So are you.' Matt leaned against the front gate. 'When are you going to retire?'

This street, like all the streets in the town, was wide. At intervals on both sides of the street were wattle trees, some of them still sprinkled with the spring gold. At bloom time the trees formed arches and Keith had once dryly suggested the street should be re-named McDonald's Street. None of the houses were large, but they were all solid-looking, even the weatherboards, and stood in their own gardens. A few cars were parked along the kerbs, but this was a street that somehow suggested sulkies and drays would not have looked out of place. It was part of the historical map of Collamundra.

Keith turned off the hose, began to wind it in a heap, doing it with the same unhurried ease that he did everything. 'Maybe next year, I don't know. I get fed up sometimes. Bureaucrats down in Sydney set the syllabus, all newfangled ideas that make me wonder if they've ever taught a class. And the kids themselves ...' He finished winding the hose, straightened up. 'Three girls in Year 12 are pregnant. Christ knows what future they'll have. Or their kids. You'd find teaching now different from what you knew.'

'I guess so.' Matt looked at his father, looking for the erosion. But could see none. 'Dad, why didn't you ever marry again? After Mum died?'

If Keith was surprised by the question, he didn't show it. He took his time, fingered a rose, looked at the pink petal that broke off in his fingers. 'A Moss Rose, Mum's favourite. We didn't know whether it would take to the soil around here.' He looked at it as if it were an heirloom, then he looked back at Matt: 'I couldn't, Matt. She was the only woman I ever loved. We were —' He searched for the word: 'We were *complete*.'

'I wouldn't have minded if you had — I mean if you'd married again.'

Keith shook his head. 'It was never on the cards. I took out a few women — still do.' His smile was so thin that Matt almost missed it. 'But something permanent?' He shook his head again. Then, after a long moment: 'I think you and Carmel are the same. Complete.'

Matt nodded, all the answer that was needed. 'We're expecting you for dinner tonight at Cavanreagh.'

'I'm looking forward to it. How are the kids?'

The next three-quarters of an hour was a rest cure, a holiday, for Matt. He and his father, without intention or awareness, spun a cocoon about themselves. Memory was alive in the house.

Matt left and walked leisurely back to the main street. He was standing by their car, waiting for Carmel, when he was aware of an elderly man watching him. He hesitated, then said, 'Have we met?'

'Some years ago,' said the man, moving closer. At a few paces he did not look so old, just worn. He had a large frame and large features that seemed to have contracted, as if his bones had grown smaller. He was dressed in a blue workshirt, white shorts and blue trainers with white socks; he had an air of *beach* about him. 'Charlie Rawson.'

'Mr Rawson —' Which was what Matt had called him when he had been Ruby's father. 'You're back in Collamundra?'

'No. We live down at Cronulla now.' A beach suburb. Matt remembered the slow, gravelly voice, as if its owner considered everything before it said it. 'Just passing through, a sort of detour. We're on our way over to the Barossa.' He looked around, then back at Matt: 'The place hasn't changed.' A pause, then: 'You have.'

'Only older,' said Matt, treading carefully. 'Maybe a little wiser. How are Mrs Rawson? And —' He tried to remember Ruby's younger sister, but couldn't.

'Sharon. They're fine.'

Then Carmel came along the street, carrying grocery bags. She paused when she saw Matt and the stranger in conversation, but Matt reached out a hand towards her, as if to lean on her, and she moved closer.

'Darling, this is Mr Rawson, he used to own the Kurrajong Coffee Lounge —' As if afraid to mention Ruby's name.

But Charlie Rawson wasn't. 'Ruby's father. You remember her?'

Carmel nodded. 'Just to say hello to —'

'You two are married?'

What's it to you? But Matt just said, 'Yes. Some time now. Well, we've got to be getting back ... Nice meeting you again, Mr Rawson.'

'Yeah,' said Rawson and nodded. 'We're going out to the cemetery, put a few flowers on the grave ... You ever do that?'

'No,' said Carmel before Matt could reply. 'Only on his mother's grave. Goodbye, Mr Rawson.'

She went round to the driver's side of their car, opened the door and looked at Matt. He hesitated, then went round and got in on the passenger's side. Carmel got in, started the car and backed it out from the kerb. Matt said nothing, but, without looking back, was aware that Rawson was staring after them.

Carmel drove silently for a hundred yards or more, then said quietly, 'Are they moving back into town? The Rawsons?'

'No.' Matt wondered why his voice seemed stuck in his throat. 'No, they're just passing through. On their way to the Barossa, I think he said.'

'He didn't look very friendly — or sound it. What did he say to you?'

'Nothing, really. I suppose he still connects me with Ruby.' He waited a while, then said, 'He never mentioned her.'

'He mentioned her grave.' They were out of town now and she pulled the car in to the side of the road. Behind them the iron digger kept guard. 'Darling — all that is way behind us and that's where I want it to stay.'

'It will. But —' He looked ahead down the road, then back at her: 'I'm glad they're not coming back to Collamundra.'

'So am I,' she said and started up the car again.

2

Matt went back to Canberra and moved down, or up, the backbenches. He asked questions of the Opposition and next day got an inch or two in the newspapers. No television reporters accosted him; backbenchers were a waste of screen time unless they were involved in some scandal. He was making an impression, but faint, like a brush stroke in a large painting. He was still Joe Rothschild's protégé and that was why the press gallery kept an eye on him. It could be a sour eye, but so far they had spared him.

He spoke to Carmel and the children every night, his long-distance family. Occasionally he would call his father or the O'Reillys, but it was connection by wire. He felt the isolation that other members had told him about.

Then one night in early autumn he got a phone call from his father. He had gone to bed early in the cramped motel room and for relief was reading one of Richard Condon's satires, thinking the author should make a trip Down Under and let fly the daggers of his typewriter. Then the phone rang: 'Matt, were you asleep?'

'No, Dad. What's up?'

'Were you and Carmel planning to come home for the Collamundra Cup?'

Cup week was the big event of the year in Collamundra; its only big event. A ball was held on the Saturday night, the final day of the racing carnival, and for weeks afterwards there would be gossip of who had disgraced themselves and if they would dare to come again next year. Which, of course, they would and the gossipers would be disappointed if they didn't.

'Of course. We're looking forward to it —'

'Don't. Find some urgent business elsewhere ...' Matt had never heard his father as concerned as this; not since Matt's mother had died. 'We've had another murder out here. The Japanese manager of the South Cloud cotton gin — he was shot, then fed into one of the module feeders. A bloody mess. We've got two cops up here from Sydney, Homicide. And —' Keith paused, though that was not unusual with him.

'And?'

'They're expecting trouble from the Abo settlement. A couple of agitators have come into town and they're planning a protest march the day of the Cup. One of the local Koori boys committed suicide in a cell at the police station.'

'God, what's happened to the town?' But even as he said it, a shadow, Ruby Rawson's, crossed his mind.

'I dunno. There's a bit of friction between the graziers and the cotton people, about water, but not enough to bring on murder.'

'Is Paddy involved?'

'So far, no ... There are some old-timers who resent the Japanese coming in here, but I don't think they want to start shooting Japs again. As for the Kooris ... Stay away, Matt. It's not a Federal matter, let the State blokes get involved, if politics has to come into it.'

Matt considered, then agreed: 'Okay, we shan't come ...' Then to lighten the moment, he said, 'Would you like to be my campaign manager the next election?' There was silence and Matt wondered if he had blundered, trying for levity. 'Well?'

Then one could almost see Keith's small grin over the phone: 'I was trying to think of something less inviting and can't ... I'll let you know how things turn out.'

Matt hung up, pondered a while, then rang Carmel: 'Did I wake you?'

'No, I'm in bed with Richard Gere —' They had a TV set in their bedroom. 'What is it?'

He told her: 'Dad's advised me to stay away —'

She was disappointed. 'And so will Richard and Natalie be. But I think your dad's right.'

'I'm trying to imagine all this happening out there — the murder, the Kooris getting ready to demonstrate ...'

'Darling, forget it. Or at least stay away from it.'

'Okay, I'll do that. But switch off Richard Gere ...'

He went home that weekend, paused at the garden gate to look with dry amusement at the light on the porch. It had become a joke between him and Carmel, one that was just theirs and they did not share with others.

They did not go out on the Saturday night, but stayed home. He had done his surgery Saturday morning and was thankful that there were no fêtes, nursing home openings or other functions in the afternoon. The children had wanted to know why they were not all going to Grandpa Paddy's and Grandma Eileen's for the weekend, but

Carmel had given them some excuse and, after five minutes' disappointment, they had accepted it. Matt restrained himself from calling his father and asking what had happened.

They had an early dinner and while Carmel and the children did the washing-up, he went into the bedroom, switched on the set they had there, turned it to the ABC for the seven o'clock news, sat down and froze.

He was glad the children were not in the room with him; and he didn't call Carmel. He sat there and saw the lead item: the Aboriginal demonstrators marching down the racecourse straight just as the horses came round the bend. He wondered how the TV camera had been stationed at exactly the right point and guessed the agitators from Sydney, experienced in getting covered, had organised it. It was all there in thirty seconds of carnage as the jockeys tried to avoid the marchers and the horses went pitching into the rails and the jockeys were thrown. It was horrible to see, almost unbelievably horrible because Matt knew the course, had once or twice ridden horses around it, had seen a dozen Collamundra Cups, had gone to school with, had taught some of the Kooris. He got up, switched off the TV as Carmel came in with the children.

'Anything on the news tonight?'

'Nothing special.' He caught her eye, gave a slight shake of his head. 'Have your shower, kids.'

Then he told Camel what he had seen and she put her hand to her mouth as if she were actually looking at what he was describing to her. 'Oh God, I'm so glad we didn't go! The kids would've seen all that —'

'There's still the murder out at the cotton farm —'

She shook her head, hand still to mouth: 'Don't let's talk about it . . . Are you going to call your father?'

'No. He'll call us —'

Which Keith did on Sunday night: 'You saw what happened yesterday? It was on the news?'

'In full colour. Christ, Dad, what a pile-up! Has anyone died, the jockeys or the Kooris? It was in this morning's papers but they didn't say if there were any deaths —'

'No. Half a dozen of them are in hospital, but no deaths. Except the horses — they had to put six of them down. I didn't call you last night because I spent the time moving around town. Things are pretty edgy, you did the right thing not coming out here . . .'

'What about the murder out at the cotton gin?'

There was a pause, almost for theatrical effect: 'They arrested Chester Hardstaff . . .'

'They *what*? Chester? You're pulling my leg?'

'This isn't a weekend for leg-pulling —' Keith sounded like a stern schoolmaster.

Hardstaff was the uncrowned king of Collamundra country. His family were the biggest landowners, the oldest family in the district; he had been a war hero and he ruled the local National Party with an iron hand. He had been an emperor never without clothes. Matt realised that it had been a good time for him, a Government MP, to be far distant well away from the scandal that was sure to break.

'The Sydney cops tied up the case, but they've left it with the locals,' said Keith; another pause, then: 'Matt, stay away for a few weeks. It's none of your concern, but if you come back someone is sure to start asking you questions.'

'Dad —' He was suddenly worried for his father. The older man sounded depressed, as if illusions had suddenly been shattered. Philosophically, Keith Durban lived in another age. 'How do you feel about all this?'

Keith, as always, took his time: 'Shattered. The whole town has just fallen apart this weekend. We're not used to shocks like this. You're lucky to be outside of all of it. Stay there.'

'Wally Mungle — I went to school with him. He's a cop now, in the middle. How's he taking it?'

'I had a word with him — I used to teach him, remember? He's okay, but it's hard, being the man in the middle . . . Like I said, Matt. Stay out of it.'

So Matt did, getting no closer than to offer some sympathy to the National Party backbencher from the Cawndilla-Collamundra electorate. But couldn't help adding the barb: 'Chester Hardstaff — who'd have believed it?'

'Don't rub it in, Matt. Right now I'd like to be offered an overseas posting. Say, ambassador to Tristan da Cunha.'

'I'll talk to the PM about it. How about Easter Island?'

'You bastard —' But the Opposition MP was smiling, though with an effort.

Two days later Collamundra was out of the news. Saddam Hussein, a name as unfamiliar to voters as that of a European conductor or a Chinese novelist, invaded Kuwait. The PM called a Caucus meeting, which, as one old hand remarked, was the political equivalent of a cattleyard. Bellowing and shoving would prevail.

'Cabinet and I have decided to offer troops —' said the PM.

'Why?' That was from a backbencher from the Victorian Left, a body that wouldn't have gone to war with Lucifer. War was only to be fought against capitalist bosses, a dodgy foe. 'It's no business of ours —'

'Get real, Rusty,' said the Minister for Energy, a pragmatic man from South Australia, who was said to carry a calculator in the pocket that other men kept for handkerchiefs or combs. 'We don't want to finish up buying all our oil from the Yanks or the Brits. This brawl is about oil, not the Kuwaitis.'

'Whatever happened to principles?' asked Joe Rothschild piously and several members looked at him as if he had thrown up.

It was Matt's cue to stand up and say, almost as piously, 'States have interests, but no principles. Cardinal Richelieu said that back in the seventeenth century and things haven't changed.'

'Thanks for the history lesson, Matt,' said the PM, but he was grinning and looked as if he wished he had said it.

'Who the hell's Cardinal Richelieu?' asked the Victorian backbencher. 'Another bloody Vatican busybody?'

'A Frenchman,' said the Minister for Energy, who knew his cynics.

'The bloody French,' said someone and everyone murmured agreement.

Matt went home at the weekend, did his surgery and flim-flammed his way through questions about the war in Kuwait. The voters were wary of sending their troops overseas; many of his questioners still remembered Vietnam. Matt was not a belligerent, but he saw the sense in backing the Americans in coming to the aid of the Kuwaitis. He managed the morning's questions without too much anguish.

At lunch Richard asked about the war, then announced, 'I'm going to be a fighter pilot. Flying F-One Elevens.'

'Last week you were going to be an actor,' said Carmel, pushing toasted sandwiches towards him. She was not a mother or wife who believed in big lunches.

'I read up on it. You're outta work most of the time, being a waiter or something. You'd have to keep me.'

'Be a fighter pilot,' said Carmel practically.

'I think I'd like to be a fighter pilot,' said Natalie. 'Swanning around the sky in a F-whatever-it-is.'

'Swanning?' said Carmel. 'Where'd you get that?'

'Mrs Fawcett, at school, says I do it all the time and very nicely, too.'

'Well, you don't go swanning in F-One Elevens,' said Matt. 'Not at umpteen million a plane ... You'd really like to join the Air Force?'

'Yes,' said Richard. 'Seriously. I have to get my HSC, then I go to the Defence Academy —'

Carmel looked along the table at Matt. 'I think we're getting ahead of ourselves ...' Then to Richard: 'We'll talk about it when you've got your HSC.'

Later when they were alone, close to each other on the lounge in the living room, the TV set blank in front of them, Matt said, 'How would you like a trip overseas?'

She had been reading an Isabel Allende novel, her escape. She put down the book, then said, practical-minded, 'Where to?'

'Right round.' Now that he had mentioned it he became expansive; he waved a hand, taking in the world. 'America, then England, France, Italy. But not Kuwait,' he said, pushing that region off the globe.

'What's brought this on? You've kept putting off trips —' She was cautious, not unenthusiastic.

'I know,' he admitted. 'When the kids were young, it would have meant gallivanting off on my own. Joe Rothschild says it's time for me to go now. He'll be retiring soon and the chances are I'll get the Ministry ... We'll go in the winter break, the kids can go out to Cavanreagh ... What do you say?'

She leaned across Isabel Allende and kissed him; he was offering her escape: 'I thought you'd never ask.'

Then he came back to earth; or the mundane: 'How are things out at Collamundra? Have you spoken to your mum or dad?'

'Things are settling down, Mum says. But Collamundra will never be the same again. It's changing ... '

His arm round her shoulders, he stroked her upper arm. 'Everything's changing, love. Kids are growing up sooner, chasing money is now a national sport, nobody these days looks any further back than the Sixties ... If ever I get to be PM, it'll be another country —'

'Are *you* changing?'

'I dunno,' he said honestly. 'Am I?'

She considered for a long moment. She knew as well as anyone that in love vision is often blurred; one can be too close to the other. But, with him away five days of the week for so much of the year, the vision had sharpened: 'I think so. You don't have the, I dunno, the illusions you once had. Maybe I mean ideals ...'

'I couldn't find the Altruists' Society —' She looked at him and he said, 'It's a Joe Rothschild joke ... But you're right —'

'Try and find them again,' she said.

Then he changed the subject: 'Have you talked to the kids about the birds and the bees?'

She looked at him in surprise. 'What brought that on?'

'I dunno. Just looking at Richard tonight, him wanting to be a fighter pilot. He's growing up —'

'I'm glad you noticed,' she said without rancour. 'Yes, I've talked to both of them — something you should've done with Richard.'

'Don't rub it in. How'd he take it? And Natalie?'

'She took it in her usual dreamy way. Airily, I think is the word. I had to tell her about periods and all those sort of things and she as much as said, What's new, Mum? As for Richard — when I brought up the subject, he asked me if I'd read the *Kama Sutra*.'

'He *what*?'

'One of his mates brought a copy to school — he'd taken it out of his father's library. We started from there and worked backwards —' Suddenly she was laughing.

'Did you tell him I'd read it and got a sprained back from trying some of the positions?'

She thumped him. 'Of course I didn't! You shouldn't be laughing —'

'You are —'

Her laughter subsided, she settled back into the lounge. She took her time, then said, 'Matt, I was angry at you — you should've been talking to Richard, not me. It's things like that —'

'What?' Without thinking he adopted a political pose: look for the hidden barb.

She hesitated again, as if she saw him drawing up his barrier; then she went on, 'I'm the one bringing them up, you're not sharing it with me. Georgia Peal once said to me, don't let yourself become a political widow. If you don't watch out, that's what I'm going to become.'

Hesitantly, he reached for her, put his arm round her again. 'No, I'll never let that happen —'

'It's happening —'

He knew she was right; but he couldn't let slip his fragile grip: 'I think this trip round the world has come just in time —'

'We'll still be leaving the kids behind —'

'Agreed.' That sounded like a political assent; he would have to be more careful. 'But by the time we come back, we'll be family again — I promise.'

She looked at him (measuring him? he wondered), then she leaned towards him again and kissed him. 'Sometimes, when I'm alone, I think, What a bastard he is . . . And then I look at my luck and you're forgiven.'

In his heart he knew he didn't deserve to be. But there are moments in all relationships when a silent tongue is the wisest friend. And that, he told himself, was not a political judgement.

3

The Gulf War lasted only long enough to be called a long battle. It filled the TV screens for several weeks and a new generation of viewers got a view of what tanks and guns and planes could do to a landscape and the people in it. But the viewers were safe from the bomb-bursts and the black oily smoke from busted pipelines: all that was happening behind the plastic screen.

Matt and Carmel took the children out to Cavanreagh, where Richard and Natalie looked upon their abandonment as a release.

'Oh God,' said Natalie, 'I can swan all over the place!'

'Do that,' said Carmel. 'And if Nanna clouts you over the ear, don't tell her you're just swanning. What are you going to do?' she asked Richard.

'Help Pa cut the balls off the bulls.'

'Enjoy yourself,' said Matt. 'And imagine the bull doing it to you.'

'Go away,' said Eileen, already beginning to enjoy herself. 'We'll see you in a month.'

'Enjoy America,' said Paddy. 'It's a great country, despite some of the mugs who've run it.'

Keith Durban had come out to Cavanreagh to say goodbye. 'Make this your first big step,' he told Matt. 'Next year you'll be a Minister.'

'I occasionally catch glimpses of that light on the hill.'

'Keep your eye on it. Give my regards to George Bush. That must be the worst job in the world, being in the White House.'

'I'm always amazed at how Americans revere the Oval Office. It's been filled by some mugs and some bastards, but the voters still bend their knee to the Office.'

'Not all of them,' said Keith. 'It amazes me, who believes in compulsory voting, how half the population never seem to vote . . . Would you have run for President if you'd been born in the States?'

'I'd have run *from* it.'

Next morning Matt and Carmel left to drive back to Sydney. The children waved goodbye without tears, were already turning back into the house before the car had turned out of the long driveway. It was a fine cold morning, some frost like white shadows beneath the trees. Collamundra and its surrounds looked as peaceful as Matt remembered it from his youth.

As they came into the main street of the town, Matt slowed the car.

'What's the matter?' asked Carmel.

'There's Wally Mungle. I want a word with him.'

'Why?'

Matt pulled the car in, angle-parking, switched off the engine. 'Love, Wally has one of the worst possible jobs — an Abo cop in a country town, the man in the middle. I sympathise with him. One day I may find myself the man in the middle.'

She nodded. 'I see your point. Give him my regards.'

He got out and approached Wally Mungle, who had stopped as if waiting for him. They shook hands, equals; each had always had respect for the other. 'G'day, Matt. You're looking well. Canberra agree with you?'

'Up to a point — it's the voters that are the worry. You're looking well —' Then Matt looked at him more closely: 'No, you're not.'

Wally Mungle smiled his beautiful smile, but it looked a little weary. 'It's been a tough few months, Matt. But things are settling down.'

'How are things out at the Camp?' It was the local name for the settlement of tin shacks and humpies out along the Noongulli.

'Better. The council got a grant from the State — there's an election coming up —' He grinned again. 'They're gunna build houses, they've already started. Things are looking up.'

'How are your wife and kids?'

'Fine. Yours?'

'Fine. Well —' They shook hands again. 'Keep your head down.'

'You, too. It must be tough down there in Canberra.' He was smiling again.

'In the trenches all the time.'

Matt got back into the car.

'Well, do you feel better?' Carmel sounded tart, as if her mood had changed.

He started up the engine, but didn't put the car into gear. He watched Wally Mungle go off down the street and, though he nodded and spoke to people, Matt saw him as lonely, the outsider still. Then he looked at Carmel: 'Yes, I do feel better. It's people like him, not just the Kooris but the battlers, who keep my feet on the ground when I get carried away with other things down in Canberra. Yes,' he repeated, 'I feel better.'

She looked steadily at him, then she said, 'I'm sorry.'

He put the car into gear and they headed out of town for Sydney. They passed the Southern Cloud cotton farm and it struck Matt that he had not enquired who had replaced the murdered Japanese manager. It was as if he had closed his mind against it, had, as his father had advised those months ago, stayed out of it. He drove on towards the coast and the ground there that was continually shifting, where keeping your feet on it was a constant dance.

Two days later they flew out for California. Carmel walked up and down the streets of Beverly Hills, stared like a teenager at the luxury goods in the windows of Rodeo Drive, while Matt went down to the district coast guard base and marvelled at the organisation and the money available there. Compared to what he knew was available back home, it was Rodeo Drive against Main Street, Collamundra.

The officers at the base welcomed him, showed him everything he wanted to see, explained their routines, and he went back to his hotel in Beverly Hills boiling with enthusiasm. The PM and the Treasurer would *have* to listen to him when he got back home.

He and Carmel did the Universal Studio tour, but both said no to Disneyland: 'Mickey Mouse and Snow White weren't my childhood,' said Carmel. 'I was five years old when I discovered Elvis Presley and I shook my little hips and swung my fanny —'

'What a disgusting child!'

'Then it was the Beatles and the Rolling Stones and the Who . . . '

They flew on to New York, the huge river-fed continent beneath them, and Matt couldn't help but remember the droughts that came and went so regularly back home. They checked into a boutique hotel in the East Fifties and went sightseeing next day, hicks from the sticks. Matt, alone, went down to Wall Street and smelled the money and watched the pit of the stock exchange where anonymous men raised their frantic hands and affected stock exchanges all round the rest of the world.

He made a polite call on the Australian consulate, spent half a day at the United Nations, observed the sleek, well-fed, well-dressed delegates who represented the poor and the starving of the world. Then on the next day he and Carmel flew down to Washington.

He went investigating while she went sightseeing. He went to the Department of Transportation, a huge office complex where the coast guard service was part of their administration.

'We used to be under Treasury,' said the young officer showing Matt around, 'but I suppose your Treasury is the same? Always querying the cost of everything?'

Matt nodded, grinning. 'Ain't it the truth?'

He went away, armed with notes, met Carmel and they went up to the Capitol. They sat in the gallery of both the House and the Senate, the latter, Matt remembered someone saying, 'the best club in the world'. He and Carmel met several Representatives and Senators, all of them with that courtesy that many Americans show to total strangers. There was a decorum in both the House and the Senate that amused and impressed Matt after some of the exchanges he had heard in that other House under the hill back home.

He talked with a senator from New England, another courteous man: 'We appreciated Australia coming in with us on Kuwait.'

'We had it explained to us why we should join you,' said Matt, not mentioning oil. 'But why didn't your President go into Baghdad, wrap up Saddam?'

'Politics,' said the senator and looked as if he knew Matt would understand. 'The President didn't want a big casualty list. I remember Vietnam, when the first body bags were shown on TV —' He shook his head at the memory and Matt forbore to ask if he had been in Vietnam.

'How many casualties were there? We count 'em by the dozen now. I was a teacher before I got into politics, I taught history. On a single day in 1916 at the Somme there were 60,000 casualties, killed and wounded. God knows how many you lost in World War II in the Battle of the Bulge or in the Pacific, Saipan and Okinawa . . .'

'Different wars, different attitudes. We'll keep an eye on Saddam. He's learned a lesson, we think, he won't give us any more trouble . . . Well, what do you think of our Congress, our parliament?'

'I envy you,' said Matt, but didn't specify.

'I'd better take him back to New York,' said Carmel, who had just joined them and raised Matt's status as a chooser. 'He'll be running for the Senate if I don't get him back to reality.'

'Reality?' said the senator with a big American smile, teeth as beautiful as sculptures. 'What's that?'

The flew off to New York, went to a Broadway show, and on their last day, before they were to fly out late afternoon for London, they had lunch in the restaurant on one of the top floors of the World Trade Center. They had a window table and they sat there and stared out at the scene below them and the vista across the Hudson and into New Jersey.

'Sometimes,' said Carmel, 'I think America is unbelievable.'

Then as she spoke a helicopter, NYPD in big letters on its fuselage, came up beneath them, like a huge insect crawling up the immense glass wall. It hovered opposite Matt and Carmel and she lifted her hand and waved. The two officers in the helicopter smiled, gave brisk salutes and then the chopper swung away, this time like a great bird, and went out over the Hudson to the Jersey shore.

'Only in America,' said Matt without rancour or sarcasm.

'If ever we come back this way again —'

'*When*,' said Matt, and suddenly missed the children. 'This won't be our last trip. We'll bring the kids next time.'

'On study tour expenses?' She smiled, knowing some of the rorts that were rumoured in Canberra and that Matt had told her about. '*When* we come back, let's have lunch here again. I'll always remember that helicopter coming up from *below* us. I felt like the Angel Gabrielle —'

'Gabriel? You had a sex change while that was going on?'

'Gabrielle — his sister.'

They were like honeymooners: nothing but happiness lay ahead. At least for the next three weeks. They flew on from New York to London.

They checked into a boutique hotel in Knightsbridge, where Matt's credit card, now he was paying his own expenses, shrivelled at the edges. They played tourists, Carmel as guide: the Houses of Parliament, the Tower of London, Hampton Court, the Tate Gallery, the theatres. Not once did she mention whom she had been with when she saw all this first; the man, or men, in her life before Matt, were ghosts in her own memory. He had always had the sense never to ask about them.

They went out into the countryside on a beautiful summer's day and Matt saw why so many Englishmen dreamed of home when they were abroad. They stopped to watch a cricket match on a postcard village green and ate dinner in a sixteenth-century inn. It was idyllic and they both savoured every moment.

They called the children, as they had each weekend, who sounded as if they didn't miss their parents — 'Pa's teaching me to shear a sheep,' said Richard.

'I'm just swanning around,' said Natalie. 'Nanna says I'm the best she's seen.'

Then a couple of days before they were to move on to Paris, Matt rang Sir Donald, the ex-High Commissioner, now retired and living in a village in the Thames Valley — 'Getting croup every winter and hay fever every summer and dreaming of Nirvana,' he said.

'Would you and your wife come up and have lunch with us at the Connaught?'

'My wife died, dear boy. Just after we came home. But yes, I'd be delighted —'

Matt hung up, turned to Carmel. 'His wife died. I felt I'd put my foot in it.'

'How were you to know? Did you meet her?'

'A coupla times. I don't think she ever enjoyed the diplomatic circus. But he did — every moment of it.'

'When you retire, try for an embassy. I'll show you how to enjoy it. Why are we going to the Connaught? That's pretty pricey, isn't it?'

'Someone told me they make the best bread-and-butter pudding in the world. I've always thought my mother did.'

So they went to the Connaught, met Sir Donald, who seemed delighted to see them — 'Any reminder of Nirvana will do.'

'Nirvana?' said Carmel.

'Canberra, dear lady.' He had not met her before and was visibly impressed.

'You could have fooled me,' said the dear lady.

Then, a politician and a diplomat together, Matt and Sir Donald talked of the state of the world. Matt asked, 'Did President Bush do the right thing, not going on into Baghdad?'

'Yes, but for the wrong reason. He didn't want any more casualties — an admirable idea, politically. But if he had gone on to Baghdad —' Sir Donald shook his head. He looked much older than Matt remembered him, and his face showed more than it had ever had when he was a diplomat, as if he had at last rediscovered truth. 'The Americans have never understood the Arab mind. Never will.'

'What about you, the British?' said Carmel, no diplomat she.

Sir Donald smiled benignly on her. 'A good question, Carmel. Yes, we understood them. What they never understood about us was our natural air of superiority. We had the same attitude towards you Australians, till 1942 when your PM, Mr Curtin, told us to get — forgive the expression — stuffed. Churchill never forgave him, you know.'

'He never forgave Attlee for giving away the Empire,' said Matt. 'Do you miss it?'

'I only saw the end of it, dear boy. We had a talent for taking a map and drawing new countries on it. We drew Iraq out of Mesopotamia and there is a story that Lady Lugard, the wife of the then G-G, created Nigeria with a red crayon one night after dinner. Oh, we had fun with our natural superiority.' He smiled at them both, free of croup and hay fever. 'Jolly good bread-and-butter pudding. I hated it at school, but this —' He raised his wine glass to the pudding.

Carmel looked at Matt: 'As good as your mother made?'

He nodded. 'Good as, but not better.' Then he raised his own glass. 'To natural superiority.'

Sir Donald smiled at Carmel. 'Does he have it?'

'Not at home,' she said, liking this old man waiting for Nirvana. 'He'd be a dead duck if he tried it.'

Two days later they went over to Paris. They booked into another boutique hotel, this time on the Left Bank. Matt, still counting his own money, felt that the hotel cost *un bras* and *une jambe*. But he said nothing, seeing the light in Carmel's eyes at being in Paris again. And wondered, jealously, what adventures, romantic adventures, she had had here.

She took him by the hand and showed him old haunts of hers.

'Those French fellers — how'd you go with them?'

'Wouldn't you like to know! Don't torment yourself. I went out with a gendarme twice, but he was too serious. He was looking for a wife, not a girlfriend.'

'A gendarme? You went out with a cop?'

'He was an inspector. He didn't wear his uniform when he took me out. Don't torment yourself — that was another life and you weren't even on the horizon. Now let's head for the Louvre and you can see where I got my Mona Lisa smile . . .'

He took the city in with an admiring eye, marvelled at the boulevards, the squares, the circles, wondered if Burley Griffin had, subconsciously or otherwise, had Paris in mind when he designed Canberra. The French might be the most arrogant nation on earth, but certain things had to be admired.

On their last night, at Carmel's insistence, they went to dinner at Le Grand Véfour:

'Napoleon and Josephine exchanged confidences here. You and I can be Napoleon and Josephine when we get to the Lodge, we'll exchange confidences about the proletariat —'

'The proletariat were Romans, not French —'

'Who cares?' said Carmel, Natalie-like.

The dinner was sumptuous, but cost Matt *deux bras* and *deux jambe*. As, limbless, he was helped into a taxi, he asked, 'Did your gendarme bring you here?'

'No, we ate at Les Halles,' she said and kissed him. 'I told you, don't torment yourself.'

They flew home, over the Middle East with Kuwait and Iraq, still smoking after all these weeks, down there on the right. Matt looked out the window of the plane and saw how easily the map could have been drawn; Babylonia, Parthia, Carmania were all buried beneath the sands on which the new maps had been drawn. Flying the last leg over the plains and sluggish rivers of the Outback, he wondered if and when this homeland map would ever be re-drawn.

They got home to rumours of warfare in the Party itself; the generals were crossing swords. They went out to Cavanreagh to pick up the children and Keith Durban was there: 'You should have stayed away for a while longer. You're going to be asked to take sides.'

'I think I'll just sit on the sidelines.' Then he turned to the children: 'You miss Mum and me?'

'Occasionally,' said Richard.

'Have you been away?' said Natalie and it seemed that she, too, now had a Mona Lisa smile.

Matt went back to Canberra, to the gathering of the cadres. First he went looking for reminders of Paris, but they were too faint and in the end he thought that maybe Burley Griffin had not been thinking of the French capital. But what was going on up the hill was as bloody as anything in the French Assembly.

'Don't take sides,' advised Joe Rothschild. 'Sit there and look as if you might vote for both sides — it's called the Janus look by those of us who know our Mediterranean voters. I'm keeping my seat warm for you, no matter who comes out on top.'

The PM and the Treasurer had fallen out over some agreement they were said to have made. It was a repeat from history: the top men were always, at the last minute, reluctant to go. Churchill had hung on; Nixon would have stayed forever if the rules had allowed it; kings had clung to thrones like drowning men to pontoons; it would not be the last time it would happen. Matt took Rothschild's advice and tried to look neutral, if not neutered.

The Treasurer came out on top and the Party got ready for him to lead them into the next election. He was not a popular Leader, but he was strong-willed and any tears he had were well-hidden at the back of his eyes. He had a wife everyone admired and children who were no problem and everything looked set for a return to government. Then things started to go wrong and the media *savants* predicted a victory for the Opposition. Matt wondered if the ministry warmed for him by Joe Rothschild might prove to be a punctured air cushion.

The election came and Matt went back to his electorate and glad-handed his way around shopping malls, nursing homes, everywhere but jails. Carmel accompanied him sometimes, trying to be not too obviously charming to male voters in case their wives were watching, chatting with women voters as if men were the enemy. Danny Voce guided them both through the maelstrom with a firm hand.

Against all predictions, the *savants* with egg on their faces, the Government was re-elected, but only just. Matt had a reduced majority in his electorate, but that was to be expected; swinging voters move from one party to another like call girls looking for another bed; though, of course, one never made the comparison. The faithful still thought of Matt as their man and they celebrated with a big party at the social club.

Carmel brought the children, because 'family values' was now a new battle cry. Richard took it all in as if the seat were just being kept warm for him — 'If there's anything I hate,' his mother confided to Danny, 'it's a juvenile politician.'

Natalie gave up swanning for the evening, just looked bored: 'It's like a big kids' party, only there's no music. Can we go home now?'

Danny Voce, bigger in the face and belly now, thumped Matt on the back, almost causing a by-election: 'God smiles on the honest!'

'Are you praying or between prayers?'

Danny's laugh was a thunderclap: 'Who could be an atheist on a night like this?'

Back home, in bed, Carmel said, 'How different is it going to be if you get a Cabinet post?'

'More work —' He turned his head on the pillow, looked at her. 'Are you tired of it all?'

'No-o —' It was stretched out. 'But I'm afraid of losing you —'

'I've told you — I'll give it all up the day you ask me —'

She turned to face him. She was still beautiful, her beauty seeming to grow rather than fade, as it does with some women. 'Darling, I'll never ask — it'll be your decision —'

He kissed her. 'I'll know when I need to do it. Trust me.'

Then Parliament reconvened and Matt went back to Canberra and was invited by the PM to be the new Minister for National Security. Joe Rothschild, all relaxed, cynicism retired as well as himself, came back for a last goodbye. He took Matt on a farewell tour of the House and the Senate and then, down the long slope, to the old House where they had met:

'I'll miss all this. Not just the stoushes in Parliament, but the Houses themselves. Halls are made for messengers and, well, even the dumbest of us deliver a message or two over the years.' He stopped. They were in the main chamber of the old House; it was morning and the tourist parties had not yet arrived. He looked around, then back at Matt: 'Always respect the message, if not the messenger. I've heard fools deliver gems of wisdom, utter nongs made wise for the moment by where they stood.'

Matt looked at him with affection. 'You know, you *are* an idealist. The Altruists' Party would welcome you.'

'I'll look for it,' said Joe Rothschild and for once the smile was not that of a moneylender but of a man who was lending, no, giving his faith to a younger man.

And so the routine began again. Matt took Doris with him into his new, much larger office; she organised it as if it were her own kitchen. He had inherited Rothschild's liaison staff, his minders, the principal of whom was Tony Casio. He was a bony man who had been middle-aged since his teens, as cynical as Satan's secretary.

'I'm a practical man, Matt —' No *sir* or *Minister*. 'I throw up when I hear the word *idealism* and I believe that every man, like Judas, has his price. But I would never sell my boss down the river, no matter what the price, not while I worked for him. I am, believe it or not, an honest man. Do you want me to work for you?'

Matt laughed, bonhomie suddenly coming to the surface: 'Tony, how could I let you go after that character reference? I do have ideals, but I won't let them get in your way ... Do you think I'm up to the job?'

'Joe wouldn't have recommended you if you weren't.'

'Good enough. Then we're a team. But —' The bonhomie was dropped. 'I'm boss. Okay?'

'I couldn't have put it better myself.' Tony Casio's grin was a replica of Joe Rothschild's.

Matt settled into the new routine and the new responsibilities. He held meetings with the various Intelligence branches, found that there was only wary consultation between them ...

'That's the way it is,' said Guy Fortague, who stayed behind after one meeting with ASIO. 'The Americans have fifteen different Intelligence bodies and I doubt if they ever sit down together and exchange notes. I guess it's the nature of our game —'

'That's the way you look at it? A game?' said Matt.

Fortague smiled. 'No, not really. We're bloody serious about what we do. But we're a long way from where the real world of Intelligence operates ... Look at the map there on your wall —' He pointed to the large map of Australia that Matt had inherited from Joe Rothschild. 'We're all down here in the south-east corner and the whole bloody continent stretches north and west beyond us. It's an illustration of how far we are from the game, from the world of espionage. But we keep trying ... '

'Do that,' said Matt.

But when he was alone he began to wonder at the flimsy structure of his Ministry, a thin muslin curtain protecting — what?

Still, he was busier now than he had been as a backbencher. His diary had less and less time for Carmel and the children and once again he got the feeling he was slipping away from them. She said she understood, but Matt, more and more experienced now to the nuances in a woman's voice, heard the reservations.

'Am I neglecting the kids? Do they complain to you?'

She took her time before replying: 'Occasionally. Not directly, but they'll say things like, I wonder what Dad would think of this or that.'

'And you?'

Again she took her time: 'You know the answer to that. I miss you every minute you're away.'

He held her to him. 'I promise you — when I get to be PM, we'll live in the Lodge and never be separated.'

He got on well with the new Prime Minister, as he had with the old. But the PM still had a Treasurer's approach to money; he was reluctant to spend it, except at election time. The submarines that had been okayed some years before were proving a headache in development and were running over costs. So a coast guard service was put on the back burner and Matt had to look around for other things for a Minister for National Security to do.

He no longer stayed in the motel during the week, but had rented a one-bedroom flat in Manuka, where he could go to the local oval for his morning exercise and where there were one or two good restaurants. He saw Bernadette occasionally, but she had moved on from her former Minister to another one, a younger man, and all Matt got from her, and was glad, was a distant wave.

He went back to Sydney each weekend, did his duty calls, bought enough raffle tickets to have started his own lottery, spread the bonhomie like marmalade. And winced sometimes at his own double-face.

He had finished one such surgery and was sitting in Danny Voce's office with him and two volunteers, all of them with a beer in hand. Matt enjoyed these rare moments, when he could take off the less-than-shining armour and relax without having to impress anyone.

'I heard a good yarn the other night —' Danny, though a heavy man, had once moved with grace; now he seemed weighed down by his body. The gold curls round the sides of his head had turned grey and straightened. He was tiring, but so far had not complained. The big laugh was still there, but it sometimes came now in gasps.

'I haven't heard a good one in ages,' said Matt. 'Somehow, they don't seem to tell as many good jokes as they used to.'

'It's all smartarse quips these days,' said Kel O'Hare, one of the volunteers. He was a wrinkled Irishman who hinted he had once belonged to the IRA; but Matt couldn't think of a more gentle man. 'I should go back to Dublin, they still have the great stories there, my word.'

'Anyhow,' said Danny Voce, not to be denied, 'there's this girl in the army, she's so rank-conscious she salutes even corporals. Anyhow, an officer takes her out one night, gives her dinner and then on the way back to barracks —' He started to laugh at the joke. 'On the way back he puts the hard word on her and she, still rank-conscious, can't say no.' He was laughing again, red in the face. 'They're at it like rabbits and her forehead keeps coming up and bumping his. He stops, looks down at her and says, What's the matter? Are you epileptic? No, sir, she says, I didn't like to mention it, but you've got my tie caught in it —'

And then Danny Voce stopped laughing, his mouth a silent cup, his eyes just marbles. He dropped his beer and fell off his chair in a terrible tumble.

'Oh Christ!' Matt dropped on his knees beside him. 'Danny!' He began to thump the broad still chest. 'Ring for a doctor! Oh Christ, Danny!' He was crying, the tears rolling down his face. 'Danny!'

But Danny Voce had told his last joke, was beyond laughter or the appeal of his friend.

4

Danny had died between prayers, but the local priest, a friend, could not think of him as an atheist. So he was buried from a church. Relatives came whom Matt had never met; friends by the hundreds were there. The church was packed and there were a couple of hundred people out in the churchyard. Matt gave the eulogy — 'Danny had more jokes, as he said, than Bob Hope's stable of writers ever had. He saw life as a joke, but he knew that so many jokes are based on tragedy, that we laugh to fight against the tears —'

Then a young niece, in a clear and beautiful voice, sang *Danny Boy* and all the mourners wept.

'The saddest love song ever written,' whispered Matt, tears in his own eyes.

'If you go first, I'll write an even sadder one,' murmured Carmel and dug her nails into his hand like small, sharp anchors.

Outside the church, waiting to go to the cemetery, Matt stood while friends, voters, strangers came and complimented him on the eulogy.

'He loved to joke —' he said for the thirty-third time.

'Matt —' said Fleur Tan.

He focussed on her, shook his head in embarrassment. 'Sorry, Fleur. I've been on automatic — I'm not functioning too well —'

'Maybe I'd better come back and see you another time —'

'No, I'm going back to Canberra tonight.' The prospect suddenly didn't appeal to him; he would rather be going home to Carmel and the kids. 'What is it?'

She bit her lip, then said, 'Would you consider letting me take Danny's place? I could do the job —'

He frowned. 'Fleur, what about the *Gazette*?'

'Didn't Carmel tell you?' Carmel still worked there occasionally, but not as regularly as in the past. 'We've been struggling for months. We've had an offer from one of the suburban chains and we're going to accept it. I'll be out of a job.'

He looked across at Carmel, surrounded by people he didn't recognise. Friends of hers he hadn't met? He wondered why she had not told him of the *Gazette*'s failing fortunes and influences; then wondered, with shame, why he had never asked how it was going. He looked back at Fleur:

'Why come to work for me?'

'I want to be a political journalist —' She was hesitant, as if regretting she had chosen this time to speak to him. 'A year or two with you will be terrific training. Then maybe —' She smiled, almost shyly. 'Maybe some day I'll be down there in the press gallery.'

'God forbid,' he said, but he, too, smiled. He had to admire this small, plain girl who had come so far, out of the killing fields of Asia and had made good in an environment completely foreign to her. 'I'll have to talk to some others, Fleur, but as far as I'm concerned, the job's yours.'

'Thanks,' she said and stood on her toes and kissed him on the cheek. 'You're a lovely man, Matt.'

But, looking across at Carmel, distant yet close, he wondered.

Later that day Carmel drove him to the airport. They said little during the journey, she concentrating on her driving through the early peak-hour traffic. At the airport they sat in silence in the car till he said, 'What's the matter? Is it Danny's death?'

'Partly.' She wasn't looking at him; her gaze seemed to be on something out of sight. 'I just wonder if it's an omen.'

'An omen?' He was treading carefully.

'Things are — *different*.' She turned to look at him; it seemed to him that she was altering her focus. 'Haven't you noticed?'

'How?' She didn't answer that and, after a moment, like a footballer looking for an opening, and as clumsily, he said, 'Why didn't you tell me the *Gazette* was going bust?'

She stared at him as if wondering where that subject had come from; then she said, 'Would you have cared?'

'Oh, for Crissakes!'

Then a parking officer was at Carmel's window. 'Will you please move on, ma'am? This is a No Stopping area.'

'My husband is the Federal Minister for National Security,' said Carmel, and to Matt's suddenly apprehensive ear, she sounded sarcastic. 'We are looking out right now at what security this airport needs.'

'That's why we have No Stopping signs,' said the parking officer, not to be outdone, and moved on.

Carmel looked back at Matt: 'You were saying?'

For a moment he had nothing more to say; he realised, with sudden shame, that he would not have cared that the *Gazette* was going under. But he said, 'Yes, I would have. If it was something you still liked doing —'

'But you never asked me about it. Not in weeks. It was always your bloody interests, what you were doing —' She looked away from him again. 'It's not just that. It's — it's so many things.' She looked back at him. 'Richard and Natalie. Do you know, you don't know any of their friends, never ask if they have any.'

He had enough shame to feel that as a punch in the guts. 'Have they complained?'

'Richard has. Natalie — no. But that's her — swanning

even through her disappointment in her father ... You'd better go, you'll miss your plane.'

'I can't go — not when it's like this —'

'Go, Matt. We'll talk about it when you come home at the weekend.' She leaned across and kissed him on the cheek, a social kiss. 'Go. Here comes that parking officer again.'

He stared at her, saw nothing in her eyes that encouraged him; then he opened the door of the car and slid out quickly, as if trying to escape before it crashed. He went into the terminal without looking back, not in anger but in shame.

He flew back to Canberra, silent all the way, burying his head in papers, glad that the woman in the seat next to him did not want to talk. The hostess, recognising him from previous flights, brought him coffee, smiled at him, hoped that he would have a good day, even though it was the end of the day. Platitudes were part of the service.

The hostess went away and the woman beside him, closing the book she had been reading, said without looking at him, 'They always treat the men better.'

'Not always,' he said and turned away to look out the window at the landscape below fading under night like a watercolour under spreading ink.

Back at the flat in Manuka he rang home, but there was no answer other than: *We can't take your call, but* ... He hung up, leaving no message, because he had none.

Then he realised he had had nothing to eat since an early lunch. Remorse can fill the mind, but the belly has a mind of its own. He went out to dinner at a restaurant in Manuka, got a table to himself by the wall and gave his order to the waitress, another woman who recognised him.

'The steak is particularly good tonight, Mr Durban. It's local.'

'Harmony —' He had found out that was her name, though he wondered how much harmony there was in her life; she wasn't always bright and happy. 'Is it sliced off the Coalition?'

'It could be,' she said, who read the press gallery.

He was just about to taste his pre-dinner light beer when Bernadette Brown sat down opposite him. 'May I join you? I'll pay for my own dinner.'

He was not in the mood for company, especially hers: 'Have you been stood up?'

'Not at all. At the moment I'm — what's the word? — at liberty. Fancy-free, I think my grandmother used to call it.'

'What happened to your man?' One didn't drop names in Canberra restaurants. The local ears could pick up messages from Mars.

'His wife got to hear about us.' She showed no embarrassment or discomfort; she was a seasoned love-warrior: you took your conquests when and where you could. The waitress came back and Bernadette, after a glance at the menu, gave her order. Harmony went away, leaving no harmony behind her, but Bernadette arranged herself as if settling in for the night. Then she looked back at Matt and said, 'I'm thinking of giving up and going back to Melbourne.'

'There'd be more choice there. But I hear the young blokes today don't want to settle down. They want to spend their money on themselves.'

'If I find the right one, I'll settle for a middle-aged man. How old are you?'

He grinned. 'Senile, Bernadette.'

She smiled in return. She was still good-looking and it was surprising how charming, almost innocent (well, almost) her smile could be. He could see why men fell for her, besides the attraction of the bosom. 'No, I wasn't trying to seduce you. You may not believe this, but I like to see a happily married man.'

'My wife wouldn't believe you.'

'I know.' You couldn't insult her. What a courtesan she would have been, he thought. But Canberra didn't breed courtesans, they weren't among parliamentary perks. She went on, 'Most wives wouldn't believe me. But I never went after happily married men —'

You went after me.

She read his mind and smiled again. 'I soon realised you were happy. And when I saw your wife, I realised the competition. Not all men are as lucky as you.'

Suddenly he liked her and was sorry for her. The waitress brought them their dinner, smiled at them as if she *knew what was going on*, and went away.

'There'll be gossip out in the kitchen,' said Bernadette, smiling. She bit into her *veal saltimbocca* as she might have bitten into her men, chewed on it like a woman who loved her food, then said very casually, 'Was there any gossip about you and June Herx?'

He chewed on his own rare-to-medium steak before he said, 'What brings her up?'

'You were observed —'

'Observed?' God, she hadn't been an ASIO *observer*!

'Okay — *seen*. It must've rocked you when she was murdered —'

'It did.' He took his time, chewed another mouthful of steak. Then: 'Bernadette, there was absolutely nothing between me and June Herx. It was political business, strictly. I had an interest in national security and so did she, coming from up north. That was all it was.' He chewed another mouthful, then said, 'My wife knew all about it.'

She smiled. 'I'm glad to hear it. But there was talk about you and Mrs Herx. You were lucky it didn't get in the papers or on radio. You know what they're like.'

'Indeed I do. The medieval hatchet has been replaced by gossip. It's supposed to be more civilised, but I dunno.' He looked around the restaurant, half-full, then back at her. 'You think they'll gossip about you and me?'

'No. I checked before I came and sat down here. I know all the media guys and girls, there's none here tonight. We're safe. *You* are safe.'

He relaxed, smiled again. 'Bernadette, if it hadn't been for your chest, we could've been the best of friends.'

'It's an asset,' she said and looked down at it in the pink sweater she wore. 'But other women see it as a deadly weapon.'

'Never,' he said and they both laughed and out in the kitchen Harmony, looking at them through the porthole in the door, remarked how well Mr Durban and the stacked girl were getting on.

When Bernadette had finished her meal and her coffee, she asked for her bill, paid it, then stood up. 'Stay and have another coffee. That should convince those watching us that nothing's going on.'

'Has it convinced them in the past when you've gone out separately?'

'No. But tonight I feel innocent.'

'It doesn't show,' he said and they both laughed. 'Good luck in Melbourne,' he said and meant it. He was in a mood tonight to feel sorry for women.

She walked away, hips provocative, even if tonight she felt innocent. She would go to her grave with men looking at her, he thought. Then he caught the eye of Harmony and ordered another coffee.

'The steak was great, Harmony. Right off the best part of the Coalition.'

'Did the lady enjoy her meal?'

'You know, I forgot to ask her.'

Later, he paid his bill, stood up and looked around for *observers*. But there appeared to be none, no one was interested any more in him. He went out into the cold night air, glad he had brought his overcoat, a scarf and a tweed cap. He walked back to his flat, eyes watering as the wind came down from the ranges, let himself in the door and went straight to the phone, as to a confessional.

'Did I wake you?'

'No,' said Carmel. 'I'm re-reading *The Female Eunuch*.'

'Don't rub it in. I called earlier —'

'I took the kids to Pizza Hut.' There was silence for a long moment, as if her voice was taking its time over the couple of hundred kilometres between them. Then she said, 'I forgive you.'

'I love you.'

'How could you not?' she said and laughed and hung up.

The rest of the week seemed a month, but at last Friday came and Matt went home. The porch light was on and the door was opened by Natalie before he could put his key in the lock. He looked at her with bursting heart and, beyond her, in the hallway, at Richard and Carmel. He stepped in under the light.

'Daddy —' said Natalie dreamily. 'One of the girls at school asked if you ran Australia?'

'Just occasionally,' he said.

Chapter Ten

1

The weeks, then the months, then a year slipped by. Fleur Tan came to work in Matt's electorate office and proved as popular and efficient as Danny Voce had been. She didn't laugh as much as Danny had, was not as expansive, and she had no jokes. But she arranged the Saturday morning surgeries as efficiently as Danny had:

'Who have we got this morning?' he asked.

'Eight people,' said Fleur. 'First, there's Mrs Lucastopolous —'

'Who?' He envied the old-time politicians who had had to attend only to the Browns and the Smiths and the O'Hanrahans. He was not racist, not in the least, but he had difficulty sometimes in getting his tongue round some of the names that came before him.

'She runs two fruit shops, gives us a donation every year ... She has a family problem,' said Fleur and looked at him warily.

'Just what I like,' said Matt, already weary before he had begun. 'Send her in.'

Mrs Lucastopolous was well-dressed and carried a handbag that could have held a watermelon. She was plump, dark-haired, flutter-handed and a bundle of worry.

'Mrs Lucastopolous —' The name rolled off his tongue like Greek marbles. 'What can I do for you?'

'My son, Andrios, he'sa in love!'

'Well, that's a nice state to be in, Mrs —'

'He'sa sick and sad, he'sa in love with a man —'

This was sticky territory. 'He's gay?'

'No, no, he's notta gay, he'sa sad! He'sa in love with Brat Piddi!'

'Brat Piddi? A friend? He'sa — he's gay, too?'

'No, no, he's a new fillum star. Always taking his shirt off. Andrios, he'sa moody every time he seesa Brat Piddi. Ombra, too.'

'Ombra? Another gay?'

'No, no, she'sa my daughter. Always falling in love, except Wednesdays —'

He didn't dare ask why Ombra was loveless on Wednesdays.

'My whole family, they're fillum fans. My husband —'

Now this was really sticky territory: 'He's not gay?'

'No, no! He likes dark women, the darker the better, he say. He gotta thing for Whoopsie Goldenburg!'

'Mrs Lucastopolous —' The syllables were becoming more difficult. 'I'm not a counsellor —'

'Councillors — phooey! I go the council about the rates, the garbage not collected —'

'Mrs —' He didn't try her name again. 'Why don't you send Andrios back to Greece for a holiday? Greek men are handsome, look at all the statues — he might forget Brat Piddi —'

'Excuse me, Mr Durban, you right in the head? He go back to Ithaca, where I come from, he go on the dole, there'sa no work. Why I come to Australia? Start the fruit shop, makea the money —'

Matt sighed. 'Send Andrios in to see me, Mrs Lucastopolous.'

She kissed his hand, making him feel papal, and was gone, sure now that her family was safe from the temptations in fillums. Matt looked at Fleur, who was grinning broadly. 'Do you have a thing for Brad Pitt?'

'Jackie Chan is my cuppa tea. He'd be so athletic in bed.'

'The mind boggles. Who's next?'

She looked at her list. 'Charlie Henke.'

'*Again?*' He was a voter who thought one had to vote at least once a week; or at worst, complain. 'Send him in.'

'My pleasure,' said Fleur and smiled sadistically.

Pages peeled off the calendar. Matt did not blot his copybook as Minister for National Security; but that was because there was so little in the book. Terrorism was a new word not yet frightening to the voters; it broke out, like terrible sores, in parts of the world still remote from Australia. Defences were planned, but it was like putting up latticework against an approaching windstorm.

The Opposition had a new leader, which was of more concern for the Government than shadowy terrorists. He had run several times for the leadership and been defeated; he was a practised politician, a strategist and tactician who could have drawn the map of politics. He had one drawback in Matt's estimation: he looked back to the Fifties as if they were the Golden Years. Unfortunately for Labor, there were also a growing number of voters who were looking backwards. Nostalgia, Matt was coming to realise, had its dangers.

But all he did was look forward; without registering it, he began to change. Whether it was the bigger office, the wider influence as a Minister, or just expansion of ego, Matt Durban slowly became more flamboyant. The glad hand pressed the flesh of every mitt that couldn't escape; he hugged people like the hooker in a rugby front row; the smile grew several more teeth. Cameras caught him, wide-screen.

Carmel's own smile was wifely critical: 'I could see your back molars at that reception tonight.'

'Geez, was I that bad?' They were in bed, the place not only for secrets but for home truths. 'Am I turning into a celebrity?' A new breed that had begun to appear, an epidemic of cloning.

'No. Celebrities have huge smiles and tiny talents. You have talent, but it's getting lost in your bonhomie.'

'My bonhomie, eh? Is that an Aussie characteristic?'

'Only with TV hosts. Just watch it, pull your head in.'

Which he tried, though not always with success. He coasted through the months, then the years. The PM continued his knack of rubbing voters up the wrong way, giving them Mahler when they preferred Meatloaf, and prospects for Labor at the next election did not look good.

The children grew older and, though he hadn't expected it, grew closer to him. Both of them were getting exceptionally good marks at school; Richard was ambitious, but Natalie was still swanning. They were not handicapped by having a famous father; he was just well-known, which was bearable, they told him. It was a handicap that he was a politician, Natalie told him, but the girls at her school didn't blame her for that.

Jobwise, he was in the doldrums and found he liked them more than he had expected. A good salary, expenses and perks, rising income from his investments: the blankets kept him warm and comfortable. The light on the hill dimmed.

And Carmel didn't complain: 'You've lost your ambition, you know.'

'I haven't, you know —'

'Okay, you haven't lost it. But you've put it on the back burner. And I don't mind. You're a better husband and dad.'

He wondered if that were true, but was pleased to hear it. The ambition was still there, an ember maybe, but still there. But he had become lazy.

Then, one Friday evening just as he and Carmel were about to go out, Fleur Tan having come to babysit the kids — 'Oh Mum,' Richard had wailed. 'Not *baby*sit! Kidsit, if you like, but not babysit —' the phone rang. Matt almost did not answer it: he wanted no politics tonight.

But it was Paddy O'Reilly: 'You'd better come home, Matt. It's your dad, he's had a massive stroke —'

'Dad?' The most relaxed man he had ever known.

'A blood clot. It looks bad, Matt, he's in intensive care. Doc Hennessy has called in two specialists.'

Matt hung up the phone, stood in the hallway, trying to believe the unbelievable. Carmel, ready for their evening out, came out of the bedroom. 'What's the matter? Not bloody parliamentary business?'

'No —' He had trouble getting his voice out. 'It's my dad, he's had a massive stroke. That was Paddy — he didn't sound hopeful.'

'I'll pack,' said Carmel, turning back into the bedroom. 'Break it to Richard and Natalie. Gently.'

Which he did, as gently as he could, with Fleur sitting there in the most uncomfortable of possible positions, the outsider to bad news. 'Can you move in for the weekend, Fleur? Cancel my surgery tomorrow.'

'Dad —' Richard was biting his lip; he and Natalie had had great affection for the quiet man with the quiet smile. 'Can't we come?'

'You and Nat don't want to be standing around in a hospital.' He held the two of them to him. 'Just pray Pa comes out of it okay.'

'Who's Pa's favourite?' asked Natalie. 'Jesus or Mary?'

'Try both. I'm sure they're listening.'

The drive that night was the longest journey Matt had ever taken. He drove, sitting quiet most of the time, Carmel just as quiet; there are times, between life and death, when the words suddenly dry up. They stopped once to get petrol and a cup of coffee, and even then they hardly spoke. It was one o'clock in the morning when they drew up in front of the hospital in, not Collamundra, but Cawndilla. Paddy and Eileen were waiting for them.

'Doesn't look good,' said Paddy, and Matt knew the worst at once. Carmel took his hand and held it tightly, almost as if afraid that she was losing him, too.

He and Carmel, still hand-in-hand, as if protecting each other, went into the small intensive care ward. The man in the bed, masked and tubed, was almost unrecognisable. Matt broke down at once and Carmel's grip tightened on his hand.

'Oh Christ,' Matt whispered and it was a prayer, not a curse.

'Let's go outside,' said Carmel. 'Dr Hennessy is out there.'

The doctor was waiting for them in the silent corridor with Paddy and Eileen. He was a small man, with thin grey hair and the look of someone too familiar with death. He had practised in Collamundra for almost forty years and was part of the life and death of the town.

'I'm speaking for the specialists we called in, Matt. Dick Lester and Joe Parrish. We're agreed —' He hesitated, as if afraid to say what he was about to say; but he had been saying for years: 'It'll be better to take him off the life support. He'll be speechless and bedridden for the rest of his life . . . I knew Keith well. He wouldn't like that.'

2

Keith Durban was buried on a beautiful summer morning. The service was held in the Catholic church in Collamundra and mourners came from within a hundred miles of the town, old friends, old pupils, for he had been a man who, in his own quiet way, was an example of a dying breed, the man of exemplary honesty. Neither the priest nor Paddy O'Reilly nor Matt mentioned that in their short eulogies, because each knew that Keith would have shaken his head and remonstrated with them. He had been a teacher, not a lecturer, he would have told them; that men, like history, repeated themselves and some day, maybe soon, honesty would once more be the yardstick. What went on in the financial capitals around the world was a long way from this small church on the rim of a country town. Perspective, as he had taught, had to be kept.

Carmel had flown back to Sydney, collected the children and brought them back to Cavanreagh the night before the funeral. On the morning itself Matt drove into town, went to the home where he had been brought up and picked a dozen Moss Roses, just come into bloom. At the cemetery he laid half a dozen on the new grave of his father, half a dozen on that of his mother. Then he stood back and, with his arms round Carmel and the children, wept for the past.

Walking back to the cars parked on the road outside the cemetery he passed Ruby Rawson's grave. Carmel and the children had gone ahead of him with the O'Reillys. He paused; and then was aware of Wally Mungle beside him. The grave was untended, overgrown, Ruby dead beneath weeds.

'A long time ago, Matt,' said Wally.

Matt nodded, made no comment on Ruby. All the mourners had passed on and the cemetery had that loneliness that is all its own. Matt looked around him, then started walking, Wally Mungle falling in beside him.

'We'll miss him, your dad,' said Wally. 'He was the best friend I had in this town. Him and you.'

'Thanks, Wally . . . How are things? Out at the Camp?'

Wally's smile was gentle. 'They don't call it that any more. You wouldn't recognise it. Thanks for the grant you managed to get us. My mum thinks you're St Vincent de Paul.'

'The poor bugger died a miserable death.'

Two years before, Matt had prevailed upon the Treasurer to put through a building grant for Aboriginal settlements; it had been outside his portfolio and he had not got the public credit for it. But certain people had known, including Wally Mungle.

'Is your mother still out there?'

'Still there. She'll never move. Her story is our family has been there for umpteen generations, she couldn't count 'em. The Noongulli was a big river in those days, there was plenty of food around ... Our family has owned — well, not *owned*, we didn't think in those terms. But we make the Hardstaffs and the O'Reillys look like Johnny-Come-Latelys.'

Matt smiled. 'Some of the families would be upset to hear that.'

Wally Mungle, too, smiled. 'Mum used to keep an eye on all you young fellers coming out there with your girls —'

Ruby and me in the silver Mercedes?

'She used to joke she could of written a gossip column.'

Time to change the conversation. 'How are things on the police front?'

'Quiet. One or two break-ins, a coupla brawls. Very quiet ... Chester Hardstaff died in jail, did you know that?'

'One of the fellers in the National Party told me. I was never quite able to get my mind around the fact he killed that Jap manager.'

'I'm not experienced in murder, even though I'm a cop. But I've read a lot about it. Not detective stories, true stuff. True crime, as they call it. Nearly most murders are committed on the spur of the moment and half of them by people who've never been violent. Chester was a hard man and I don't think he ever did anything on the spur of the moment. He was right out of Shakespeare.' Matt looked at him and Wally Mungle smiled again. 'Remember, your dad taught me English? I've read all the Shakespeare plays.'

'How do they stack up against Koori legends?'

The smile widened. 'About equal. We had less bastards in our legends . . . Give my best to Carmel. I haven't spoken to her, I didn't want to butt in —'

'I'll tell her.'

Matt paused at the cemetery gates, watched the slim dark figure walk away. And thanked God he was not Minister for Aboriginal Affairs, the toughest role in Government, trying to make the past understand the present and vice versa.

A wake was held at Cavanreagh; funerals, as Eileen remarked, being a reunion for the living. Then in mid-afternoon the Durban family, what was left of it, began the long drive back to Sydney. In the back seat the children were unusually quiet and Carmel looked back at them and said, 'Think of Pa when he was alive. That's the way he'd like it.'

'Is dying hard?' asked Richard.

Matt, at the wheel, glanced sideways at Carmel, glad he had not been asked the question.

'Sometimes,' she said. 'It's harder for us who are left behind.'

'I think I'll take all of you with me,' said Natalie.

'Thanks,' said Matt and laughed and then all four of them were laughing as the car climbed into the mountains and a door closed on the other life Matt had lived.

He went back to Canberra next day and the life there closed its grip on him again. Rebecca Irvine, the Minister for Health, came round to his office and offered her condolences: 'I lost both my parents when I was sixteen.

They were in the Granville train crash.' A major disaster back in — 1977 or '78? But Matt didn't ask. 'I hope your father died quietly.'

'Very. No raging against the dying of the light ...' She looked blank and he said, 'Dylan Thomas, a Welsh poet. I taught English at school.'

'I was never one for poetry. Just Bob Dylan.'

She went away and he wondered if he should have asked her what had brought her to politics, what ambition she had. But here in the House he was still something of a loner, something he had only just begun to realise. He would have to start increasing the bonhomie if he wanted to go further.

The following weekend, back in Sydney, he told Carmel he was going back to Collamundra. 'We can't put the house up for sale till probate comes through, but I'll have an agent look at it. I'll get your dad to give away the furniture and Dad's clothes to one of the charity crowds. Then I'll bring some of his books and his record collection back here and you and I can dance to Bix Beiderbecke and *Riverboat Shuffle*. You can shake your fanny again —'

'Mum's going to shake her fanny?' said Natalie. 'Disgusting!'

Matt cancelled his surgery again, took Richard with him and they left at seven on the Saturday morning. Richard was now fifteen and was slowly changing from the brash know-it-all he had once been. Matt glanced at him as they headed down the long stretch of motorway leading up into the mountains.

'You still keen on the RAAF? Be a fighter pilot?'

'Yeah. What did you want to be at my age?'

Matt tried to remember. 'I dunno ... Yes, I do. I think even then I wanted to go into politics.'

'Jeez —' Richard shook his head. 'You must've been a pain.'

'We all are at fifteen, one way or another.'

They made it to Collamundra in good time and went straight to the Durban house. 'We'll go out to Cavanreagh for dinner, but come back here to sleep. That okay with you?'

'Last look around?' Richard was fast growing up.

Matt nodded. 'I won't come back here, after this.'

Richard nodded as if he understood. 'Okay, where do we start?'

Matt looked through the wide range of books his father had collected. 'I'll give most of these to the Cawndilla library. But —'

He then took out the ones he wanted to keep and wondered at how he and his father had had such similar tastes. *The Power and the Glory*, *The Sun Also Rises*, *The Great Gatsby*, *All the King's Men*, *The Catcher in the Rye*, *Gossip from the Forest*: he had read them all and enjoyed them and would again.

'*The Complete Works of Shakespeare*,' said Richard, holding up two books. 'And *Anthology of Welsh Poets*. Why Welsh poets?'

'Pa thought they were the best. They could be melancholy and Pa was sometimes melancholy after Grandma died.'

Richard was suddenly grown-up: 'Would you be melancholy if Mum died?'

'Very,' said Matt, but was abruptly happy that at last he was beginning to talk to his son.

They went out to Cavanreagh for dinner, where Eileen fussed over Richard as if he were already a decorated fighter pilot. Teresa was there and looked upon her handsome young nephew with amused affection.

'You got a girl?' she asked.

Matt was surprised to see Richard blush; the boy was indeed changing. 'No special one.'

'You've got a harem?' said Paddy. 'I tried that when I was young, but it was too much trouble.'

'Don't listen to him, Richard,' said Eileen. 'He's been telling me that for years, but if there ever were any, they've all left the district.'

'Stick to one,' advised Teresa. 'One at a time.'

Matt and Richard went back to the house in town. Matt slept in his father's bed and Richard in what had been Matt's. Before he fell asleep, Matt felt the comfort of the arrangement. In the morning, before they left, he went around the garden and gathered all the Moss Roses, wrapped them in wet newspaper and plastic and put them on the back seat. They were the last he would collect, flowers on two lives.

They drove out of town, into the sun coming up from the coast. A mile out of town, suddenly on the spur of the moment, Matt turned the car off the main road.

'Where are we going?'

'Down to look at the Koori settlement. I came out here when they first built it, but I haven't seen it since.'

'Why are you interested, Dad? You don't have anything to do with the Aborigines?'

'Wally Mungle, the cop, is my friend — his mother lives out here.' No need to mention that out here there had also been a happy humping ground.

What had been a rough track down to the Camp was now a gravelled road down to the settlement. Matt took the car down the road cautiously, as if intruding and not sure of his welcome. He pulled it up some fifty yards short of the weatherboard, tin-roofed houses, some with neat attempts at a garden, others already neglected.

'I don't understand the Abos,' said Richard.

'Neither do a lot of people. But that's the way it is all over the world. I don't think they really understand us.

Sometimes I wonder if Jesus Christ ever came back, whether He'd understand everybody.'

'Why don't you write the Pope and ask him?' said Richard and grinned.

Then Matt saw the woman, grey-haired, heavily-built, flat-footed in slippers, coming towards them. It was a moment before he recognised Nell Mungle.

'You looking for someone?' She had a soft, gruff voice. Then she peered at him and suddenly smiled: Wally's smile. 'Mr Durban! Howyagoing?'

'Fine, thanks, Mrs Mungle. This is my son, Richard.'

She peered in at him: 'You look like your dad — and your ma.' She looked back at Matt: 'She all right — what was her name?'

'Carmel O'Reilly.'

'Yeah, that's right. I seen her when I used to go in to Dr Hennessy for my pills . . . You look well.'

'You, too, Mrs Mungle. You happy with —?' He nodded past her at the settlement.

'Yeah. Yeah, it's better'n things used to be.' Then she smiled again. 'We don't get the young fellers bringing their girls out here no more, like they used to.'

'Those were other times, Mrs Mungle —' And I'd rather you didn't mention them in front of my son. 'Well, we've got a long way back to Sydney. If there's anything you ever want —' He nodded past her again, at the houses. 'Let me know.'

'Yeah,' she said, but sounded as if she never would. 'Look after yourself. And him, too —' She smiled at Richard. 'Give my regards to Mrs Durban.'

As they drove away Richard said, 'She sounded nice. Did you bring girls out here when you were young?'

'None of your business,' said Matt, and they both laughed.

3

The seasons slid into one another and then it was an election year, a fifth season of windy rhetoric. Back in Parramatta Fleur said, looking Confucian, he thought, 'It's going to be tough, Matt. You'll get back, but the word is other seats are very dicey —' An un-Confucian word. 'How's the PM feel?'

'Up and down, his minders tell me. Our mate, Charlie Henke, called me in Canberra the other day, reversing the charges, said we'd sold out the working classes. Other MPs tell me they're getting the same message. It's all this easy money being made at the top, Fleur. The IT kids making fortunes overnight. Why aren't you into it? You're a genius on the computer, whereas I'm still using a quill pen.'

'I'm Asian, Matt — we're supposed to have been using money before you Westerners knew what it was. My mother and my grandmother can't understand I don't know how to make money. Put my grandmother into IT and she'd have Microsoft playing second fiddle in no time.'

'You think she'd like a job in Cabinet?'

'She'd run rings around the Treasurer. But don't quote me.'

Picked up one morning at Canberra airport by his new driver, Des Lake, Matt asked, 'What's the tip amongst the workers, Des? Are we going to be tossed?'

Des Lake had been driving Commonwealth cars for twenty years; he had seen power passed hand to hand like a relay baton. He had lent his ear to Labor and Coalition, showing interest in both; but none of the Ministers and Shadow Ministers he had driven knew how he voted. He was a wiry, tall man whose face, it seemed, had been lined for years. Experience was stamped all over him and he was the ideal man for testing the waters.

'I think so.' He had never called any of his Ministers *sir*; which hinted he might even be a Communist, a now almost extinct tribe. 'You're in trouble. Not you, but some of your mates. Quite a lot of them.'

'What do the voters want?'

'I dunno that they know themselves. Jesus Christ, maybe.' He took the car out of the airport, drove towards the city at a steady speed, as deliberate as a tumbril driver. 'But I can tell you — don't quote me — they know what they don't want.'

'Us?'

Des Lake nodded. 'But I hear you're safe.'

'If I finish up a Shadow Minister, you still want to drive for me?'

'It'll be a pleasure,' said Des Lake and for the first time gave a hint he might be a Labor voter. Or at worst a sympathiser.

Parliament broke up and Matt spent the next month mending fences in his electorate, glad-handing his way around shopping malls, even pausing by Mrs Lucastopolous' fruit shops to let her kiss his cheek and to shake the hand of Andrios, the lover of Brad Pitt. He was a handsome youth, younger than Matt had expected, and Matt couldn't resist asking: 'Still a movie fan?'

'Sure.'

'Got any favourites?'

Matt was treading dangerous ground, but he couldn't help himself; though Andrios didn't seem to notice: 'Sharon Stone.'

Glory be, he had been saved! 'Nice girl. Enjoy her.'

'I wish I could,' said Andrios Lucastopolous and leered like a Greek satyr.

Carmel lent her help and the voters appreciated her, especially the older women voters. Carmel kept the children out of sight; the violins could be overworked, she said. She gave the male voters a good look at her, but never too much encouragement; she was aware of the wives and girlfriends hovering by 'like Praetorian guards', she told Fleur. The latter worked like a peasant in the fields back home, ten and twelve hours a day. But all to no avail in the wider cause of the Party. Labor went down with a gurgle and Matt was returned with a further reduced majority.

The morning after the defeat Fleur came to the house and after some hesitation announced in a small girl's voice, 'I'm leaving, Matt. I was offered a job a month ago, but I said nothing till — till yesterday was over.'

Matt was disappointed and surprised; this was a day for defeats, political and personal. 'What's the job?'

She named a radio station. 'As their State political reporter. It's what I've always wanted, Matt. Well, maybe not radio, but it's a start —'

Fleur hadn't meant it as a cruel blow; but it was. She and Danny Voce had been his staffs, in every meaning of the word. All at once his world was crumbling; or so he felt. 'I'll miss you, Fleur.'

She nodded, then put her arms round him and wept. Carmel came out to the grape arbour where Matt and Fleur were, smiled and went to say something; but Matt shook his head. Carmel said nothing, just stood there till Fleur had dried her eyes and Matt had told her of Fleur's new job.

'I couldn't be more pleased, Fleur,' said Carmel and the truth was there in her face. 'We'll tune in every day to you.'

Fleur, eyes dry now, thanked them both, then said, 'I've found a guy who'll be a good replacement. Ham Jessup — Hamilton. He's worked in a union office and he knows what works and what doesn't.'

Matt trusted her judgement: 'Ask him to meet me next Saturday morning.'

When Fleur had gone, Matt and Carmel looked at each other.

'Well,' he said, 'we're at the bottom of the hill again.'

'We'll survive,' she said, took his hand and kissed his knuckles. 'I spoke to our accountant last Thursday. Do you know that, plus the house and your salary and all the rest of it, our portfolio is now worth almost two million?'

'Sh-h —' He put his fingers to his lips, looked right and left. 'I'm the battlers' friend —'

'How much did you say Dad was worth?' asked Richard from the doorway. 'Mr Carrol says I'm a genius at maths —'

'Genius, phenius,' said Natalie behind him. 'Who cares? Are you going to be a nobody again, Dad?'

The voice of the public, the mole in the house. 'Not quite. I'm still the battlers' friend around here —'

'How much did you say you were worth?' Richard persisted.

'Get outta here,' said Carmel.

At midday Matt called the Prime Minister, the *ex*-PM, who was gracious but sounded tired and very, very disappointed. 'But these things happen, Matt. What other professionals have to line up every three or four years to find if they still have a job?'

'Football coaches?' ventured Matt.

The PM still had enough spirit in him to chuckle. 'I'll see if the Raiders have got a vacancy ... Carry the flag, Matt.'

'I'll try,' said Matt and hung up, wondering for the moment if to be PM was worth the effort, if the disappointment at losing was so much greater.

Before he went back to Canberra he met Hamilton Jessup. He was a young man with a sense of humour but no jokes. He was a toucher, an encourager; he would have patted the Pope on the back and told him to hang in there. He had a thin veneer of cynicism, a coating from his time as a union worker but he also had faith in the future.

'Well, you'd better put that on hold,' said Matt. 'This new

Government is going to hang on for as long as it can and we have to start picking a new team.'

'No worries,' said Ham Jessup, and Matt shook his head at the optimism of the youth. Then remembered he had once been like that.

Keith Durban's house was sold and that added to Matt and Carmel's fortune. Occasionally, when he was home, Matt would take out some of his father's LPs and play them. But he felt Benny Goodman and Artie Shaw fade away as ghostly music, contemporaries of Blondel and other medieval cats.

The new PM tried to revive Doris Day, but a deaf ear was turned to him and her. The voters did listen to his message for the future, and tried to understand what economic rationalism meant.

'What it means,' Matt tried to explain to Ham Jessup, 'is we'll have three economies. The one out of the ivory towers, the one the Treasurer puts down every so often and the one the rest of us live under.'

The other disturbing feature as far as Matt was concerned was the sudden changing attitude of some older, and even younger, voters. A red-headed woman came out of the north and revived the White Australia policy under another name. History went back for a re-run, as it has a habit of doing in even the better-educated countries.

And information technology was the new mantra, a new language understood in every corner of the world. Matt settled back to study it, like a caveman struggling over the new scribblings on the cave wall.

Chapter Eleven

1

And then, suddenly it seemed, Richard was seventeen, had got top marks in his Higher School Certificate and was ready and eager to enter the Defence Academy.

'He must be a pain in the arse to a lot of people,' said Matt. 'The girls all think he's a better-looking Brad Pitt, his rugby mates think he's another Campese, his teachers think he's Isaac Newton —'

'He's not conceited,' said Carmel.

'He doesn't need to be. He couldn't hide his light under a tonne, let alone a bushel. Sometimes I'm blinded by the sight of him.'

'Have you told him?'

'Of course not. I'm proud of him.'

'You men!' said Carmel and rolled her eyes.

Matt drove Richard down to Canberra and the Defence Academy in the summer break. He pulled the car into the parking lot, switched off the engine and looked at the collection of buildings that would be his son's home for the next three years. There he would come under the influence of strangers, taught the arts of war, how to hold the leash on the dogs of war. Then he looked at Richard:

'It's not going to be easy, mate.'

'I know, Dad.' Richard was built like his father, tall and broad-shouldered, looked older than his years and sounded older. 'Just as well you're not the Shadow Defence Minister.'

'It's bad enough I'm in Parliament, a politician. You'll be hazed, you'd better expect that. But try out for the rugby and cricket teams, you should make both of them. Aussies will cheer a serial rapist if he's good at sport.'

Richard smiled. He was no longer the swaggering know-it-all he had been when younger. He was still confident, though not brashly so. 'I'll try and remember that.'

'You want me to come in while you report?'

'Cut it out, Dad. I don't want you holding my hand.'

'They may want to see me —'

'Let's wait till they ask.'

'Okay. But if the other cadets start hazing you, let me know —'

Richard looked at him. 'Where do you think that would get me? Relax, Dad. I know what I'm letting myself in for.'

Matt looked back at him. 'Yes, I think you do. Good luck.'

As Richard walked away, carrying his bags, Matt realised another door was closing. Richard, the boy, the youth, was gone; when he came back through that door in another three years, he would be a man. At the entrance to the administration building, Richard paused, then looked back and waved. Then he was gone through the doors.

Over the next months, if Richard was hazed at the college, he made no complaint. He progressed with good marks, made both the college rugby and cricket teams, seemed to be certain to be no less than an air marshal. Back at Parramatta, Natalie swanned through high school, getting average marks in everything but boys' attention, where she was dux of parties. She appeared to have a new boyfriend every week, but Carmel told Matt not to worry:

'Our girl, for all her vagueness, has her feet on the ground and her knees together —'

'You're talking about my daughter —'

Carmel gave him a comforting kiss. 'Don't worry about her. She'll tell me when she loses her virginity.'

'Are you going to ask her?'

'No. And neither are you.'

But each weekend when he was home he kept a watchful eye on Natalie. She, in turn, kept an eye on him, more amused than watchful:

'Dad, I'm no longer seven years old — I'm a big girl now. Put away the shotgun.'

He had to smile. 'It's the National Security attitude I have. You'll come to Mum or me if ever you're in trouble?'

'If ever I'm pregnant, you mean?'

Had he had this sort of conversation with his father when he was Natalie's age? The world, and customs, were galloping past him. 'No, I didn't mean that. But you may find some boys — well, difficult —'

'Dad,' she said, Cleopatra on the Parramatta, 'relax. Boys are easy. Girls are the difficult ones.'

'You mean *lesbians*?'

She went away laughing and Carmel came in and said, 'What joke did you tell her?'

'None. She thinks I'm the joke . . . '

Then Carmel said, 'I think it's time we took Georgia to dinner again. We haven't seen her in months . . . '

So they took Georgia Peal to dinner. She had sold up her house in the electorate and moved to a flat in Milsons Point. They picked her up there and took her to dinner at Level 41.

'I like dining high in the sky,' Carmel told her. 'Matt and I once had a wonderful lunch in New York, where a helicopter came up from *underneath* us and I waved to the pilot over my dessert ... Georgia, you look terrific. What have you been doing to yourself?'

Georgia looked as if she had set out again for the shores of Bohemia. She had not one scarf but several; jewellery gleamed on both wrists and round her throat; she even wore a modest turban. 'I've taken a lover.'

That, for a moment, took the breath out of the Durbans. '*Taken?*' said Matt. 'I can't remember ever being tooken as a lover —'

'Shut up,' said Carmel. 'That's great, Georgia. Who is he?'

'He's a doctor, a specialist, a gynaecologist. He's married, but separated from his wife — she won't give him a divorce. We met in his surgery and one thing led to another —'

'I'll report you to the AMA,' said Matt.

'I reported it to my starched shirt son and his snobby little wife and they're both horrified that I'm taking a lover at my age, as they put it. They think I should stay home and knit my own knickers. I'm only sixty-two and I'm still lubricious.'

'Do you mind?' said Matt. 'I'm in the middle of my vichyssoise.'

'Enjoy it,' said Carmel. 'Not you, darling. You, Georgia. Do you go away for dirty weekends?'

'Every chance we can —'

'I've forgotten what a dirty weekend can be —'

Matt put down his spoon. 'Would you like to hear how I voted in the last Ways and Means bill?'

'Matt, my dear —' Georgia patted his hand, leaning close to him. He could smell her perfume and recognised it as Arpége. Which he would not mention to Carmel later tonight. 'Matt, my dear, I know all about the ways and means of living. I used to tell that to Walter time and time again. You remember that with Carmel and you'll never have any problems. Now finish your vichyssoise.'

'Yes, Ma,' he said and picked up his spoon.

'Are you into the menopause yet?' Georgia asked Carmel.

'I haven't been through the Fontainbleau yet,' said Carmel and told Georgia the joke.

Then Georgia gave up being lubricious and became political. All the years with Walter were still with her, another scarf round her throat. 'How do you get on with your new Leader?'

The new Leader had been a Minister in the team when it had been in power. He was an amiable man from out of the West, highly intelligent but as long-winded as a sirocco. But everyone, including Matt, liked and respected him.

'He's what we want, while we settle down. No friction.'

Back in Canberra things went quiet on the Labor benches. Being neutered, if only figuratively, is sometimes a relief for experienced politicians. Tossing balls continually, especially your own, can be exhausting.

Elsewhere, the world shifted its tectonic plates. A small vicious war was being fought in history's battlefield, the Balkans. In Central Africa hundreds of thousands were being massacred, but they were only blacks and had no oil and the major powers tut-tutted at the Tutus and looked the other way. The Soviet republics, no longer having to be wary of the enemy to the west, began to be wary of each other; crime increased tenfold and the *Communist Manifesto* became a comic book. Across the Atlantic the CIA, under the mistaken idea that Central and South America were southern states of the real America, interfered in politics right down to the tip of Cape Horn. Asian countries became the offshore factories of Western business. China was a giant awakening to disturbing dreams of capitalism. In South Africa, the memories of apartheid were pushed further and further back by a black man who made other, white leaders look small and mean. The world was just repeating itself, but with new characters.

In one winter break Matt took Carmel and Natalie north with him to Cairns. They hired a Land Rover, with the understanding that it could be returned in Darwin, and drove west into the Gulf country. Matt had introductions and they stayed on cattle stations and were made welcome. A senior MP from *Down There*, even from the wrong party, because this was National territory, was welcome. Particularly if he had a good-looking wife and daughter. In the distances between their stops Matt was once again amazed at the vast loneliness. Down south the cities were spilling over, facing land shortage, water shortage and waste problems. Up here empty land stretched away for hundreds of miles.

'Why do people want to live up here?' asked Natalie as they bumped along a rough road with plains and hills stretching away forever on either side of them. Odd-shaped trees mocked these outsiders from Down There; a boab looked like a fat woman turned into a tree, black cockatoos in the hair of its branches. Natalie was in the front seat with Matt and so far had taken all the bumps and discomfort without complaint. 'It's so — so *lonely*. How do people not go bonkers?'

'Everyone has a different idea of loneliness,' said Carmel from the back seat. 'I get lonely sometimes . . . '

Matt looked at her in the driving mirror; she stared back at him. Natalie, if she was aware of the sudden small tension, passed over it. 'I guess so. But up here, so far away from everything, couldn't people get on each other's nerves?'

Matt, one eye on the mirror, got in first: 'There are families down in the cities, six or seven of them in one house, don't you think they get on each other's nerves occasionally?'

Natalie considered that, then nodded. 'I guess so. But I don't think I'll ever be a cattle baron's wife.'

'Cattle *baron*?' said Carmel. 'What about a station-hand or a jackeroo?'

'Phooey,' said Natalie and airily dismissed the plebeians.

They stayed that night at a camp that catered for tourists. The place was full, American Express explorers from overseas. The owner of the camp, an escapee from Melbourne, where, he told Matt, he had felt trapped, introduced the Durbans to the foreigners, who were intrigued that a *politician* would come this far looking for votes.

'Our Congressmen back home, they wouldn't leave Washington, DC, if we didn't hold a gun to their heads. That's why the NRA comes in handy.'

'NRA?' asked Carmel.

'National Rifle Association.' He was a cynic from Cincinnati, a wizened man who, the Durbans learned later, was a violinist with one of the world's best orchestras. 'It has its uses.'

Matt and Carmel escaped, leaving Natalie to hold court, which she did as if born to it. As Matt and Carmel began their walk, the owner's wife, a pleasant plump woman in her thirties, warned them: 'Don't go down by the river. The crocs come out at night.'

'Have you ever lost a guest?' asked Carmel.

The woman smiled. 'Just a leg or two ... No, not so far. We have some trouble with some of our English guests. They think crocs like being patted.'

'The old Empire touch,' said Matt.

He and Carmel walked away from the river, stopped on the edge of the plain that stretched away dark as a dead sea under the slowly rising moon. The mosquitoes had not yet risen to work and the warm air was comfortable on them.

He put his arm round her waist, still slim, and said, 'I get lonely, too.'

She put her hand on his, the one on her hip. 'I know you do. I was just feeling a bit shirty today ... Sometimes I wonder ... '

'What?'

'You're in Opposition again, you may stay that way for another six or eight years, who knows? You're standing still — or sitting still —'

He had thought about it. The light on the hill was now just a flickering candle. 'What would I do if I gave it all up? I'm a political animal, love. A leopard can't change his spots —'

'Don't start quoting clichés at me ... I don't know. You're right — what *would* you do?'

But he had no answer to that. They stayed another ten minutes, enjoying the loneliness because it increased their closeness, then the first shift of mosquitoes began to arrive. They went back to the camp, where an elderly couple from, as they declared, Grand Rapids, Michigan, the Furniture Capital of the World, told them: 'That daughter of yours, you got a treasure there. You got your shotgun ready, Mr Durban?'

'Ready and fired,' said Matt. 'Hit the targets both times. They haven't been back.'

'We've got four sons,' said Mrs Grand Rapids. 'Pains in the butt, each one of 'em.'

'Watch your language,' said her husband, then smiled at the Durbans. 'Her father was a politician, State Assembly. A Democrat. I'm a Republican, so are our sons. Makes for a feisty marriage, forty years of it. I understand you're Labor, Mr Durban. That the equivalent of our Democrats?'

'No,' said Carmel. 'They like to think they're the Twelve Apostles.'

'She's a fascist,' said Matt.

'Women are,' said Mr Grand Rapids and ducked as his wife whacked him. They moved on, laughing, and the wife flung back over her shoulder, 'Take good care of that daughter of yours.'

Next morning, before they left to continue west, Matt took the camp owner aside: 'Do you get any uninvited guests down through the Gulf?'

The owner looked hard at him; then nodded. 'I see what you're getting at ... Yeah, occasionally. Illegal fishermen from Indonesia. Illegal pearlers from Christ-knows-where. Drugs from West New Guinea ... It's open slather up here, Matt. That why you're here?'

'I've been trying for years to get a coast guard service, but they tell me every time there's no money.'

'There's plenty of bloody money for sport —'

'Justin, old man, that's heresy. If ninety-five per cent of the population heard you say that, they'd feed you to the crocs down there in the river ... Well, I'll keep in touch. Some day we may be lucky and have a coast guard service.'

The Durbans moved on, through the Northern Territory and across the Kimberley to Wyndham, made welcome everywhere they stayed. Then they headed north-west towards Darwin, staying this time in several Aboriginal reserves, where the elders told Matt of the intruders who came out of the sea.

'Dunno where they come from,' said one old man, a thousand years of lines in his face. He gave them a gap-toothed smile. 'Not like you white buggers. You come, you stayed.'

'Blame our ancestors,' said Matt and shook the old man's hand. 'What was it like in the Dreamtime?'

The old man's smile widened. 'Better'n now. Where you going this time?'

'On up to Darwin.'

'Good luck,' said the old man and sounded as if he thought they were heading for hell. Certainly not for the Dreamtime.

On the way up the coast Matt took a detour, drove the Land Rover out to the edge of a low cliff, got out and took Carmel and Natalie with him. They stood on the cliff and looked back south-west.

'I was here, exactly *here*, I dunno, twenty, twenty-five years ago. With some blokes from teachers' college. Nothing's changed, not a bloody thing.'

'What's out there?' Natalie waved a hand towards where the sea and sky met.

'We're still guessing,' said Matt. 'This is our frontier. A couple of thousand miles of nothing. Oh, a few small towns, but most of it looks like that. All emptiness.'

'Nobody patrols it?' said Carmel, reading his thoughts.

'Some gunboats from the Navy, some Customs boats, one or two aircraft ... Do they teach you anything at school about this?' he asked Natalie.

'Nothing. Little bits of the geography, but that's all.' She stared down the long coast, with its cliffs and glimpses of deserted beaches, at the sea stretching away, a blue highway waiting for the invaders. Then she looked at her father: 'Does it make us unsafe?'

'It will. Eventually.'

They went on to Darwin, a city as foreign to Natalie as Seoul or Beijing. They stayed two days, Matt given a stiff welcome by the locals, who had not had a good word for Canberra since the national capital had been established. Matt's gladhand got just a nod in exchange; nobody knocked him down, but nobody bought him a beer. Beer louts leered at Carmel and Natalie, but that was as far as the welcome went. Matt turned in the Land Rover and he and Carmel and Natalie caught a cab out to the airport. The cab driver was friendly, but he was from Adelaide, newly arrived, and still had southern prejudices.

As they buckled themselves into their seats on the plane, Carmel said, 'The bonhomie didn't work back there, did it?'

'It's another country. Maybe some day they'll welcome me when I bring a coast guard service to Darwin.'

But back in Canberra two weeks later his report and suggestions were acknowledged by the National Security Minister and then disappeared down the Black Hole of parliamentary papers.

Matt settled back on the Opposition frontbench, put his feet up and watched the light on the hill glimmer more dimly.

2

Then came the Olympics — 'the best ever' said everyone with no reservations. The Games, happening in a Labor State, meant no problem for Matt in the matter of getting tickets; mates look after mates. The PM, not needing a ticket, being a self-proclaimed sports fanatic, attended every event except the tae kwon do — 'too much like a Cabinet meeting', said Tony Casio, with not much to do these days but whet his cynicism. Gold medals were won, then the Games were over, the flame doused and the crowds went home, leaving the huge Olympic complex empty and with a debt that no pole-vaulter could jump:

'But it's all on the altar of sport,' said Tony Casio, 'and where are the heretics?'

'Hush, hush,' said Matt and settled further back on his haunches, now lying almost flat on the frontbench.

The new millennium came in, a word not heard for a thousand years. Old-fashioned economics and books and film scripts were branded as not having the 'millennium edge', whatever the hell that meant. Information Technology companies, perhaps sliced by the millennium edge, began to collapse. Executives of major companies in the US suddenly became bandits, making the robber barons of a hundred years before look like pickpockets. Again history began repeating itself and historians, as ever, proved unshockable.

'What's the millennium edge?' Matt asked.

'You missed it by about two centuries,' said Tony Casio. 'But we'll cover it up.'

'Up yours,' said Matt and mused now that jokes filled in the time.

Then came another election and suddenly Labor sat up, buoyed by faint hopes and some blunders by the Government.

'We can do it!' Matt told Carmel, showing more enthusiasm than he had for over a year now. 'Attack the bastards! Shoot 'em down!'

'You've been looking at too many of those old John Wayne movies,' said Carmel. 'Calm down. How is he in our electorate, Ham?'

'Safe. We may lose a few votes, but not many. Elsewhere —' Ham Jessup shook his head; the crystal ball was clouded, the star charts murky. 'We may pull it off, barring accidents.'

Richard came home on leave and the four Durbans sat around the dinner table, as they had not for months, and discussed Dad's chances. Richard said, 'If you get tossed, Dad, what'll you do?'

'I'm not even thinking about it.' Where did his kids get their lack of faith? He looked at Natalie: 'You're old enough this time to have a vote. Are you going to come and work for me on polling day?'

'No.' Natalie had lost her dream-like quality, had even cut down on her swanning. She was eighteen, about to step into not just the voting booth, but womanhood. 'I won't be working for them, but I'll be voting for the Greens.'

'Watch it,' said Carmel. 'You've just turned my crème caramel sour . . . Yep, it's definitely gone off.'

'The *Greens*?' Matt couldn't believe such treachery. He thanked God she hadn't said the Coalition, otherwise he would have had to kick her out of the house.

'Yes. I'm not a tree-hugger —'

'You're too well-dressed, too,' said Carmel, wondering if she should pour oil on these troubled waters.

'— Labor hasn't done enough —'

Where had this stranger come from? Matt wondered.

'— for the environment. You've planted a few trees, but you still let them chop down old growth. You've encouraged cotton and rice farming, drying up our rivers. Pa O'Reilly told me the cotton farms out at Collamundra have almost dried up the Noongulli —'

'Cotton and rice are two of our biggest money-earners —'

'Why didn't you get them to start growing up north, up where we have plenty of water?'

'They started rice production on the Ord River in West Australia. They forgot about the water birds that came and ate all the plantings.'

'Did they consult the conservationists? They could've told them about the birds —'

'More crème caramel, anyone?' said Carmel. 'You can hand out cards for the Greens, darling, but wear dark glasses and don't tell anyone your name. How are you going to vote, Rich?'

Richard, totally grown up now, grinned. 'I'll vote for Dad. I'm all for his Leader, he's a man for defence.'

'He believes in submarines,' said Matt and made *submarines* sound like *galleons*. 'I'm surrounded by subversives.'

Then, out of the blue, out of the blue Timor Sea, came an election issue that no one had contemplated. Some leaky, overcrowded fishing boats, loaded with would-be immigrants, were interrupted by Navy vessels and all at once the Government had an issue. *Send 'em back!* yelled sixty per cent of the population, all of them immigrants or descendants of immigrants. And Aborigines, all over the continent, blew into their didgeridoos, *send all the bastards back*!

Matt went looking for publicity: 'Sending a warship to intercept some old fishing boats! If we had a coast guard service —'

But he was a voice shouting into a gale; even his Leader said the invaders should be turned back. 'They can't jump the queue' was the clarion cry, while in the northern hemisphere several million refugees milled around looking for the queue. The country went to the polls and the Government was returned. Matt kept his seat, but the margin was now down to danger level.

Mrs Lucastopolous met him outside a polling booth: 'You gotta keep 'em out, Mr Durban! You dunno wherea they comea from — they gotta join the queue —'

It was no use arguing; it was a lost cause: 'Yes, Mrs Lucastopolous, the queue's important —'

He would need to spend more time in his electorate, glad-handing everyone in sight, offering help in all directions.

'You should've encouraged the Greens' support,' Natalie told him.

'Now she's a bloody political analyst!'

Natalie, blood pressure always at a languid level, kissed him. 'You'll survive, Daddy-o.'

Richard rang from the Defence Academy: 'You're still there, Dad — you must be one of the old-timers —' Jesus! 'Some of the guys down here thought you sounded *honest*.'

'Gee, thanks,' said Matt, but had to smile. 'How're things going? You think you'll make the Air Force?'

'I think so.' Richard had never lacked confidence.

'What are the women like at the Academy?'

'Defensive.' Richard could sometimes laugh infectiously. 'Don't worry, Dad. I'm playing the field.'

Matt hung up and turned to Carmel: 'He says he's got a squadron of girlfriends. He's starting to sound like a male version of his sister.'

'Or the son of his father,' said Carmel. 'But you're starting to sound more and more like a parent. Welcome to the club.'

'I dunno why I love you —' He hugged her and kissed her.

'Because, as your dad said, we're *complete*.'

The leader who had led Labor into another defeat was replaced by another leader, a grey-haired, grey-suited man with a grey aura from which no sunlight was reflected. And who would fall short of his own short-comings. The Opposition benches looked ineffectual against a now suddenly powerful PM. Matt sank back on his haunches once again and began to realise that the glimmer on the hill was almost gone.

Out in the real world money had begun to smell; huge firms were suddenly full of holes, bushrangers came back into fashion. Labor, defenders of the battlers, sat up, railed against the robbers, but they were just the voices on the wind. The voters had other things to think about.

Fashion, for instance. Designers and hairdressers began to shave their heads; bald skulls bobbed amongst the crowd like floating cobblestones. Another fashion hit Matt, a man still proud of his head of hair and his smooth cheeks:

'I had to send Tony Casio home the other day to shave. He had three days' growth of beard, said it was the latest fashion —'

'It must make for raspy oral sex,' said Carmel.

'You're getting vulgar in your middle age —'

'It's listening to the young. I'm likely to get vulgarer. At that reception the other night one of your volunteer helpers had too much to drink. He rubbed his gravelly cheek up against mine and almost took the skin off. If he does it again I'll kick him in the crotch —'

'That should rasp his sex ... Love, are we getting out of touch?'

'No-o.' Then she looked at him, taking her time as she so often did. He had learned to live with these pauses of hers, knowing that she did not often jump to judgements. 'Do you want to give it all up, try for something else?'

They were out at Cavanreagh, having come without Natalie. They were here for the christening of Teresa's second child. She had not become the station agent she had aspired to; she had come home and unexpectedly, at least to her, fallen in love *with* a station agent, Colin Hailey, a quick young man who looked as if he wrestled bulls when he wasn't selling them. She was, Teresa told Matt, very happy — 'Just like you and Carmel.'

Now, on the Saturday evening before the christening, Matt and Carmel were sitting out on the verandah of the homestead. There was still light in the sky and down over the paddocks a flock of currawongs flew home, like moving punctuation marks against the pale page of the sky. It was cold and they were both wearing thick sweaters and sat side-by-side under a rug. They still treasured their moments alone.

'I don't know.' He had thought about it, but they had been idle thoughts drifting on another lake. 'I think I would wangle the chair of some commission — but that would still mean going to Canberra. Or I could go on one or two company boards — there are some who think I've got business acumen. But — I dunno —' Again.

Carmel looked out at night that had suddenly descended, looking west to infinity. Thousands of miles as empty as the future seemed to be. Then she said without looking at him, 'Give it till the next election. Then we'll decide . . . '

'Yes,' he said, gazing in the same direction as she, seeing the emptiness. Silence came out of the vast night almost like a pressure against the ears. Fancy taking flight, he wondered how the last man in the world would feel.

She sensed his listlessness. 'Let's have another overseas trip, you must be due for one. We'll take Richard and Nat, take 'em to lunch at the World Trade Center —'

'That'll be the end of next year — I'm not going to New York and those other places in winter . . . This is cold enough.' He moved closer to her, looking for the warmth of her. 'What are you wearing?'

'Two pairs of pants and a hot-water chastity belt.'

'You really encourage a feller . . . '

The christening next morning was a big success — 'Eleven grandkids,' said Eileen. 'How are we going to cut up Cavanreagh between them?'

'They can have eleven boutique vineyards,' said Matt, holding up the Cowra chardonnay with which the newly christened Stephen Patrick Hailey had been toasted.

'I'll come back and haunt the buggers if they do,' said Paddy, a sheep-and-cattleman to his hoofs.

Matt and Carmel went back to Sydney that afternoon and that evening Ham Jessup rang: 'Can you come up from Canberra Thursday evening, Matt, instead of Friday?'

'Why, what's on? Not a two-day surgery, I hope?'

'No, they're opening the new Sunplex development, the biggest thing we've had in years. A shopping mall, offices, apartments —'

Matt knew of it, had seen it as it had been built, but hadn't taken much interest in it; it was a State development and he knew not to wander into *that* territory. 'Sunplex? Isn't that run by that bloke Badon?'

'That's him. You know him?'

'Only by repute.' Developers rarely came to Canberra; they knew where development power lay, with the State MPs. But now was not the time to bring up Luke Jamieson's disappearance and the possible connection of Badon with it. 'Okay, I'll be there. Do they want me to cut the ribbon, make the speech?'

'Are you kidding? Macquarie Street is going to be there in full force, everybody but the Minister for Pigeons. But I'll let 'em know you'll be putting in an appearance. They might give you a cuppa tea. Bring Carmel, she improves your presence.'

'Ham . . . Just why do you think I should be there?'

'Matt, right now our federal image wouldn't light up a dark closet. I think you need to be *seen*.'

'You'd better watch yourself or you'll be back pretty soon in a union office.'

'You need me —' Ham Jessup was laughing, but it sounded hollow.

So Matt came back from Canberra on the Thursday night and Friday morning took Carmel, who did improve his presence, to the opening of the Sunplex complex. Ham Jessup drove them, but they arrived outside the development to no red carpet treatment.

'Around the back to the parking entrance,' said a security guard.

'This is Mr Durban, the Federal Shadow Minister for National Security —'

'You don't have an official invitation sticker on your windscreen,' said the security guard, unimpressed by national security. 'Around the back!'

Ham Jessup was about to get out of the car, but Matt, laughing, leaned forward and restrained him. 'Easy, Ham.

Or you'll have me on Channel Ten for the wrong reasons. Here comes their camera crew —'

Ham Jessup started up the car, drove it round to the rear of the complex and, belligerently, parked it in a *Reserved* slot. 'I could shoot the buggers —'

But Matt and Carmel were both laughing. 'Ham, this is the first time in twenty years it's happened. Let's enjoy it . . . '

Ham looked at Carmel. 'I'm sorry to embarrass you like this —'

She patted his arm. 'It's good training for when we're all retired. Retired and forgotten . . . '

They went into the complex, found their way to where the ribbon would be cut and the speeches made. The area was crowded. 'Like a football match,' said Carmel.

'Glad you could grace us with your presence, Matt —' The State Minister for Development was muscular, bald and gay, something that puzzled the older officials at party headquarters in Sussex Street, old homophobes who wondered what a real man's man, like Jack Lang in the Thirties, would have felt. 'Do you know our good friend Nick Badon?'

Matt had had in his mind's eye the usual caricature of a developer: fat, cigar-chomping, fingers be-ringed. But Nick Badon was small, grey-haired, quietly dressed and not a ring in sight. He had a small, soft voice: 'Mr Durban, I admire you for what you do for us down in Canberra. Always working for the voters.'

'One does one's best,' said Matt, the words like thistle-balls in his mouth. Out of the corner of his eye he saw the State Minister grinning. 'You've done a fine job here, Mr Badon. Any other developments in mind? Apartments down by the river?'

Badon played that one with a dead face. 'That would spoil the view, Mr Durban . . . I admire your stand in Parliament on those poor immigrants up north. I was an immigrant once.'

'Poor?'

This time the stone face cracked in a smile; but only a crack of a smile. 'Absolutely. I washed dishes — isn't that the cliché?'

'You're to be admired, then,' said Matt, almost choking on the two tongues in his mouth. 'Good luck.'

'You, too,' said Badon and somehow it sounded like a curse.

Matt moved away, bumped into the State Minister again. 'How'd you get on with him, Matt?'

'I think he could be sitting on a cartload of bombs and still hold his own at a disarmament conference. How do you suffer him?'

'Isn't that what we politicians are supposed to do? Suffer?'

And the two of them laughed and shook hands and parted and the voters in the big crowd, like zoo visitors allowed in to see the gorillas gambol, said, 'Ain't it nice the way the State and Federal MPs get on so well together?' And somewhere in the ether dead politicians laughed hollowly.

Matt went back into the crowd and found Carmel looking for him. 'Let's go home,' he said.

'You upset about something?' She looked around, then back at him. 'Who was that you were talking to?'

'Nick Badon. The bloke who probably paid for Luke Jamieson to disappear.'

She peered through the crowd at the small, quiet man. 'Is that what Menace, with a capital M, looks like?'

'Shakespeare should have lived to see some of our villains. His were always so obvious.'

'Did you teach that to your students when you were at school?'

'Are you kidding? Classes, audiences, like their villains to be obvious. I'll have to watch out for Mr Badon. Ham tells me he donated ten thousand dollars to my last campaign.'

'Did you give it back?'

Matt looked at her as if she had suggested one should pay more taxes. 'Wash your mouth out . . .' Then he turned away to a voter: 'Mrs Lucastopolous!'

'Mr Durban! Thisa lovely lady — she'sa your wife?'

'No, just the girlfriend —'

Carmel whacked him, smiling at Mrs Lucastopolous: 'I'm his wife. He has told me about you. You're moving in here?' She gestured at the mall around them.

'A café. I'm outa fruit, inna cake and coffee. My son Andrios, he's gotta thing —'

Matt escaped, left Carmel to listen to Mrs Lucastopolous. He moved amongst the crowd, suddenly felt unrecognised, a stranger amongst his own. But these were not his own: they were the strangers, power brokers from another kingdom. He was a Federal MP, a Shadow Minister but — of what? National Security. And where was the money and the influence in that?

He went back into the crowd, found Carmel again. 'Let's go home —'

'You look tired —'

'I am,' he lied.

They went home, had lunch and went to bed, where everything was as usual as usual.

3

It was a midweek morning and Matt was still asleep when the phone rang. Even as he groped for it, he was thinking bad news: Natalie or Richard had been injured, her mother or father was dead ... 'Have you seen the news?' Carmel sounded incredulous. 'Two planes have crashed into the World Trade Center —'

'The where?'

'New York — the Trade Center, where we had lunch that time ... Turn on the TV, it's on now. Call me back —'

He was wide awake now, the personal fear gone. He got out of bed and switched on the television, which he kept in his bedroom. The images, unbelievable, came up on the screen. For the moment there was no commentary; the pictures were enough. He looked at what was a silent end of a world. Clouds of smoke and dust, like a headlong storm, billowed towards the camera, threatening to burst through the screen and envelop the watcher. He saw people, wide-eyed with fright, covered in dust like resurrected mummies, running towards him. Then a voice came out of the screen:

'There are reports of other planes crashing —'

He switched off the TV. He had not seen enough to have it all explained to him, but the images were so terrible and unreal he knew they would be run again and again throughout the day. Then the phone rang again: it was Richard.

'Have you seen the news, Dad? Jesus, who'd believe it? The guys here are crowded around the TV ... Is it going to mean war?'

'Calm down, mate. I dunno, I don't think anyone would know right now. Don't start thinking you're already in an F-One Eleven ... I'll call you back later when I know more ...'

Then he called Carmel: 'I've seen it — it's unbelievable —'

She was calmer now: 'They say there's a plane crashed into the Pentagon. And another one, they think it was on its way to crash into the White House, it's crashed somewhere in Pennsylvania. Nobody seems to know where President Bush is ... What's happened to the world, darling?'

'I dunno. I should imagine people right around the world are asking that question. The Americans more than most ... I'll call you later in the day, when I know more.'

He showered, dressed, made himself some toast and coffee, then headed for his office, catching a cab and not waiting for Des Lake to pick him up. The cab driver, a Turk, said little, as if he, a newly arrived immigrant, was now an outsider.

Matt paid him off, said, 'Don't worry, Ahmed.'

The driver bit his lip, shook his head. 'Is bad. A guy on the radio, he say it's gunna be a holy war.'

'Maybe,' said Matt. 'Let's pray it's not.'

Every TV set in Parliament House was turned on: saturation images of the bombings. Matt closed the door of his office and, after three calls, got through to Guy Fortague at ASIO: 'What have you blokes got on what's happened, Guy?'

'It's an outfit called al-Qaeda, run by a guy named Osama bin Laden — you'd better get used to his name. He's a Saudi, but he doesn't operate from there. We've had him on our list for some time, but that's all — just his name. The CIA and MI6 have had him on their lists, but they've never been able to pin him down. He's been responsible for earlier bombings, but nothing like that. They think he operates from Afghanistan —'

'With the Taliban?'

'We're not sure on that, but we think they support him —'

Matt began to realise how little he knew.

As if sensing Matt's lack of knowledge, Fortague went on, 'Matt, you'd better get used to what's going to happen. You and your opposite number, the Minister, are going to learn what National Security is all about. Come to me and I'll try to get you everything we learn —'

'How much do you know right now?'

'Two-thirds of five-eighths of fuck-all. You just do your best to enlarge the fractions. I'll be in touch . . . '

Parliament came alive again. The Minister co-operated with Matt, keeping him informed; this was no time for politics. The term 9/11 was suddenly shorthand for a terrible event. Richard graduated and was posted to Amberley in Queensland for air training; he came home one weekend in uniform, a reminder of war to come. It did come: the Americans sent in bombers and troops to Afghanistan; the British and the Australians sent in special units. Matt noted the irony: years before, the Americans had been aiding the Taliban to get the Russians out of their country; now they were bombing the Taliban, demanding that it tell them where Osama bin Laden could be found. But irony weakens patriotism and Matt said nothing.

One Saturday afternoon when Matt was back from Canberra, Natalie brought home the latest boyfriend. She was now a woman, even if only one step inside the door, and more and more of her mother was showing through in her. She no longer swanned, but there was still an occasional airiness in her.

The new boyfriend had a homely face, a change from the handsome sheikhs she had sometimes brought home, and he had the build of a middleweight wrestler. He was not Julian nor Tarquin nor any of the other exotic names that had come to the house: he was plain Bill Jones.

'Mum — Dad —' Natalie was holding Bill Jones' hand, as if to comfort him. 'I'm moving out and moving in with Bill. He's my first true love,' she said and sounded like the dreamy Natalie of long ago.

'Is that true, Bill?' asked Carmel with her usual directness. 'Are you her first true love?'

The homely face had a redeeming smile. 'How would I know, Mrs Durban? I'm taking her word for it.'

'You'd better,' said Natalie, sounding like her mother.

'Then that's good enough for us,' said Matt. 'Where are you going to live?' He didn't want his darling daughter living in some squalid room in some shared house.

'Bill has a flat in —' She named an expensive block of apartments on the edge of the CBD.

Matt was impressed, but still cautious. 'What do you do, Bill? What work?'

'I'm an IT consultant.'

A new occupation, on a par with astronomy consultant. 'How much do you earn?'

'Da-ad!' Natalie was shocked.

It was interesting that modern youth believed everything should be out in the open, but didn't believe in direct questioning. Matt was becoming more Victorian by the minute: the period, not the State. He didn't want his daughter working her fingers to the bone for some geek fiddling with a computer. 'Can you keep the two of you, Bill?'

'I think so, Mr Durban.' Bill Jones seemed amused, but was too polite to be open about it. 'I earn between ten and fifteen thousand a week.'

Five times or more than Matt himself earned. Out of the corner of his eye he saw Carmel laughing silently, like Salome when the seventh veil was dropped. He capitulated: 'Okay, you win, Bill. But you can't blame me for being cautious . . .'

'Of course not, Mr Durban. My own dad doesn't believe I earn what I do. He leases a service station and says his income goes up and down with petrol prices.' Then Bill Jones looked at Carmel. 'I'll take care of her, Mrs Durban.'

'I'm sure you will,' said Carmel and moved forward and put her arms round her daughter's first true love, 'and we'll knacker you if you don't.'

Bill looked at Natalie and raised his eyebrows and she said, 'You'd better get used to them. They're unpredictable and sometimes downright embarrassing.'

'Pull your head in,' said her father. 'Bill, are you getting any international business? World trade?'

'You mean the terrorist scare?' Terrorism was now part of the weekly vocabulary. 'Who can bomb the Internet?'

Matt looked at this new breed. 'Isn't there something called a virus?'

Bill Jones looked at his lover's father with new interest. 'Natalie told me you're the Shadow Minister of National Security. Do you think software viruses will be a weapon of war?'

'Yes, I think so.' Matt was no expert yet, but tried to sound like one. The young had to be impressed or they wouldn't vote for you. 'Computers may one day be weapons of mass destruction.' Another new word construction. 'Be ready, Bill.'

Later Natalie came to him and kissed his ear. 'You'll like him, Dad. He's gen-u-ine . . . '

'You're sure he's the one?'

She nodded emphatically; the old dreamy girl had gone — where? 'When were you sure about Mum?'

He considered: 'Not right away. I had to take my time with her — she took her time, too . . .' For a moment he looked back into those dim ages, wondered if the love then had been what it was now. Then he looked at his daughter fondly: 'I hope you're as happy as Mum and I have been. Has he proposed?'

'Yes. It was my choice to try living together first. That's the drill these days. Didn't you and Mum live together?'

'Come to think of it —' He kissed her cheek. 'Be happy.'

He went back to Canberra, where eyes were now turned on the northern hemisphere, more so than for years. The war in Afghanistan was dragging on; the Taliban was supposedly defeated, but an awful (in the real meaning of the word) lot of warlords had been left behind. And Osama bin Laden was still just a six-foot-six ghost in the mountains. The new interest was Iraq and the suddenly revived target of Saddam Hussein. The threat of a big war started to spread like a rapidly growing dark cloud. The Administration in Washington began to beat its drums.

Then in October Natalie rang him to say she and Bill had decided on a quiet holiday in Bali. 'Bill likes to surf and it's cheap. We're going for only a week. You want me to bring you back anything?'

He was not a lover of Indonesia, or at least its military. He had watched its intervention in East Timor and had been pleased, though not vocally, when Australian troops kicked them out. 'No, I don't wear batik or whatever it is they wear. Sarongs.'

'You'd look cute in a sarong. Those Canberra secretaries would rush you. I'll call you and Mum from Bali.'

So off they went and five days later the phone rang in his flat at six o'clock in the morning. It was Carmel, voice shredded: 'I've heard from Natalie. They're okay —'

'What are you talking about?' He was still only half-awake.

'Someone bombed a bar and nightclub — there are two hundred or more dead —'

'Jesus!' He sat up on the side of the bed, feeling the quivering in his chest and belly. 'Nat and Bill are okay?'

'Yes —' Her voice was calmer, but still strained. 'They'd been at the bar, but left about an hour before the bomb —'

'Are they on their way home?'

'No-o . . .' She sounded as if she thought Natalie and Bill had made the wrong decision. 'Bill says he learned first aid at the surf club. He's helping out. So's our girl —'

'If they call again, tell 'em to be careful.' Suddenly, even in his own ears, he sounded pompous, the schoolteacher still beneath the skin. 'I'll call you later today when I know more —'

When he got to his office, driven there by Des Lake, who commiserated with him when told the news, Tony Casio and Doris already had a list of media calls.

'Forget 'em for the moment,' said Tony. 'The Minister asked for you to go around and see him. This is collaboration time, Matt —'

'Sure, I'll do that. But get me Guy Fortague at ASIO, Doris ... My daughter and her boyfriend are in Bali. They missed the bomb by an hour.'

'We'll make something of that —' Tony Casio was already reaching for the phone, his weapon of choice.

'No!' Matt's voice was sharp. 'Wait till I hear from them again. They're working with the rescue squads. I don't want to make capital out of this, no matter how indirectly ... Wait till I've talked to Guy Fortague.'

Fortague, it seemed, had been in his office since six a.m. He sounded tired, as if Intelligence had suddenly become a huge weight. 'It's bad, Matt —'

'Anyone claimed responsibility? Was it Jemaah Islamiah?' Since 9/11 he had been doing his homework on terrorist organisations, had been shocked at the spread of the net of them.

'We hear they're claiming credit — or about to —'

'Guy —' Matt tried not to sound judgemental. 'Didn't you blokes have any idea of what they might get up to?'

'Matt, we pass on what we know to the ONA —' the Office of National Assessments, with which Matt had only a passing acquaintance, despite his National Security posting. 'They make their own judgements. Matt — don't quote me — but I think we all stuffed up.'

'Guy, I'm not going to pass an opinion — this isn't the time for political point-scoring. But I'm worried at the way things are going —'

'Who isn't?' said Guy Fortague, wished him luck and hung up.

Matt put down the phone and looked at Tony Casio: 'How did all this start, Tony?'

Tony shrugged. 'Christ knows. You could name a dozen incidents over the past twenty years that got under the skin of these guys — but who knows?' He shrugged again. 'There were probably terrorists when we were still living in caves.'

'You make National Security sound like a cushy job. Get outta here!'

Over the next few weeks the voters realised they now had terrorism on their doorstep. It was a good time, politically, to be in Opposition; but Matt, wisely, did not joust with his opposite number. Natalie and Bill came home, their rescue efforts leaked, not by Matt, but by media reporters who had rushed in droves to Bali. They had their moment of small glory, taking it modestly, and Matt bathed in its reflection. But then Carmel took charge and the curtain was pulled down:

'You both did wonderfully and we're proud of you. But the media could make a long story out of this —'

'Mum,' said Natalie, 'relax. Are you relating all this to Dad?'

'No, I'm not,' Carmel sounded almost fierce. 'But the media might — and you don't want to make capital out of it, do you?' She glared at Matt as if challenging him.

He held up his hands in surrender. 'No. It's their story, not mine. But the papers and TV these days spend more time looking at politicians' families than they used to. You understand, Bill?'

'Of course —' The young man was relaxed; whatever he had experienced in Bali had left no visible scar. 'All I want is to get back to a normal life —'

'It's not going to be the normal life we used to have,' said Matt. 'Not for any of us. The trick is going to be to act normal — with one eye over your shoulder.'

'Dad, you're exaggerating —' Natalie shook her head at the dramatics of her father. Then she looked at him again, as if remembering what she and Bill had been through: 'No, you're not.'

'No,' he said. 'I'm not. From now on I'm going to be working twice as hard as in the past.'

Then Natalie left them alone, went into the house to help Carmel with lunch, and Matt and Bill sat out on the patio under the grape arbour and sipped beers. Matt looked at the young man and said, 'You haven't talked much about what you saw and did in Bali.'

Bill looked pensively at his beer, like a man deciding whether it was half-full or half-empty. 'No-o. I haven't talked about it with Natalie — that night after the bomb went off, she was helping mums calm their kids, the villagers in the nearby shops. What I can't forget, it's still in here —' He tapped his nose. 'The smell of burnt flesh. They don't teach you that in first aid classes.'

Matt said hesitantly, 'Do you get nightmares about it?'

'No. But sometimes, it's crazy, when I'm in the kitchen and something burns, a steak or something —' He closed his eyes for a moment, then opened them and blinked. Then he said, 'Matt, I'd like to marry Natalie.'

'Have you asked her?'

'Yes. We'd like it as soon as possible.'

'Did Bali bring this on?'

Bill nodded. 'Suddenly it seems that everything might move faster.'

'Good thinking,' said Matt and reached across and shook the hand of the first addition to the Durban family.

Bill and Natalie were married the week before Christmas and went away to Noosa, a safe haven for honeymooners. It was a quiet wedding, Natalie's choice; Paddy and Eileen came down from Cavanreagh and Richard came down from Amberley with yet another girl, Charlene (or was it Darlene?) who, Matt guessed, would be replaced by New Year.

The moving staircase started to quicken. On the other side of the world Osama bin Laden was still lost somewhere in the bomb-dust of the Afghan mountains; with him still on the loose, Washington had resurrected the threat of Saddam Hussein. Teams were searching, under UN control, for weapons of mass destruction in the sands of Iraq. But the Bush Administration, not a hive of steady-as-she-goes, grew impatient and then it announced it was sending troops into Iraq to topple the tyrant. With them would be going British and Australian troops . . .

'I can't bloody believe it!' Matt shouted, and Doris closed the door of his office and waited for the tempest to die down. 'Christ Almighty, why *us*? Why not the French or the Germans or the Canadians — the Canadians have a closer alliance with the Yanks than we do —'

'Cool it, boss,' said Tony Casio. 'We've done our poll and there's a slight majority that think we should go with the Yanks and the Brits —'

'I had a friend, an expert —' But Sir Donald, the expert, had died six months ago, gone to another Nirvana and, in the current circumstances, probably glad to be there. 'He said the Yanks never understood the Arabs and never would. And I don't think the PM does, nor his mates. I can't believe there's not someone in the Cabinet who's worried we're heading for a mess —'

'Okay,' said Tony Casio, 'beat your drum, but not too loudly. I've tested the water — you can be accused of being un-Australian. Or anti-American . . .'

'Jesus!' Matt slumped back in his chair. 'Is that going to be the catch-cry? Anti-American, just because one thinks they've done the wrong thing? The Americans revere the Oval Office, the presidency, as they should. But the blokes who move into it are only politicians, nothing more, nothing less. There was one bloke, Chester A. Arthur, when he succeeded Garfield, who'd been shot, reporters went to his mother and said, "What do you think of Chester being President?" and she said, "Chester Who?" There was Harding, who turned a blind eye to the crooks in his Cabinet. And Nixon, a manipulator who'd have stayed in the White House forever if they'd have let him —'

'Okay,' said Tony placatingly, 'but nobody is going to remember them. We have short memories in this country, but the Yanks have shorter ones. I'm your minder and I'm minding that the voters out there are getting out their little flags and starting to wave them —'

A flag was waved from Queensland. Richard rang from Amberley, where he was now well into his training: 'Geez, Dad, I wish I was through the course — this is what I've always dreamed of —'

'Pull your head in. I'm dead against this war —'

Richard's voice suddenly turned more sober: 'I guessed you would be. But up here all the guys are busting to go — this is what we've been training for —'

How to argue with him? 'I know that, mate. But there are just wars and stupid wars — I think this is a stupid war —'

'Dad, Saddam's a tyrant — geez, I never thought I'd use that word! But that's what he is — he's a danger to the world, he's got those weapons of mass destruction —'

'Oh, for Crissake! A feller who's just come back from Washington told me a joke that is going around there. How does the White House know Saddam has got WMDs? Because Rumsfeld has the receipts. That's an American joke, not one of ours. Rumsfeld was in Baghdad in, I dunno, 1988, I think it was, shaking hands with Saddam while American firms were selling chemicals for use in weapons —'

'Dad, you once told me history is a hall of mirrors, that all you see is a reverse image of what happened before —'

Why do your kids have selective memories? 'Yeah, well, there's going to be some cracked mirrors this time ... The Americans don't understand the Arab mind.'

'Do you? How many Aussies understand it?'

'That's the point — we don't. I heard one of Bush's Christian pastors, sitting there with Bush beside him, say that the only way to heaven is through Jesus Christ. How do you think the Muslims are going to take that? Not to mention the Buddhists and the Shintos and Christ knows how many other religions. I've got no time for Saddam, but I also had no time for Pinochet in Chile and the bastard generals in Argentina and we didn't declare war on them. No oil, mate ...'

'I think you and I are going to agree to disagree —'

Now he was talking like a politician! 'Okay, we agree to disagree. But don't try and excuse me to your mates — I'm going to be pretty vocal on this —'

As he was over the next few weeks, but his voice had no effect. Back at Parramatta some voters came to him and said he was right, we shouldn't be going into Iraq, we should stay home and mind our own business; but, and it was Ham Jessup who pointed it out to him, many more stayed away, didn't come with either encouragement or argument. The first contingent of troops left for the war, not many, not more than a token contribution, but the country was now part of what was called the Coalition of the Willing. The PM was photographed farewelling everybody but ferry passengers.

Then the war was over in a month. Television showed President Bush, kitted for the occasion, flying in in a warplane to land on the deck of a carrier and declare the war was won.

'Madison Avenue meets the Pentagon,' growled Matt.

'You want to try that on the *7.30 Report*?' asked Tony Casio. 'And lose another twenty-five per cent of your votes?'

The peace process began. Saddam Hussein couldn't be found and it looked as if he, like Osama bin Laden, had disappeared into the bomb-dust. Then, at last, he was dug out of a hole in the ground and finally the war looked to be over.

'Bullshit,' said Matt. 'It's only just beginning.'

'Darling —' said Carmel; she had come down to Canberra to, as she said, keep him company and throw cold water on him. 'Stop trying to sound like an expert, a clairvoyant. I agree with you, we should never have gone into this war, but it's done and you're banging a drum that's gone a bit slack.'

'I dunno, I seem to spend most of my time down here banging my head against a brick wall, not a drum.'

'You think you're the first MP who's never been listened to? I'll bet MPs have been making that complaint since Federation.' Then she looked around the small living room in the small flat, as impersonal as a railway waiting room. 'Are you happy here?' She gestured around them. '*Here?*'

He knew her too well not to recognise that it wasn't an idle question. 'You mean the flat or Canberra in general?'

'The flat.' She got up and began to walk about the room, though it was a tiny march. She stopped by a photo taken of them on their honeymoon: a beautiful young couple, the sun shining on them as if they owned it. 'Sometimes I think we had more then than we've got now —'

'How long have you been thinking like this?' He felt uneasy.

'I dunno. A month, a couple of months —' She stopped by the door that led into the only bedroom. 'I'm into the menopause —'

'Been through the Fontainbleau?' he said and was instantly sorry. 'I'm sorry — that was stupid . . . Is it affecting you much?'

'I get depressed . . .' She suddenly sat down and, to his surprise, began to weep, moving her head side to side in her hands.

He fell on his knees beside her, put his arms round her. 'Oh Christ, love — why didn't you tell me?'

She shook her head, seemed unable to say anything. He had never seen her like this; she had always been — in *control*. It distressed him more than he had ever felt. He was suddenly hit by the inadequacy that men feel when they realise they can't get inside a woman's emotions, that there are secrets there that men will never penetrate.

He put a hand under her chin, lifted her face and looked into the eyes that were now clouded with tears, more than he had ever seen. 'How can I help?'

'Come home —' It was just a husky whisper, choked in her throat.

'Give up —?' He waved a hand that took in the flat, Canberra, ambition, everything.

She dried her eyes, looked at him, beyond the flat, then back at him. 'Back home I'm there in our house — and it's got bigger since the kids left home — I'm there on my own and you're down here and what have we got? Bugger-all, I sometimes think. A long-distance marriage . . .'

'You think I don't sometimes think like that?'

She studied him a long moment, then she raised her hand and stroked his cheek. 'I'm sure you do ... I'm just not myself. I'll get over it, but sometimes ...'

'I know,' he said and knew it was a half-lie; he *didn't* know, never would, not fully. 'Spend more time down here — we'll work something out —'

She looked around again, this time only at the flat. 'It's like starting all over again —'

'No,' he said gently, 'we've got too much to remember ... Let's go out for dinner.'

She smiled, kissed him, her voice clearer and lighter: 'I thought you'd never ask.'

She went into the bathroom, washed her face, then he saw her looking at herself in the mirror above the wash-basin. She was unaware of him, still out in the living room: there was just herself and her reflection and for a moment he felt he was a Peeping Tom staring at a stranger. She was looking at the reflection of someone only she knew.

He took her to dinner at the restaurant in Manuka that had become his regular eating stop. His usual waitress greeted him with a smile and a second smile even wider when he said, '— and this is my wife.'

'Welcome, Mrs Durban. Your husband is one of our favourite clients.'

'Mine, too,' said Carmel, re-establishing priority rights.

They ordered, then Carmel looked up and across the crowded room. 'Isn't that Bernadette? I thought you said she'd gone back to Melbourne.'

Matt had already seen Bernadette, but had studiously ignored her. 'She did. But that bloke she's with brought her back here as his secretary. He won a by-election, he's new. And not married.'

Bernadette saw them and fluttered a hand across the room to them. Matt just nodded, but Carmel fluttered a hand in reply. 'It's hard to see from here, but I think her bosom's dropped.'

'I hadn't noticed —'

'Not much. But if it ever does drop, she'll need a forklift truck to get it back up again.'

'Are you having milk for starters, pussy-cat?'

The dinner improved the mood between them and they left the restaurant hand-in-hand, the waitress smiling on them like a marriage celebrant. Carmel fluttered her fingers again at Bernadette, who gave a flutter in exchange.

'You're like Catherine of Aragon and Anne Boleyn,' he said, remembering his history.

'I'm not going to lose my head,' said Carmel. 'Bernadette and I understand each other.'

'I thought you were sworn enemies.'

'Not now. I won.'

Back at the flat she came out of the bathroom naked, stood in front of him, chest out. 'Have they started to droop?'

'Actually, I thought they were on the rise —' Then he grinned. 'No, they're as good as they ever were.'

'They're not, but I'm glad you think so.' She got into bed beside him. 'Why are men always so interested in women's tits? Is it retentive, are they still hankering for their mother's milk?'

'When I'm nuzzling you, the last one I'm thinking about is my mother —'

'— in primitive societies the women go around bare-breasted and the men don't get horny —'

'How do you know?'

She ignored that. 'Georgia Peal told me what some of the older women, the ones here in Canberra, used to tell her. A Governor-General, for instance. He used to accidentally —' She made quotation marks with her fingers. 'He used to accidentally brush up against women's bosoms at receptions and garden parties. He was known as the titter that ran through the crowd.'

He laughed. 'Where do you get this sort of dirt?'

'It's all that makes Canberra interesting for wives —'

He kissed her. 'What are you going to be like when you come out of the menopause?'

'Lubricious.'

'Love —' It was more than an endearment, it was his comfort.

Chapter Twelve

1

The end of the war in Iraq was now a joke, a tragic one.

'I can't see an end to it,' Matt told Tony Casio. 'It's just dragging on and the Yanks don't seem to have any idea of how to end it. They're a contradiction — they've organised themselves into the biggest economy in the world, there's never been anything like it, but when it comes to organising a war, a small one, not a major one, they don't seem to have looked even a week ahead.'

He put the same argument to Richard when he and Carmel went up to Queensland for their son's graduation as a pilot. 'Rich, it's a mess, a huge swamp —'

'The Iraqi people are better off —'

'How do you know? I keep hearing from people who haven't been within a thousand miles, five thousand miles of Baghdad —'

'I think we should be increasing our forces there —'

'You're just busting a gut to fly your plane in there. What's it going to be — an FA-Sixteen, not an F-One Eleven?... Rich, I'm not a peacenik, I just think our going in with the Yanks and the Brits was a mistake —'

'Dad, you and I'll never agree on this, so can we forget it? Come and meet my girlfriend —'

'This week's?'

Richard grinned, almost too handsome in his uniform. 'Her father's a banker, just to the Right of Genghis Khan. He's all for the war in Iraq, any war, anywhere. Mum —' He looked at his mother. 'Tell Dad to put away his red flag for the day . . .'

'I should have worn my tiara,' said Carmel.

Richard's girlfriend was Rosemary Blanchflower, all long blonde hair, a model's figure and big blue eyes that didn't seem to have a longer range than beyond her whitened fingernails, which she kept admiring as if they were white diamonds. Her teeth were perfect, her voice was thin and she seemed to have no other interest in the world but herself.

'No wonder he wants to go to Iraq,' said Carmel as they left the girl and Richard. 'If I could fly an FA —' She stopped. 'An FA? Does that mean what I think it means? A Sweet FA airplane?'

'Relax about the girl. She's just his weekly ration. It goes with the uniform.'

And so it proved. When Richard came down a month later on a three-day pass he had with him a black-haired Italian girl.

'This is Rosa, Mum and Dad. Rosa Poncelli, she models lingerie and swimsuits —'

I can believe it, thought Matt. 'A hazardous occupation, Rosa?'

She smiled, experienced in men; Richard suddenly looked like a highschool cadet beside her. 'I carry a gun, Mr Durban.'

'Don't shoot our boy,' said Carmel. 'Where are you staying?'

Richard laughed; it was a good laugh, almost as infectious as his father's had grown to be. There was no sign yet of bonhomie, but it might come in middle age, an air commodore glad-handing Senate committees for more money for Defence.

'Not here, Mum. We're booked into the Sheraton-on-the-Park. We're going on the town tonight with Natalie and Bill. But can we come and have lunch tomorrow? Nat and Bill said they were coming. I've told Rosa what a terrific cook you are. Her father's a chef, you might've seen him on TV.'

'At last count there were ninety-three chefs on TV,' said Matt. 'We must have missed him.'

Rosa laughed, a pleasant sound that probably sounded even better when in lingerie. 'That's what I tell Papa. Have you got a favourite, Mr Durban?'

'Only Nigella,' said Carmel. 'And not for her cooking.'

But Sunday, for lunch, she excelled herself; Nigella, as she said, would have been proud of her. No barbecue for her: it was *coulibiac de saumon* and *poires Grand Véfour*. 'Just something I threw together,' she said, having worked till midnight Saturday throwing it together. *Put that in your pipe, Signor Poncelli, and smoke it*. 'Matt and I had it one evening at the Grand Véfour in Paris. We often have it, don't we, darling?'

'Every second night,' said darling.

Ham Jessup and his wife Jenny, a plain, cheerful girl, had also come to lunch. While Jennifer talked with Carmel and the two young couples, Ham led Matt down to the rear fence of the garden. The fence was festooned with a choko vine, a vegetable from ancient times that Nigella and the other TV chefs had probably never heard of.

'Matt —' Ham and Matt both held a light beer in hand, something probably not recommended by Le Grand Véfour. 'There's a rumour about getting rid of our Leader.'

'That's all it is, a rumour.' Matt sipped his beer. 'Who's going to stand up and oppose him?'

'Why not you?'

Matt looked hard at him. 'At the moment, with all the talk I'm doing about the mess in Iraq, who'd vote for me?'

'I think you'd get more than you expect — public feeling about the war is changing and there are people in the Party who now think you've been right all along. Who'd be your competition?'

'Rebecca Irvine. She'd have all the moderate vote sewn up.'

'Not as many as you think. Give it some thought, Matt. The Party needs shaking up. We're halfway up our own arse trying to outwit the Government and we're getting nowhere.'

Matt looked around him. Was this where political rebellion started, here by the choko vine in the backyard? Did Cromwell start by the Brussels sprouts in his back garden when he plotted against Charles the First?

'Well —' The dream had almost died, the light on the hill gone out. But . . . 'Test the water. Have you got any contacts?'

'Plenty. Keep Tony Casio out of it for the time being — let me do it from here. I'll run up a huge phone bill —'

'Why not e-mail?' Had Cromwell sat down with a quill pen and written to the Roundheads?

Ham tapped the side of his nose. 'It's easy to see you know nothing about intrigue —'

'Where did you learn?' Machiavelli under the choko vine.

'Matt, I came to you from union business. Leave it to me . . . That a was nice fish pie Carmel made.' He had, according to his wife, the palate of a camel. 'You live well —'

'I'll tell her. The white plonk wasn't bad either.' A Loire Sancerre at fifty-five dollars a bottle. All that to impress his son's girlfriend who, in either her lingerie or swimsuit, might be gone next week. 'Let me know how you go with your *intrigue*.'

That evening, after their guests had gone, while they supped on what was left of the salmon pie, Matt said, 'Ham wants to see how I'd go for the leadership.'

Carmel paused with a forkful of salmon and brioche halfway to her mouth. 'Is it on? A challenge?'

'I've heard rumours of it. The livestock are getting restless, as they say. If I declared, it'd be uphill — I'd be running against Becky Irvine and maybe one or two others.'

Outside a thunderstorm had come out of nowhere. The sky cracked and drummed and beyond the kitchen window lightning came and went through thick curtains of rain. Just the night for intrigue. Or to be cut up by Frankenstein ... But his wife was too practical: 'She's got two strikes against her —'

'Such as?'

'She's a woman and she's divorced. If ever we have a woman PM here, she's got to be tougher than any man, a sports lover and as chaste as the Virgin Mary. Rebecca is tough, but as far as I've read, she's had a string of men-friends since her divorce and she's no sports fan, she wouldn't know a cricket ball from a basketball. Right?'

'Right. But she's as tough as Maggie Thatcher was and if she's had so many men-friends, as you say, then she should know how to handle men —'

Carmel laughed, spitting out crumbs. 'No woman can handle crowds of men — even Boadicea had trouble —'

'Catherine the Great handled them —'

'By taking them to bed, a couple a day —'

'Well, I still think Becky will be tough competition. The women will vote for her, those in the Party.'

'And how many of them are there? Not enough ... But don't underestimate your own appeal with the women. Pour me the last of the Sancerre.'

'Can you imagine how that would go down with the voters? A Labor MP drinking French wine ... Ham is going to test the waters, then we'll get Tony in on the act. If they get a good reaction, then I think I'll make a run for it. Will you mind?'

'Darling —' She reached for his hand. 'After all this time, after all the effort? No, I shan't mind. Be a Leader.' There was a tremendous clap of thunder outside. 'There, hear that? De Lawd's on your side.'

'That'll upset George W. Bush — he thinks he's got that market cornered.'

Over the next couple of weeks Ham Jessup came back with encouraging news: Matt was, as Marlon Brando had once claimed, a *contenda.* One day in the House dining room, Rebecca Irvine sat down at his table. They were alone together and Matt was aware of other diners in the room looking at them.

'I hear you're going to run —' Like him, she had been listless and colourless over the past few months. But now she was the old Becky Irvine. Famous for her off-the-cuff remarks, though the cuff had been polished as if it were steel. She was never precipitate, she took her time even to sneeze. 'I hope we can be civilised.'

'I'd never expect anything less from you, Becky.' He had become an experienced charmer.

'Cut out the charm,' she said, but she was smiling; she had been reading men ever since she had discovered there was an opposite sex. 'If we fight fairly with each other, we can get rid of Buggerlugs.'

Everyone in the dining room, eyes sideways, was watching them. Even the waitress hovered like a media hawk.

'If I win,' said Rebecca Irvine, 'you can have any Shadow Ministry you like. Foreign Affairs — how'd you like that?'

'Whatever you offer. I'll do the same for you. How about Minister for Sport? I heard someone say you didn't know the difference between a cricket ball and a basketball.' They were both smiling, much to the puzzlement of the covert watchers.

'I'm very keen on synchronised swimming. Everyone arse-up in the water. Like we've been in the Party the last few years.'

'I think I might enjoy losing to you, Becky.'

'I'll feel the same towards you,' she said and again their smiles locked together, an advertisement for any toothpaste. And the kibitzers in the crowd marvelled at how, sometimes, just occasionally, the Labor Party could breed such friendly enemies.

Joe Rothschild rang from Melbourne and retirement. 'Give it a go, Matt. You've got the talent and the experience. And the Party, for Crissake, needs shaking up. You've been letting the PM and his mob walk all over you.'

'You know how to encourage a feller, Joe. How's retirement?'

'Boring. I've even taken up bowls. It's so different from throat-cutting.'

'I miss you, Joe,' said Matt and hung up laughing. Old-timers like Joe Rothschild were fading from the scene, would soon be just pale figures, maybe even invisible, on the pages.

The reports that Ham Jessup, and then Tony Casio, were bringing back were encouraging: 'The women are for you,' said Ham. 'The voters, I mean. We're not sure about the women MPs.'

'What we're suggesting,' said Tony, 'is that you get out and we'll test the voters. If they're for you out there, then we'll bring that into the Caucus room and press the facts of life to those who are going to vote for Leader. In the end, it's the voters out there in the real world who'll see you as the next PM.'

'I loves youse both,' said Matt and spread his arms, an offer they refused. 'Shall I gird my loins?'

'You'd better,' said Tony. 'I can't remember an MP who got in on a bare dick.'

'I can remember one or two who got tossed out for it,' said Ham and the three of them leered like celibate deacons.

Then one day Doris appeared at the doorway of Matt's office. She always looked as if she owned that space. 'A lady to see you, Mr Durban,' she said and stood aside to let Fleur Tan come in.

Matt jumped out of his chair, crossed the room and hugged Fleur. 'Where have you been? We haven't seen you in ages!'

'I've been up in Brisbane, I'm with the ABC now. Radio. I've just been posted down here. I'll be interviewing you —'

'Doris, you remember Fleur ... All my pigeons, the nice ones, are coming home to roost.'

Doris, whose last show of respect had been to her kindergarten teacher, raised an eyebrow to Fleur. 'That's all we are — pigeons.'

'But the very best,' said Matt. 'Bring us some coffee, Doris, and go easy on the arsenic in mine.'

'A comic,' said Doris to Fleur and went out.

Matt seated Fleur, then went round behind his desk. He had real affection for this small Asian girl and he could not have been more pleased at the fact she was climbing the ladder. 'Are you enjoying it?'

'Loving it,' she said and he could see the confidence in her. There was a toughness in her that she had brought with her from the fields of Asia and it was coming to her advantage. 'You politicians love the TV, the doorstop thirty-second interview — you can dodge all the difficult questions, get by with blah-blah-blah —'

'Fleur, you are in a politician's office right now,' he said with a grin.

'In radio we get you to sit down and really talk. Answer questions.'

He was still grinning. 'You going to ask me questions now?'

'No, Matt ... Well, yes. You're running for Leader of the Party?'

Then Doris came back with the coffee and biscuits. 'Real coffee, Fleur, not instant. I had to wean him off that ... You look well.'

'You, too, Doris. Is he keeping you busy?'

'He thinks so —'

'Would you two like me to leave the room?' asked Matt.

'Always the same,' said Doris to Fleur, dismissing the boss. 'Drop in on your way out and I'll give you the real dirt.'

She went out and Matt said, 'I couldn't get by without her. You should do a piece some time on the women who keep Canberra on the rails.' Then he looked at her and said, 'So?'

'So you're running for Leader? Speaking of women, how does Carmel feel about it?'

'She's backing me.'

'Should I put *my* money on you?'

'Off the record, yes.' Then he shrugged, sipped his coffee. 'You know how it goes. Someone changes his mind at the last minute.'

Then Fleur suddenly stopped smiling, sipped her coffee, looked as if she didn't care whether it was instant or not. 'Matt, I've heard rumours ... '

'Rumours?' They were heard on every change of the wind in this city. 'What about?'

'Past history. Yours. Someone trying to dig up the dirt on you.'

He frowned. 'What, for instance?'

'I'm not sure. I tried to find out, but when the guy who mentioned it to me found out I'd once worked for you, he clammed up. But whoever they are, they are at work on you. Have you got any secrets?'

'Am I being interviewed now?'

'No. This is just friends together.'

'I apologise, Fleur — I shouldn't have asked that, about being interviewed.' She had looked hurt and he would never want to do that to her. 'No, I've got no secrets —' Then he changed his mind: 'I once knew a girl back in Collamundra who was murdered, but I was never under any suspicion. They charged a bloke, someone from the town, I knew him, but he was acquitted and the murder was never solved. Why would they drag that up?'

'Matt, you know what it's like these days. We're not as bad as Fleet Street, but we're heading that way ... If I find out any more, I'll let you know. Give my love to Carmel. How are Richard and Natalie?'

'Living their own lives — which is good.' She nodded and he went on, 'Do you want to do an interview with me? I've got the time —'

'Not today. This was just a social call ... '

They talked for another five minutes, then she rose to go. He noticed she was much better dressed than she used to be, had a quiet assurance that made her seem older. 'If you get to be PM at the next election, could I come and work for you?'

'Of course.' He rose, put his arm round her. 'You and I were a good team.'

'So were Carmel and I at the old *Gazette*. Seems such a long time ago ... '

She left and he went back to his desk and sat there pondering. Then Tony Casio came in and Matt said, 'Tony, Fleur Tan has just been in. She tells me someone is trying to dig up dirt on me.'

Tony didn't look surprised; he had spent half his life in excavations. 'That's par for the course these days. Have you got any sins you haven't told me about?'

'None that I can think of ... Where do they spread this dirt when they dig it up?'

'On the Internet, mainly. That's the equivalent of the backyard fence these days. I'll keep an eye out ... '

'Do that,' said Matt and put the matter out of his mind as he left for a Caucus meeting where dirt was just a joke between friends.

But when Matt went home at the weekend Natalie and Bill Jones were at the house, both looking perturbed. Carmel said, 'They have something to tell you —'

'You're pregnant?' Matt looked at Natalie.

She shook her head. 'Not yet. Why, do you want to go into the Lodge as a grandfather? No, Bill has something to tell you ... '

They were all out under the grape arbour again; it seemed to have become the village green for meetings. Sunlight streamed through in soft rays like a benediction: the meeting place for gentle family discussion. Carmel and Natalie were sipping white wine, Matt and Bill light beers. All very relaxed; but ...

'Have you heard of a website called Scorn?' asked Bill.

Matt shook his head. 'Don't be offended, Bill, but I hardly look at what's on the computers. I leave that to Tony Casio and Ham.'

'Well, they'll probably pick it up —' Bill took his time. Matt could see him in front of a computer screen, deliberate and error-free. 'Scorn is run by a guy out of Brisbane. Up till now he's been pretty harmless, just relaying gossip most people have seen in the newspapers or heard on radio. But now ... '

Matt paused with his glass halfway to his mouth. 'Now?'

'He's asking why you were connected to two murders. A girl you knew in Collamundra and that woman MP down in Canberra ... '

Matt somehow swallowed his anger, looked at Carmel. 'Has the bastard mentioned you? Somehow dragged you into this dirt?'

'No.' She looked worried for him; she put down her glass and reached across to take his hand. 'Can't we just ignore it?'

'I dunno.' He looked at Bill, who was uncomfortable at what he had had to tell. 'Can you be sued for this sort of crap? Would it come under the head of libel?'

'I'm no legal expert, but I don't think so. He just asks questions ... Here's a transcript I took.' He handed Matt a sheet of paper. 'See for yourself. He's not accusing you of anything. Just asking questions.'

Matt looked at the paper; Ruby Rawson and June Herx were both mentioned by name. He read: *On both occasions Mr Durban was well acquainted with the dead women and was interviewed by State and Federal police. Both murders have not been solved, but are still on the books ...*

'It's just mud,' said Natalie, 'but mud sticks.'

'I'll have Tony look into it ... Thanks, Bill.'

'I can't say it's my pleasure. But —' He waved a shy hand. 'We just want to see you there in the Lodge.'

Natalie got up and kissed the top of her father's head. 'I hope you'll invite us down there when you and Mum are in the Lodge —'

'There's some way to go yet,' said Matt and was suddenly aware of potholes in the road.

When Natalie and Bill had gone, Matt and Carmel sat on in the dying light beneath the arbour. Carmel was silent and at last he said, 'Are you upset at this dirt?'

'For you, yes. These days, they twist things so much —'

'Becky Irvine won't do that. It's been a clean fight between us so far ... I just don't want you touched by all this.'

She picked up his hand, bit the knuckles, an old habit. 'I love you.'

'If ever I meet the bastard on this website, I'll tell him.'

'Try not to worry too much about it. From now on, whether you get to be Leader or even Prime Minister, they are always going to be gunning for you.'

'You sound cynical —'

'No, darling. I've just come to know what it's like.'

He went back to Canberra on an early morning flight, got in touch with Fleur as soon as he was in his office: 'Fleur, do you still have some contacts in Brisbane?'

'Yes. This is about what's appearing on Scorn?'

'How'd you guess? Yes. Can you have someone check where this bastard is getting his dirt from? Someone's feeding him.'

'I'll be back to you, Matt —' As she hung up he could hear the concern in her voice. He had more friends than he had enemies, but wondered if that was enough.

As he put down the phone Tony Casio came into his office. He was now clean-shaven, fashion out the window for the time being. 'Boss, we go down to Melbourne tomorrow —'

'Did you know about the dirt that's been on a website about me?'

Tony nodded. 'I was going to bring it up . . . A guy from the *Age* phoned me Saturday morning. It's dirt, Matt, but we can hoover it out of the way.'

'I'm not so sure. There's nothing to it but innuendo, but that's often enough. I wouldn't be the first politician who's gone down under innuendo.'

'Okay, I'll look into it. In the meantime, here's your schedule. Tomorrow down to Melbourne, give the Victorians a look at you, since that's where Becky comes from. Then Thursday we head west out of Sydney, giving the voters in the Blue Mountains and Bathurst a look at you. We'll finish up at Collamundra — future PM comes home. Then it'll be back here on the Monday for the vote in Caucus. My tip is that you'll toss Becky by about four votes . . . '

'It's going to be close. It might be the other way around if Caucus has been listening to that dirt.'

Two hours later Fleur rang: 'Why didn't we guess? The Scorn creep is getting his feed from another creep. That guy Urling, who was Nick Badon's dirty tricks man. Still is . . . '

Matt gestured for Tony to pick up the extension; then he said, 'Can we prove that?'

He saw Tony shake his head and Fleur said, 'Not a chance, Matt. They're paying him and he'll swear blind he's never heard of Nick Badon.'

'Okay, Fleur, and thanks very much. I'll be in touch —' He hung up and looked at Tony Casio, who, for the first time, looked as if he might be worried. 'History never dies, does it? Not even small history. That bugger Badon has been carrying his grudge all these years.' He had told Tony of the fight over the riverside development and the disappearance of Luke Jamieson. 'This is when I wish we had a Praetorian guard that I could send out to run a sword through the bastard.'

'The old ways were the simplest,' said Tony regretfully, suddenly looking Roman, though his family came from the Dolomites, once a place for warrior tribes who were never devious. 'Well, in the meantime we forget him and the Scorn shit merchant. Melbourne is getting ready to shake hands with you —'

So Matt went down to Melbourne, gave them subdued bonhomie, since the southern capital prided itself on its moderation, except for its gangsters. Local party stalwarts told him they would vote for him, but with their fingers crossed behind their backs, just in case. Matt told them that

Melbourne was still the hub of the universe, his own fingers behind his back, and they agreed with him. He went back to Sydney, hoping he had done all he could to get the nomination as Leader.

Next morning he headed west.

'We've got the ABC and Channel 9 to lend us their presence for a coupla days,' said Tony Casio, who could have rounded up stormtroopers if they had been required. 'And the *Sydney Morning Herald* are sending a guy. Two days of saturation coverage, Matt, shaking hands, reading fairytales to the kids, talking to oldies in retirement homes like their favourite grandson, spreading the bonhomie as wide as you can . . .'

'Tony, I think you're becoming cynical at last —'

'Heaven forbid!' said Tony and tried to look innocent.

The Blue Mountains towns didn't hang out any bunting or flags for Matt, but the voters he caught in the streets were polite and wished him well. Those in Bathurst were more interested and asked him questions about what Labor would do for rural communities, especially them, and he glad-handed his way through promises he hoped he could keep, if and when the time came.

Then the tiny caravan moved on and there, at last, though unexpected, hanging between the trees outside Collamundra, was the big calico sign: GOD IS OKAY — MATT DURBAN BLESSED HIM.

He was home, back where it had all begun.

2

Matt had just started the engine when the unmarked police car pulled across in front of him and Wally Mungle got out. Matt hesitated, then he switched off the ignition and got out of the Ford. He glanced back up to the cemetery: Bert Carter was now on his knees beside Ruby's grave. It was impossible to tell at this distance whether he was praying or just pulling out weeds.

'Wally —'

'How's Carmel?'

'She's fine. I'm going out to pick her up, she's coming in on the morning plane. We're going to have a coupla days' rest before I go back to Canberra for the stoush on Monday.'

'Good luck.' Then Wally Mungle nodded up towards Bert Carter. 'He comes out here every week, sometimes twice a week. How was he with you?'

'Okay. Awkward at first, but I couldn't blame him for that. I hadn't seen him since — well, since before his trial. He's still grieving for Ruby, after all these years.'

'Yeah —' Wally had always had a quiet personality, often a little unsure of himself; Matt had put it down to his colour in an all-white police station. But now he looked uncomfortable: 'You're gunna run for boss of the Labor Party?'

'That's the idea,' said Matt, wondering what Wally was getting at. 'It's a toss-up who'll win . . . How's your mum?'

'She died —' He put his hand on the fender of the Ford, as if testing the paint. 'Two months ago. Nothing serious. She just give up and died.'

'I'm sorry to hear that, Wally. Really. She was a good woman.'

'Yeah —' He had been looking at his hand on the fender. Now he raised his gaze, seemed to straighten up as he faced Matt. 'One of the blokes at the station told me you been getting some shit on the Internet.'

'Muck-raising, Wally, that's all. There's no substance to it, it's just a bloody nuisance.'

'Yeah ...' Again he looked uncomfortable. He looked away, nodded up the hill into the cemetery again. 'He's still there. Every week.'

'So you said —' Matt looked at him: what favour was Wally going to ask him? 'Something on your mind, Wally?'

Wally Mungle looked back at him, seemed to take a deep breath. 'Yeah ... Matt, I talked to my mum just before she died. She had all her marbles, it was as if she was trying to settle everything before she went ... She told me something —' He straightened up again. 'Remember she used to watch you guys from the town, you'd come out there along the Noongulli with your girls?'

'Yes —' Matt felt a sudden silence come down out of the cemetery; or was it his imagination? 'Yeah, you told me —'

'The night Ruby was murdered —' He stopped and nodded up the hill, as if he was hoping Ruby would hear. Or Bert Carter. 'She saw Ruby's car — remember, the silver Mercedes? Her old man's?'

Matt nodded, said nothing.

'Mum said she saw who was with Ruby that night. It was a woman.'

Somehow Matt managed to say, 'Why didn't she tell the police?'

'You know what my mum was like. She said it was white fella's business. That was how it was with her, always. White fella's business.'

'She'd have kept quiet, even if Bert —' It was his turn to nod up the hill. 'Even if Bert had been found guilty?'

'No, I don't think so. She knew Bert, like she knew you —'

'Who was the woman, Wally?'

This time Wally Mungle's deep breath was like a sigh: 'Mum used to go to Dr Hennessy's surgery once a month to get her pills ... '

3

'Why didn't you tell me?'

He had left Wally Mungle and driven out to the airport, driving in a fog of shock and despair, like a drowning man who sees the shore receding. Out along the main road the big calico sign proclaiming Matt's blessing of God had disappeared; God had gone, not wanting to be any part of Matt Durban. Ribbons of Catholicism wrapped themselves round him. He uttered a prayer as he turned the big Ford into the tiny airport and he saw the twelve-seater plane coming in to land.

Matt got out and stood by the exit gate and watched as Carmel came down the steps from the plane and came towards him. A stranger: he was looking at her as if seeing her for the first time. She was wearing an Italian knit suit, a Missoni she had told him, carried a coat over one arm and had a small suitcase in the other hand. She was still beautiful, still had men, and women, look at her. She looked, as they say, a million dollars; but then, a million dollars was no longer worth what it had once been. She was his one true love and now he wondered if he had ever truly known her.

They kissed and some of the other passengers recognised him, smiled and thought how lucky he was, and how lucky were they, that some time this year their local boy might be Prime Minister.

He took Carmel out to the car, they got in and she said, 'You're quiet. Things not going well?'

'Well enough. A good trip?'

'Cramped. I don't know how people with big bums fit into those seats.'

He took the car out of the airport and on to the main road back to town. He played the careful driver, concentrating while other drivers came out of the parking lot, all eager to get home to reunion, lunch, love. Once out on the road she said again, 'You're quiet.'

'Yes,' he said and turned off at the side road, now gravelled, that ran down to the banks of the Noongulli and the Aboriginal settlement. He brought the car to a halt, doing everything deliberately: switching off the ignition, putting on the handbrake. Switching off everything . . .

'Why didn't you tell me?'

She looked at him, no puzzlement, just a steady stare. Then she looked out at the settlement and the red gums along the river, then back at him. 'What?'

'Why did you kill Ruby Rawson?'

She didn't flinch; it was as if she had been expecting this blow for years. But there was a sudden stillness in her; she didn't move, but he had the feeling she had slid away from him. 'She tried to kill me —'

He shook his head; not in disbelief but like a man coming out of water. 'For Crissakes — why didn't you tell me?'

She was still distant, no attempt to reach out a pleading hand to him. 'How do you know what happened?'

'That's it!' Anger was taking hold of him and he didn't want that. 'I don't bloody know! Wally Mungle's mum saw you that night — she saw Ruby come down here in the silver Mercedes — she saw you jump out of the car and run away —'

'Who told you this?'

'Wally — less than an hour ago —'

'What's he going to do about it?' She was still distant, but he recognised now that this was her way of keeping control of herself. He had seen it before and admired her for it. But now it angered him.

'Nothing — he told me to talk to you first . . . Jesus, love, why have you kept it from me all these years?'

Then, suddenly, she broke. She put her face in her hands and began to weep, silently but with her shoulders heaving.

He reached for her, but she still didn't come to him. His hand rested on her shoulder, an almost impersonal touch. Out of the corner of his eye he saw two women and a man come out of a house on the edge of the river and stand staring at them. But they didn't approach, not into white fella's business.

At last she raised her head, dried her eyes, looked suddenly like the woman he had known for so long. She swallowed, got control of herself.

'She tried to kill me, that's the truth ... She was waiting for me that night when I came out of Dr Hennessy's. She said to get in her car, she wanted to talk to me. I dunno, I really don't, why I didn't turn my back on her ...' She stopped, stared out at the two women and the man, all three as still and unmoving as tree trunks.

'Go on,' Matt said and even in his own ears he didn't sound encouraging.

She looked back at him, frowning, as if wondering whether it was worthwhile going on. Then she said, 'We drove out here and then she started in on me, about my stealing you from her, that you were hers and nobody was going to take you away from her. Then —' She paused, swallowed again. 'Then she took out that nail-file of hers, that bloody long stabber, and swung it at me. She was berserk, that's the only way I can describe her ...'

'I still don't understand — you could have told me, I'd have understood then ...' But at the back of his mind, the rat in reason, was the doubt. Would he have understood back then?

'Darling —' For the first time she put her hand on his. 'I wasn't sure — I really wasn't — that I was the one you wanted. You know what your reputation was — before Ruby you had a team of girlfriends —'

'None of them meant anything — I told you that a dozen times —'

'Yes, you did. But you'd gone off — you asked me to marry you, but I still wasn't sure you meant it ... I'm not blaming you. But if I'd told you, would you still have married me?'

He didn't answer that, because he could think of no answer. He had been a different, a much younger man back then; could he remember now how he had thought twenty-five years ago? He, too, looked out at the three Aborigines, then he looked back at her.

'If Bert Carter had been convicted of her murder, what would you have done?'

She looked straight at him. 'I asked myself that all the time he was on the charge. And each time I told myself the same — I'd have gone to the police.'

'Tell me exactly what happened.'

'I don't think you are believing me —'

'I am,' he said and pressed her hand. 'Tell me. Exactly.'

'How can I tell you *exactly*? It was — what? — twenty-four, twenty-five years ago ...' She closed her eyes, as if that old scene might be there on the inside of her lids; then she opened them and went on: 'We were arguing — or she was. That you were hers, not mine ... Then, all of a sudden, she had that nail-file, I'd never seen it before, in her hand, she — she lunged at me. I dunno how, but somehow I managed to grab her wrist ... ' She stopped, didn't seem to be breathing; then she took a deep breath and continued: 'We fought there in the front seat of the car, then she was on top of me, she was really out of her head ... I'm not sure what happened next. I still had hold of her wrist — I must have turned her arm or something ... It went into her chest — I can still see the look on her face, after all this time ... Suddenly she was — *frightened*. She fell back behind the wheel and it was, I dunno, five minutes at least before I could bring myself to check that she was dead.'

He was trying to picture the scene; but all the violence in movies and on television doesn't educate one in the real thing. 'What did you do?'

'Just sat there — I was, I guess, I was paralysed. Then, and I know this sounds cold-blooded, I got out my handkerchief and wiped where I thought there might be fingerprints of mine —'

'Jesus!' He was shocked. Then he wondered what he would have done. Maybe all the fake crime on television was a primer after all.

'I know — it makes me sound like a real murderer. But I did it. Then I got out of the car and went up the track — remember it was just a track in those days — to the main road back there.' She nodded back over her shoulder. 'Fortunately, I was wearing flatties — I threw them away a couple of days later, somehow they were a reminder ... It started to drizzle and I walked all the way back into town. Every time I'd see a car coming, I'd lie down in the grass. I was wet through by the time I got back to town and the ute. Then I drove home ... '

'What did you tell your mother and dad?'

'Nothing. They had gone over to Orange to some farmers' meeting. By the time they came home I was in bed, pretending to be asleep. I didn't sleep, you've got no idea how I felt ... I'm not a murderer, Matt.'

He believed her; he touched her cheek. 'I know that, love. But why did you keep it bottled up inside you all these years? That I just don't understand —'

'I don't know. There were times ... The longer you keep a secret, the more secret it becomes. As if you are burying it deeper ... A couple of months ago, when I was feeling pretty low about the menopause, I almost broke down and told you ... What are we going to do?' She looked at him despairingly.

'Well, first —' He bounced both hands on the steering wheel. Over by the red gums the man and the two women were still there, like jury members waiting to be called. 'Wally Mungle is up on the main road. I promised him I'd let you tell your story . . .'

'Oh Christ —' For a moment it looked as if she would refuse. Then she shook her head. For the first time he noticed the grey hair in the black; or was it imagination or a trick of light? 'No, I understand. Let's go —'

He turned the car round, looked in the driving mirror as he drove away. The man and the two women were still standing there, dark statues, unmoving. But somehow judgemental.

Wally Mungle was waiting for them where the side road joined the main road. He got out of his car as Matt pulled the Ford in behind it. Matt switched off the engine, took a deep breath. 'Just tell him what you told me.'

'Will he want to take me into the station? I can't face anybody else — not yet —'

'I don't know. I don't think so . . .'

They got out, Carmel shook hands with Wally and the three of them stood a moment in silence. Then Matt said, 'Carmel has told me what happened. Now she'll tell you . . .'

Two cars went by, horns blowing; hail, hail to Matt Durban! Wally looked at Carmel, as uncomfortable as if he were the one to be charged. 'What happened, Carmel?'

She told him, flatly, almost calmly; her story didn't deviate from what she had told Matt: 'I didn't kill her in self-defence, Wally. It was an accident . . .'

'You should have reported it.' But Wally said that as if reading from the police manual.

'I know. I didn't and I've lived with it all these years —'

There was a long silence. Another car went by, no horn-blowing this time; but two children in the rear of the car looking back, faces pressed against the window. *Who's that, Dad? Why's he talking to that Abo man?* Then a semi-trailer, loaded with cotton bales, went by like metal thunder. Then there was silence but for the distant croak of a water bird down on the river.

Then Matt said, 'Well, Wally, what do we do?'

Wally said, 'Carmel, if Bert Carter had been convicted, would you have come forward then and told your story?'

'Yes,' she said without hesitation.

'Good.' He looked away from them, obviously ill at ease in the situation. He, the man in the middle of white and black, was being asked to be judge and jury. Then he looked back at them, seemed to gather himself: 'It was a long while ago . . . Like my mum said, white fella's business.'

Matt felt the tears in his eyes. He put out his hand, shook Wally's. 'Thanks.'

Wally Mungle nodded again, shook Carmel's hand, said nothing till he had walked back to his own car. There, he paused and looked back at them: 'There's that guy with his muck-raking on the Internet. You better watch out for him . . .'

He got into his car, a little hurriedly as if he wanted to be gone before he changed his mind, waved to them, then swung out on to the main road and headed for town.

Matt and Carmel stood a while; it suddenly struck Matt that they were standing by the trees from which the big calico sign had been hung. Though it was only a day ago, it seemed that a lot of water had flowed down the Noongulli since then.

'We'll keep it to ourselves —' said Matt.

'Whatever you want.' She was standing apart from him: like one of his students of long ago. 'Now I've got it off my chest at last . . . Do you want to tell Richard and Natalie? My parents?'

'No. No, it's our secret — and Wally's.' He was surprised at his own sudden vehemence, but he had been making decisions for the past twenty-odd years on matters affecting other people; now he was deciding on their own future. 'We'll think about it and talk about it over the weekend — I've got two days off —'

'What about what the scum on the Internet is saying? Could they dig up more that would hurt you?'

'Where from? Who do they talk to — Wally? But —' Scorn, well-named, lay there beyond the horizon.

They got into the Ford and looked at each other before he turned on the ignition. Her eyes had a faint veil of tears: 'Do you still love me?'

'I've never stopped,' he said. 'I never will.'

She leaned across and kissed him on the cheek, said nothing but it was all there in her silent lips.

4

They drove on into town where Des Lake, Tony Casio and Ham Jessup were waiting to take the Ford back to Sydney. The tiny media caravan had gone out on the early morning plane, the Durban odyssey already just jottings in their notebooks. The *Sydney Morning Herald* man had filed his piece last night and it had been in this morning's edition, though the papers had come in only on the plane that had brought Carmel. But Tony had read to Matt what the *Herald* man had written: *Matt Durban has the approval of voters, including many who will vote for the Coalition, but whether he or Rebecca Irvine, whoever becomes Labor's Leader, will have the clout to oust the PM is a toss-up*. Matt had not been impressed. Lukewarm is not a water politicians like to bathe in.

The three men greeted Carmel warmly; they liked her for herself and, particularly, because she was so easy to sell to the voters. She had regained her poise and Matt, standing off, looking at his wife as he had not looked at her before, a stranger whom he knew intimately, had to admire her.

'You're quiet, Matt. Something on your mind?' Tony Casio could read changes in the wind better than any weather forecaster; Matt had once remarked that Tony could see the changes in a statue's expression. 'Everything's gone well —'

'I'm just doing some homework ... I'll talk to you tomorrow night.'

'Sure ... Well, enjoy your rest. Nice seeing you again, Carmel. It'll be even nicer seeing you in the Lodge come October.'

'I'm looking forward to it,' said Carmel and again Matt had to admire her composure.

The three men got into the Ford, Des Lake started it up and they drove away down the main street, swinging round the iron digger still guarding the town against invaders from the coast, then they were gone from view. Carmel watched the big car go, as if it were a film ending, then she turned to Matt:

'How do we get out to Cavanreagh?'

'Your dad's coming in for us. Here he comes now ... '

Paddy O'Reilly kissed his daughter, whom he didn't know, though he didn't know that, and patted Matt on the shoulder. 'Last night went well, you made an impression. But you need a coupla days' rest. You look buggered.'

'It's been a tough week. Sometimes —' He stopped, seeing Carmel turn back as she was about to get into the ute.

'Sometimes what?' said Paddy, getting into the cabin, not really interested.

Matt shrugged, waved a dismissive hand and got in beside Carmel. He could feel the warmth of her body and, even though she looked at ease, he suddenly knew she was sweating inside.

They drove out to Cavanreagh, the paddocks stretching away on either side of them, pale brown like shores from which the sea had receded. The sheep and cattle stood in tight clusters, as if seeking strength from each other, and further out kangaroos were as motionless as bent trees.

'Bloody roos,' said Paddy. 'They're fighting the cattle and sheep for grass, what there is of it. This drought is really knocking us this time. And the bastards down on the coast complain because water restrictions stop 'em from hosing their lawns or washing their cars. We're becoming two nations, you know that, Matt? I hope you can do something about it when you become Leader. Or PM.'

'I'll try,' said Matt and felt Carmel press her hip against his, some comfort growing again between them.

They drove up between the avenue of coolibahs and Eileen was waiting for them on the steps of the homestead. She looked at her daughter and said, 'You look peaky.' She sometimes used words that Matt thought had slipped out of dictionaries. 'You in the middle of something? The 'flu?'

Carmel smiled. 'Yes, the Fontainbleau.'

'The what?'

'A joke, Mum . . . '

The rest of the day Matt spent on the phone. He went into Paddy's small office, spread a list in front of him and began soliciting, like a whore, he thought, but smiled at it, feeling no shame. He called Labor MPs as far away as north Queensland and the western shores of West Australia. He was fishing and the lines were long and sometimes there were no bites at the other end. Politicians are nervous of commitment in their own party, unless in a body; isolated at the end of a phone line, they tread water cautiously. But when Matt got off the phone at the end of ninety minutes, his ear dead or anyway deaf, he had ticks of commitment against three-quarters of his list.

He sat back. The race with Rebecca Irvine would be close, but he had the edge. But was it enough? He sat there, going through his thoughts as if going through old files. Ambition was there, the file with the biggest lettering; but he ignored it as he looked through the rest of his life, past, present and future. It occurred to him at the same time that he had never done this before.

He looked at the list again. The ticks against the names were enticing: *It's yours, Matt.* He stared at the paper, then he folded it, neatly, and put it in the pocket of his shirt. Against his heart.

In the late afternoon he was sitting out on the verandah when Eileen came out and sat beside him. There were only traces of what she had once been still left in her; she was now in her sixties and the signs were there. But the old directness was still there, too: 'What's the matter with our girl? She's not herself.'

Matt looked for an answer, found one: 'She's into the menopause . . . '

Eileen considered that for a moment, then nodded. 'You helping her through it?'

'I'm doing my best.'

'It's a handicap for some women. I got through it like a breeze —' He could see her doing it, treating it as no more than a slight cold. 'But I know a coupla women, it was hell for them. They got depressed — badly — and one of them told me she thought of suicide. I'd have kicked her bum if she'd tried it in front of me . . . '

He laughed, though it was an effort. 'I can see you doing it, too.'

'In some women, it, the menopause, it brings on a chemical imbalance, they call it. Plays hell with their nerves. You think she's building for that?'

'Could be . . . I'll watch out for it. But don't worry, Eileen. She's my girl and I'll look after her.'

'I never thought otherwise.' She stood up. 'You look peaky, too.'

He grinned, loving her for her stability and her efforts to stabilise others. 'I'm going through the Fontainbleau.'

'The where? Oh, that what you call it? Where'd you get that from?'

'A feller told me, a long while ago. He's dead now,' he said and suddenly wished Danny Voce was still alive, to talk to and to advise.

He sat there alone, watching the sun go down behind the distant hills and in the late light the countryside looked softer, less drought-stricken. He sat there staring into space where there was no comfort.

Then he got up, slowly like a man stricken with arthritis, went down the verandah steps and walked, also slowly, down between the coolibahs to the stone gateposts on the main road. He stood there, remembering that it was on this very spot twenty-five years ago that he had first asked Carmel to marry him.

What to do? He had chosen a path before he had met her, but, once met, there was no separating them. Ambition is a blood-disease; he knew he could never rid himself of it. But love, too, is a blood-disease: an agony sometimes, but the pleasure and the comfort outweigh that. The light on the hill would always beckon, but, at the end of his run, would he have got close enough to touch it? The political road is littered with casualties; he had seen many even in his own time. How many people would he disappoint if he turned his back on the light on the hill? Not many: he suffered the isolation of the loner. He would have disappointed Danny Voce and Walter Peal; but they were both gone, safe from voters. Joe Rothschild might remonstrate with him, but he doubted it. Joe was Jewish, a race that knew the agonies of choice.

A semi-trailer went by, lights blazing, like a cruise ship run amok. He remembered one of his father's old records: Roger Miller's *King of the Road*. He looked after the disappearing truck, another king of the road. Then he wondered what his father, that man of quiet advice, would say to him now. Keith had lacked ambition, but he had understood it. He had also understood the power of love. *We were complete*: the echo was clear.

The sound of the truck died away and somewhere in the coolibahs a bird croaked, as if its sleep had been disturbed. Matt stood there in the silence, wanting to weep but dry of tears. If he resigned he would turn his back forever on politics: he could not go on tasting the lure of it. But, as he had begun to realise over the past couple of years, the taste was sometimes bitter.

Then he saw Carmel coming down the avenue, ghostly in the dark. Not hurrying, something she never did. Just coming towards him, as she had out of all the years behind them.

She reached him, put out her hand and took his. 'You've been quiet all day.'

'Thinking.' He took his time. 'Looking both ways, the past and the future.'

'Am I forgiven?' Her voice was quiet, but he could feel her hand digging into his.

'I just wish you hadn't kept it to yourself all those years. As if you didn't trust me —'

'I know —' She looked out into the night beyond the road. 'But I never wanted to hang it round your neck. You've kept secrets from me, haven't you? Small ones?'

He dodged that question, keeping the temptations of the past to himself.

She waited for an answer, then said, 'What have you been thinking while you've been down here?'

He began cautiously, as unsure of himself as of her: 'You said something to me a long while ago. One night at Palm Beach. You said, morning's gone. It's true. It's gone.'

He could see her face only dimly; he could read no expression. But he felt her hand tighten a little more on his.

'It was in another context,' he went on, sounding in his own ears like a politician talking to someone from the press gallery. 'I had illusions, once. No, better than that. Ideals.'

'I remember,' she said; and he felt encouraged.

'But the world has changed, love —'

History, he knew, was cyclical; honesty and selfishness were seasonal. It had all started maybe at the very beginning. When Cain had clobbered Abel he had gone home and lain with his wife (who was she? his sister? his mother Eve? incest in the eastern suburbs of Eden?) and she had begat Henoach and Henoach begat Irad (who with?) and honesty and selfishness and charity and greed came and went . . . But he couldn't explain all that to Carmel here in the deepening darkness. He suddenly realised his decision had to be immediate.

'I could handle the way the world has changed. But I'd feel differently about it. And somewhere down the road I might, because it was politically expedient, do something you wouldn't be proud of —'

'You're looking for another excuse,' she said practically. 'Trying to make me feel better —'

'No —' But he had to be honest: 'Well, maybe. But I'm trying to — I dunno. Rub ointment on my disappointment.'

He heard her giggle at that; her hand relaxed a little on

his. Then she said, 'Don't, darling — please. You're doing it for me and I feel terrible —'

'Never. I'd never want you to feel that because of me.'

Another truck, another blaze of lights, went by and when its sound had died away she said, 'What else have you been thinking while you've been down here?'

He took his time; they were re-building fences: 'Thinking it was here I first asked you to marry me and you said No. Not yet, you said. Was Ruby here with us that night? Her ghost?'

Her hand tightened on his again. 'Yes —'

He waited for her to say more; the silence hung between them like a net. Then he said, 'I'm going to retire. From parliament, from the lot —'

Her hand now dug into his. 'Why?'

'Love —' He turned his head. In the darkness her face was dim, unable to be read. 'Like I said, morning's gone. If I don't fade away, that creep sheet Scorn, with Nick Badon at the back of it, it will sooner or later dig up what happened that night with Ruby. Even though it was an accident, there'll be people who'll have other thoughts. Half the world is always looking for scandal —'

'I don't want you to give it all up —'

'Carmel —' Formal, almost as if she were not his wife, not his love. 'It's not just me giving up something — we don't want Richard and Natalie ever to know ... The fact is, I'm afraid of what shit will come out on that website. We'll find a reason why I'm giving up —'

'Giving up what? Everything? Or just running for Leader?'

'Everything. I'll say I'll retire at the next election —'

'What reason are you going to give?'

'Your health. Your mum has given me an idea ... Some women suffer depression quite badly from the menopause, there's a chemical imbalance —'

She was distant, there in the darkness. Then she said, 'It wouldn't be the first time someone has retired because of his wife's health. But I'll feel like a cheat — I'll have cheated you —'

'No, love. I'll never think that.'

She lifted his hand, held it close to her almost invisible face, then he felt her bite his knuckles.

'Love —' he said, and was glad the tears in his eyes were invisible in the darkness. A dream had gone, but he would never let her know the depth of his disappointment. But he knew that happiness was not tied up in dreams alone.

5

Sunday at lunch, just the four of them around the table, Matt told Paddy and Eileen of his decision. Both of them looked at him and Carmel as if meeting them for the first time; it suddenly struck Matt that his dream had been theirs, too. But all Paddy said was, 'You sure?'

'I'm sure. Carmel's health is worth more than anything I might achieve down in Canberra. And even if I beat Becky Irvine for the Leadership, there's no guarantee I'd oust the PM. He's hanging on there for dear life . . .'

Eileen looked at Carmel, not interested in the politics: 'How do you feel?'

'I know it sounds selfish, Mum, but I want him home with me. You've had Dad every day, every week —'

'Sweetheart —' Eileen put a hand on her daughter's. 'That's what counts.'

Paddy said, 'A lot of people will be disappointed. But in the end, it's your happiness, not theirs. What'll you do?'

'I haven't looked that far yet,' said Matt. 'But we'll be okay financially —'

'You wouldn't like to buy a property? Five thousand acres of dirt —'

Matt laughed. 'No, thanks. I've got my pension, our dividends, I think I can land a directorship or two ... We'll be okay.'

'Your dad would've been disappointed,' said Paddy, reluctant to let go of the knife.

'I'm not sure. I think he would have understood.'

Eileen raised her wine glass. 'Here's to a new life.'

Matt and Carmel flew back to Sydney that afternoon. The plane took off, banked over the cemetery and Matt looked down at the anonymous graves. His mother and father lay there; and Ruby Rawson. The past that still influenced the present.

That evening Matt rang Tony Casio and told him the news. There was dead silence at the other end of the line and Matt thought they had been cut off. Then Tony said, 'It's something I never expected, Matt. We've worked bloody hard —'

'I know that, Tony. And I appreciate it. But Carmel's health is more important to me ...'

'I appreciate that. No, I really do. But I'll always think you might have made a bloody good PM ... How do you want me to handle it?'

'With as little fuss as possible, Tony. Word it somehow so that women will understand it. If they understand, then maybe they can convince their men. But don't make a big thing of it — this isn't the surrender at Waterloo or in the Forest of Compiégne —'

'Don't start quoting history at me. The last surrender Aussies remember was when we lost a Test match ... Okay, I'll make it quiet and dignified. Like a Pope retiring.'

'When did that ever happen?'

'You can tell Becky Irvine when you come back to Canberra tomorrow. But I'll keep it under wraps for another coupla weeks, unless that bastard on Scorn kicks up more dirt.'

'Why wait?'

Tony's sigh could be heard down the line. He gave a short lesson in national psychology: 'Matt, the Olympics start in another ten days. The voters will hardly look at anything coming out of Canberra. You'll just be another politician taking his pension —'

'Tony, why are you so cynical?'

'It's my elixir ...' His tone changed. 'I enjoyed working for you, Matt.'

'Likewise,' said Matt and hung up before the moment got too emotional.

Then he rang Ham Jessup, who, after a moment, suddenly wept. 'Jesus, Matt, you would've made a great PM! Every fucking crystal ball I looked into, you were it!'

'You'll get over it, Ham. I have to think of Carmel —'

'Sure, sure. But she'd have looked great in the Lodge, too.'

'I know. Could you get in touch with Fleur Tan, tell her I'll talk to her, but I don't want anything announced just yet.'

'Sure, I'll do that. She's gunna be as disappointed as I am —'

Richard and Natalie took the news with more composure than Matt had expected: their mother's children.

'I'm sure you're disappointed, Dad,' said Natalie. 'But Mum is the one we have to look after.'

'Thanks, darling,' said Carmel, who was on the extension. And Matt knew, from her voice, how difficult it was going to be for her to keep up the impersonation for the next twelve months.

Richard was equally sympathetic: 'I admire you, Dad — it's a big sacrifice. But Mum's the important one in all this —'

'All the way,' said Matt.

Back in Canberra some Labor members, all male, were up in arms at his caving in to female opposition. But they meant Rebecca Irvine, not Carmel. The situation was explained to them and they went home to their wives and came back chastened if still disappointed. Rebecca Irvine accepted his retiring with her usual grace: 'And I admire you, Matt. For being a husband before anything else.'

'Thanks,' said Matt, stepping into the first act of what might be a long year.

Two weeks later Tony Casio released the news to the media. Ian Thorpe had just won his first gold medal, Jodie Henry had just broken a world record. And Matt Durban sank beneath the waters with just a few bubbles to show that he had once, might have been, a contender.

6

In bed Carmel noticed the long streak of light between the bedroom curtains. 'You've left the light on on the porch.'

'I know,' said Matt and held her to him.